Elizabeth Lavender's

DAGGERS
AMONG THE STARS

Book 4 of the Sunspear Series

Ebook ISBN: 978-1-951741-09-9

Paperback Print ISBN: 978-1-951741-10-5

Hardcover Print ISBN: 978-1-951741-11-2

ACKNOWLEDGEMENTS

My thanks once again goes to Arcane Book Covers for continuing to transform the concept in my head into an astonishing masterpiece. Countless thanks go to family and friends, whose constant enthusiasm about the series encourages me daily to continue to write the story. They are those with the heart and spirit of the spear-bearer, the heroes in my world that inspire me each day, though they would dismiss their impact. Special thanks to my husband and my two children for their patience and encouragement as I continue to write the story and all the time it takes. Thanks especially to my husband for his feedback on the manuscript.

And as always, I am thankful for you, the reader. We traveled together in this journey for a fair distance now, and you are incredible company. This journey is for you. Stay. You have come so far with me and our spear-bearers. The road continues to be difficult for them, not unlike places in our own life's journey. Perhaps the roads intersect in more ways than it appears at first. Certainly, I can't say the battles will get easier. Quite the opposite. However, I've seen it's easier to be victorious when you don't fight alone or journey alone. So, thank you again for traveling with me, my friend.

Fear's eyes pierce the deepest parts of us to bring forth our most unimaginable,
dreaded vision into being and delights in capturing the broken spirit left behind.
Yet over the beast's roar, a whispered vow is heard.
I will protect you for you are my heart. I will hold you beyond the grasp of Fear's
claws. I will come for you, to stand between you and Fear's deadly dagger.
Always. Beyond the endless starry sky.

CHAPTER ONE

Boisterous laughter greeted her from one end of the lounge while raised voices claimed another arena. *I know which of those deals is going smoother,* she thought as she strolled through the entrance undaunted by the ruckus and headed straight for the open bar area. The colony's hangout mimicked the setup of numerous others strewn across the galaxy. The walls were relatively plain except for scattered hangings showcasing sayings, ranging from the clever to the crude. Several hid evidence of the patchwork done after a stray blaster shot or a fist missed its mark. She could sit in one of the cushy swivel chairs encircling the center of the bustle, but she wouldn't stay long enough to make it worth it. Besides, she spied her target the instant she stepped inside, settled in one of the booths away from the activity. One of the young bartenders rushed to serve her, and she flashed him a smile as she leaned against the counter.

His eyes roved appreciatively over her before meeting her eyes and grinning. "What can I do for you today?"

"Get me a drink?"

"Love to. How adventurous are you feeling?"

"Very little. I'll be disappointing you."

"Not remotely possible. You haven't done that since you walked through the door." He winked at her.

Laughing, she indicated her selection. "So, you say."

"Don't want something with fire to it?" He angled in closer. "You can handle it."

"No doubt I could, but I'll stay with my choice. My beverage, now?"

"Of course." He filled a glass and handed it to her, intentionally brushing her hand with his. "How did I get lucky enough to have such a gorgeous woman like you come in?"

"Business."

"There are lots of businesses. Where do your enterprises lie?"

She met his gaze. "The kind I'm not a part of the package, and I don't mix work with pleasure."

"You're unusual to be on that side of the shop." As his eyes traveled over her again, he added, "And that's a crying shame."

"I hear that a lot."

"Not surprising." He leaned up from the counter, "What else can I get you, miss?"

She smiled at the shift as he gave her the respect due to a shipping dealer. "You delivered fine."

"How about I tempt you with a bite to eat as well?"

After tapping the pay port with her data pad, she said, "Nope, I'm good."

"A generous tipper too. You get better every second." He grinned. "If you change your mind, let me know. I'll come running."

"I won't hesitate. Thanks." Taking her drink, she resumed her path to the intended booth and slid into it.

The man seated in it didn't look up from his data pad as a grin played at the corners of his mouth. "That bartender didn't take his eyes off your backside until you sat down, Chris."

"I'm used to it and felt it too, Christopher."

"I'd call you a liar if you said differently."

"Catch any trouble lately?"

"Of course not. No doubt you managed to attract plenty."

She sipped her drink. "Really no issues?"

At last, he looked at her. "You expected otherwise."

"Maybe."

"It's like that, huh?"

She stared back at him in answer. "When is the rest of your food coming?" She motioned in front of him to what amounted to an appetizer.

"This is all I ordered so far. Probably best since it's clear we won't be sticking around."

"No, go ahead with your lunch. That won't fill you up."

"I'll be fine. After all, we both have reserves on our ships. Comes with the business. Help me finish this."

"No, it's yours. You'll be starved as it is."

"You already ate? That's what I thought. I'm not taking another bite until you do. Chris, it's got every topping imaginable piled on it. Stop wasting time."

"Why are you such a pain?"

He grinned at her. "I'm the one being a pain? Next, you'll tell me you're watching your girlish figure."

"I could be."

"I may be at least ten years your senior, but ... "

"Just ten?"

"Don't push it. As I started to say, though I'm older than you, even I saw from our first meeting you don't have an ounce of anything in the wrong place."

She couldn't suppress her laughter any longer and popped one of the topping-covered chips into her mouth. "Happy, now?"

"It's a start. With your various business enterprises and the insane schedule they demand, you barely eat as it is. You need to take care of yourself." Shaking his head, he dug into the appetizer.

"You're beginning to sound like someone else." She ate another chip. "For your information, I did well in that area the last few days. Two real meals a day. Worked in a third a couple of times." She grinned at him. "Even got dessert."

"Really?"

"I meant desserts."

"Intriguing. There are lots of desserts," he lowered his voice, "and since I know where you went, what kind of dessert are we talking about?"

"I never got the name of it because I ended up distracted a fair amount of the time. I've tasted similar, but never this combination. It's … the individual's favorite and rightly so. It was delicious."

"Any other dessert you indulged in, Chris?"

"Yes, but none I'm telling you about."

He dissolved into laughter. "Sounds like you need more sugar-filled days on your horizon."

"Probably, but I'm back to my old ways, Christopher. That sky is a long way off for me." With a sigh, she took another sip of her drink and stared out into space.

"That bad?"

"Yes."

"We'll get you back there."

"Impossible to see how."

He didn't push further. "This deal needs most of my time today?"

"Afraid so."

"And you want me all to yourself for this one?" he joked.

She chuckled. "Absolutely."

After making a few swipes on his data pad, he showed it to her. "Is it secluded enough for you?"

She studied it and did the same on her device. "It's perfect."

"Time to head out." He motioned to her as they rose from the booth. "Ladies, first."

"Always the gentleman."

"I try despite the shipping business," he said as they walked out. "Poor bartender. His day goes downhill now that you're leaving."

❧

Chris watched from her cockpit as Christopher's vessel landed moments later at the rendezvous spot, and he strolled towards their ship. She turned to Alena. "This place remains under the radar."

"Because there's nothing here but miles of dirt and those weeds trying to pass as flowers. Even Black Dragon isn't interested."

"Let's hope we can keep saying that."

A beep originating from the ship's computer announced his entrance as the door opened for him. "Catch me up with what you two lovely ladies have been up to, besides finding trouble."

Alena said, "She's exceptional at that, with no end in sight."

He laughed. "Glad to see you two in one piece."

Chris said, "I'll get us drinks."

Christopher and Alena sat as she did so. He watched Chris for another second and turned back to Alena, "It's eating at her, isn't it?"

Alena nodded.

"Should it be?"

"With what we discovered, yes. Then with the images raging in her head added to what already happened, it got bad. Worse than what you saw from her the last time you were with us."

"Here you go." Chris handed them their drinks and joined them.

"Thanks." He took a sip. "Doubtless you've returned with plenty of doom and gloom. I'm hoping there's no impossible task for me to do." He groaned as the two women exchanged a look. "Of course there is, but there's time for that." Placing his drink on the table, he grinned. "First tell me about something pleasant recently, Chris."

"What do you mean?"

"Don't try that on me. Details, now."

"Totally unfair."

"You want my help, right? Come on. Everyone has heard all about the spear-bearer Dante decimating an army in record time, and thanks to Black Dragon, more are getting to see him in action on that front. I'm guessing there's a softer side to him, and you drew it out. What's that Dante like, the one who got to meet the woman of his dreams and is utterly smitten?"

Chris stared at Christopher, but she didn't see him anymore. The mention of Dante transported her back to the previous few days spent with him. She recalled his soft brown eyes gazing back at her. They were sometimes teasing, other times intense and passionate, but always holding her in his loving gaze as if she were the only person who mattered in the galaxy. She felt his arms around her again, his lips brush hers, and his hands playing in her hair. She sighed and opened her eyes, realizing they had closed and said, "Dante is incredible. I never imagined how much. The hardest thing I did was leave him, and I miss him so already."

"I can see, and he certainly feels the same way." He reached over and clasped her hand. "I'm happy for you, Chris. If ever two people deserve this, it's you two." He released her hand. "Your visit went well then, and he's pining away until you return."

"He can't afford to do that, not with the Black Dragon's threat." Her eyes suddenly twinkled. "I'm not the only one who caught an admiring eye while at the fortress."

"Is that so?" He grinned at Alena and turned back to Chris.

"Are you going to tell him, or shall I?"

Alena laughed. "You're having so much fun doing it, so I'll let you."

"She attracted the attention of a certain commander as soon as she entered the room, and they were inseparable from then on."

"A commander, huh? Caleb would be there, but he's happily married to Lana. Everybody knows that, and the Ancient One help anyone crazy enough to cross her to lay a hand on him. There's only a couple of them unattached out of the bunch. From gaining the inside scoop from you two, my guess would be the commander Dante and Caleb consider friend foremost and their next in command second. So, Ryan's softer side is uncovered as well?" He laughed. "What you two managed in a few days."

"It was an unexpected, but wonderful surprise. Ryan is amazing," A smile lit up Alena's face.

"I'm betting you two found the best men left in the galaxy. Both are fierce in any fight, but more importantly, they can be counted on when it matters from what I've heard. Sounds like an enjoyable visit all around." He put his arms out in a mock sign of surrender. "Lay it on me. How is it worse?"

Alena said, "We should start from the beginning."

Chris said, "You're right." Together they chronicled the four days spent with Dante and Ryan and the others. Christopher interjected sparingly with questions about the events and to clarify what they had learned, but primarily he listened while a myriad of emotions played across his face.

"That's it?" he asked as they both fell silent.

"Yeah, that covers it," said Chris.

"Let me see if I got this recap straight. Chris, you got a dagger put through you."

"No, it wasn't me. I saw ... "

"Fine. You felt a blade go clean through you. Before that, you tried to plummet down the cylinder to your death."

"That was an accident."

"Not another interruption. Then you wandered off and almost got stabbed through your heart while being strangled. Another near dive down the cylinder to end it all the next day. Followed by letting someone else get another chance at cutting you open. Oh, and scattered in all of it is the nightmare you had and images that kept you in a state of ... I can't come up with the word."

"You make it sound so ... "

"Scary? Terrifying? Because it is. Chris, Dante is young and can take an awful lot, but are you trying to give your man a heart attack?"

"Of course not. I'd never do anything to hurt him."

"Not deliberately, but you have to be more careful. After all that, he probably planned on locking you up in his quarters and keeping you there."

"He wouldn't."

"Only because you'd find a way out. I've witnessed you and a data pad at work." He shook his head but then grinned. "The thought occurred to him; I guarantee it. Other reasons come to mind for him to keep you locked up in his room."

"You're bad, Christopher." She laughed. "He behaved."

"Two elders would beat you two if not. Even without that threat, I've seen enough from him to know you're right. However, there are many ways to romance a girl where he's still safe with the Elders, and I'm sure he found them all."

"In record time."

"Clearly he did from your expression. So, for his sake, ease up on trying to get yourself killed."

"I'll do better."

"Time to see this science experiment you brought me."

"It's ugly." She motioned to Alena who retrieved an average-sized metal box. "Not the best thing after lunch. Sorry about that. Ready for this?"

"I've seen nasty a'plenty in this business." He opened the box, pulled out a metallic-shaped cylinder first, and took out the sealed clear beaker container inside. Rotating it in his hands, he watched the black element masquerading as blood crawl along the beaker's sides. "You weren't kidding. Not the slightest swish. Slime texture all the way. The color doesn't bother me. The consistency we can mimic it somehow with me and your teacher brainstorming it. I've already got ideas forming. Mimicking the substance isn't our big problem. It's the fact it has to go into you two and come out looking the same, without killing you when you're injected with it."

Chris said, "We can insert a minuscule amount first to see if it works before we go full in."

"How are you suggesting we do that? We still have to inject you two first to check."

"We modify it until it works."

"Not if you two don't live through it."

"I'll volunteer to be the one to test it."

Alena interjected, "No, and that's not what this is about."

"Chris, how many lives do you think you have?"

She stared back at them, at a loss for words momentarily. "This is too important. It's worth the risk."

Christopher shook his head and clasped her hand. "No, it's not. If Dante were here, you know what he would say to you and Ryan would second him." He unclasped her hand. "I'll help you two figure this out, but I won't sacrifice either one of you to do it. I don't aim to have a blade in my back from Dante or Ryan because I'm the reason one of you dropped dead."

"They would never do that. They wouldn't blame you."

"Why wouldn't they? Because they should. I would, Chris." He paused. "We do this my way, or I'm not helping." Only after a sigh of surrender finally escaped her did he forge ahead with examining the second item in the box. He extracted the small case from a larger metal container. "The pound of flesh?"

Alena nodded. "Yes, and remember the warning."

Christopher opened it and whistled. "Took a chunk out of him, didn't they? The elders preserved this to perfection. The pattern is a little intricate, but there are ways." He took his fingertips and traced over the image. "The pocket of black ooze underneath could prove a brain teaser to work out, but then again as long as it feels like it's there, that might work. Yeah, I'm seeing it." He peered up and caught the expression on Chris's face. "Chris?"

She stared at the sample, and the design moved before her. The eye revealed itself and bore into her. It doubled as a familiar face appeared along with a dagger racing towards her chest, causing her to gasp and jump back in her seat. Christopher's voice broke through in that instant. "Chris, what's going on? Say something." She looked up to see their concerned faces and each of them gently gripping one of her arms as she struggled to refocus on the two. "Nothing. I'm fine."

"That was far from nothing," said Christopher. "Try again."

"It brought back the encounter with the Black Dragon agent."

Alena scanned the room and turned back to her. "Is he here again?"

"No, it just popped into my head again. Vividly, like it does."

Christopher reassured her, "He can't hurt you again. This is all that's left of him, a slab of flesh. Remember that."

"You're right. I'm sorry."

"Don't apologize. I wish I could get my hands around the neck of this Trey thing terrorizing you from the dead."

Alena sighed. "Stand in line."

"Yeah, I expect Dante wants a first shot," he paused, "and, Chris, I know you didn't tell me everything Trey said to you like you wouldn't tell Dante."

"I can't, Christopher."

"I get it. I mean I don't, but it comes with the territory with you. However, if you have a change of heart, I'll listen. More importantly, Dante will. Give him the chance."

She looked down. "I'll keep that in mind."

"Please do." He studied her for another moment before repacking the items into the metal box. "How will we do this? I don't want to work at cross purposes with your teacher."

Alika's voice rang out through the comm system, "You won't, Christopher."

"Glad to hear from you as well."

"We'll be talking a great deal until we uncover a solution. You'll be given an encryption code for us to communicate. You can guess the expiration date for it."

"Of course. Safety first."

"Speaking of that, we were worried about you and made you our first stop once we returned."

"Much appreciated. Blaster-immune mutated Black Dragon agents and killer discs are scary additions. As if we didn't have enough problems. I'm skilled with a blade, but I'm not feeling nearly as confident now. I'll watch my back, more than before."

"See that you do, my friend."

"Let me start cracking on this. Thanks for the hospitality. I'll return it next time we're on my ship." He rose with the box in hand and paused to look around as if searching for someone. "Hey, and for crying out loud, would you keep your students out of trouble?"

Alika laughed, "I try, Christopher. In fact, Seth and I both did this last time."

"We don't make it easy on them," said Chris. "Stay safe, please."

"I will," he said as she engulfed him in a hug.

"Yes, because I have to bail her out enough as it is. Don't add to my workload," Alena joked as she hugged him goodbye as well.

"Don't worry. See you two soon," he said as he strolled off the ship.

⁓ eℓℓ ⌐

Dante pushed the button on the wall beside the curtain in his room. What appeared to be a solid piece of construction slid out of the way to reveal a view to the outside through a deceptively fragile-looking surface. He glided the drapes open in his quarters and scanned the morning sky. There wasn't a hint of the trouble they had recently revealed. "Why did I ever agree to this? Are you okay? Angelina?" He sighed, knowing there would be no answer.

"Even I can't get into mischief that fast, Dante." Her hands glided over his bare shoulders.

He spun around to find himself face to face with a gorgeous smile, two beautiful blue eyes, and a stunning form he would know from a million lightyears away. "My Angelina, what are you doing here?" His arms encircled her waist.

"You asked for me, so I'm here."

"That easy, huh? I'll continue requesting you." He nuzzled her neck and grinned back at her. "Sorry, I haven't hit the shower yet."

"I see, but I like you shirtless." She slowly encircled both arms around his neck and whispered in his ear. "I imagined the view would be impressive, and you don't disappoint."

"I intend for you to keep saying that." He brushed a stray strand of hair over her shoulder. "You're really, okay? No trouble?"

"None, my Dante."

"Stay."

"You know I can't."

"I worry about you."

"Don't." she leaned in. "There are so many better ways to spend the time with me."

"You're right." Pulling her against him, his eyes grew heavy and closed as he kissed her. Suddenly they flew open, and he gasped. He no longer looked into those beautiful blue eyes he loved. Instead, his eyes focused on the ceiling of his quarters, and he realized he lay in his bed. Sitting up in it, he confirmed being alone in his room, and a glance at the display on the table showed his wake-up call approaching. "You've got to be kidding me. All that was only a dream." He groaned as he settled back down and burrowed his head into his pillow. Unable to force himself from the covers, he remained there for several more minutes, wallowing in his disappointment. "How am I supposed to get out of bed after that? If she was here, she'd tease me to the end of the galaxy." On cue, the display sounded its reminder, and he delivered a more forceful tap to it than needed. "Yeah, I'm getting up."

He stood by the open curtains again, this time showered, dressed, and armed with his sunspear. The skyline appeared unnaturally calm as in his dream. "Angelina, where are you? Are you okay?" Silence was his only reply, and the memory of her caress made him miss her more. Still staring out, he said, "Stay safe, my Angelina, please." He closed the curtain and strolled from his quarters.

CHAPTER TWO

Commander Austin sat at his desk, going through a final mental checklist as he prepared to leave. He looked up and smiled as a familiar young man leaned against the doorway.

"Sanders, come talk to me before I head out."

Sanders settled in the chair across from Austin. "Dad, how long are you gone this time?"

"I don't know, son. Considering recent events, this could be lengthy. My hope is Lana has answers to help us fight this, and that's why she called all the commanders."

"It didn't matter the last time for those planets."

"Son, don't do that. Not to Lana or any of us. We're all trying to come to grips with what happened. Lana most of all, and she doesn't need reminding."

"I didn't mean to make it worse." he paused. "Do you think they figured something out?"

"I'll see soon enough. By the way, where's Simon? I hoped to say bye before I left."

He shrugged. "Where is my brother ever? I don't know, dad."

"I spotted him at the meeting earlier with us. He couldn't have gone far."

"Don't bet on it. He couldn't wait to leave it. I caught him dozing off a couple of times. The Black Dragon could destroy us all, and he wouldn't know the difference."

"That's not true. You two approach it differently, but it doesn't mean he ... "

"Doesn't care at all? If you say so, Dad. But we should be doing something. Like going straight at Black Dragon and hitting them with everything we've got instead of sitting back and waiting for them to strike. I'll volunteer to command a fleet myself."

Austin's eyes drifted to a picture of a young man on his desk, one who clearly bore a resemblance to both Sanders and Simon. He stared back at Sanders with sadness. "Why are you so eager to go into battle? To put yourself in harm's way further?"

"I don't need protecting, just because of what happened to Galen. I'm not him."

"No, you're not," Austin whispered as his eyes strayed to the image again before refocusing on Sanders. "But you're my son. Attempting to protect you is my responsibility. I'm proud of your help with managing affairs here and your training progress with the Freedom Fighter army, but you're where you should be. Don't volunteer to take an unnecessary risk, and don't begrudge your brother because he's not taking the same path."

Sanders got up. "Dad, I get it, and don't worry about things here. Mom and I will take care of everything," he let out an exasperated sigh, "with Simon's hand of course. We'll see you when you get back and anticipate good news."

Austin watched Sanders walk from the room, and then he turned to trace the young man's face in the photo. "I wish I had done a better job at protecting you, son. I don't know what else to say to him. Maybe he would have listened to you, Galen."

"I thought you would have left by now, honey," a female voice interrupted Austin's musing.

He smiled and rose. "Trying to get rid of me, Docia?"

She strolled over to him and wrapped her arms around his neck. "Never. You know how much I enjoy having you with me."

His arms encircled his wife's waist. "I'd rather be here with you any day."

"It's been a minute since you showed me." She winked at him.

"Let me fix that." He kissed her. "Although you know this doesn't help me leave, " he murmured as he kissed her again.

"I know." She stared up into his eyes and stroked the side of his face. "We can handle everything here like we always do. It'll be okay. What was that about with Sanders?"

"Him itching for another confrontation with Black Dragon and not understanding why everybody isn't rushing in too."

She leaned against her husband and closed her eyes, "To that again, huh?"

"Yes. He's deaf to whatever I say to him about it."

"He's got to see it on his own, without it ending terrible for us again. I miss Galen too," she whispered and took a deep breath. "Have you talked to Simon since the meeting?"

"No, I'm hoping to before I leave."

"He's around here somewhere." She stepped back from him. "Time to get you moving for real."

~~

Simon replaced the bottom half of the cockpit panel and rose from the floor of his ship to swipe his hand over the control console. "Let's see if that works." Settling into the cockpit chair, he studied the front display. "Seems it did, but I'll run a scan to be sure." Two people on another screen caught his attention. "Already time?" He grumbled. "I can hear it now, so I best make an appearance." He secured his vessel and exited.

"See, I told you, honey," said Docia as she glimpsed a figure in the huge hangar near Austin's ship. "Simon!" she called and motioned for him.

Simon appeared to take a moment to register the source of the call but then waved as he came bounding towards his parents. "Hey mom, dad. What's up?"

"Don't you remember?" asked Docia.

"Remember what?"

"Son, you were at the meeting earlier," said Austin.

"Yeah, I was." His face scrunched up as if trying to dig up the detail deemed important by the two.

"I'm leaving today. As in now."

"Oh, for your talk with the other commanders. It didn't hit me how soon you'd head out. You're all set?"

"Yes. Where did you go off to afterward so quickly?"

He shrugged. "Here and there."

"Son, I need you to help your brother and mom while I'm gone. There's a lot to manage."

"And as normal my brother wasted no time whining about how I'm not pulling my weight."

"Simon, it doesn't matter what he says."

"You know I can't stand all that, not like Sanders does." He smiled at his dad. "Hey, but you can count on me, Dad. We got it covered."

Austin smiled. "I know you do."

Simon hugged him. "Go do all your commander stuff, and make us proud."

Austin laughed. "I'll do what I can, and you all hold down things here."

Docia said, "We will. Now it's time for you to go, honey."

"I am, but first to give my wife a proper goodbye." He reached over and kissed her. "See you when I get back."

"I'll be right here."

They watched as the ship lifted off carrying Austin.

"Mom, I hope they find out what to do."

"Me too."

"Do you think they will?"

"We believe they do, Simon. Three planets say they must." She looped her arm through her son's. "Come back in with me. I've hardly seen you all day."

He glanced over in his ship's direction but then smiled back at her. "Sounds great, Mom."

CHAPTER THREE

Lana and Caleb watched as the remaining commanders made their way into the fortress's main room to join Seth, Dante, and Commander Ryan.

Lana's gaze shifted to two men as she said quietly to Caleb, "They seem at ease, despite my concerns."

He followed her eyes to Ryan and Dante. "They're still worried, but they were laughing with us earlier. Both of them bounce back fast when they have to." He leaned in and kissed her. "Ready to work this room with me, sweetheart?"

"Only with you, Caleb." She smiled up at him as she took his hand, and they approached the full table. Turning to the group, she said, "Gentleman, thank you for gathering so quickly. There's a great deal to discuss with you today. Note any questions you have, but refrain from asking them until we have been through it all."

Caleb nodded. "Our battle against the Black Dragon is nowhere near over, and they changed the battlefield on us again."

Dante listened as his cousin and her husband dispensed the information to those gathered, consciously leaving out a crucial piece of the intel. He glanced at Ryan, who met his eyes, clearly echoing his thoughts. They all agreed to it, at least in the initial presentation to the other commanders. Lana and Caleb finished and silence greeted them as the full weight of the situation engulfed their audience.

"Blaster-proof Black Dragon. Colonists turned into mutant soldiers and we're looking for a mark on them," said Commander Aegeus.

"And you said a couple pretended to be on our side and put up a convincing act before they attacked," said Commander Conrad. "We thought they were done when we got rid of the Dark Lord or more specifically when you did, Dante."

Commander Cephas turned to Dante. "Are we sure about there being someone else taking over the reins?"

"Yes. It's the only theory that fits."

"From simply looking at the events of that day? No one has seen or heard news of anyone replacing the leadership, so maybe that's a leap through a portal that's not there."

Seth said, "Unfortunately there are several elements of the Black Dragon that have only of late been disclosed to us. This inside agent, Black Beauty, who carried out much for the Dark Lord is a prime example. Lana and I had a close encounter with her, and we can vouch for her existence. Two of our men are dead because of her work, and she would have claimed Abigail too if we had arrived a second later."

"If they didn't broadcast that one to the galaxy, what or who else did they keep under wraps?" said Ryan.

"It scares me to answer based on what I've heard today. We just thought we knew the enemy," said Austin.

Gabe sighed. "We've paid the price already for that, three planets of innocent, precious colonists. Gone." His eyes grew misty. "We can't allow it to happen again. What's our next move?"

Caleb said, "Keeping the colonies safe when an attack comes will be our main goal."

Austin asked, "How do we possibly do that against a threat of this magnitude? We've already seen we're no match against it."

Gabe nodded. "Shouldn't we locate and go after the device again?"

Lana paused before answering, "We have other resources working on that end of it."

"Other resources," Gabe murmured.

Austin continued Gabe's unspoken thought. "This is more than just piecing together. Even with gathering intel from the planet, I wouldn't have made the connection with the soldier and the wound and the discs. Then there's this inside agent and her visit to the Elders Hall. Granted, you don't know why she went, but the fact you know she went at all leads me to believe there's more you haven't told us."

Caleb looked at Lana. "We knew we couldn't leave it out. Go ahead."

Lana said, "You're right, Austin. However, our other resources do not go beyond this room. Not to anyone, including those closest to you. Our circle of who we can trust is becoming increasingly suspect. If they accidentally speak out of turn and our enemy is close by masquerading as a friend, our advantage is gone. Literally. We will have a specific script for you to report back with, and it will not include any mention of this resource. Does everyone understand?"

A chorus of answers in the affirmative followed from each commander in the room, even Ryan, though he knew what came next. Satisfied at receiving the desired response, she said, "You are acquainted with our resources, both of them. They have been instrumental in assisting us thus far and will continue. However, the only way to keep them safe is the knowledge of them staying within this group." She paused. "Our resource is our two friends, the spear-bearers."

Gabe gasped, "They sent you all this information."

"No, they were here and helped us discover much of it during their visit. The rest they already uncovered before they arrived and shared."

"They are obtaining the location. How are they to do it without ... ?"

"With great caution."

Austin's eyes widened. "The only way is to go straight into Black Dragon."

"Yes, that's the case. They understand and are preparing to do so." Lana's shoulders slumped.

"What if they can't? What if Black Dragon catches them, Lana?"

Gabe stared at her. "We know what will happen to them."

"We do, and they have accepted that as well. It was their decision, Gabe." She bowed her head as Caleb put his arm around her shoulder.

Seeing the collection of somber faces, Seth said, "Everyone, take a break, and we'll proceed in thirty minutes."

Dante got up and Ryan started to follow him, but Caleb motioned Ryan over. Ryan settled on mouthing to Dante, *"You, okay?"* Dante nodded as he walked over to a corner of the fortress, lost in his thoughts.

"Even with seeing them in action, how do you think they will pull it off?" Gabe's concerned voice startled Dante from his worry for Angelina.

"Same as they always have, Gabe. They'll find a way."

"You couldn't talk them out of it?"

"No. We tried, myself included. It didn't matter what I said."

"I thought with the one rescuing your mom, you could convince them. Maybe that connection would be of help."

"Me too, but I'm afraid not. A colossal failure with that one."

"You gave it your best attempt. I hope they make it. Although I spent a short time with them, they left an impression. I would hate to lose them."

"Me too. I can't imagine if I ... " he looked down. "It would be a terrible loss for ... our cause."

"No, for him, Gabe. It would shatter his heart," whispered a voice. Gabe thought he imagined it at first, but he knew the truth as sure as Dante stood before him. For him? His heart shattered? Gabe continued staring at Dante, and the pieces fell into place as the meaning took hold. He met the two spear-bearers that day, but they were covered from head to toe in armor and apparently were using voice changers. Dante was concerned, but Gabe knew that look that had flickered across Dante's face seconds ago. Then when they discussed the possible outcomes of what could happen to the two spear-bearers, Dante tried to hide his anxiety. On the surface, it appeared normal considering the situation. Gabe glanced over at Ryan and recalled observing the same quiet settle over him. He refocused on Dante. He didn't have a clue why the Ancient One revealed this to him, but he needed to proceed delicately with his friend.

"Dante, don't you mean it would be an unimaginable loss to you?"

"To me?" He stared at Gabe again. "Of course. Like you said, they leave an impression. They saved my mom."

"That's not what I meant." He paused. "Every time there's a confrontation with Black Dragon and I have to go to command the fleet, there's a fear I won't make it back. I see it reflected in the eyes of my family, but most of all in my wife's eyes. It's something you can't hide. Your cousin and Caleb go through it each time when she sends him into battle. No matter how brave of a front you put on, you can't help but worry when the one who has your heart faces the battlefield." He placed a hand on Dante's shoulder. "She'll come back to you safely."

"What are you talking about? I didn't say ... "

"It wasn't anything you did or said. Or Ryan either." He paused at the mounting anxiety possessing Dante's face. "Yes, him too. The Ancient One wanted me to know, but I don't know why. I put it together from there."

Dante looked around to ensure everyone stood a distance from them and then lowered his voice, "Gabe, if He wanted you to know, He has His reasons. You can't say a word though. I'm begging you. If it got out, it's an automatic death sentence for them, or Black Dragon could use one of us for bait to draw them out and capture them. You're right. I can't lose her. I don't know what I would do without her now that I've found her. Ryan and I are both worried sick, but we couldn't change their minds. The woman is a magnet for trouble. She scared me to death while she was here." He grasped Gabe by the arm and locked eyes with him. "Promise me, not a word."

"I promise, Dante. Tell me what happened when she came."

"What didn't." A sense of relief washed over him with simply being able to talk about it. "She came within inches of getting a dagger through her twice. Almost fell down the cylinder. I can't put into words the other because we still don't know what she encountered."

"That sounds strange. I can't see either one of them overcome with a dagger, not with the way they handle a sunspear."

"None of us knew about the blasters not working, so she thought she killed him. The other one was a turned colonist pretending to be on our side, and it fooled her. The cylinder was all her, deciding she had to see inside right then."

"Sounds like she kept you running."

A smile played at the corners of his mouth. "She only knows full throttle, but I managed to keep her close with no complaints about that part."

"Someone finally snagged you. Remember I didn't get to see either one. Once you got a look?"

"She's absolutely stunning, Gabe."

Gabe chuckled, "Well the look on your face says it all, Dante. Both of them proved amazing in a fight, but I'm curious. The one who gave the rousing speech and took down the squadron leader, who has the claim on that one?"

Dante laughed, "She's all mine, and I couldn't be happier." He lightly slapped Gabe on the back. "Thanks, for the talk. I feel better."

"Anytime, Dante. Ryan too. Everyone is finding their way back to the table."

"That's our signal too."

CHAPTER FOUR

The Premier sat in the small conference room of the command ship and looked up as the door opened.

"Sir, as you requested," said the Black Dragon soldier as he motioned to the two individuals standing beside him.

"Leave us, please," the Premier said and then turned to the other two. "Take a seat, now." He waited until they did.

Black Beauty stared at him and made no effort to hide the triumphant smile forming. "We're back so soon. You realize you needed us."

"That's quite the assumption on your part." He addressed the cloaked masked man beside her. "Destroyer, what do think of her conclusion?"

"I assure you she does not speak for me."

"Noted." He approached them to stand directly behind Black Beauty. "Your short recall tests my patience." Leaning down to talk in her ear, his hand simultaneously wrapped around her neck and his sword's edge found her midsection. "You are dispensable. Surely you see how true that is now, or do I need to prove it to you?"

She tried to struggle out an answer, but the grip on her neck tightened.

"I can't hear you. Do you require proof? Answer me."

Using all the air left in her, she gasped, "No."

He loosened the grip on her throat, but his hand remained there as he resumed speaking into her ear, "I do not require you for anything. Do not make that mistake again. It will be the last time you do." He slid his hand from her neck and twisted the blade to slide the dull side across her midsection before standing back up and returning to his seat. "Now that we've wasted time with pleasantries, we'll conduct business. I have questions, and let us hope you have answers. We all agree there has never been a powerhouse, but rather an empire, built as impressively as Black Dragon. Equally impressive was the architect, the Dark Lord, but he's gone now. In one day, he was eliminated. How the mighty fell, which brings me to my question. How does such a one collapse?"

Black Beauty said, "How would we know? None of us were there when it happened."

"True, but you are adamant this man is the Dark Lord."

"And you would hear none of it. So, what does that have to do with this? Have you changed your mind?"

"Watch your tone, Black Beauty. No, I haven't modified my opinion, but I've concluded there is a reason you insisted so. Also, from my observation of Destroyer." He turned to Destroyer. "Your manner in certain ways reminds me of the Dark Lord, and I don't think that's by accident. Furthermore, your traveling companion is rumored to dabble in areas beyond her skills, if desperate enough. Possibilities have surfaced for me to hint at what I see before me. Therefore, I'm inclined to believe the two of you can enlighten me on what happened to the Dark Lord."

Destroyer turned to Black Beauty, but she remained quiet. He focused back on the Premier. "My apologies for the squandered time because of her. When I awoke I was this, but I don't know what occurred beforehand. However, I discovered pieces of another memory inside my own and small fragments filled in at random. At the onset, it seemed strange until I realized what she tried to do. You're correct. She had a grand vision of her abilities, but she fell flat in the resurrection of her Dark Lord. Instead, she got me and became furious at her failure. The side effect is gaining portions of his memories."

"I had the right idea. Excellent. Do you have the memories of his final moments? The events that led to his demise?"

"Pieces of it, but it's enough I can tell you what appears to have taken place. The specifics I can't because of the way the memories formed."

"It will suffice, Destroyer. The Dark Lord and Black Dragon Commander watched and monitored everything from the Elders Hall. Then I received no further communication from them, so whatever transpired took place there."

"Dante, the Black Dragon Commander's son, arrived and convinced his father to change sides. Together they battled the Dark Lord. The Dark Lord managed to run the commander through, but Dante used the moment to sunspear the Dark Lord."

"The Commander had been the Dark Lord's second for many years. How would he switch loyalties so readily?"

"His wife, Premier. You're aware of her imprisonment and recent missing status from the facility?"

"Yes, a botched job by the supervising agent as I recall the Dark Lord saying." He glanced at Black Beauty. "He was most unhappy about the turn of events. How does that tie in with what occurred at the hall?"

"Dante found out and showed his father."

"His father believed him?"

"Not at first. I had him. I mean the Dark Lord did. Pardon me, it's hard to keep from doing that since his memories are so numerous now."

"An easy mistake to make. I understand your meaning. Continue."

"At first the commander didn't believe his son. The Dark Lord did what he does best and subtly spun a tale of other possibilities of what happened. He pulled the commander back into his fold and proceeded to successfully use the same tactics on the son. Spectacular to watch. A master at his craft. He had the boy, preparing to give his allegiance as well." Destroyer smiled as he remembered the scene of Dante on his knees before him.

"Then how does he lose both of them?"

Dante's words echoed in his head, "I will not break your heart, spear-bearer." Destroyer's eyes flashed in anger at the memory. Yes, those spear-bearers interfered again, but he wasn't ready to reveal all of his secrets yet to Black Beauty or the Premier. They didn't need to know the exact sequence of events. "The Ancient One interceded. He got through to Dante at the last moment and revealed to both that I, I mean, the Dark Lord was the one behind all the misery to their family. I could do nothing. The Ancient One bound me somehow while he showed them."

"That's when Dante dealt the death stroke."

"Yes, beaten by a youth."

"He is far from a mere youth and not to be underestimated. We all know that, Destroyer." He paused. "The Ancient One intervened, and the Dark Lord could do nothing. You're sure?"

"Yes. The Ancient One's chains held long enough for Him to take back the two."

"Most unsettling. I know of few instances of Him interceding on his followers' behalf directly. I'm not sure how to counter such an attack."

"Agreed. With that being the case, you go after the ones you can eliminate."

Black Beauty hissed, "Dante."

The Premier said, "Decided to rejoin the conversation, Black Beauty? Luckily Destroyer has been helpful in your absence. Target Dante for certain."

"His companions too, including that cousin of his and the Elder. I had Abigail as sure as dead if not for them barging in at the last."

"Of course, Black Beauty, you would have succeeded except for that," mocked Destroyer.

"Yes, the only person who believes that is you, Black Beauty, so your excuses will not work in the future. Yet, eliminating any or all of them is a worthy goal."

Destroyer said, "But they are also the hardest to bring down in a fight. There is a reason they are such a power to the Freedom Fighter cause and drew the Ancient One's direct assistance."

"But if we could, a great deal of our problems would disappear. It would take time for them to regroup."

"I agree they were considerable headaches for the Dark Lord."

He stared at Destroyer. "What are you not saying?"

"Another source caused him as much fury in his plans. The two spear-bearers."

"Yes, the day before the final confrontation he recalled to me again what chaos they had created. I understand they broke out Abigail and came to the aid of the Freedom Fighters in one of the attacks, but he never told me their identity."

"He didn't know, and Black Beauty failed in her task of tracking down that piece of information."

For the first time, Black Beauty took no offense to the slight. "I tried, but they are no amateurs and proved exceptional at covering their tracks. They penetrated through the security twice, once at a Black Dragon facility and once with the hired non-Black Dragon troops. Also, only one battle occurred as far as we know where they outright assisted the Freedom Fighters. The rest of the time they were satisfied to let it play out."

"Impressive except they are aiding the other side and only as they choose to. I wonder what determines their involvement. They should be considered as big of a danger as the others."

Destroyer said, "Or larger in a sense. There are too many unknowns about them and how they accomplished what they did. They could hold more power than we realize."

"You believe that?"

Inside Destroyer screamed, *"Yes of course! One of them pulled Dante from my grasp. I had him, and she ruined it."* Instead, he shrugged and said, "I'm not sure, but the Dark Lord saw them as quite the threat."

The Premier stood up. "I will too. You gave me the information I sought, and I'm confident in how I wish to proceed now. We will be in touch soon. Await my call. Until then, take your leave and the troop outside will escort you back to your ship." He watched the door shut on the two as the troop took over their care, and he sat back down in the chair. He wondered aloud, "What else didn't you tell me, and why did you keep it to yourself? Eventually, if it matters, I'll find out, Destroyer. The games continue." He laughed.

CHAPTER FIVE

"We're back, Alika," said Alena as she came through the door with Angelina on her heels.

Appearing from a side room, he said, "As I expected. Remember, I maintain a close eye on you two."

Angelina said, "That you do. Anything broke the monotony of today?"

He chuckled. "You have found ten different ways to ask me the same question in the past two days. It's amusing."

"Sorry, Alika. I'm … "

"Impatient. Who knows how short our time is, so it's understandable." He sat with the two following suit.

"Alena and I went through more of the downloads."

"But we would've snapped if we did any more. Doing a couple of shipping deals after our talk with Christopher was a good change of pace," said Alena.

"There's always a dealer or two that needs a last-minute bailout."

Alena grinned at her. "And you sense them even in a crowded bar."

"One of my many talents. We completed the second and final delivery of the day just now. Those two deals gave me a chance to get people talking too, but it didn't net any useful intel."

Alika said, "Keep in mind the Dark Lord and Black Dragon Commander haven't been dead long. There's still an adjustment time for Black Dragon and their operations. However, back to your original question." With a swipe across his data pad, an image of Christopher sitting on his ship appeared above them. "Chris is wondering if anything broke up the boredom of our day."

Christopher laughed, "Again? How many times today? I never would have pegged her for having such an interest in science, particularly glorified slime."

Alena giggled and Chris teased, "And you only thought you knew me. How about a nice surprise, and you give me an update about the pile of goo?"

"Alika and I are ready to deliver on this deal."

"Wait. Really? You figured it out?"

Alika laughed. "Patience is the lesson I have yet to impart to you, Chris." He turned back to Christopher. "We'll see you shortly, Christopher."

—ele—

"What have you got for us, Christopher?" Chris's eyes shone as she sat in Christopher's ship with the rest of the group.

"There's something wrong with you."

"What?"

"You shouldn't be eager to go running into an army of Black Dragon."

"Come on, Christopher, stop wasting time. Let's see it."

"Stop wasting time." He mimicked while making a face at her. "I'll regret this at some point, but here goes. Besides we already tested it." He tapped his neck with his hand.

"You did what?" She almost screamed as his words registered. "What did you do to yourself?"

"Why are you upset? Nothing worse than what we're doing to you two. I ensured it works, and it's safe. Alika supervised the whole time. Now watch." An image radiated from his data pad above them, poised to play.

Alena laid a hand on her arm. "Calm down. Everyone is okay. Come, let's take a look."

"Sorry. I overreacted. Go ahead, Christopher." She forced a smile for him.

The recording revealed Alika and a shirtless Christopher in the back quarters of Christopher's ship with an assortment of bottles and a handheld medical device on a nearby table.

"There's a lot of stuff out to test this." Chris' eyes scanned the numerous items as she glanced over at Christopher with renewed concern.

Alena looked over at Christopher and nodded at his image. "Not a bad-looking profile, Christopher. Have you been working out?"

He grinned. "Thanks for noticing, unlike some people. It's what I do in my spare time."

Chris gave up and dissolved into laughter at their joint effort to lighten her mood. "All right you two. You win. See, this is me not worried."

Christopher smiled and continued the projection. "We'll start with the mark. Fairly easy to replicate."

"It didn't look like it," said Alena.

"If I had to come up with it from scratch, yes. People do that often. Describe a picture in their head and one of those impression artists can translate it onto paper or skin for them. A talented group of people. Then there are others like me with a picture already and technology."

He played the video, and they watched as Alika took a thin film-like square and using tweezers placed it on the back of Christopher's neck. Next, he pulled out a small bottle with a screw top and bristle end to brush the substance over the square.

"It's the exact image. It's on skin squares?" Chris wrinkled her nose.

Christopher paused the recording. "Are you kidding? You wear something which works the same way all the time, and you don't recognize these?"

Alena laughed as she finished it. "Yes, silly, think of it like the skin clothes we wear under the armor breathe."

"Fine. Maybe it was the way the light hit it."

"Please do not ever use that line to escape one of your failed enterprises because you'll surely meet your end," said Alika.

"Now I'm getting it from you too. Quite unfair." Chris slumped in mock defeat as a faint smile appeared.

Christopher winked at her. "The image is unique on the patch, at least the ink we used to make it. Once we imprint it on you and brush the sealant on top, you'll be certifiable Black Dragon."

Chris stared up at the recording and slowly her words came out, "We'll truly be marked Black Dragon. We're stuck with it."

Christopher looked at her closely. "That's the idea. It's not made to just come off, then you two would be in trouble." His eyes widened. "Oh, Chris, no. Not that permanent." He reached over and grabbed her hand. "I would never do that to you, to either of you. Especially with the stuff already going through your head that you've told me about. We have the means to get you back in your skin after every operation. Promise. But against the normal elements, it'll hold up. We're good?"

She took a deep breath. "Yes. Still, I would've done it, if we had to."

"Alika and I know you would, but it won't happen. That's why we're here, to keep you from your own ... " Trailing off, he squeezed her hand before releasing it. "Next in line is you bleeding black. That one proved easiest to solve. Just a variation on a dye that's been used in the past within the medical community. Changing the color isn't an issue, and it goes both ways. One to change it to black and another to return you to normal."

Alena asked, "Even in large quantities and repeated? I mean, who knows how many trips we end up making?"

Alika nodded. "A legitimate concern on the surface, but you'll be fine. An equivalent of a syringe is all we'll need to use for the desired effect. The dyes were used in certain medical scans before we found less invasive methods to obtain the same information. Physicians always had different substances on hand because of allergies someone might have, so a variety of colors were the natural result."

"And we benefit from it now."

"Exactly."

Chris asked, "And the consistency?"

Christopher sighed. "Yes, the slime part. That almost became the breaking point. As I said in the beginning, the problem isn't creating the consistency. There are tons of ways, but none meant to be in the human body."

Alika nodded. "Agents to thicken or thin the blood have been around for ages. Certain circumstances call for it. However, to thicken one's blood to this extent, would result in deadly clots instantly."

"When we stayed with the idea your blood had to be slime consistency inside of you, we got nowhere."

Chris waved her hands in front of her. "But it does have to be. There's no way around it."

"I'm confused too, guys. How else will it work?"

Christopher smiled. "As long as when your blood spills it's slime consistency, you'll pass. It will thicken, but only in that situation."

"An agent will activate and react with it," said Alika.

"A Black Dragon soldier will see the black slime with the prick or in the syringe, and everyone is happy."

Chris asked, "How quick is it?"

"Instant. It must be to fool them."

"You're sure?"

"Watch." He resumed the video. "The first syringe is for blackened blood. The second one is for the slime consistency." They observed as Alika emptied two syringes into Christopher. A minute later, Alika pricked Christopher's finger, and it oozed a black slime. Next Alika used a syringe to siphon out a small sample of Christopher's blood, and the two exchanged a grin at the perfect match to the finger prick. "Told you."

Chris said, "Sounds like it's all figured out. The image, black blood, and the slime."

Alena shook her head. "There's still the slime pocket underneath the image."

"If you'll let us go on with our demonstration." Christopher continued the footage again. It showed Alika with another syringe filled with a black substance which he plunged into Christopher sideways at the mark's location. Alika felt the mark on Christopher and nodded his approval.

"What is it, really?" asked Alena.

Alika said, "A derivative of a mixture commonly used in human implants in medical circles which has been perfected over time."

"Entirely safe." Alena nodded.

Chris looked from Alika to Christopher. "You two have outdone yourselves. I'm impressed."

Christopher grinned. "Now that takes doing."

She smiled. "Does it? I'm sorry Alika had to stick you all those times. How long will you be Black Dragon?"

"Already back to normal."

Alika nodded. "Yes, for everything we did, there is an identical rapid means of reversal. Regrettably, it did involve more sticks for Christopher. The effects will remain from a couple of days to a week without needing a booster. The slime consistency of the blood was the hardest to produce and will break down first. It's also the one we were most hesitant to have continued for a long period. The rest have the extended life. However, we would not want you under enemy lines for more than a couple of days."

"You're sure everything is good again on you?" Chris turned concerned eyes on Christopher.

"See for yourself." He turned around and removed his shirt to reveal an image-free back. "Go ahead and feel where it was."

Chris reached over and felt nothing but the expected solid wall of muscle where the mark previously resided. "You're right as far as that."

Christopher slipped his shirt back on and faced her again. Then he retrieved his dagger.

"What are you doing?" Her voice rang out.

Ignoring her, he made a tiny incision on the pinkie finger of his left hand. It flowed a bright red. "Convinced?"

"A simple yes would have sufficed."

"Not with you." He grinned at her as he held a napkin on the cut to stop the flow.

"He's got you there, Chris." Alena paused. "You and Alika perfected the recipe for a complete transformation."

"Appears they have." Chris turned to Christopher. "Will you be okay if you run into Black Dragon?"

"Chris, I can handle a blade."

"Of course, you can. But what we're up against now is a whole other level of dangerous."

"I get it. You and Alena volunteering to give me pointers?"

"Whatever we can do to keep you safe."

"Under normal circumstances I wouldn't take weapon training from a couple of women," His teasing comment elicited a mock glare from the two. "But I realize I'm looking at two of the best individuals who ever touched a blade, so I won't pass up the offer."

Chris said, "Appreciate the compliment, but I've seen a few others that could put us in our place."

"No way. On even ground with you two, yes. Fortunately, those people are on the same side as us."

⁂

"That was something to watch." Christopher shook his head in awe as the two walked over to him and Alika after their impressive demonstration.

Alena grinned. "Your turn, Christopher."

"You two are here to help me, right? Cause I'm not matching up at all."

"I promise I won't let her chop you to bits."

"Counting on you to keep your end of that, Alena." Christopher moved forward. "Chris, go easy on an old man."

"Don't try playing that card now."

"It's the perfect time to play it."

Chris laughed. "You have a point. No worries, Christopher. We're going to take care of you. Ready?"

He smiled. "Ready."

"Begin," said Alika.

Christopher attempted to catch his breath as he jumped back to avoid another swipe from Chris. They had practiced for at least twenty minutes now. Terrifying enough he knew she wasn't fighting anywhere near her normal abilities. Also, he had another advantage, which resounded behind him.

Alena's calm voice instructed him, "You left yourself open. She could've gone low and taken you out. If you were the enemy, she would have."

Christopher said as they continued, "You're right. So, like this instead?" He adjusted as Chris helped by recreating the move.

"Better. If she gets you, it's only an ugly swipe this time."

Alika looked over at Alena. "Time to switch?"

Alena nodded and stepped forward.

⁓ꝏ⁓

Christopher sipped his drink as he stood inside his ship with the other three after his practice session. "I feel more confident about my chances now thanks to you two."

"Although if you run into trouble, you know we'll be found," said Chris.

"Somehow it's always the case. I'll be careful. You two do the same if you need my help."

"We will."

"Got everything?" He pointed to the rolling luggage bag in Alena's grasp.

"Yes. This should keep us supplied for at least twenty operations, and we know how to make more if necessary. Of course, we'll reach out to you if we get into a time crunch."

⁓ꝏ⁓

Ryan plopped down on the couch in Dante's quarters. "Two days of this, and I'm beat, Dante."

Dante answered as he sat down with his drink. "Me too, and I'm not sure if the other commanders are jumping onboard with the plan."

"Let's see them come up with better."

"True. Just organizing the teams to take over the weeding out and getting them trained for it and any weird situations they might run into had half of them sweating."

"How I hope that was a one-time thing your girl stumbled across. Alika seemed certain about that." He paused. "Gabe still keeping our two under wraps?"

"Yeah, and he will. He knows what's at stake." Dante ran his hands through his hair. "I wish we knew how it panned out so far with them."

An exasperated sigh escaped Ryan. "My mind won't let it loose either, what they're walking into and everything that could happen."

"What are we going do? How are we supposed to keep our sanity?"

"We don't have a choice but to hold it together."

CHAPTER SIX

Alena came over to Angelina, seated at the table. "You need to get sleep. We have an early start tomorrow."

"I'm about to. Just wanted to make sure our access is in order."

"Because the hundredth go-over is finally deemed enough? Stop doubting yourself."

"I wonder what they're doing in that building."

"Likely we won't find out."

"Such a missed opportunity. We're right there, Alena. How can we pass it by?"

"We discussed this how many times today? This is a simple run to see how things are being done now, to verify we can pass inspection."

"Anything more is a bonus."

"Finally. Go to bed." Alena crossed her arms and stared down at her.

"You really will won't you?"

"Like you have to ask?"

Angelina laughed as she closed down her data pad, got up, and headed for bed. "Fine, you win."

"Of course I did, but I always do."

Angelina lay in bed and drifted off quickly. It seemed she had only been asleep for minutes, when she opened her eyes with an iron grip on her sheet that she managed to twist into a mangled knot. Relief poured through her as she let out a deep breath once she took in her surroundings. Her eyes met Alena's who approached her bedside.

"Get some sleep?"

"Enough."

"Nightmares?"

"Not back to full force yet, but the time with Dante is losing its effect." She got up. "I'll shower and everything, so we can get this operation in the air."

Alena put a hand on her shoulder. "I'm sorry."

"It's okay. This is my world. I got a reprieve, but we expected nothing more."

"Still doesn't make it easier to take," she said as she watched Angelina walk away.

"That's the final stick," said Alika as he laid the syringe aside. "My apologies for the frequency. I don't anticipate it being this close together in the future."

Alena said, "No way around it. We had to test it out last night and today."

"Now to see if it all pays off," Angelina said as she put on the Black Dragon gear.

Alika inspected the two before they boarded their ship. "You look and sound like Black Dragon. Be safe, and I'll be monitoring as always."

Angelina stared out into space from one of the cockpit chairs. Would this work? Black Dragon possessed new leadership. What if they changed things? Like the security? Was she flying both of them to their death? Dante's concerned face appeared in her mind along with his voice begging her not to go through with another operation. What if he proved right? Suddenly she missed him anew. What she would give to be caught up in his arms now and feel his reassuring touch. A beep from the console interrupted her thoughts, and she scolded herself for being distracted. It was rule one in any mission, and she already broke it. Forcing Dante from her thoughts, she focused on the scene before her. It was a large building with two huge areas attached. Black Dragon personnel strolled in and out of the structure, but seemingly in no particular pattern. "Pretty busy again."

"They should be questioning us soon. We're about to eliminate one of the places from our list."

"If Black Beauty visited here, there must be something of interest."

"Maybe, but the Black Dragon scene has changed since we dropped in on this place."

"It's a starting point." Another beep signaling an incoming communication interrupted Angelina's thought and she said, "Permission to land, sir."

"Transmit your information, and we'll initiate your clearance to do so," commanded the Black Dragon troop.

"Transmitting, sir."

A minute later the troop said, "Land where indicated quickly."

"Yes, sir," said Angelina.

"That one still opens doors," said Alena.

"So far. Those two areas are hangars like we thought. Makes sense with seeing personnel, but no ships out in the open."

Alena and Angelina took only a few steps out of their ship before a Black Dragon soldier blocked their path and commanded, "Step forward."

Immediately the soldier grabbed hold of Alena, and violently spun her around to horse collar her, inducing a light gagging sound from her. Angelina forced herself to remain standing at attention, as she witnessed the harsh treatment of her friend by the soldier.

"You check out," said the soldier as he released Alena and shoved her forward.

Of course. The soldiers were checking for the mark as expected. Angelina braced herself for her turn, but it never came.

"Now your business here?"

Angelina said, "We need to make a repair to the ship and retrieve a part to do so."

"Fair enough. I'll leave you to it."

The two headed for the entrance that took them further into the facility.

"Stop you two," the Black Dragon soldier called, and his footsteps closed in on them.

They froze in place and turned to face what new crisis awaited them.

"You said you had a repair to complete?"

"Yes, sir," said Alena.

"What type?"

"At least one of the ion coils needs replacing in the control panel."

"Sounds reasonable."

Angelina watched him take entirely too long to ponder their story, and her thoughts roamed to the Black Dragon sword that could be in her hand.

He turned to a nearby soldier. "Take over for me. I'll be back shortly." He returned his attention to Alena and Angelina. "Come with me now. Down the hall. Move."

They obeyed but finally, Angelina asked, "Sir, is there a problem?"

"Yes, but I have the solution." He opened a door to the right and motioned them. "In here, now."

Resistance would prove pointless. The room wasn't horribly busy, but enough Black Dragon troops hovered around that the two would make a scene. Even if they escaped the room, getting back to the ship would be a larger challenge with the racket they would create. Boxes of various sizes filled the room, but there was an order to them. It appeared a strange place to serve as a holding area or carry out an interrogation. So, despite their misgivings, the two walked inside the room as instructed.

"Continue moving. Down that way," said the soldier as he followed them. "Ion coils, correct?"

"Yes, sir," said Alena.

"Third shelf down in front of you." He tapped his feet on the floor. "One of you grab it. Now."

Angelina quickly did, not wanting to fuel the soldier's impatience further as she realized they had anticipated danger where none existed.

"Keep coming. One of you gets that part too." He pointed to another box before continuing down the row as he occasionally consulted his data pad. "Retrieve that as well, and one more piece should do it." He ushered them to the next aisle and zeroed in on the last box. "This one too." After routing them back to the front, he pointed to a small rolling cart. "Stack it all on here. That's everything you need for the repairs."

"Sir, we only needed the one part."

"Yes, to repair your ship. However, there is another vessel, and we're behind schedule. The orders that came through are adamant we get caught up. A coil can take considerable time to replace, but with both of you, it will go quickly. Then you'll have ample time to fix the other ship and move to whatever additional duties you are assigned. Understood?"

"Yes, sir," said Angelina.

Alena pushed the cart of supplies as the soldier led them from the room and said, "I'll direct you to the second ship needing repairs once we're back to the hangar area. I'm fortunate you two showed up today."

Angelina stared from their ship's cockpit in dismay. "We won't have free rein of the place."

"No snooping for you." Alena giggled.

"Aren't you unhappy about this?"

"A little, but we accomplished our goal. We established we pass inspection. I could've done without getting stuck repairing one of their ships, but we have no choice if we wish to keep up appearances."

"I still don't have to like it. How much time do we stay in here to make our repair believable?"

"Give it thirty minutes."

Alena and Angelina all too soon stood inside the Black Dragon ship needing repairs. Alena hovered over the control panel and watched as the internal scan finished. "You think we'll need all these parts?"

"Don't know. I got the impression he didn't know the extent of the problems with it. What's the scan say?" Angelina came closer to study the screen with her.

"A fair guess on his part, but the reading doesn't line up if it's something in propulsion."

"It would be showing skewed as well, but it's not. Over here it's showing strangely too."

"The combination points more to navigation." Alena swiped a button and listened. "The propulsion isn't charging up right though."

"So, a problem with ... "

"You two already hard at work on this one?" The Black Dragon soldier stood at the entrance of the ship.

"Accessing it now, sir, " said Alena.

"Your findings?"

"Our assessment is leading us to an issue in propulsion and navigation or the connection between the two."

"Based on?" He came closer to the screen, and they explained while motioning to various points on the monitor. After listening, he nodded. "Agreed. Excellent work. I got pulled away as I started delving into it."

"Considering that you made a reasonable assumption. Of course, we haven't done the repair yet, so we could find another issue once we begin."

"That's always an unpleasant possibility, and our leadership is unforgiving about delays. The Dark Lord and Black Dragon Commander were impatient, but the current one is proving their rival."

They scanned the ship further to conceal their eagerness for what they hoped the soldier might reveal.

Angelina casually ventured, "Yes, it's been impressive how everything continued to flow, despite the loss of them both."

Alena said, "I'm sure it surprised those Freedom Fighters."

"They thought us beaten. Losing the Dark Lord and the Black Dragon Commander were unimaginable blows, but our leadership prepared for the unthinkable. I sure wouldn't want to cross this one in charge now."

Angelina asked as she worked with the control panel, "You estimate he's tougher than the Black Dragon Commander?"

"Certainly, he is equal in that regard and could be as scary. He's more hands-on with wanting updates than the Dark Lord. In that respect, he reminds me more of the Black Dragon Commander."

Alena nodded. "I noticed that too."

"With everything that's happened, we need a strong hand at the command now," said Angelina.

"Or a fist," the soldier laughed. "However, not everyone agrees with us. Black Beauty for one. She didn't care for her demotion."

"I imagine she wouldn't. She doesn't back down," said Angelina.

"At least not that I've ever seen," said Alena.

"But this new head of Black Dragon made it clear he's giving the orders now, and she's taking them like the rest of us. She left quite unhappy from her visit."

"You were there for the whole thing?" asked Angelina.

"No, I haven't been on the command ship, but I learned from another soldier what happened. The remainder of what I needed to know I heard like everyone else. Our new leader left no doubt we're to take commands only from him unless he says otherwise. No more from Black Beauty."

Alena said, "Anyone that puts fear into Black Beauty is worthy of our respect and to hold the Black Dragon leadership."

"He means to. I'm glad I didn't witness any of it. I know what he said about her, but she still scares me. Although maybe we won't see too much of her or the other one."

"The other one?" asked Alena.

"Yes, she brought somebody with her. Left with him too."

Angelina said, "Strange. I've never seen her with anyone else unless commanding one of us, and those days are over now."

"Wonder who he was," said Alena.

"Nobody knew, but he had the creepy vibe going too." He shrugged as he looked down at his data pad. "I need to get back, but if you require additional supplies I'll bring them to you."

"Thanks for your help," said Alena.

Once he exited the ship and was out of earshot, Angelina said to Alena, "That turned out better than snooping."

"Agreed. I take back what I said about the repair."

A couple of hours later, Alena swiped the cockpit controls and watched as the viewscreen changed. "That's got it."

"I hope so." Angelina groaned as she pulled herself off the floor. "The panel is secure."

"The final scan is coming through, and it shows clear."

"And that's what a working propulsion sounds like," Angelina grinned inside her helmet, but it quickly disappeared. "Although it grates me it's on a Black Dragon ship. Let's gather up the spare supplies and check out."

"Finished you two?" asked the soldier as the two approached.

"Yes, sir. Here are the unused items still in their boxes, and on this side are the defective ones," said Angelina.

"Well done." He took inventory but stopped at one of them "Wait, this is the one you took for your ship."

"We didn't need the coil as an electrical issue within the system turned out to be our culprit. The coil would have been the easier repair," said Alena.

"You're right. Locating those can send your head into a maze."

"Although if we hadn't found it, we would have needed the part too. Electrical problems are a sure way to overload a coil," said Angelina.

"We'll go now, sir. We don't want to make the new leadership unhappy and fall behind in our duties," said Alena.

"That's a smart policy to adhere to."

CHAPTER SEVEN

The man landed his ship as directed with the realization he never would have located the place without the supplied coordinates. An open field stretched out before him, except for the Black Dragon vessel parked alongside his own. He stepped from his ship, and directly several Black Dragon soldiers greeted him.

"Leave your vessel here. We'll ensure it remains safe." The soldier motioned to a couple of those with him, and they positioned themselves around the man's vessel. "Move, now."

The man walked into the Black Dragon ship, wondering about the wisdom of his current decision.

"Sit."

He did as a hood slid over his head, and he stiffened.

"Comfortable?"

"No complaints here." He felt the ship lift and had no choice but to settle in for the ride. His dealings with Black Dragon always ended with a sweet payoff, so he had no reason to think otherwise this time. Of course, he expected there would be adjustments after the recent events. At least what the rumors said had happened. Perhaps he would get the full story, but truthfully he could care less.

"Get up and walk."

They landed, and he rose as instructed. Black Dragon troops on either side of him guided his steps from the ship to an unknown location. Their footsteps sounded like those on the surface of a hallway of a building or maybe a large ship. He couldn't be sure. Moments later, he heard a door open and close and one of the soldiers barked, "Sit in the chair, now." Only then did the soldier remove the hood from his head so he could inspect his surroundings. Four soldiers stood in a room with him and a table stationed in front of him with a cup and a pitcher on it. The soldier motioned him. "Eyes on the screen and listen."

The man stared up at the black viewscreen mounted in the corner wall.

"Welcome. I am the leader of Black Dragon now. Your unique skills have been useful to us before, and I mean for that to continue." The distorted voice emerged from the blackened monitor.

"I see no reason it can't."

"Excellent to hear. Feel free to have a drink. I promise it's not tainted." He chuckled. "It wouldn't be to my advantage to eliminate the person I wish to employ, correct?"

"Makes sense." The man took a sip of it. "I'll get used to your changes, like the hood over the head routine."

"New management. New procedures. However, I'll advise you many things about Black Dragon remain unchanged. You will do well to remember."

"Understood."

"Then we can begin. I have a deal to propose to you, one well suited to your area of expertise. I warn you to consider it thoroughly before accepting my offer."

"I'm listening." A soldier handed him a data pad.

"Read the information on the data pad, and then we'll proceed."

His eyebrow arched as he read the details from the data pad and then slowly put it down on the table to stare back at the viewscreen. "Quite a target you're aiming for. She's not just coming down. She's deadly with the sunspear. I've heard the stories. Taking her out is a tall order."

"Everything you said is accurate. Head-to-head, I agree you lose the battle each time. Another approach is necessary to secure her. Eliminating her is a lofty goal, but it's not what I'm asking of you. My request is more difficult. She is more useful to me alive."

"That is more challenging. She'll fight me every inch even if I capture her unless she's … " A slow grin spread on his face.

"Exactly."

"Once you have her?"

"Do you care?"

"No."

"What is your true question?"

"There's a reason nobody has gotten to her. This job will cost Black Dragon a hefty amount if I take it. A significant dent in the budget."

"The real question as I guessed. I am prepared to pay you handsomely if you deliver her. See for yourself the updated information on the data pad."

The man picked up the device and stared at the payout. He forced his hand to remain steady and to keep his business-like façade. Inside though his heart raced, and his thoughts went a million miles at once. He wouldn't have to take another deal for months if he delivered on this one. They wanted her bad, and this new leadership was determined to make it worth the galaxy to see it happen. After laying the data pad back on the table, he looked back up at the viewscreen. "It's an enormous amount to secure one woman."

"She's an impressive target with much to offer Black Dragon. Yet she's only part of the plan, an end to a means. If we have her, we won't just obtain her. In time, the game will play out."

"And Black Dragon wins the whole house. I see why you're willing to put such an expensive price tag on her."

"Can you deliver this prize and are you agreeable to the deal, or do I look elsewhere?"

"I can deliver, and I want the deal."

"You are confident and have shown yourself capable in the past, which is why I requested you. However, you should be aware of all conditions before you agree. As I said, some things about Black Dragon have not changed. Failure will not be tolerated, especially with a mission of this utmost importance. Just as there is an impressive payoff for success, there will be an equivalent dire consequence for failure. You do not wish to see that vision come to pass; I assure you. Pick up the data pad again to read the new information. Make sure you understand it. If you have reconsidered, you can walk away and no hard feelings."

The man picked up the data pad, and his eyes widened, weighing the deal in his head with the additional information. It was a huge gamble. The more he thought about his target and her fighting abilities, the more doubt that crept into his head. However, a plan had already begun coming together to avoid a confrontation with her. His determination soared again. He could do it, deliver on this heist like the past ones. Yet his eyes focused on the data pad again to remind him of the consequences of he didn't come through as promised. With a job as big as this, he shouldn't be surprised. It was an ugly part of this business and worse so with Black Dragon as the employer. He had always known, and it never stopped him before. The sweet payoff came back to him, whispering in his ear like a lover enticing him. With his mind made up, he put the device down and stared back at the viewscreen. "I understand what happens if I fail, but I don't intend to. I'll take your deal and make your delivery."

"Excellent. Decide how long you need to have the target delivered. There can be no mistakes. It's important to allow yourself sufficient time."

"I'm figuring it out as we speak."

"Now for the last piece of business."

"Of course," He couldn't help tensing up as the Black Dragon soldier came closer to him.

"My extra assurance. After it's done, you'll be escorted back. Best of luck with your endeavor. Your success will make life easier for all of us."

The viewscreen went silent, and the man concentrated on his imagined future payoff.

CHAPTER EIGHT

"It's a relief to be back in my skin again." Angelina reclined in the chair at home.

"That soldier took way too much pleasure in checking for the mark. Whiplash on demand is a truer name for it," Alena scowled as she rubbed her neck, and Alika set aside the syringe.

"Rather surprising they didn't check everyone, but apparently they're only random checks. It'll be my turn next time. Sorry though, Alena." Angelina's eyes turned mischievous. "Too bad Ryan isn't here to take your mind off it."

"Kiss and make it better." Alena grinned. "I'd go for that now."

"I bet so." Angelina laughed. "I wonder what they're up to right now." She turned to Alika. "You would know."

"The greatest danger is their dying of boredom."

"Really? That doesn't sound like Lana," said Alena.

"I exaggerate, but it can't be helped with the current circumstances. Your two men find it easier to solve the problem with a swing of a blade or a shot from a blaster. Instead, they are preparing to face a threat where none of those things will be of much help to them."

"It must be frustrating to them. The Black Dragon holds all the pieces now, and we ended up helping them today. That ship will be pointed at a Freedom Fighter vessel and could shoot it down," said Angelina.

"We had to or else our cover was blown," said Alena.

"You know who ends up in the sky when there's an attack. Not usually my Dante. It's always Caleb and probably Ryan again, your Ryan, Alena. What if the ship we fixed downs one of them?"

"It won't. They'll take it out before that happens. It doesn't matter. That ship makes it back into the air with or without our help. They planned to repair it, so it's back for use today rather than tomorrow. Besides Dante is in as much danger as Ryan or Caleb with those disc weapons."

"She's correct. Child, you cannot make everything your fault," said Alika.

"Because it's not. We had no choice but to do it, right? I'm not sure how much I can keep telling myself that. I think as many times as I've … " she stopped and shook her head.

"What is it?" asked Alika.

"How often did I hear, 'Know your role. Learn it. Own it. Always play it to its end.' If I didn't understand anything else, I learned that. It became my childhood incantation, the only thing that mattered to both of my parents. It always struck me strangely that they spoke the same words and meant them so differently. Although I hated it, I couldn't do what I do now without perfecting that lesson. In that sense, I should be thankful to my father and his teaching methods."

"No, child, you should never be grateful for anything your father put you through. No child should have endured what you have."

"Where would I be without playing my role though, Alika? The identical advice from both. Perhaps I'm a fool to believe there was a difference."

"There is a great contrast, and deep down you know that." He reached over to clasp Angelina's hand. "One used it for power, to serve a darkness that consumed him. Then he forged it as a tool to manipulate you, to create a waking nightmare for you, his daughter, for his brutal purposes. The other utilized it to fight that darkness until her last breath. She wielded it to survive his cruelty, to teach her daughter to do the same, and protect her as long as she could."

Angelina released Alika's hand. "The difference is clear when you describe it. She sounds as noble as I remember her, but would everyone see it like that? Or would they see it as a mother's misguided love, the mother who risked too much for her daughter? What would she have done differently if she didn't concern herself with protecting me? Was I worth the cost?" she bit her lip and paused,

"After all I'm the daughter of my mother and my father. What if one is stronger than the other in me?"

Alena said, "One is. You are your mother's child."

"And if you're wrong?"

"We're not." Alika stared back at her. "Your mother's spirit shines through you, but your father's shadow covers it before your eyes. You must see beyond it to the truth as your mother did."

"Maybe I can't. His shadow is larger than you realize." She paused. "I fear I'm more of my father's child than either of you admit."

"Child, don't."

"I need to shower and change, and we'll go over more if you wish. Decide where Alena and I want to head for tomorrow." She rose, ending any further discussion.

~ele~

Opening her eyes, she stared down at her hands. They were different, smaller as those of a child. She knew before she looked up, and a wave of panic swept through her as she confirmed her surroundings. Then the shove came, accompanied by the impatient voice she dreaded, "Move, now. Don't make me say it again, you insolent child." Her father towered over her, glowering at her.

She quickly fell into step beside him, scolding herself for already angering him since he usually delivered on his threats. As they continued to walk down the corridor of the huge ship with the Black Dragon escort, she attempted to calm her younger self with the knowledge she would be okay. She had done all of these visits and lived through them, some better than others. Over half of the encounters had been routine if any involving Black Dragon could be considered such. However, there were other visits. She pushed those from her mind, but part of her pleaded it wouldn't turn out to be one of those. Although she was no longer the child, the memory of the broken state those times left her brought it all back anew. Yet no one would know the turmoil going on inside of her by looking at her exterior. From the moment she boarded the ship with her father, she made herself unreadable. Her mother's parting words still whispered in her ear, "Play your role while you're there. Do as I taught you. It's your only chance of staying safe. Please, sweetheart." Now she embraced the instructions as her face became expressionless, not a word escaped from her mouth, and her eyes were vacant. While walking down the hall, they passed another man with a child. She estimated him to be several years older than her and saw him try to catch her eye. Retaining the empty stare, she pretended to be unaware of her surroundings, including him. He pondered that one day they could end up working together for a common cause, and he scoped her out as a desirable ally for the future. She accessed him too, but for a far different reason. Know your enemy as well. Another lesson imparted to her early. She cataloged him as she had done the rest without appearing to do so.

They stopped in front of a chamber door. The Black Dragon soldier nodded and turned to them. "He will see you now." The door opened, and she entered the room with her father.

A cloaked figure appeared from the shadows and seated himself on an imposing, ornate chair.

She maintained the same blank stare as she wondered again how the chair could be comfortable and knew it couldn't be. It simply served as another show of how he thought everyone should cower before him. Not that he needed it as she forced herself to keep her stance despite the solid black eyes drilling into her.

"The last visit went beyond the anticipated hour. I know you had no problems waiting."

"Of course not, Dark Lord. We are at your service," said Draco.

"Yes, you are, and you brought the child too as I requested."

"I anticipate the request as it's often now."

"Both of you sit." He continued only after the two did so. "First business is in order. It'll be boring to the child, but she'll manage."

Internally she briefly relaxed as she pretended not to register the back and forth between her father and the Dark Lord as they discussed shipping schedules and incoming deliveries which her father needed to ensure happened. The conversation went from mundane to heated.

"Draco, let me remind you I have taken great pains to make your area a safe and lucrative location for my enterprises. I will not see it wasted."

"It's not. The shipments are secure coming through, and they suspect nothing."

"You better trust you're right, and keep your end of the ploy going. However, I believe you're slipping on your duties."

"In what way, and I'll rectify it at once."

"The first rule of Black Dragon, play your role. I hope you are not neglecting your child's education as much as you are forgetting how to practice it."

"The child is told every waking moment and is shown as often. Whether she is smart enough to incorporate it fully, is beyond my control. So, in what area are you concerned I am losing my way?"

The Dark Lord leaned closer to Draco. "You will lose more than your way in an instant if you do not watch your speech." A dagger appeared from underneath his cloak to point at Draco. "I would hate to expose your daughter to such a scene."

"We both know that's not a consideration for us. However, I do care for my skin, so I apologize for how I misspoke. What do you wish me to do, my Dark Lord?"

The Dark Lord turned to her. "See, how agreeable your father can become? They all can be, and I know how to bring it out of them."

Angelina did not acknowledge his comment.

"As I'm sure you did with your last visitors. We saw the pair leaving as we came."

The Dark Lord forgot Angelina and returned his attention to Draco. "Yes, they are particularly interesting. I see high potential for them in Black Dragon service. Both are eager to serve, and the child is quite trainable." He glanced over at Angelina. "Some prove resistant and take more time. However, I haven't found one that can't be trained, and I won't see it happen." Turning back to Draco, he continued, "You are to get closer to those who would seek to undermine my efforts."

"I already do."

"Increase your engagements. More private ones."

"That's why I have my family I adore so." Draco's voice dripped with sarcasm. "To take care of that nonsense."

The Dark Lord resumed as if Draco had not spoken. "Specific families. Target them. Like this one. An administrator on one of the planets that would be useful to us and this family too. They are friends with one of the commanders." He motioned towards Angelina. "Use the girl. They have a brat about her age. Although if she acts like this, she'll be a poor companion to any child."

"I assure you she doesn't behave so but only shuts down here."

"She's happy at home?"

"That's going too far. She does as she's told. She plays her role and if it's pretending to be a happy child to any visitor that drops in she does so. I've made clear the consequences for failing to fulfill her role in our house."

Angelina felt the Dark Lord's eyes searching her face and eyes for a clue to unlock the wall he repeatedly encountered. His eyes suddenly gleamed. "Walk with me, girl."

She stayed seated as if she hadn't heard him. Yet she couldn't ignore the menacing tone of his next words, "I meant now."

"Do as he says," roared Draco.

It proved unnecessary as she already stood up. The Dark Lord placed his hand on the small of her neck, guiding her across the room to his display window.

"What do you see?"

She stared out at the starry expanse and remained speechless.

"Perhaps that is the proper response for once. Some are amazed by the beauty of the stars and space in all its glory. It is quite the view. Do you know what I see though? A galaxy of possibilities. An endless domain waiting for the perfect moment, for the right person to seize and hold it captive. That person must only create the means to do it and then the one cannot be stopped. Look there. It's coming together. I'm creating that instrument, that army, that iron fist which will resound throughout this sea of stars and beyond. It will be the manifestation of all power in the galaxy, and it's mine to command." He turned her around and forced her chin to look up at him. "This is what you are a part of, one way or the other. You will choose it in time. They all do." He moved in closer to her. "What do you care about, dear? I'm starting to see. Those are dangerous to hold close to your heart. Soon it won't matter. What I desire is what you will as well. You will serve me." He whispered, "I can wait."

She was falling, drowning as the terror flooded her frame and darkness covered her eyes. Then she jerked up, and her eyes flew open. A half scream emerged from her, and her eyes dropped to her clenched hands fisted around the bedsheets again. She released them and stretched her hands, relieved to find them back to normal size. Two hands grasped her shoulders, but she jumped at it. Only then did she register Alena's voice, "Hey, it's me. It's okay." She stared at Alena as the other voice echoed in her head, "You will serve me. I can wait."

She whimpered, "No."

"Yes, you're safe. I promise." Alena wrapped her arms around Angelina in a hug.

"You're sure?" she asked as she encircled her trembling arms around Alena.

"Always," said Alena.

After a minute, Angelina pulled back. "Sorry. Did I wake you?"

"No, I was already getting up." She forced a smile. "What woke you?"

"What doesn't?" Curling her arms around her legs, she rested her head on her knees. "A blast from my childhood. One of those field trips to the Dark Lord with my father." She caught the look from Alena. "Don't worry. One of the normal visits."

"Any time with that man consisted of only the terrible."

"Not like the other visits, Alena."

"I know."

"I need a shower, and we'll start in on it." She shook her head as she headed for the other room.

⎯ ℓℓℓ ⎯

"Alena told me how you met the morning," Alika said as he looked across the table at Angelina as they all sat at it.

"I expected she would, but I'm fine. It was one of the routine visits with him."

Alika's eyes flashed with anger. "There is nothing routine about twisting the mind of a child like those two did to you as well as the others the Dark Lord toyed with. There will never be a defense for it, and you endured far more than ... " He took a deep breath as he reached over to clasp her hand. "Are you all right, child?"

"Yes, Alika." She smiled at him.

He squeezed her hand and released it. "Where would you like to go from here?"

She pulled her data pad out and projected an entry onto the wall. "That one."

"Still intrigued to see where Drew leads you," said Alena.

"Quite the dangerous starting destination. A point I agree with Dante on," said Alika.

"He wouldn't approve of any of these operations. If he decided for me, he'd go with Christopher's suggestion."

"Dante would gladly, and I am not convinced you should continue refusing him." Alika laughed as Alena joined in.

"Alika!" Her pretended reprimand ended in her laughter.

Alena teased her further, "Alika and Seth would make it happen for you two. One ceremony. Say the word. Dante won't need any urging."

"If only it were that easy."

Alena turned back to the screen. "Black Dragon ruins everything. What about where we just left?"

Angelina shook her head as she displayed another image above them. "I downloaded a basic blueprint of the place while we fixed the ship. The facility felt like a stop-off to me, like a way station, and that's true from what I saw. Black Beauty's appearance there makes sense. I don't see us finding anything useful there. Maybe put a tiny dent in their supplies if you blew the building up, but our weapon isn't there."

"What do you believe is uncovered by following Drew's path?" asked Alika.

"I don't know. The center of it all. Where the weapon is. How they're creating the Drews of the galaxy. How to turn the tide. The one holding all the strings, Alika."

"What will you do if you find that one?"

"Tear him and his whole empire to pieces once and for all. End this. After everything, I should be the one that gets to do it."

He studied her before answering, "Perhaps so. Let's consider it further while we fix lunch."

CHAPTER NINE

Commander Austin took a deep breath as he stood at the head of his conference room back on his soil and tried to determine the thoughts of those with him. Satisfied with what he sensed, he wrapped up his update, "I wanted to share with you the high points of my conference with Lana as soon as I returned, and I've covered everything. I will be meeting with all of you in varying degrees once we strategize how to put into play the information I have given you. It will change the way we do many things. We need to prepare for the worst if it occurs but hope it doesn't end up being the case. Since there is nothing else," his eyes focused on Sanders whose question froze mid-sentence, "you're dismissed for now."

The room cleared except for three individuals.

Austin said, "You could have made that easier, Sanders."

"You told us everything?"

"I told you what you needed to be told."

"Unbelievable." He crossed his arms across his chest. "I knew it."

Simon said, "Give Dad a break, would you? He just got in."

"Get off it, Simon. You half listened as usual, so you didn't notice he gave us nothing."

"I paid attention enough to see you're being a pain in the rear. Do you think you have all the answers? You're scared too but won't admit it like the rest of us."

"I'm not afraid! I just don't aim to sit here, and wait for them to come at our door." He marched to stand in front of his brother.

"Because your idea is to take a fleet of ships and shoot at the stars and hope you hit something. Brilliant, Sanders. What a strategy." Simon stared into his brother's eyes, undaunted by the anger raging in them.

Their mother's voice softly commanded, "Enough, boys." She came to position herself between them, and one of her palms rested on each of their chests. "I said stand down you two, now."

"Your mother is right." Austin moved to stand beside his wife, grateful again for her ability to bring peace to chaos. "No more discussing this here. I mean it." He directed his gaze to Sanders. "I'm open to continuing this calmly in my private study but not here."

"We can discuss this as your father wishes, right?" She paused as both men nodded. "You will abide by what your father says, what he is willing to share or not share?" She waited again as they nodded before motioning them towards her husband's study.

Austin wrapped an arm around his wife's waist and smiled at her. "Thank you, sweetheart."

She kissed him on the cheek. "You're welcome. I missed you."

"You too, and I'll show you how much later." He winked at her.

"Now that we're comfortable, how about you try again with your father?" Docia looked at her two sons from her place seated on the couch leaned up against Austin.

Sanders said, "Dad, you stayed there for a few days. There had to be more than what you reported in that room."

"I repeat I told you what you needed to know."

"Did you lie to us?"

"No. Everything I said is true."

"But you didn't tell us everything."

"No, I didn't."

"Why not?"

"In this area, I am a commander first, Sanders. There is certain information that must remain with me only. You aspire to command one day as you've indicated numerous times. With that calling comes responsibilities and trusts which have to be kept. This is one of those situations. I can't break that any more than I would ask you if you find yourself in the same position."

"We're your own family, and it feels as if you're saying you can't trust us."

"Is that what this is about?"

"A little bit." Sanders took a deep breath. "Okay, yes, particularly, with your mentioning of the Black Dragon spies."

Simon patted his brother on the back and grinned. "Come on bro, Dad doesn't think that badly of us."

Sanders grinned back at Simon. "Not yet, but if I keep being a pain in the rear he'll reconsider."

"You were in your element today, but I could've taken you down."

"You wish." He laughed. "Simon, I'm sorry about earlier. You know how I get."

"I've stopped keeping count. Already forgotten for me, but maybe not for everyone else." He glanced over at his parents and back at his brother.

Sanders nodded and turned back to his parents. "Sorry to both of you, especially you, Dad. You're right. That's really all you can say?"

"Yes, and it has nothing to do with a lack of trust in any of you. The Black Dragon spies have always been from what we're being told, but it's coming to a head now. They could be closer in our camp than we realize. An overheard conversation could jeopardize things further and give Black Dragon another advantage."

Simon shook his head. "That's the last thing we need to do with the death shot they have targeted at us." He paused. "It does seem strange there's no effort made to prevent that shot from firing. That's one part I agree with Sanders on."

"We have our role in this, and we must concentrate on it. Information should stay in a tight circle for everyone's safety."

Sanders' eyes widened. "Dad, you're not really suggesting there's a spy here? Some of our advisors have worked with us for years."

"They have, son, but it is a new world," said Austin.

"And this is where it leads us," Docia murmured, shaking her head.

Austin turned back to his sons. "We'll discuss the necessary adjustments to be made with you and the others that were here. Please be careful. Keep your blade close. If you listened to nothing else today, take that to heart."

Docia nodded. "You heard your father, and he's done now. He barely had a chance to breathe before the meeting." She looked at her sons, her meaning clear.

The two rose with no further questions.

"Sorry about earlier again, Dad," said Sanders.

"It's fine. You're passionate at times, and it got the better of you."

"Don't worry, dad. I'll keep him from causing trouble for you," boasted Simon as Sanders punched him playfully in the arm for the comment. "Glad you're back, dad." Simon turned back to his brother, "Come on, let's leave them alone for a while, Sanders. They're sick of us now."

"Maybe of you."

"You're the pain in the rear, remember?" He pretended to drag Sanders from the room as they both laughed.

"Lie down for a bit," said Docia as the two were in their bedroom as Austin put the last thing away from his visit with Lana.

"Remembering my earlier promise to you?" Austin murmured as he wrapped his arms around his wife.

She wound her arms around his neck. "I am and I intend to hold you to it later tonight, but you look tired. Rest for a while, and then we'll eat."

"You're right. I am exhausted, but I must get the advisors and our sons back together to start planning."

"Austin, there's time." She stroked the side of his face. "If just an hour. You'll feel better and be refreshed for your long to-do list."

He kissed her. "I'll let you win this round. Although, it'll work better if you lie down with me." His eyes twinkled.

"Sleep, Austin. That's what you need." She laughed at his expression. "All right, but you promise ... "

"Promise." He laid down, and she cuddled next to him. "Told you." He paused, " I hope the boys listen."

"You're worried."

"Yes. If the worst happens, I don't know if anything will matter that we do. But this is our part in it."

"Our part in it is this." Realization crept into her face. "Someone else received a different assignment."

"Nobody knows where this Dark Lord's creation is now."

"And locating it will take time that no one has. Austin, whoever must take that burden for us, the Ancient One be with them. Although I'm relieved it's not you, and I know that's selfish, but I can't help it. It's wise you didn't tell the boys, mainly Sanders. He would have pressed for more, tried to volunteer for it."

"That's why they said not a word. They can't chance Black Dragon getting an inkling. Lives hang in the balance."

"We've lost enough, so we won't be the cause of any more. I'm glad I don't know who took on that task, and I don't want to know."

"Stopping it before Black Dragon can use it again could be impossible. I don't know, Docia."

She smiled up at him. "Have faith. Black Dragon always underestimates us. We're stronger than what they see and what we realize."

"What would I do without you?" He kissed her.

"You'll never find out. Now rest, Austin." She cuddled closer to him, and in a few minutes, they both fell asleep.

Simon sat in his ship's cockpit. It had been easy to part ways with his brother. He did it regularly, but he didn't have much time now. He slid his hands over the communication panel. "Sorry, I got delayed."

"I began to wonder," said the male voice.

"I need to stay close to home for the next couple of days."

"Why the change?"

"My father arrived back today from his meeting."

"The one with Lana and the others."

"Yes, that one. He's been edgy since he returned."

"Has he? Does he suspect you?"

"Not at all, but we intend to keep it that way."

"What did he find out?"

"Hard to tell because he's keeping quiet. He didn't say anything unexpected. It's what you would anticipate they would piece together from what's happened."

"There must be more. Press your father harder."

"Already tried. Actually, my brother did the work for me. My father didn't budge, but he started to get angry with him."

"Your father has a great deal of patience as I recall, so your brother must have been persistent."

"Exactly."

"Intriguing."

"I have to get back to the house. I don't want to miss anything."

"Of course. Update me as you can."

Simon leaned back in the cockpit chair as the communication ended, and he contemplated his next move. "Yeah and tread carefully while keeping up appearances." He got up and walked out of the ship as he headed back to the house.

CHAPTER TEN

Lana stood in the small meeting room of the fortress, staring at her data pad again, her mind pondering the possibilities.

Caleb wrapped his arm around her waist. "Any clue of what's up?"

"Not a one. At least we finished with the commanders and sent them on their way. Except for Ryan, of course. He relayed the script to his father, and it's being taken care of for him. I can't imagine what this is about."

"What is it, cuz?" Dante strolled up with Seth and Ryan.

"A call from one of the ruling families that administers Dairo."

"Which one?"

"The Santiagos."

"They have always been helpful and willing to give whatever support they can," said Seth.

Ryan nodded. "My family would say the same if you asked them. So, what's going on with them?"

"I don't know."

Dante raised an eyebrow. "You talked to them, but you don't know?"

"He said it was important, but he couldn't go into details virtually."

"Then the only question is, when are we leaving?"

"As quickly as it takes us to get ready."

"We're ready, so let's go."

Ryan slapped Dante on the back and laughed. "Think again, buddy. Not according to Angelina's definition for you."

Dante grinned at the mention of Angelina and ran a hand through his hair. "Guess you're right, and I don't want her mad with me when I see her again."

Lana smiled. "I imagine not. Everyone, make it quick with the armor breathe underneath, and we'll meet back here to fly out. I'll confirm with the Santiagos that we're headed their way."

⸺ele⸺

Ryan jabbed Dante in the ribs on the ship. "Falling asleep over there? Dreaming again of Angelina?"

"I never should have told you." Dante laughed as he sat up in the chair.

Caleb turned around from the cockpit. "Dreaming of her now? You've got it bad, Dante."

"The only unpleasant part was it ended too soon."

"Like that, huh? Catch us up. We haven't landed yet."

"Caleb, stop teasing my cousin."

"No way. I'm just getting started, and I'm waiting for his answer." He grinned back at Dante.

"I woke up just as I pulled her in for a kiss."

"Man, that does hurt. I'd be disappointed too."

"She told me she was safe in it, and I wish I could believe that. The wondering is about to drive me insane."

Seth touched his shoulder. "It's expected, but you must trust. You and Ryan both. Angelina and Alena can take care of themselves, and Alika is watching them."

"I know they can. I mean, I've seen them fight. It's obvious what they're capable of, but it doesn't work as well as hoped."

⸺ele⸺

Caleb unconsciously put a guiding hand at the small of Lana's back as he continued scanning the surrounding area when the group approached the entrance of the Santiagos, "Nothing screams trouble so far."

"I haven't seen anything either, Caleb," Lana turned and smiled back as the escort motioned them inside the mansion and down the hallway to a large open room. "Our thanks."

"My pleasure, Lana. Please make yourself comfortable at the table. There are refreshments set out for everyone. Mr. Santiago should be here any moment." He gave them one last smile before leaving.

"Appears he's busy as usual," said Caleb as they all sat.

"It's barely lunchtime, so I'm sure his day is already full of managing a dozen things," said Lana.

"Perhaps it would have been easier for him to meet us in one of the administration buildings," said Seth.

Ryan shrugged. "We do meetings often out of our house too. Use the conference room attached to it, like this one. Depending on what you want to discuss, it's the better option. More private."

Dante poured himself a glass of water and said, "Makes sense, I suppose."

"We'll find out soon enough," said Lana as she nodded at Dante's offer to pour her a glass of water too.

The door opened and a tall dark-haired man in his early thirties walked into the room, closing the door behind him. A broad smile broke out on his face as he strolled towards them, and they all stood in greeting. "Lana and Caleb it has been too long." He clasped Lana's hand for a second before giving Caleb a firm handshake. "And you told me you were bringing the others. This is a treat. Dante, Seth, and Commander Ryan, always a pleasure to see you as well." He greeted them with a similar firm handshake which they returned with a smile and his same enthusiasm. He turned back to Lana. "How are you holding up, Lana? I wanted to reach out before now, but I didn't know what to say."

"I'm as well as can be expected with what happened, but I appreciate your concern."

"Of course, but you're wondering why I called you here today. Please, let's sit." He glanced towards the door.

Dante caught the motion and asked, "Are we waiting on someone else?"

"My wife and son are on their way down, but I expected they would beat me here. She always wants everything perfect. Probably stopped to bring more refreshments."

A knock on the door came.

He rose from his seat to open it. "There they are, but they should have simply come in." He opened the door. "Why didn't you ... "

"Sir?" responded the man at the door.

"Oh, it's you. I thought you were Braydon and Teresa. It doesn't matter. Come in. What is it?"

"It's your son. There's another incident."

Mr. Santiago's face tightened. "Where's my wife?"

"With him in his room, but she's having difficulties managing the situation. She asks for your assistance."

"I understand." He turned to Lana. "I hoped to speak with you about this more leisurely, but I won't get the luxury."

"Sir, there's something else."

Santiago turned to him, frustrated by the interruption.

"I'm sorry, but scanners show possible trouble on the horizon."

"And it would have to be today."

"What do you wish us to do?"

"Give me a moment." He turned to Lana. "My son is ill, but not in the traditional sense." He paused, visibly struggling. "He's been having episodes, horrible waking nightmares since everything happened with the three planets. My wife and I are beside ourselves. We come to you, pleading with you as devastated parents to one who we know will one day be a parent themselves." He looked down and then stared back at her with tears in his eyes. "I'm embarrassed to ask this of you, but you've always had a way about you, Lana."

The weight of what had occurred fell on Lana's shoulders again, and she saw this grieving father, unable to help his hurting child because of what she failed to prevent. "Of course, I'll do anything I can to reach your son. Take me to him."

"Sir, the other?" the man reminded him.

"Evaluate the threat. If it's what we think, dispatch what we have and send out the alerts."

"Sir, we could use help." The man stared at Dante, Caleb, Ryan, and Seth.

Lana nodded. "Yes, it sounds like you could." She turned to the others "Go with him, and lend whatever aid. If there's an attack bearing down on us, the colony needs you. If they require additional forces to handle the danger, make it happen. I'll stay and manage from here."

Caleb said, "Lana, are you sure you'll be okay?"

"I got this. Go. This is what we do."

"Okay." Dropping a quick kiss on her cheek, he rushed out with the others.

"Now let's see about your son."

Mr. Santiago put his head against the closed door of his son's room and turned back to Lana. "Strange. I don't hear anything. There's usually a lot of commotion when he's like this." He knocked on the door but received no response, so he opened it to discover a deserted room. "Braydon. Teresa," he called. He continued searching the room with Lana. "Did you check that closet door, Lana?"

"Just did."

"I need to find out what's going on, where they went. Let's head back to the conference room," said Santiago, as he did a final scan of the room before exiting it.

"Sir, you needed something?" asked one of Santiago's staff.

Santiago turned from Lana in the conference room to approach the attendant. "Yes, where are my son and wife?"

"In your son's room."

"No, they're not. We left there moments ago."

"That's where I last saw them, but I'll track them down and be back."

Santiago sighed and sat back down, forcing a smile for Lana. "It's a big house. They're here somewhere."

She smiled back, hoping to reassure him. "I'm sure you're right and worrying for no reason. How old is Braydon now?"

"He turned five a month ago. He's a great kid. I'm surprised you and Caleb aren't parents by now." He paused, "Sorry, that's not my call. I didn't mean to make you uncomfortable."

"No, it's okay. We keep putting it off for a better time, one when the Black Dragon isn't always there."

"Don't we all, Lana? Keeping a family safe with them lurking is almost impossible. I worry every day about what could happen, especially after the lives lost on those three planets. If I lost my family, I ... " He stopped and stared up at her, deciding it best not to say more. "I admit I'm frightened like ... "

The door opened, and the attendant returned. "Sir, if I could speak with you for a moment?"

"I gather you found them."

"We need to speak with you." He paused. "Out here, please. A few minutes and you can rejoin, Lana."

"If you'll excuse me, Lana."

"I'll be here. Let me know if you need me before then."

⸙

Caleb and his group followed the officer and exited the maze of hallways making up the Santiagos' home. They continued their brisk pace to the communication center in the nearby administration building.

Caleb asked, "What's headed for us?"

"We're getting mixed reports."

"Scanners are tuned to pick up Black Dragon, so they should be able to tell us that much," questioned Ryan.

"We've been having issues with the scanners."

"How long have you been encountering these issues?" asked Seth.

"Since the attacks. It's one of the many things bugging our administrator."

"If it's not Black Dragon, then it turns out to be nothing?" asked Dante.

"No, we've sustained attacks by non-Black Dragon ships, and that ends up being the villain. They can best be described as mercenaries that target supplies from our warehouses."

"They attack the warehouses with the ... " Caleb trailed off, clearly confused.

"Sorry, no. They land, hit them, and take the goods. Their other strategy is to use the air battle as a distraction while another team goes for the warehouse. We've tried stiffening clearances on what gets through to the surface, but it's a job keeping the warehouses safe and not disrupting the shipping traffic coming through. Those shipping dealers can be a pushy bunch."

Dante hid a smile. "We've heard, but you need them to maintain the flow."

"The unfortunate reality. We have to get supplies in and out like everyone else, but it's hard to tell enemies from friends nowadays." As he opened the door to the administration building, he motioned them inside.

"Doesn't the administrator have a mini command center where he can see what's going on? I mean how much further to the communication center's scanners?" Caleb's frustration became evident as they continued following their guide.

"He does have one in his home, but like I said it's been unreliable of late."

"Sorry, you did say that, but that's a horrible setup for times like these."

"For that reason, he's been spending more time at the administration office during the day, so he can be close to the command center while he sorts out the problem with the scanners. However, he felt he needed to do the meeting today in his home, then it all fell apart."

"I get it. How much further?"

"To the left, through this door."

He opened the door, and they followed him. Several screens surrounded the room with equipment, but with only one man managing it. The individual turned and nodded when they entered the room.

Ryan exchanged a look with the others, knowing they all wondered the same thing. "Pretty quiet for a command center."

"You know everyone here, right?" their guide asked the officer at the post, never addressing Ryan's query.

"Of course. I'm sorry you walked into this."

"What have you got for us? Did you get it figured out?"

"Yeah, as we suspected they're not Black Dragon, but a few of the distraction ships. They're putting up a decent fight for show, but our forces have that handled. I'm sure they'll make their escape soon enough if the pattern holds. We spotted a group on the surface that I'm guessing is doing the haul-away end of it. It's an average-sized team as usual."

"But our best fighters are in the air. Where are we going?"

"There." He pointed to a location that popped up on the screen.

"Let's take care of them," said the man as he rushed from the room with the others.

"How far is it?" asked Caleb.

"Not far."

"That's what you said about this place. Now how much further?"

"About a mile."

"That's enough in a situation like this. I saw speed gliders outside. How about we use them?"

"Oh yeah, we can pick a few up on the way out."

"About time," said Ryan.

"Have you figured out what they're using the supplies for? Like what kind of items they're going for?" asked Caleb.

"It varies. Could be with the Dark Lord and his second-in-command gone, it threw his thugs into chaos and they're making trouble. Of course, there will always be people ready to take advantage of a bad situation. Those three planets being destroyed doesn't get much worse. Everybody is already quaking in their boots, and this adds injury to insult. It's anybody's guess."

"Perhaps," said Seth.

"Shouldn't we be over there?" asked Dante, pointing to a building a small distance from them as they dismounted the speeders.

"Yeah, I thought you said a warehouse," said Ryan as he scanned their sparse surroundings.

"No, they're down here," said the man.

"Look, there's a speeder here," said Dante, focusing a few feet away.

"Likely one of the runners is using it." He motioned them. "Follow me."

"What's down here?" asked Caleb.

"Step on the platform with me, and keep your voices down," he lowered his own and waited for them to do so. "Get your blasters ready. It's mines. Often we store the goods in temporary underground warehouses, and once the haul is large enough a separate group moves it to the above-ground ones you see. This crew knew that system. Be careful with blasting down here. It could get tricky."

They reached the bottom, and the platform made a slight scrape as it hit. The man put a finger to his lip, reminding them of the need for quiet. He pointed to a group of men filling and hauling boxes, unaware of anything else. He whispered, "Stay here. I'm going around the other side and sneaking up on them. There's another platform. Give me six minutes from the time I step on this one and then move in from here. I'll do the same on my end."

"Are you certain one of us shouldn't come with you?" asked Seth.

"I'm sure and given more time they'll be gone. Six minutes." He crept away from them and onto the platform as it lifted him from sight.

Once he reached the top, he stepped from the platform and peered down at the group. Rubbing the sweat from his forehead, he restrained a chuckle. That had been easier than anticipated. He retrieved a metal cylindrical object from his belt and precisely placed it in the lifting mechanism. He murmured, "That should keep them held up and in case that's not long enough, this will do it." Then he delivered a single shot to each one of the control panels of the speed gliders that were outside. "Caleb, you were right. This is the best way to travel." He grinned as he walked towards the single speeder a few feet away, mounted it, and sped off.

⸎

"I've got under two minutes," said Caleb.

"I do not see any sign of our guide, and he should be in position by now," said Seth.

Ryan said, "Agreed. Something is off with this."

Dante said, "Tell me about it. None of these people are panicked to pack this stuff or rushed."

"And how long can a distraction last?" asked Ryan. "We've seen for a while with the whole Black Dragon supply switch, but those were full-scale attacks."

"Which these aren't close," said Caleb, as his eyes swept the area again. "Spot our guy yet?"

Seth said, "No, I do not, and we're down to seconds."

Caleb said, "Go in easy on my mark." With a nod, he eased out of his position, blaster raised and his other hand fingering his sunspear hilt as the others followed him. His voice rang out, "Put the supplies down, and don't think about drawing your weapon."

The men exchanged bewildered expressions as they stopped their activity and cautiously laid down whatever they held.

Suddenly a man emerged from a side entrance and called, "What's going on out here? Problem with the equipment or something?" He halted at seeing the drawn blasters pointed at the men. "Hey, none of my people need to get hurt. They're simply doing their job, and they have families to go home to when their day is done. Please, can we figure something out?"

"You're not smuggling these goods out of here?" asked Caleb, but he already knew the answer as he lowered his weapon.

"No, we work here. I'm the foreman, and you're Commander Caleb?" His voice registered recognition with disbelief.

"The same. Stand down, guys." Caleb replied, visibly frustrated.

"And Commander Ryan, Dante, and Seth. Why were you pointing blasters at us?"

"Because we've been played," said Dante.

"This felt wrong, but I couldn't put my finger on it." Ryan shook his head.

Seth turned to the foreman. "We must return to the surface. This was an elaborate ploy by the man who brought us down here. Our apologies to you and your workers."

"No harm done. Do you know who he is?"

"No, but I'll choke it out of him once I get a hold of him," growled Caleb.

"I believe you, and it sounds deserved, Commander Caleb. Take the platform back up. Be careful though if this guy is as tricky as you say. He could be waiting on you."

Caleb and the others were already on it, and Caleb initiated the lift. It rose the tiniest bit and groaned in the effort. Another foot off the ground produced the same disturbing noise.

"It didn't sound like this last time, right?" asked Dante.

"Sure didn't." Ryan squinted, trying to see to the surface.

The platform crept up an additional foot followed by the smell of burnt wires, and an explosion resounded that sent the platform plummeting back to the bottom.

The foreman ran to their aid along with several of the other workers.

"Everybody okay?" asked the foreman, as he scanned their faces.

Dante nodded. "We jumped clear when it started falling. We weren't high up yet."

Caleb said, "Tell us there's another way out. We need back up now. The fastest route."

"There's another lift on the other side." He pointed across the way.

"Seriously? Wow, the weasel told us the truth about something," said Ryan.

"Come with me. I'll get you back up, so you can take care of him."

"I've still got first dibs on him," scolded Caleb.

"We appreciate your help," said Seth as they emerged from the mine and stepped off the platform.

"Happy to assist. Track down your troublemaker. Somebody like that is bad news to have around for any of us."

"Don't worry. We'll take him down," said Dante.

"There's the speeders, over there." Ryan motioned ahead.

"In a few minutes we can be there," said Seth.

———eℓℓ———

Alika, Alena, and Angelina dove back into determining their next destination after lunch. Alika's and Alena's efforts to nudge her in another direction continued to prove unsuccessful.

"How about one of these other targets first?" Alena pointed to the viewscreen.

"I don't think it yields what checking out Drew's trail will."

"What happened to easing into it? Isn't that what you said to Dante?"

"I know what I said, but we're running out of time."

Alika turned to her. "Or perhaps this is about something more personal?"

"No, it's not. Like I said before, would I like to strike the death blow after everything? I won't deny it, but I wouldn't endanger anyone to do it." Her voice drifted off, and her eyes suddenly became far away.

"Child?" Alika clasped her hand and glanced at Alena as they both recognized the familiar look crossing Angelina's face.

"There's trouble. There's no time."

Alena touched her arm. "No time for what?"

"She's in trouble. We must go now before it's too late."

"Who, child?"

Angelina looked up at them as if waking from a daze as she sprang from her seat. "Lana. Where's she now?"

Alena jumped up too and took her by the shoulders to stare straight into her eyes. "Tell us what we need. You know. We don't."

She nodded and gave instructions as she rushed through the room with Alena to gather the essentials for their sudden mission. "Alena, we must be disguised like when we went as Lana's advisors. Alika, get us Lana's location and clearances to land. You have to reach the others and direct them to Lana."

"They're not with her?" asked Alika as he set out to locate the group.

"Somehow, she got separated from them from what the vision showed," said Angelina as the two made their wardrobe transformation.

"Lana is on the planet visiting the Santiago family from what I can see. I sent the coordinates to your ship."

"We're gone," yelled Angelina back at Alika.

"The other requests will be done before you land. Go!"

CHAPTER ELEVEN

"I don't believe this! All of them!" Caleb hollered as he stared down at the worthless speeders, his clenched fists at his sides.

"I'm guessing there's one working fine." Ryan shook his head.

"Seth, it's Alika. It's urgent," Alika's voice blasted through Seth's earpiece, and Seth froze. He put a firm hand on Caleb to stop him further and answered Alika for all to hear. "Alika, we're here."

"Lana is in trouble. Get to her now." His instructions now sounded through all of their earpieces.

Caleb's face paled. "Oh no. We left her back at the Santiagos."

Ryan said, "These speeders aren't moving for us."

"Looks like we're on foot," said Dante.

"What do you know, Alika?" asked Seth as they ran back towards the Santiagos.

"Only what Angelina saw and had time to share. She witnessed Lana in danger and said somehow Lana became separated from the rest of you. She and Alena landed and are attempting to reach her."

"Your two are already here?" panted Caleb.

"Yes."

"Can they get to Lana in time?" asked Ryan.

"They are hoping."

"Can you plug us into their system too, so we can hear what's going on?" asked Dante, struggling as well to talk while keeping the current pace.

"I could, but now it would prove distracting for them, so I won't. If you need to change course, I'll alert you."

Lana waited at the table, still wondering if something happened to Mr. Santiago's wife and son. The expression on the attendant's face didn't bode well, but he said to stay. Once again the burden of what occurred with the three planets weighed on her. She remembered the devastation mirrored on Mr. Santiago's face, the utter brokenness pouring out from his plea for help. This planet wasn't even one of those hit. Just the threat hovering over them as the possible next target was enough to have his child in this heartbreaking state. The father placed such faith in her, that she could say something, do something to bring back the happy child he possessed before what the enemy had unleashed. She wanted to be able to, but what assurance could she offer? Any day it could come again because she hadn't prevented it in the first place, this world the Black Dragon created for this little boy, for a galaxy of children. Her thoughts drifted to another child; a little girl named Emily whom she had given assurances. She still saw Emily's radiant smile and heard her sweet voice that promised to be brave in this scary world. Yet in an instant, Emily had been taken from them. A tear fell down Lana's face, and she quickly wiped it away. Renewed hate surged in her for the Black Dragon. What they had done and continued to do was unforgivable. How many more times would it be repeated? How much more will we sacrifice? Not solely her and Caleb either. Dante came to mind and his mother still lay in a tortured sleep, representing the last pieces of his family. What about Alika, Angelina, and Alena as well? They had become family to her, and they were putting themselves in the center of danger to pursue this device. What if they became the next sacrifice in this war? Dante and Ryan would never be the same if something happened to them. Taking a deep breath, she forced herself to leave the frightening possibilities behind for now. It wasn't the time to turn this over in her mind as she had done on countless occasions. The Santiagos asked for her help, and she would do everything in her power to aid them. She couldn't help but wonder if an attack commenced and thought about contacting Caleb for an update, but she dismissed it. If he was in the middle of a battle, she didn't want to divert his attention. He'd call if needed. She heard footsteps outside the door as it began to open. "Finally," she murmured as she stood.

Seven armed soldiers entered the room, shutting the door behind them and closed in on Lana. One stepped forward. "Mr. Santiago regrets he will not be returning, but he sent us to finish your visit."

She ignited her sunspear. "I don't care for how Mr. Santiago chose to end this briefing."

"We didn't expect you would, but you're terribly outnumbered."

"If you think that, you haven't seen me fight."

"Such spirit." He chuckled as he launched himself at her with his sword.

Lana's sunspear flashed as she parried the initial blows with ease, but the others surrounded her. Time to go in for the kill before she found herself on the wrong side of a blade. She felt her sunspear go in clean and observed the horrified look on the man's face as his blood blanketed the floor. "Like I said, I'm not outnumbered. Your mistake." Her sunspear continued in motion. She rolled on the ground to avoid the army of blades that came enraged at her, and she instantly sprung up behind them, slicing another one through.

Suddenly, the door flung open again to reveal the man who left earlier with her husband's group. "What in the galaxy is going on?" His face went from confusion to disbelief to grim acceptance as he yelled, "Guards, get in here!" He rushed towards Lana, unsheathing his blade at the same time and commanded the armed men who attacked her, "Put your weapons down now, and get away from her."

"We can't, but if you leave now, we'll let you live."

"Not a chance. I don't know how you got this far, but I've got a security problem to clean up." He smiled. "My thanks to Lana for already beginning the process."

"You're welcome." She finally had a friendly blade in the room but no time to ask him where her husband and the others were. "You take that half, and I'll take the other."

"Works for me and our reinforcements are on their way."

He never got another word out as the remaining armored troops surged forward and attacked him and Lana with new rage.

Lana continued to fight, sending her attackers to the ground, creating a myriad of wounds on them with her sunspear. In the background, she registered the reinforcements' entrance as she delivered the death blow to a third attacker.

Her newfound ally said, "Now to wrap this up."

"Of course, sir. Here to help."

The remaining armored soldiers lowered their blades as the reinforcements approached them. She took a deep breath when she watched the situation come under control. The next moment she felt the sharp plunge of something into the back of her neck as an arm encircled her waist from behind and heard the whisper in her ear, "I'm sorry, Lana, but we all know this is the only way to bring you down. We'd never win a fair battle with you." She attempted to fight it, but it proved useless as she collapsed to the ground and her sunspear dropped from her hand.

He eased her onto the floor and addressed the group, "Well played. This delivery goes as planned."

"She still killed three of our men," complained one of the armored guards.

"They should have learned better fighting skills."

"We get their share?"

"No, they forfeited it when they bled all over the beautiful carpet. Maybe I'll use it to have the carpet cleaned for the Santiagos." He rolled his eyes. "Stop being stupid and finish this. Nobody gets paid anything until I see this through, and that means delivery is completed. Where's the crate to transport our lovely cargo in?"

"Here." Two of the soldiers brought out a large rectangular wooden shipping box with a few holes discreetly made in the side of it and laid it at the man's feet.

"Looks to be a perfect fit. Get her bound and gagged. The whole bit."

"Why bother? She's out for the count, right?"

"Because I'm not taking any chances with her. I won't end up like those three."

"He has a fair number of staff. Surprising someone just waltzed in," said Angelina as they rounded a corner.

"Like we did," said Alena.

"We're special though. You have me." She teased.

"Lucky me." Alena grinned. "Or maybe we look official enough to blend in."

"You had to dash my shining star moment?"

"That's what you're calling it now? More like a flickering star."

"That hurt."

Alena jokingly jabbed her and nodded up ahead. "Don't worry. Here comes your chance to shine again."

"They do look like the gatekeepers, and that's the one we need through?"

"Yes, once we're in that corridor beyond their guard."

"Got it."

Alena scanned the hall. "Surely, they would've heard something."

"That's what I'm wondering too."

The two walked towards the door as if the two guards were invisible.

"I'm sorry, but you can't come through here," said one of the guards as he blocked the door.

Alena and Angelina stepped back slightly as if suddenly aware of the guard.

Angelina asked, "What do you mean we can't come through here?"

"Because people wander through here all day long from what we see," said Alena.

"Not on our watch."

Angelina shot back, "Clearly you haven't been paying attention today. We need through the door, now."

"Why?"

"Official Freedom Fighter business."

"How do we know?"

Alena snapped, "If you take us to the person we're here to see, she'll confirm it."

"So, stop wasting our time."

"Who do you need to see?"

"Lana. She has a meeting here, but of course, you knew since you're such amazing gatekeepers," said Angelina.

"You can't see her."

"Why not?"

"Mr. Santiago said not to disturb his meeting with Lana and her group."

"Did he now? You said her group." Angelina turned to Alena. "Hear that?"

Alena nodded and turned to the men. "You think Lana's group is still there with her? Say goodbye to your job."

"I know you two aren't getting through. His assistant came and reiterated they were not to be disturbed."

"The plot thickens," Alena said sarcastically. "What's this assistant's name?"

"I can't remember. He just started."

Angelina shook her head. "Of course, he did." She waved her hands in front of them. "We don't care, because we've done this long enough with you. We're seeing Lana now. Get out of our way."

"Who do you think you are?"

"We would be her security team, and we're necessary today because you failed at your job. Move aside."

Angelina and Alena looked at each other while keeping one eye on the two guards.

Angelina said, "They're not moving."

"A shame."

"Thoughts?"

"Hard to believe they missed so much."

Angelina made a sweeping motion around the corridor. "Not if everyone didn't come through this way."

"That would explain it, but I'm still not sure about these two."

"Me either, and I can usually tell."

The guard looked between them bewildered, but interjected, "Hey, we told you that you're not getting through."

Angelina turned to him. "Shut it. If we want your input, we'll ask." She turned back to Alena. "Try to find another way?"

"Is there time?"

"No, and Dante and the others will come through this same way."

"No point in leaving them to deal with it."

Angelina turned back to the guards. "You should've moved." Before the guards could react, Angelina and Alena pulled their blasters out, and a single shot brought the men down. The two knelt and took the men's blasters.

"They're staying down. An encouraging sign. Should be out for a while with that setting." Angelina lowered her voice as they strolled through the door.

Alena shrugged her shoulders. "We gave them the chance to move."

Angelina pointed to the end of the hall. "That's the door we want."

"There's nobody in this hall. Too quiet."

They slowed their footsteps as they crept to the door.

Angelina mouthed, *"You hear it?"*

Alena nodded and mouthed back, *"On my mark."* They both unsheathed their swords as Alena counted to three on her fingers, and they heard voices floating from the room.

"She's ready like you wanted. You want us to load her?"

"No, I'll put her in."

Alena and Angelina flung the door open and stifled a gasp at the scene. At seeing Lana's crumpled body on the floor, Angelina screamed, "Lana!" With swords raised, they reached her and found themselves encircled by an armed force.

The man who had started to place Lana in the box stepped forward. "Just when I thought I wrapped this up. Now who might you two be?"

"What did you do to her?" demanded Angelina.

"What does it look like?"

"Is she … ?"

"She's too dangerous on all cylinders. You see her handiwork. She's asleep." The man held up an emptied syringe.

"Asleep?" Angelina's mind latched onto one possibility, and Alena's face mirrored her panic.

Alena asked, "How asleep did you put her?"

"Not forever. She'd never agree to accompany me, so I found the solution. She'll awaken with a monster headache, but that will be the least of her worries."

Relief poured through them as their fear went unrealized. Angelina asked, "Where were you taking her?"

"Doesn't matter. Now you should be concerned about yourselves." He stepped from the circle and motioned to the troops. "End this. We need to go."

Angelina and Alena stood with their backs to each other, only about a foot between them. In that space, laid Lana's unconscious body and the box they had meant to transport her.

"We have to be careful with Lana being underfoot," murmured Angelina.

"An added level of difficulty. Terrific," muttered Alena.

"Eleven plus the one who doesn't get his hands dirty."

"Three more if not for Lana. I like our odds." Alena struck at the same time as she heard Angelina's sword find a blade.

Angelina swung her sword, rarely missing a mark. However, so far it fell short of the final blow she needed on her opponents. Her mind was distracted with ensuring she kept Lana's body secure, and it put a chokehold on part of her training. Alika's words rang in her head, "Use your surroundings to your advantage. See the possibilities." She glanced longingly at the table on the other side of the room. There were a few other pieces in the room, but it placed too much distance between her and Lana. She determined no more hacking them a piece at a time. It had to be clean shots all the way through, even if it forced her to take chances.

Angelina yelled, "Taking too long over here!"

"Same here. Time to go all in."

Their swords rang with new energy and although Lana still lay between them, they made themselves extend the length.

Angelina's sword found the sweet spot seconds later, and her attacker collapsed dead at her feet as Alena's blade claimed victory in almost the same instant.

"He left a mark," railed Angelina as she stepped back a little too late from an approaching troop's blade.

"Okay over there?" hollered Alena.

"I am now," she growled as her blade cleaved straight through the soldier.

"It's unwise to lower your guard," sneered the soldier fighting Alena.

"I didn't," she said as her sword went clean through his abdomen, "but you did."

Angelina placed a punishing slice on another fighter, but not enough for the kill and left herself more open than she should. The blade started to come through, and she groaned at the minor pain compared to what it could've been.

The soldier stared at her. "What gives? That should've gone all the way through you." He grinned. "I'll put more force into the next one."

Still recovering from the impact, but grateful for the extra layer of hidden armor she wore, Angelina stepped back to get reorientated. However, she stumbled into something, resulting in her on the floor on her backside despite all efforts to catch herself. "That box!" she fumed. In the same instant, she realized the soldier towered over her with his blade ready to plunge her through. She reached to bring her sword up before he could, but his boot crashed down on her hand that held it. Screaming in pain, her sword slipped from her grip and she stared up as his blade resumed its downward stroke.

"No!" yelled Alena, but she couldn't reach Angelina.

CHAPTER TWELVE

"Been a while," panted Dante, "since I've run that hard."

"You're not kidding," said Ryan, catching his breath too.

Alika's voice came through, "Hurry! I fear it will go badly soon."

"We're in. What about Lana?" asked Caleb.

"She's alive, but I'm not sure they can keep her secure before they meet the blade point."

"We'll reach them in time," said Seth.

Caleb flung open the door to the Santiagos' residence, and his entrance was met with startled gasps. "Out of our way now!" He ran through the few people in his wake. "I'm getting to my wife! Make a path for us, or I'll make one through you!"

"Continue down the hall, Caleb," said Seth.

"That weasel tried to turn this place into a maze in our heads leaving out of here." Caleb yelled again to someone, "I said out of our way!"

"Two downed soldiers at this door. More of his handiwork," said Ryan as they stopped at the scene.

"No, that's from my two," said Alika.

"Great. Is there anybody we can trust in here?" Caleb stepped around the troops and slammed open the door to resume his pace with the others following suit.

"Almost there. Down the hall," said Seth.

As they reached the door, they heard a scream and Dante turned pale. "That's …"

A split second later another voice yelled, "No!"

Ryan's face reflected the same look, "And that's … "

Caleb flung open the door, and they looked in horror at the scene.

Immediately with her free hand, Angelina had the blaster out and hit the soldier point blank with it. A desperate plea raced through her that these soldiers stayed down with blasters. As he began to fall dead on her from the blast, she rolled away from him at the last moment and purposely into the side where her sword lay. Forcing back the lingering pain in her hand from the soldier's boot, she picked up her sword and sprang up to shout to Alena, "Under control as usual."

"Far from it. We've been over this!"

Angelina addressed Caleb's group rushing forward now. "You're finally here!"

Dante asked as he joined the fray, "Sorry, are you hurt?"

Angelina ignored him and called, "Seth, get Lana clear of this now! Please!"

"Consider it done!"

"Lana!" Caleb rushed with Seth to Lana's unconscious body.

Alena's voice rang out, "She has been drugged, but she'll be okay, Caleb."

Seth turned to Caleb. "You heard her. I'll see to Lana. Help them."

Caleb nodded and rushed ahead with his sunspear while Seth moved Lana behind the table in the room.

From the corner of her eye, Angelina spotted the man responsible for drugging Lana now creeping towards the door, and she yelled, "Oh no you don't!" All eyes focused on the door as the man made his escape through it. She rushed toward it, hollering back to the others, "I'm going after him!"

"Not by yourself you're not!" Dante exclaimed but too late as she had already flown from the room. "I have to help her."

"Go, we've got this!" said Alena.

"Get that weasel, Dante!" growled Caleb.

"You guys named him?" asked Alena as Dante ran from the room.

"We'll fill you in once we finish off his help," said Ryan.

Dante raced through the corridor. How did she get ahead of him so fast? Suddenly he heard her scream, "Duck!" as several blaster shots boomeranged off the walls of the hall, forcing him to stop his progress until they settled down sufficiently. "I'm going to lose track of her if this keeps up."

Alika's voice came through his earpiece, "I won't allow you to, Dante."

He sighed in relief as he rose and resumed his pace, following the sound of running feet ahead of him. Once he exited the house, he halted and scanned the area. "I don't see her anywhere. Wait. Forgo that." He picked up the faint footsteps again near a group of people who appeared irritated, but curious by whatever transpired. He ran straight in that direction and yelled, "Out of the way, now!" Yet after a couple of minutes, the trail went dry again. "I lost her again. This woman is going to drive me to insanity."

"She's close. Keep going, Dante." Alika chuckled. "Your sanity remains intact, despite her efforts."

"I'm glad one of us is certain." He slowed his pace to reveal several buildings ahead of him. "Is she inside one of the buildings?"

"No, she remains outside."

"That must mean she followed him down one of these alleys between them." He quickened his pace, but with enough time to glimpse through the alleyway while continuing to come up empty. A crashing sound prompted him to run to the next one. Hiding a smile, he walked up to the scene. "You have this under control I see."

"Yes, as I have all day, no thanks to you and your crew. Rescuing your rears again."

Dante barely hid his surprise at the hate radiating in her words.

While keeping the man pinned to the ground, she briefly turned to Dante to mouth to him, *"Play along."* Then her features returned to their coldness. "What took your crew so long to find their way?" She returned her focus to the man on the ground, not trusting her attention to be diverted from him.

Dante understood now. No way either one of them wanted a man like this knowing how familiar they were with each other, so he fell unhappily into his role. "As swell as it is to see you again too, he's to blame for our delay."

"Can't wait to hear this excuse. How is it his fault?"

"He took us on a chase to stop an imaginary attack when we arrived, minus Lana and abandoned us on the hunt."

"Did he now? Surprisingly, I believe you, Dante." She stared into the man's eyes. "You've been busier than I thought today. Led them astray. Separated their crew. Somehow managed to get the best of Lana. That doesn't happen. She fights like a whole army. I'm impressed. Who did you do all this for?"

"I'm not telling you anything."

"That's what they all say at first." Her boot near his side shifted.

He yelled, and his body came off the ground as her boot dug into him. However, she controlled the force exerted at the same time as she watched him in amusement.

"You're breaking," his voice came out in gasps, "my ribs."

"I assure you I'm not. Broken ribs are painful, much more than what you're enduring now, but I can give you that experience. Just the right amount of pressure," she paused as she moved her foot again, and the man let out another yelp, "is all it takes." She laughed. "I didn't do it yet, and you can't tolerate pain well, so I suggest you answer my questions."

Dante glimpsed the glint of metal and rushed to Angelina's side the same instant she caught the motion. She grasped the man's hand which he had ripped free to reveal a hidden dagger he had retrieved. Her boot crunched down on his ribs again, and the wail erupting from him sent chills through Dante. The blade fell from his hands. "Dante, you mind grabbing that dagger? We wouldn't want anyone getting hurt."

"Got it." Dante scooped it up and stepped back, attempting to resume his unconcerned stance.

"Another move like that and my foot will break every rib in your body, one by one. Did you think Dante would stand there and allow you to seriously hurt me?

He may not care to deal with me any more than I do him, but have you forgotten what you did to his cousin today? The reason you didn't succeed is due to me and my comrade. That's not lost on him either. If nothing else, he owes me. His noble Freedom Fighter ideals wouldn't let him live with himself if he didn't intervene. Unfortunately for you, I'm not idealistic."

"Who are you?"

"Think of me as the hired help, the kind no one wants to claim to know. I see we understand each other." She then addressed Dante, "We're not getting anywhere with him here."

"Then I'm assuming you want to relocate him."

"Get up now! Yes, this interrogation continues at the Santiagos." She yanked the man up, and he groaned in pain. "Give me a reason, and I'll take you out." She signaled to Dante. "Flank him on the other side, in case he's stupid enough to try anything again."

⁓

"How's Lana?" Caleb rushed over to Seth as the last soldier lay dead.

"Unconscious still. Once I know what drug he injected her with, I can determine approximately how long she'll be out and what I can do for her."

"I can help with that," said Alena.

"You know what he gave her?" asked Caleb.

"No, but I have an idea of how to know." She walked over to the cargo box, retrieved the empty syringe from it, and handed it to Seth. "Your weasel bragged about using it on Lana to sedate her. The residue is probably enough for one of the handheld scanners."

"You two never cease to amaze me," said Seth as he began analyzing it.

Ryan smiled at Alena. "They are something." He paused, "You think she and Dante caught up to him yet?"

"I have no doubts they did, but I'm curious how he earned the name weasel."

"He came up with a story about an attack, possibly Black Dragon and left us stranded down a mine shaft."

"And he still managed to backtrack here to do this. Wow. Your weasel gets around."

"Not after today, because I'm going to run him through for what he did to Lana," said Caleb as he held his wife's hand and stroked the side of her face.

Alena touched him on the back. "No one would stop you, but she'll be okay, Caleb. So, you guys never met with the Santiagos."

Ryan said, "Only with Mr. Santiago. He greeted us and unpacked this whole story about his kid having nightmares, meltdowns or something because of the attacks. He looked like he was going to break down right there and thought Lana could help. Like clockwork, the weasel came in with news the kid was in the middle of one."

"And of course, Lana jumped to assist too. But you didn't see his son?"

Caleb jumped in, "No because at the same time, the weasel announced the nonexistent Black Dragon attack in progress he needed extra blades to take out."

"And that's how your group got separated, and you haven't seen Mr. Santiago since. This is worse than I thought. There's no one we can trust here. Lana needs treatment, but I wouldn't move her from this room with the current situation."

"She's right, Caleb. We've got to call in our armed guards that we know are uncompromised." Ryan watched him nod in agreement. "I'll take care of it now while you sit with Lana." He turned to Alena. "How many are you thinking?"

She motioned to the carnage. "Our weasel must have more somewhere. There's a lot of area for us to cover. Enough to escort Lana safely back. Factor in that we're about to have at least one prisoner, your weasel, to manage. Sounds like a distinct possibility of a second prisoner with Santiago once we locate him. We should assume this whole place is compromised."

"No argument there. The reinforcement number seemed high to me, but I agree it's on target to prevent being outnumbered again." Ryan made the call on his data pad.

Caleb turned to Ryan. "Is it done?"

"Almost," He paused and resumed his previous conversation, "Sorry, I was talking to Commander Caleb. When you arrive, come straight to this location, to this room. Do not speak with anyone besides Caleb, myself, Dante, or Seth unless they're with someone else at the time. Do not allow yourself to be stopped from reaching us or accept help from the locals. I cannot stress it enough. Consider the entire place compromised by Black Dragon. So, watch your back from the instant you enter the planet's orbit. Do you understand what you're walking into and all my instructions?"

"Yes, sir."

"See that you do and everyone with you."

"You have my word, sir. We're on our way."

"Anything, Seth?" asked Caleb.

"I believe so. The residue provides our answer. He respected your wife's fighting abilities and took no chances of her waking up early. This drug's effects customarily last at least six hours, but have been known to extend as long as twelve. It depends on a couple of factors, including the amount he gave her. I can determine that once we transport her back and retrieve a blood sample."

"What can we do for her?"

"Nothing in her current state. She'll awaken on her own with an unbelievable headache, which I can promptly treat. She'll need to take it easy for a day, which will be the bigger challenge for her. It doesn't feel like it now, but this could be much worse, Caleb."

"You're right." He turned to Alena. "Thank you for what you and Angelina did today. If I lost Lana ... "

"But you didn't, she'll be fine, and you're welcome, Caleb."

Suddenly Angelina and Dante burst into the room with their prisoner as she thundered, "Through the door now! You better have something useful to say, because that's the only reason I haven't put a blade clean through you!"

"Appears they got him," said Ryan.

"No, I got your weasel. Dante swooped in after the fact to observe my efforts. Same story all day."

"Yes, I'm beyond useless according to her."

"Okay, then ... " stammered Ryan. "Reinforcements are coming from the home base."

"I should hope so, commander. This whole place is teeming with more of his despicable sort." She scolded at her prisoner before glancing back at Dante. "Look somebody did something helpful around here today. My compliments to you, Commander Ryan."

Dante snapped at her, "Since you have this under control, why don't you and your comrade get the weasel situated, and I'll do something useful too and update the others? Does that work for you?"

"The best thing you've said all day. My comrade and I got this again."

"My friend even brought you a chair, but you don't get to sit yet," said Angelina to the prisoner, as Alena came with the chair.

"Here's a blaster." Alena began a search of him. "His data pad. I'm not seeing a blade, but that seems impossible."

"It is. He abandoned a full-sized one here when he cleared out. We already got the dagger from him after he tried pulling it on me."

Alena shook her head at him. "Terrible call. It's a miracle she let you live after that. Sit. Now."

Dante went to the others, situating himself so his back was to Angelina, Alena, and the prisoner.

Ryan turned to him. "What in the galaxy happened? What did you say to her, Dante?"

Dante motioned for them to come in closer as he typed something on his data pad and said, "Check yours."

Ryan looked up from his data pad after reading the words, 'It's an act. Considering our prisoner. Play along', "Makes sense now."

"But she's convincing," whispered Caleb.

Seth nodded. "We knew her to be an expert in this area. Today is no exception, but you adjusted quickly too. I'm impressed."

"Nothing in me likes it, but it's safer for him to believe this is how we work together. Ryan, prepare to receive the same treatment from the other one now."

"I get it, and we'll play it out."

"What did I miss?"

"Dante, we need the other two over here for it."

"There's no way we leave that man unattended, but you mentioned reinforcements?"

Caleb nodded. "They just arrived, so we can get everyone caught up now."

"You're sure they can handle him?" Angelina asked Dante as three troops stood guard over the prisoner after securing him to the chair.

"Yes. They can do this. I'm aware my assurances mean nothing to you, but can you give it rest for a second? The others need to talk with all of us."

"Fine." She grabbed the prisoner by the chin. "If you try anything, I'll come across this room and take you out myself." She walked over to the group, with Dante following behind her.

Upon reaching them and knowing she faced away from the prisoner, her face softened and she asked quietly, "How's Lana?"

Seth said, "She'll recover thanks to you and your comrade. I'm estimating six to twelve hours for her to awaken. However, I'm anxious to get her back to the fortress."

"Of course." She turned to Caleb. "I'm sorry we didn't get here in time to stop them."

"No, the two of you saved her. You got here in time for my Lana."

"Take her back now. We got this, but you be careful."

"We will and we'll leave you four to handle it." Caleb stared down at his wife laying still on the moving bed the reinforcements had brought.

Seth motioned. "This group comes with us, to ensure we transport Lana back without incident. We're leaving now."

Angelina turned back as the door shut behind Lana's escort. "Where are we at?"

After finishing rapidly comparing notes, Dante asked, "What do you think?"

Angelina said, "There are a couple of possibilities. Mr. Santiago could have the most clueless staff around him with the worst security ever, and his assistant used the situation to his advantage. If so, Mr. Santiago is probably dead considering we haven't heard a peep from him since he left this room. The other option is he changed his loyalties and played his part. If so, he's responsible for what happened, and he's still here somewhere. For how long though is the question. We locate him. It's simply a matter of what his condition is when we do."

Alena nodded. "We've got the troops now to search."

Dante asked Angelina. "Which one are you leaning towards?"

"Too much came together by chance. I hope I'm wrong about Mr. Santiago, but I don't relish the prospect of finding a dead body either. Both are terrible outcomes. I think we take back two prisoners."

"See anything, yet?" asked Dante, standing behind Angelina.

"No. How many rooms does this place have?" asked Angelina as she continued her virtual tour through the house after hacking into the camera system.

"Plenty."

"I shouldn't be surprised."

"Care to enlighten my simple mind?"

"It's not unusual for people in Santiago's positions to use their residence to conduct a fair amount of their business too." She made a sweeping motion to the current room. "Like having a mini-conference room attached to the house."

"Ryan reminded us of that same thing earlier, and I remember my parents doing it to a lesser extent."

"I missed that earlier discussion, but I'll agree some families are more comfortable with that setup than others. You act as if it's so strange, but you conduct meetings from the fortress now too."

"I only think of my corner inside of it, my quarters. I assure you it's no mansion, but comfortable enough to suit me." He watched her suddenly focus more intensely on the screen.

"I wouldn't know about your quarters." She hid a smile as her mind drifted to the evenings spent with him cuddled on the couch there.

"Of course, you wouldn't," he whispered as he leaned down on the pretense of getting a closer look at her monitor. "Me too, and I haven't found a better way to spend the evening."

"That's not surprising." She paused, not daring to look at him for fear his nearness would undo her. "Prisoner still secure?"

"Yes, he's still planted to the chair." Dante stood back up, understanding the need to give them both space.

"I should go search for him."

"No, you're not going."

She rose and turned to face him. "You think you can tell me what to do now?"

"I wouldn't attempt to. The reinforcements are combing every inch of this place for him." His voice softened. "It's safer here, and this is where you're needed."

Knowing the prisoner couldn't see her face, she smiled at Dante and asked gently, "They need me, or is it you that needs me here, Dante?"

Everything in him wanted to pull her over, so he put his arms across his chest to avoid the motion. Certain his eyes would betray him if they met hers, he looked down and whispered to her, "You know what the answer to that will always be."

"Mine will always be the same for you. We'll close this day soon, and then ... "

The door opened that instant, and Angelina spun around to see three troops with a man struggling in their grip, and she said, "You were right, Dante. Mr. Santiago has arrived."

"Where should we put him?" asked one of the troops.

"There's an adjoining room with his name on it," said Angelina.

"Sir, is that where you want him as well?"

Dante nodded. "Yes, please take him there, and we're coming."

"I got this, Dante."

"This is nonnegotiable."

"You're doubting me now?"

"I'm sick of arguing with you, and I'm coming whether you like it or not. Go."

"I'm running this interrogation."

"I wouldn't dream of it being otherwise." He waved in the direction of the room. "After you."

Once they entered the room, Angelina said to the three troops, "You can go now. We got this."

Dante said, as they turned to him for confirmation, "But stay right outside the door in case we need anything. Thanks."

"Comfortable, Mr. Santiago? You left your company earlier. Horrible manners for a host, particularly one in your respected position. But that's the least of your crimes today, isn't it?" said Angelina.

"Coming from someone that had soldiers drag me by blade point in my own house, that's a bold statement. Who might you be? Another Freedom Fighter recruit?"

"No, I don't take orders from them. I'm a freelancer, which is a bad thing for you because I believe in different methods of intel gathering than those approved by the Freedom Fighters." She smiled at the look that flickered across his face. "I see we understand each other, so for your well-being, start telling us something interesting quickly, Mr. Santiago."

He glanced at Dante before turning back to her. "He's still a Freedom Fighter. He won't stand by and ... " His voice trailed off though at the look on Dante's face.

"Ordinarily, you'd be right about him. Personally, I detest his lofty Freedom Fighter ideals and don't hesitate to tell him. But we've heard what you did today, your part in what happened to his cousin. Yes, everybody knows." She growled, "We met your assistant too, so don't pretend you didn't see him tied up."

"I have nothing to say to either of you. You can't save Lana."

Angelina slammed her sword down on the chair beside Mr. Santiago's head, triggering him to jump in his seat. "We already did. Lana's safe." She came closer to his face and lowered her voice. "Next time, you're getting a shave with my blade."

"You're wasting your time because they'll only come after her again. You can't win."

"Then you don't know me." Her sword brushed his neck. "Don't play dumb with me. How long has this charade been going on?"

"I'm not saying a word."

Angelina took the blunt side of the blade and crashed it down on his shoulder, causing the man to howl in pain. "Using your child as bait? What kind of man does that? Where are they? Where are your wife and son? No one has seen them all day. Did you get rid of them too?"

"You're not getting anything from me!"

She tossed the sword aside and yanked the man up to slam him against the wall in a single movement. "Answer me, now! How long have you been Black Dragon? Is this what it's about for you? A sick game with your family as pieces left to die? Did you make their life a nightmare every second? Were you their terror each time you entered the room? Their Black Dragon?" Her hands tightened uncontrollably around his throat.

"You have to stop! You're going to kill him! He'll be no use to us dead." Dante stepped to Angelina's side and tried to loosen her grip without success.

"You're a monster, and you deserve to die! Where are they?"

"Safe, and they're staying that way," He choked out.

"Safe, but you're ... " her voice trailed off as she stared into his eyes.

Dante touched her arm and coaxed her, "Come on, ease up, please."

She removed her hand from his throat but kept him pinned against the wall as she continued to search his eyes, at long last seeing the truth. *I couldn't see it before because I judged this man by my father.* The horrible realization hit her. "You're not the monster. You've done everything today through the eyes of a father and husband, one that means to protect his family."

He stumbled out, "No, I work for Black Dragon like you said. I helped them to capture Lana."

"Because you had to," she whispered. "Where are they keeping your wife and son?"

He lowered his voice, "I can't. I never wanted this to happen. I promise I didn't."

"I believe you, and we can help you. Let us," said Dante.

"How?" he pleaded.

"Give us a minute?" asked Dante, and Mr. Santiago nodded and sat.

Dante guided Angelina over to the side and put his hands on her shoulders, resisting the urge to do more and asked quietly, "Talk to me. What just happened?"

She looked down. "There's no excuse. I allowed it to go too far, and I'm sorry, Dante."

"It's more than that. Are you going to tell me what was behind what you did?"

"You reined me back in." She stared back up at him. "That's all that matters."

"The other is important too, but you won't change your answer." He sighed and then smiled at her. "You did need my help in here, and remember, that's okay."

"Guess so." It was too long since she felt the warmth of his embrace and she longed to melt into it now, but she couldn't here.

He released her shoulders and crossed his arms across his chest again, knowing how dangerously close he came to giving in to his own emotions too. "I've got an idea for Mr. Santiago."

She stared into his eyes and nodded. "It'll work."

"I didn't tell you it yet."

"I'm certain I have the same ploy in mind." She smiled. "I'm a bad influence on you."

"You've told me, but you'll never convince me." He paused, "Can he do it?"

"He has shown he can, with the proper motivation."

They walked back over to him and Angelina asked, "Are you ready to get your family back?"

"Tell me what to do."

"We con them, like they did us all day, except this time we take it all back. We need you to yell so the man outside imagines we're beating you within a breath of your life."

CHAPTER THIRTEEN

Ryan walked back over from speaking with one of the troops, and he recognized the glint in Alena's eyes. Dante's words floated back with what to expect from her.

"Went to play commander for a spell?"

"None needed. Last time I checked, I still hold that position."

"You should work on that, since you couldn't even protect your leadership today."

"Great seeing you again too. As I remember, we came in before you and your comrade were about to be sliced down the middle with a blade."

"That's because we had to do your job. We were managing fine, so don't act like you pulled off a big rescue."

"You were outnumbered and outmatched. That's got to be the most insane idea of managing fine I've ever witnessed in my life! The two of you are full of it."

The weasel suddenly spoke up, "And I thought the other two never stopped. You're on the same side, but nobody could tell. How do you work together without killing each other?"

"Barely on both counts. It gets under his skin because he can't order me around," said Alena.

"We don't need you for any of this," said Ryan.

Alena smiled at the weasel's expression. "Oh, you still can't be clinging to that hope after meeting my comrade. Neither one of us are Freedom Fighters. We're paid help for the special jobs."

"Your comrade indicated that."

"They're glorified mercenaries, is what's she getting at," said Ryan.

"The commander will never agree with my cutthroat methods of doing business."

"And she has never come around to my Freedom Fighter philosophy because they will interfere with her deplorable practices. I choose to tolerate her."

"That's messed up. I'm guessing you two are in charge of interrogating me?"

"You have many reasons to be afraid if so, after what I said, but why would you think that's our next move?" asked Alena.

"Figured you two are competing on who breaks down their prisoner first."

She turned to Ryan. "This man led you on a goose chase? How? He's an idiot."

"I'm wondering the same listening to him now."

"No interrogation?"

"Same dumb question," Alena muttered and said, "There's no point. Did you lose your hearing too, when my comrade tackled you to the ground?"

Ryan laughed. "I think he did. What she's getting at is don't you hear how the interrogation is going in the other room even with how solid those walls are? Why waste time with you?"

"They'll have what we need. My comrade gets an unbelievable rush doing these."

Ryan stretched, contemplating checking on the troops again, as he had grown restless watching the prisoner with Alena. Suddenly, his data pad flashed a message, and he noticed Alena reach for hers as well. After reading it and holding back his surprise, he said to her, "You saw the message from Caleb?"

"Yeah, I'm glad he's there with Lana now."

"I'll reassure him it's covered here, so he stays with her and doesn't worry."

⁓ ele ⁓

Dante looked down at the reply on his data pad. *Understood. Thanks for keeping us in the loop, Caleb.* "We're all set." He opened the door and said to the troops, "We need you three back in here."

Angelina watched Dante give them instructions on guarding Mr. Santiago, grateful not to be responsible for a minute and enjoying seeing him take charge.

He really is amazing, and I can't believe he loves me. If he hadn't stopped me earlier, I don't want to imagine what would have happened. He doesn't realize what I'm capable of.

"Anything?" asked Dante, looking at her.

"Sorry, I zoned out."

"Just making certain I got everything."

"I'm sure you did. You had it under control."

He focused on her another moment before turning back to the troops to give final reminders, "This man leaves with no one unless it's me, this young woman, Commander Ryan, or this woman's comrade."

"Yes, sir."

"If anybody asks you, this man is … "

"A prisoner, working with Black Dragon, a traitor to us."

"That's the idea."

The troop turned to Mr. Santiago and lowered his voice, "We'll keep you safe, Mr. Santiago. Nobody gets to you. You have our word." He patted him on the shoulder, and the man winced. "Sorry, I didn't know."

"I got carried away with the interrogation at the start. My apologies again, Mr. Santiago," said Angelina.

"I'll be fine. Promise me something though."

"What is it?"

"Spare nothing on that man out there."

She leaned down and whispered, "I'll make him pay for what he did. You won't be disappointed."

⸺⸱ℓℓ⸳⸺

Ryan and Alena jumped as the door flung open, and Angelina marched out with Dante behind her.

"Don't get mad at me! It's not my fault it didn't work like you thought!" hollered Dante.

"Nothing of use from the man! How?" yelled Angelina.

"You're kidding, right?" said Ryan.

"Do I look like I'm joking, commander?"

Alena let out a low whistle. "Wow. It didn't enter the realm of possibility with what we heard out here. I know he's under guard, but should we just leave him in there?"

Angelina waved her hand. "That man is not going anywhere, even if there were no guards."

"With the beating she put on him, he couldn't crawl from that room if he wanted to."

"No, that we did," She looked over at Dante in triumph. "Turns out Dante's strength here, " she lightly squeezed his arm bicep, "isn't only impressive with the sunspear. He can pack punishing blows when called for."

"I don't get the enjoyment from it, like some people." He glared at her.

"I'm corrupting you. What can I say?"

"What's our next move with Santiago?" asked Ryan.

"From what he's shown today, he's a traitor, working with Black Dragon. Take him back, and make an example of him. String him up before everyone, and kill him. Show them the punishment for treason," said Angelina.

Alena nodded. "Sounds fair to me."

"Maybe we should question him more," said Ryan.

"Or ask Caleb what to do with him. After his part in almost getting Lana killed, I'm sure he goes with our recommendation," said Alena.

"He would consider it now," said Dante.

"Plenty of time to decide. Either way, you transport him back as a prisoner." Angelina turned and grinned at the weasel, who listened to their conversation. "No worries because we have another captive we can extract what we need from. Thought we forgot about you? Not a chance."

"You'll do no better with me."

"A fair assumption based on your friend in there. I underestimated him, something I seldom do. So, I'm betting I gave you too much credit, that I should have started with you. Easily remedied. You're smug, for someone in your predicament."

She turned to Alena, "You two didn't find anything else on him, did you?"

"Oddly, no."

Angelina started at his feet and began patting him down, only venturing so far up his legs. After untucking his shirt the rest of the way and pulling it up, her eyes scrutinized the lining and his chest and back for something suspicious. She felt Dante's eyes boring into her further at her hands' inspection of the man's upper body and regretted it as he watched her do it. Everything screamed wrong about this. However, with nothing discovered to confirm her misgivings, she put his shirt back in place.

He grinned at her. "If that's what you wanted, you just needed to ask. I know how to appreciate a woman with your kind of curves."

The next second the dull side of her blade slammed across his chest with enough power to send him and the chair toppling backwards onto the floor. She towered over him, as he still yelled in pain from the impact, and her boot rammed into his ribcage sufficient for another scream to erupt from him. Placing the tip of her blade to his throat, she said in a calm voice, "Don't address me like that again, or I will cut your tongue out."

As her boot lengthened his agony, she turned to Dante, "You think he got my message?"

"You like to be sure, and he should have more sense than to talk to a woman like that," Dante answered nonchalantly, but inside his blood boiled at the man's words to Angelina.

"On this occasion, I agree with Dante." Her boot found its mark again, as another cry burst from the man. "Remember, you want to keep your tongue." She motioned to the guards. "Pull him back up, would you?"

She turned back to him. "While Dante is ready for another round of using a prisoner as a punching bag, I've shown I don't need him to do so. I have plenty of effective interrogation methods of my own. So how friendly are you with Black Dragon? Middle man? Direct supplier?"

He shook his head weakly.

"Wrong answer again!" The dull side of the blade crashed down on his shoulder, followed by his howl of agony. She rotated the sword in her hands as he looked up, panting from the painful spikes still slicing through him. "Didn't they tell you how much I enjoy this? You should reconsider your decision. This won't end well for you." Suddenly she stopped. "Didn't we retrieve a data pad from him?"

"We did," said Alena.

"Anything?"

"Haven't messed with it yet."

"Mind if I try?" She smiled as Alena handed it to her. "Thanks." She turned back to her prisoner. "Could be we don't need you after all. Oh no, your data pad won't let me in. Tell me how to get into it."

"No."

She walked around with it, making a show of fiddling with it. "You must have a fancy lock system on yours. Not too savvy with those things myself. Not like those people. What do you call them?"

"Hackers, maybe?" volunteered Ryan.

"That's the word I was grasping for, commander." She addressed the weasel again, "If only I were better with this. What's that? What does it want?"

"You're wasting your time. It's all encrypted."

"That's super hard to crack from what I've heard. There have to be all sorts of interesting tidbits on here I'm itching to know. Open this up for me already." She put it in front of him and waited.

He didn't move or answer.

She resumed walking around the prisoner, messing with his device. "This is a shame, and here I thought this might be useful. Is this your only one?"

"What do you mean?"

"In certain circles, individuals keep separate ones, one for personal and one for business or if it's extra secret dealings they might use a different one for that purpose. At least it's a rumored practice. That takes us back to my original question to you."

"You have the only data pad you'll get from me."

"Such an unhelpful, cryptic answer." She circled to stand behind him. "It always seemed a great deal of trouble to me juggling more than one, but if you have enough to hide it could be worth it. I'll never get through your security." She looked over at the other three and asked, "Any of you have a knack for this hacking stuff?"

"Sorry, I'm afraid not," said Dante, holding back his laughter with the others. They knew they were looking at the best person to break into it.

She took out her data pad and concentrated on it, as her fingers flew over it and returned to the weasel's data pad. Satisfied at whatever she saw, she nodded and re-pocketed hers. Her motions on his data pad became increasingly self-assured. "Oh yeah, you're right. This encryption is beyond me. I don't see any way I'm getting past it." She rolled her eyes and held up the data pad from behind the man for the others to see a display fully open, ready for her to search. "I'd have to get lucky with it, but you never know." She made a few additional keystrokes on it and came back to stand before him. "Guess not. Another dead end it seems."

"You got nowhere?" he smiled in triumph.

"See for yourself." She put the data pad in front of his face.

"On the same screen you started on."

"Yes, and we're out of time." She turned to the others. "We'll need to close this out. My comrade and I have another engagement soon, and we can't go like this."

"A date this afternoon?" asked Dante.

"Contrary to what you and the commander think, we have a life other than saving your people's backside, and a wardrobe change is necessary for our next appointment."

"You're not done here yet."

She tapped her fingers impatiently on the table. "I did imply I'd ensure your prisoners got taken care of, and I should keep my word. It's high on the unwritten rules of best business practices when dealing with you Freedom Fighters. There's time for one. I don't trust either one as far as I can throw them from a ship hatch, but we'll go with Santiago. He'll be the harder one to move, with the beating we put on him, so I'll get him."

"Not you, we'll get him."

"Still don't trust me, Dante? You shouldn't. I've never done much of that trusting either, and today proves why that's a policy I stand by. Let's get Santiago, and we'll leave the other one here." She turned in the direction of Alena and Ryan.

Alena nodded. "We'll make sure he stays put. We're used to him now."

Angelina walked behind the weasel and whispered in his ear, "A shame we have to cut this short for now, but I'll leave you with a reminder." She crashed the dull side of her blade down on his other shoulder, to produce a yell from him that echoed throughout the room.

CHAPTER FOURTEEN

"You'll need to help him a lot," said Angelina to the three troops as she and Dante emerged from the room with them and a hunched over, stumbling Santiago in a cloaked hood.

Ryan motioned to several of the troops. "That half go with them for added protection."

"You'll still be fine?" asked Dante.

"Yeah, we're keeping this half of the reinforcements in case we catch any trouble. Like we said."

Dante nodded as the group exited the room with Mr. Santiago.

"We're far enough," said Angelina moments later.

"Agreed." Dante waved for the group to stop.

Angelina went to Mr. Santiago. "Brilliant performance, but hold on to the cloak. We need to hide who you are for longer because there's ample reason to believe we'll run into danger. You can move like normal now though."

Meanwhile, Dante turned to the troops. "Come in closer. The three soldiers who were in the room with us already know this information, but we need to share the shortened version with the rest of you. Mr. Santiago is not working for the enemy, but the Black Dragon agent inside that room had to think we believed Mr. Santiago a traitor. It's the story we stick to until it all plays out. However, everything he has done is because they have taken his wife and son hostage and threatened to kill them if he didn't cooperate. This is now a rescue operation, but it should appear to anyone watching we're escorting our prisoner back for interrogation. We must watch for enemies lurking, so your job is to ensure this man's safety while we retrieve his family. Do you understand?"

A unison of nods and yes sirs followed as the soldiers' expressions changed towards Mr. Santiago.

"Sir, do we know where they're being held?"

"Yes. Inside of the Santiagos' ship. That's where we're headed."

"Dante and I will handle the rescuing part," said Angelina. "Just keep this man safe so he can rejoin his family. Let's move."

"No problems so far," said Dante as they continued walking.

"We haven't been outside the house for long, Dante." Her eyes scanned around them as they marched to their target. "He had lots of help to accomplish all this."

"They seemed determined for sure." A blaster shot cut off any further comment. "Take cover!"

"Everybody okay?" asked Angelina.

"All fine, including Santiago," said Dante from directly behind her.

"We can take that soldier out," said Angelina as another shot fired, "but It's not coming from ground level. It originated from there." She looked up and pointed to the top of a nearby building. "Do you ... "

"Yeah, I see him too."

"I've got to get up there and eliminate him."

"Last time I checked you haven't grown wings, and no feathered friends are aiding you this time."

"Then I need that." She paused as her eyes focused on a speeder close by. "Cover me. I'm going for it."

"Not without me you won't." He tried to stop her, but she was already on the move. "Protect our prisoner at all costs, or it'll be on you," He shouted to the troops as he ran to catch up to her while shooting his blaster toward the sniper.

She jumped onto the unattended speeder and felt a familiar form climb on behind her. "As I said, you're not doing this without me, my Angelina," whispered Dante.

Despite the circumstances, a pleasant warmth surged through her at his nearness and words. "Okay, but I can't have you slipping off, so get a tight hold on me."

He had wrapped his arm firmly about her waist the moment he mounted the vehicle and whispered, "That I'll always do."

She lifted them off the ground. "I count on it."

"I wanted to get my arms around you all day, but this isn't how I intended."

"Me either, Dante, but I'll take it," she said. "That blaster is getting better with its aim."

"I noticed too, but I'll keep firing from mine. You concentrate on driving."

"I am. We should be fine." She jerked the speeder to avoid another round of fire. "You still ... "

"Not letting you go. That came from a second blaster though."

"Which means there's two of them."

"And I spotted the other one. Make a pass to come behind them. My blaster isn't doing the job. I'll make a switch."

"Do what you need to. Going straight in doesn't sound like a solid plan anymore to me either." A shot sizzled near, but something else diverted its path. "Your sunspear came close to my head, Dante."

"Not as near as that blast did. I'll keep you safe, no matter how difficult you make it for me."

"Lucky for me you refuse to be deterred."

"Only when it comes to you."

"Almost there."

He continued to deflect them with his sunspear. "What is this obsession you've got with rooftops?"

"Not sure, but it's hazardous to my health, so I need to kick it." She heard him chuckle at her assessment. "About to land. Get ready."

"Stay away from the edge this time for me."

With blades poised for battle, they sprang from the speeder upon touching down at the center of the rooftop. Angelina moved to run towards the shooters, but Dante caught her arm. "Remember we make them come off the perimeter to us. I'm not taking a chance of losing you."

"If things continue to hold today, the blaster should do it." She aimed hers with one hand towards the fighters as she used her blade to deflect the shots with her other hand.

"You're right. No mutated agents so far." He adopted the same defensive stance.

"May I venture from your protective bubble now?" she teased as the two soldiers ran at them.

"Only if you keep following instructions." He winked at her. "Come on."

"You didn't even let me," Angelina complained as she stood after taking the data pads from both fallen fighters.

"There were only two. I beat you to them this round." He replaced his weapons while grinning at her. "You got rid of more than your share today." Taking her hand, he drew her close. "Let me make it up to you."

"We're out in the open, Dante." She whispered but found herself leaning into him.

"No one can see us clearly from up here." He stroked her cheek and longed to run his hands through her hair, but it was pulled back and covered. "But you'll worry somebody managed to. Later though, my Angelina." He settled for brushing her forehead with his lips. "Let's finish this rescue before I don't care how in the open we are."

—ℓℓ—

"I wonder how the prisoner transport is coming," said Alena.

"They can handle it, but I'm sure they ran into trouble," said Ryan.

"Me too. This place is crawling with more like him." She glanced over at their captive. "Ryan, this is going to be a mess to clean up."

"Meaning more than the physical room." He sighed as he surveyed the carnage remaining. "I'm racking my brain too for the best way to go about it."

"The two people that know how to do it are both prisoners."

"I came to the same conclusion." He stopped as armed men burst through the door. "Again today!" He rushed to meet them with Alena following suit while commanding his troops, "You four guard our prisoner with your life. The rest of you are with us to handle these newcomers."

"Ready?" Ryan grinned at her as he raised his blade.

"Of course, commander." She swung her sword towards the first intruder.

—ꝏ—

Dante's group stealthily entered the hangar where Santiago's ship lay. A fair number of ships resided there, but it didn't appear to be an overly large ship hangar. Each one consisted of its own comfortable space apart from the next vessel, providing a degree of privacy.

"It's quiet," said Dante.

"Only administrator-related staff land here," said Santiago.

"Common practice. Having it deserted works in our favor," said Angelina.

"That's mine." Santiago pointed to a ship up ahead.

"I spot four outside on guard duty. Two right at the ship on one side and two more a distance on the other side," said Dante as they hid behind another craft further away.

"I see them. Mr. Santiago, any idea of how many are inside with your family?" asked Angelina.

"At least one, but I'd suspect more."

"You're probably right, so we'll prepare for the more. We must eliminate the ones outside quietly. I'm in a uniform but not one that identifies any loyalty. Also, I'm a woman, so they won't take me as a threat." She moved her dagger for easier access. "Let me handle this, at least at first."

Dante held her arm. "No, there's four of them and only one of you."

"I'll be fine. Promise."

He relaxed his hold but didn't release her. "What are you planning?"

"Spin them a story, and use my charm to eliminate them."

"You know what kind of men these are, and they wouldn't give a second thought to ... " he paused, not daring to say more. "I don't like your plan."

"Trust me. It'll work."

He stared back at her and sighed. "If I think it's going sideways, I'm coming in with weapons blazing. I won't wait."

"Fair enough. You'll hear through the earpiece if you should move in." She hesitated and smiled. "You can let go of my arm now."

"I'm insane to allow you to do this. Be careful." He released her arm.

"Sir, are you sure?" asked one of the soldiers as he read the concerned look on Dante's face.

"Just watch Santiago. If she runs into trouble, I need to get in fast."

"Will do, sir."

She slowly approached the ship. The two guards close to it on the one side regarded her with a mixture of suspicion and something else, as their eyes appreciated her form with the lightweight gear she wore. She held her hands in front of her, palms showing. "I'm supposed to deliver a message."

"A message?" asked one of the men.

Lowering her hands, she continued her approach. "Yes, this is Mr. Santiago's ship, and you're watching it, right?"

"Why do you need to know?"

"That's who I was instructed to relay the information to."

"Who's it from?"

"Mr. Santiago's new assistant."

"Who are you?"

She shrugged. "You wouldn't know me. I work with the Santiagos in the administration building, but half of the time they don't acknowledge me. We've never seen eye to eye, so they don't care for me much. However, I'm excellent at my job. Replacing me would be a huge unnecessary hassle for them."

"What do you not agree with them on?"

"Most everything, but I like the new guy and the crew he's brought in so far." She smiled.

"Do you now? We're a part of that too, you know?"

"Makes sense. He'd be a fool to trust just anybody, and I'm taking you away from your work."

"As long as he keeps you as his messenger, I'm happy. I could get used to seeing you every day."

The other guard grinned. "Certainly making my shift easier."

"I still need to pass on the message, remember?"

They moved in closer to back her up against the ship.

The first guard said, "Hurry and give it to us, sweetheart."

"There's a delay, and you'll be stuck guarding longer."

"That's not so bad, and I've got ideas on how to fill the time now," said the second guard.

Dante watched and listened as a familiar scene replayed itself. *Trey.* The man threatened to do the identical thing to Angelina, and Dante refused to stand by while these two men laid a hand on her. He never should have agreed to this crazy scheme. As he stood and prepared to intervene, he saw one man collapse to the ground and at the same moment she pushed the other man's lifeless body from her.

"Move to sneak in behind the other two," He heard her words through his earpiece. "Listen if you need to proceed."

"Got it." He let out a deep breath and turned to the soldier. "She signaled me. I'll be back."

She replaced her blaster and peeked around the ship. A fair span separated the remaining guards as she had observed before, and she closed the distance between herself and them. Making a scraping noise on the ground with her dagger, she drew the one's attention and then concealed the blade.

"You should have seen him ... " the guard stopped mid-sentence in his account. "Did you hear something?"

The other guard smirked. "Besides you running your jaw? No, nothing else."

"I'm sure I did, and it'll be our hide if something happens."

"Go check already if you're worried."

The guard rounded the corner only to be met by a frantic Angelina. "What in the blazes?"

She grabbed his arm and put her finger to his lips to silence him. "Be quiet before he hears you."

"What happened here?" He took in her blood-stained clothes and the two men lying dead.

"I was supposed to deliver a message to you. That's all Santiago's assistant said. A simple message. Someone followed me though and ... " her voice broke, "Please you have to keep me safe from him." She tightened her grip on him.

"Two of ours down. I need to get the other guard."

"No, you can't leave me here alone. I barely escaped."

"We wouldn't want something happening to a pretty thing like you, so stay close to me." His eyes roved over her. Yeah, his protection came at a price, and he decided what it would be.

"I saw a shadow over there."

"You're just jumpy now, but I'll take a look. Keep behind me."

"Okay. I'm so freaked out. Thank the stars I found you."

"Must be your lucky day, darling." He chuckled to himself. He didn't see anything though and started to turn to tell her, but the cold metal slicing through him came first as he collapsed on the ground in his blood. She knelt beside him and whispered, "Your luck changed with the flick of a blade." Then he drew his last.

"One more," she murmured.

What's taking him so long? Wondered the guard and he glimpsed in time to see the dagger headed for him.

He had to turn around, didn't he? Angelina raged as the man's hold on her wrist stopped her dagger's motion. Her eyes widened, and she stumbled out the words, "You're not him. I thought you were him. I'm so sorry." She used her free arm to grip the man's other arm and cling to him, ignoring the continuing punishing restraint on her wrist.

"You tried to stab me, and all you got is a lame apology!"

"I thought you were the one who followed me. He already got to the others over there. Please ... "

"What!" He freed her wrist and started towards the other side of the ship while she used the second to conceal the dagger again. "The men standing guard over here?"

"Keep your voice down. He'll hear you, and come finish me off. Yes, all of them."

He grabbed her arm and pulled her along. "We're checking together." After reaching the other side and taking in the carnage, he faced her, "What did this man look like?"

"Brown hair, average height, solidly built. Like you. That's why I mistook him for you."

"And you thought you'd overpower him just now."

"I was trying to avoid him, get out of here, and I thought I ran right into him. When you turned, I acted on instinct."

"Why did you come out here in the first place?"

"To deliver a message to you from Santiago's assistant."

"Why didn't he come himself?"

Angelina fumed internally at the numerous questions as she said, "He's been delayed."

"What's the delay?"

"It's taking more time to sneak the cargo from the house. He said not to worry though because it's a minor hiccup."

He stared at her blood-stained clothes. "You're pretty messy for a bystander."

"I barely got away, and I slipped in all the blood."

He backed her up against the ship. "Got an answer for everything, don't you?"

"If I did, I wouldn't be in my current situation. I never should have agreed to deliver that stupid message."

"Or maybe you have more to do with this bloody scene than what you're telling me."

"You're out of your mind. I told you what happened."

He forced her arms behind her back and ground her the rest of the way against the craft. "I've got an idea. How about I take you inside to one of the quarters, and we have a private session about today?"

"Not a chance. Let go of me."

"The Santiagos practically have their personal hangar out here, so this is secluded enough for me." His full weight pressed on her as he leaned in. "It'll be suiting you too. I tried to be a gentleman, sweetness, but we're past that now."

"Your mistake was laying a hand on my girl," Dante growled from behind the man as he threw the man to the ground and put a sunspear clean through him.

Dante turned back to her. "What were you thinking?" Then his face paled, and he wrapped his arm around her waist while guiding her back towards the group. "Why didn't you say something? We have to get you to Seth."

"Why are you acting so freaked out? Dante, this is hardly the time for a lesson from Seth." She stared up at him as she allowed herself to be led back to the group.

"You're hurt."

"Why would you believe that?"

"You're bleeding from ... "

She finally took full stock of her appearance and understood his panicked expression. "No, it's okay. It's not my blood. When I downed those first two with my daggers, they ran right up on me when I did it, so it all ended up on me."

"Yes, I saw that part fine like the last one, and what they almost did." He shook his head and snatched his arm from her grasp.

The look in his eyes struck at her heart, and she ached to reach out to him again, to say the words to bring him back to her. She couldn't here though. "Dante, thanks for coming to my rescue."

The smile never surfaced that she hoped to coax from him. "You've rescued our group's backside all day as you put it, so what else did you expect from me?"

She looked at him, trying to mask the hurt in her eyes. They had said things like this all day to each other, but they dismissed it as keeping up the ploy. Yet there was no roleplaying underneath Dante's words. *What have I done?* She bit her lip and said, "I expected nothing less."

"Let's do what we came to do. Once we're finished, I don't care if the universe is coming down on itself, I get an aside with you."

"Okay, Dante," she whispered.

Angelina reasoned they had to be quiet as they approached the ship, so it shouldn't matter. It did though, because this was an uncomfortable, horrible silence between them. He should treat her like this for things she had done she reminded herself, but he always showed her the opposite. She couldn't comprehend how, the depth of his love for her. Yet, this was unbearable, his utter coldness to her, like she represented a mere mercenary he cared nothing for.

Dante continued to rage inside at himself, Angelina, and the whole situation. *Why did I do that to her? Say that to her? I didn't mean it. I love her with everything in me. She just scared me to death, but she doesn't care how many times she does it. No matter how much I tell her, she always does it again. When I saw those men's hands on her, I lost it. What's wrong with me? This is such a mess.*

They reached the ship's entrance, and he mouthed to the group, *"Focus."* However, his eyes rested on one person. She nodded, knowing they must put aside their personal issues for now. He motioned to Mr. Santiago, who moved to the ship's access port to make the attempt.

They held their breath as he completed the last step in verifying his identity for it. A moment later the swish of the door opening signaled victory, and Dante and Angelina barged through it first with the others following.

"We never got the call." The man in the cockpit seat sprang up as he registered the unfamiliar faces and yelled, "We've got trouble!"

"That you do," said Angelina, taking advantage of his confusion and cleaving him through with her sword.

"All clear, at least out in the open," said Dante after finishing another off in the front of the ship, "Only two?"

"We eliminated one towards the back, sir," said one of the soldiers.

"There are still the quarters to clean out. That's where you said it looked like they were being held, right?" Dante pointed to the cargo hold as he gazed at Mr. Santiago.

"They purposely obscured the view they sent me, but, yes, the quarters," said Mr. Santiago, understanding Dante's misdirection.

"Let's do it, then," said Dante. He and Angelina knelt on either side of the cargo hold door and listened. They looked up at each other after a minute. Dante mouthed, *Nothing.*

She mouthed back, *Same here.* Making a motion to open the door, Dante nodded his agreement. Gingerly she did so and leaned back from it, bracing for the blaster fire that never erupted. After another moment she peered back into the opening with him and whispered, "I don't see them."

"It's a hold though, so they could be behind anything," he whispered.

"But there's not a sound. How do you keep a child that quiet?" She stopped as the exact horrible thought crossed her mind as she read into Dante's eyes. "I'm going down now."

"I'll come with you."

"No, somebody needs to be up here to lead if it falls apart. That's you, Dante. I'll check it."

He watched her go, sorry again for his earlier words but unable to make amends with the audience around him. If something happened to her, he'd never forgive himself. A racket from behind startled him from his thoughts, and he turned to discover two armed men in the back of the ship with their two hostages. He discreetly closed the cargo door and hoped they didn't notice as he eased into a standing position.

"Daddy, Daddy!" The little boy screamed as he tried to squirm from the man's grasp.

"Better pipe it down, you little brat!" yelled the man.

Mr. Santiago started to run forward, but Dante grabbed him. "Don't. Calm your child from here. You can do this."

Mr. Santiago turned back to his family, focusing on his son. "Braydon, it's all right. This will be over soon. I need you to keep being brave for Daddy."

"Promise it's over soon?"

"I promise, son."

"I can be brave for you, Daddy."

"That's my boy," He forced a smile for his son as he turned to his wife.

"I'm okay," she managed, her voice trembling slightly.

"Teresa, did they hurt you?"

"Our son is safe. That's what matters."

Santiago's eyes blazed in fury at the two men. "Why you ... If you touched her, I will make you suffer before killing you myself."

Although Dante understood the man's anger all too well, he put a restraining hand on Santiago's arm again to halt his advance. "You've got to keep it together."

"Yes, Mr. Santiago, there's a child present. I'm appalled." The man laughed. "Don't worry about your wife. We treated her well enough by our standards. Although we tried to charm her, she resisted our efforts. While tempted to be more persistent, we knew you wouldn't be as cooperative if she lodged too many complaints about her treatment from us. Still, she's a pretty one you've got." He tightened his grip on the woman's waist and brushed his lips to the side of her face as she attempted to avoid his touch.

"She's my wife, so you have no right. Leave her alone." He burst out again as his whole body shook.

Angelina didn't see anyone as she scanned the hold. Yet when Dante left her predominantly in the dark, it didn't help and surprised her. He is mad at me, she conceded as he shut the cargo door on her. I can't remember seeing him like this, letting his anger cloud his judgment. That's my department she thought, as the memory of Santiago's interrogation resurfaced with a vengeance. She cringed as she felt her hand around the man's throat again and attempted to push the image aside. Fortunately, Dante isn't like me though, so I wonder why he ... is that? She stopped all her motion and listened as she recognized a child's frightened voice originating above her. How did they get up there from here? "Of course. I must be slipping. Thanks for leaving me down here, and I never should've doubted you." She murmured as she adjusted something on her data pad and obtained the light she needed. "There's my path."

Dante couldn't watch much more. Angelina's words echoed in his head, "*Using your child and wife as bait. What kind of person does that?*" Santiago hadn't done so, but he stood helpless as his family became pawns in this deadly game. "He's right. Leave his family out of this. Hand them over. Who hides behind a child and his mother? It's despicable."

"We got a rise from the great spear-bearer Dante." sneered the man holding Santiago's wife.

As his recent encounter with Angelina painfully replayed in his mind, he stared back at the man. "No, just Dante, but I'm getting this man's family back to him like I promised. Whatever problem you got is with me and my group, so face us like real men."

"Our issue is with your group, but the Santiagos aligned themselves with you. Consider them collateral damage."

"No, receiving your kicks from terrorizing a five-year-old is called sick. Now let him go."

Suddenly Dante spotted Angelina creeping up behind the men and placing a finger on her lips to signal the others to stay silent. She looked between the men, clearly torn at knowing she had two targets, but unsure how to effectively disarm both in one swing and free the hostages. Setting her sights on the one holding the child first, she readied her blaster.

"It won't work, Dante. We know we don't win against you in a fair fight, so we'll terrorize a five-year-old all day long." The blaster shot hitting him cut off any more words.

"Run to your dad, now!" hollered Angelina as she concurrently pushed the dagger clear of the little boy's frame and sent him forward, but he fell in his shock. His father along with Dante bridged the gap to pull him from further danger. Meanwhile, she turned her attention to the other man as he knocked the blaster from her hand. She started to reach for her dagger, but the man roared as he gave up his hostage to deal with the greater threat. "Move now!" Angelina screamed to Santiago's wife, who rushed to do so.

Dante advanced towards the man as Santiago's wife got clear, but he stopped in his tracks at the man's menacing words, "Not another step, or she dies, Dante."

Angelina fumed as the man aimed his blaster at Dante, and his other arm tightened its grip around her upper body to position the dagger blade across her throat.

"Ease back, Dante. That's right."

"Release her. You're surrounded. No one is letting you leave here."

"Because you're coming after me? While I have her?" He grinned. "Yeah, that's what I thought."

"I'll kill you." Dante raised his blaster.

"Why? You got his family back, so you take them, and I keep her. Two for one. It's a fair trade."

"She's not a bargaining piece in a deal."

"Does Dante have dibs on you or something, darling? I mean, I certainly wouldn't blame him."

"This is his rescue to lead. He's the commander, so I follow his orders."

The man chuckled. "What do your orders entail from her, Commander Dante?"

"The expected."

"Really? Because if I were her commanding officer, I'd have extra sweet instructions to only require her to carry out for me. You should make better use of your authority, Dante."

"His authority is fine." Angelina snapped, struggling to control her anger.

"Not from what I see."

"Dante is a good man. An honorable one. He never takes." She turned to the man, ever conscious of the blade at her throat. She knew the cost of her next words but didn't care. "And he's no coward. He's everything men like you will never be."

Without hesitation the man fisted her in the side of the face with his blaster hand and a low moan of pain escaped her at the impact. "I don't aspire to be a man like him, but I'll make you pay for your lack of respect."

Dante shook with rage as he started towards the man, but this time one of his soldiers touched his arm and said, "Sir, remember the knife is still at her throat."

Dante stopped and took a deep breath as he gazed at Angelina. "Are you all right?"

"I'm okay, Dante. After what he's already been a part of, that didn't surprise me. "

"She's a strong one. A real fighter. I see why else you keep her around." The man laughed.

"You're about to see why I command this group if you don't release her, because I'm about to waste you right here." He readied his blaster again.

"Let me take her, and you go your way. We all go home."

"I'm not going anywhere without her."

"Why not?"

He yelled, "Because I care about her!"

The man grinned. "You do have a soft spot for her after all."

He stared at the man and forced a composure into his voice that masked the chaos swirling inside him. "I already told you, just as she did. I'm her commanding officer in this operation. She's under my protection, like all the individuals in this room. I don't espouse to your belief in collateral damage with those who put their trust in my leadership, so I'm leaving with her and everyone else I intended to today. It's as simple as that." He paused, "Final warning."

Angelina smiled at Dante as his calm settled into her spirit too, and she mouthed to him, "*Take the shot.*"

Staring back at her, his eyes said what his mouth couldn't. *If I miss and hit you ...*

She mouthed, "*You won't miss.*"

He continued, *It's so close though.*

Then he heard her in his mind, the words coming through as clearly as the day in the Elders Hall. *Earlier today you protected me from men like him. You didn't let Trey take me either, and you caught me at the cylinder. Don't you see? You always come to my rescue. I trust you with my life, my heart, so I know I can trust you with this shot, Dante.*

"You'll be worth all the trouble. I can't wait to get a close-up of you in my quarters," murmured the man in her ear.

She held Dante's eyes and blocked out everything including the man's warm breath on her neck and his hand managing to hold the blaster while eagerly roaming over the side of her body.

Dante shook with fury anew as the man's hands became more brazen, and his lips found her neck. She moved her head to avoid his advances, but it simply granted the man better access. However, it also gave Dante an advantage, an easier aim. *I won't disappoint you, Angelina.*

Her voice whispered in his mind, *You never disappoint me. Concentrate on me. On us. It's always about you and I. No one else, my Dante. Now take the shot.*

He smiled at her. *I am, my Angelina.*

The man smirked, "You won't risk hitting her. You don't have the guts."

"You don't know me at all," said Dante.

The next instant, the man lay dead on the floor from Dante's shot.

CHAPTER FIFTEEN

Angelina fell forward from the man's grasp, ensuring her body avoided the dagger that had been lodged at her throat.

Dante didn't care anymore if the whole galaxy watched as his limit of pretending had long been reached. Immediately, he caught her as she stumbled and wrapped her up in his arms, pulling her against him. He expected her to push back with the audience, but the day had taken its toll on her too, and she encircled her arms around his shoulders.

"You okay?"

"I am, thanks to you, and I knew you could make the shot, Dante."

"I'm relieved you came out on the good side of that call."

She pulled back the slightest bit to look up at him. "Me too. You were something to watch back there, and here I thought it was all due to your sunspear abilities." A teasing glint lit her eyes.

"I've been told I have other talents."

"That someone is right about you."

"That person knows me better than anyone." He smiled. "Sure, you're okay?"

She nodded and smiled at him.

He eased her out of his arms, fully aware of the group continuing to witness their exchange and await his instructions. Any further time with her like that and their troops would see it as more than a commander ensuring his comrade is unharmed and stable enough to return to duty. Hopefully, he and Angelina hadn't already pushed it beyond that point. He turned to them. "Let's get this wrapped up."

She listened as he confidently dispensed orders but then stopped.

One of the troops asked, "Something else, Dante?"

"This may not be the best way, since we haven't worked out how to unravel the mess this enemy agent made." Dante turned to her, "What do you think?"

"You have excellent judgment."

"I'm missing something, though. With this process, maybe."

"What's bugging you about it?"

"Firestones clean this up fastest, but the weasel brought a mini army of thugs for this deal. We're collecting the data pads, yet for what has to be sorted out I don't know if this is the best way."

After several seconds, she said, "It's too little. Perhaps you're afraid we're turning to ashes what you'll need to figure everything out, like making sure you accounted for all the enemy agents he enlisted for this job."

"That's it. How did you manage to pull that out?"

"You're starting to see things my way."

His eyes narrowed. "Let's not go that far."

"Too late. I already corrupted you, remember?"

He sighed. "Maybe we identify them another way in the meantime."

"Which is?"

"Fingerprints, perhaps?"

"I'm doubtful it gets you anywhere. Individuals in this line of work don't leave those around, and if by any luck you found traces, they would be under ten different aliases." She paused. "At least that's what I've heard."

"Right. How about facial recognition?"

"Same thing. Unless you're in the business and crossed paths with these players."

"If we knew someone ... " he stared at her meaningfully.

"True, but if it's only for accounting purposes there's an easier way." She gazed over at Mr. Santiago and waited for Dante to follow her focus. "You don't have to know who they are, and likely you'd come up empty on that front. The key is having the individual that knows who belongs in the neighborhood. And you're golden in that respect."

"The ones that are already down, we know their allegiance, so it's pointless."

"Or it jogs his memory if anyone is remaining from the weasel's crew. Mr. Santiago should know who's in his household and works for him or have access to it."

"Makes sense." He turned to the soldiers. "This is how we're cleaning up. Get me fingerprints and pictures, with close-ups of the faces of all the fighters we killed. We'll transfer them from your data pads when we get back. Also, confiscate their data pads and put them in one place. Search their person for anything else that could be helpful. We might get lucky. Only after that's done, use the firestones to make the bodies disappear. One group does that. The other takes care of the next task. Every corner of this ship is to be checked for enemy stowaways. The Santiagos will be taken safely to the fortress. Provide them with whatever we can until that happens, especially their kid. He's probably hungry and still scared out of his mind."

"We'll see it done, sir. Anything else?"

"Another minute. Mr. Santiago, please?" Dante motioned him over.

"What can I do?"

"I need to borrow one of your quarters for a bit. Does one of these have a table with a couple of chairs?"

"Yes, that one." He pointed to a door in the middle.

"Appreciate it." Dante turned back to the troops. "I'll be in there. If something goes awry or if you have a question about what we covered, come get me. Otherwise, handle it. This young woman and I have an issue that needs to be dealt with."

Angelina looked at Dante. "The aside still?"

"Yes, still. I'm not backing down on this. We do this now. Let's go." He motioned with his hand. "You first."

Dante scanned the room as they opened the door. "Looks clear, and there's nowhere for someone to hide." He turned to face her. "Sit down, now!"

One of the soldiers murmured, "And I thought they were finally getting along."

Another soldier shook his head and murmured, "I'm not getting in the middle of that."

"What in the galaxy were you thinking with the stunts you pulled today?" Dante continued as the door slid closed, and she plopped down in one of the chairs.

"What are you so upset about? I was trying to save ... "

"No, that's not what I saw. They outnumbered you, and you know what almost happened to you because of it!"

She looked up at him as he towered over her. "What did you expect me to do? Just wait? Lana was in trouble!"

He sat down too. "Stop it. You know that's not what I'm referring to. We hadn't gotten to you yet, so you couldn't prevent being in that situation. Any of us would've done the same. Don't you dare play me for the fool. Four against one. Those are the odds I'm talking about."

"You're still going on about that?"

"Because it didn't need to happen! We outnumbered them two for every one of them with still a couple of troops left to guard Santiago, not the other way around. You never should have been in that position, but you chose it!"

"You were in Freedom Fighter gear. I was the wiser choice, and it worked."

"No, it didn't!" He took a deep breath. "How do you not see? Look at you. No. Look. At. You. Head to toe in blood because you let them get that close to you."

"You had a better plan?"

"Give me a couple minutes, and yes. Geez, there were ten saner ones than what you conceived with none leaving you like this."

"This is what you're all wound up about? My idea didn't meet your expectations?"

He reached over and grabbed her by the shoulders. "I'm ready to shake you right now! What is wrong with you? You know me like no one else does. What is this about? It's you being within a breath of getting killed in front of me and having several men almost do unspeakable things to you while I stood by! It would've been my fault, and you brush it aside as though it were nothing."

His words finally registering, she stammered out, "No, you wouldn't be to blame. How can you think that?"

"Because I let you do it. I went along with it when I knew … " He paused, "I saw Trey all over again. If a man did that to you, took that from you, and I had a part in it, Angelina … " He looked down for several seconds before staring back up at her. "How do you not see what that would do to me?"

"I do, Dante. I'm so sorry." Her eyes shimmered with tears.

"Now I'm wondering about the other. The shipping deals. You said you stay away from the more dangerous ones, but are you telling me the truth? How close do you allow them to get? How far do you let it go? What touch is too much?" Releasing her shoulders, he put his head in his hands before staring back at her. "Or can you stand to tell me?"

"Oh, Dante, no. I told you the truth, I promise." Her voice broke and she reached out her hand, "Please don't, you're the only one." A sob escaped from her, and she started to withdraw her hand when he didn't respond.

In that instant, he took both of her hands in his and brought them to his lips. "You're the only one for me too, but I'm scared of losing you. Today I was reminded again of how deep that fear runs. All those men see only one thing about you. I mean, I'd be lying and blind if I said you weren't drop-dead gorgeous." He elicited a smile from her. "But you're so much more than that. The much more is what I see every time I look at you and each second I'm with you and why I cared for you, before I ever had my first stunning glimpse of you. I refuse to see any part of you taken, bargained away as a ploy, as compensation for a piece of intel."

"It won't be, because I'll give myself to the only one who holds my heart, and that's you, my Dante," she whispered.

He stroked her uninjured cheek. "You have all of me too."

"You're welcome to use your authority any time now." She leaned towards him.

"I don't take, remember? But I'll go with what I've already been given, my Angelina." He reached over and softly kissed her.

She didn't realize how much she longed for his kiss until now, but she wanted him nearer, to wrap her arms around him and really kiss him. However, she felt him let go of her hand and his other hand leave her cheek. Disappointment ran through her as she reasoned his commander duties caught up to him, and the kiss would end. Instead, the chair moved underneath her as he maneuvered her closer to him, and he wrapped one arm around her waist. His other hand returned to her uninjured cheek as he reignited the kiss. He murmured, "I hate your hair being up. I miss playing in it." A light giggle escaped her at his comment before his lips found hers again, and she reached her hand out to stroke the side of his face.

She whispered teasingly, "You told the others they could come get you if needed."

He kissed the side of her face and whispered back, "But if they're smart, they'll stay away."

"Then you shouldn't have given them the option."

"That's the only reason I haven't simply put you in my lap right now." He grinned as he kissed her again.

She remembered. It brought back another time when he took a terrible memory and replaced it with his comfort and care for her. His embrace had erased as much as possible the encounter with the turned colonist and all the pain from her past it resurfaced. "You would have a hard time explaining that one."

"I suppose." He leaned his forehead into hers and took her hands into his. "They should be about done if they're not already. Ryan and Alena are probably wondering too. Santiago's family has to get back safe and stay that way, which is a tall order after today."

"You've got this." She smiled at him.

He released one of her hands to retrieve his data pad. "Seth, it's Dante. Angelina is here too. It's just us, so we can talk freely."

"Good to hear from your group."

"It's been rough. Hey, how's Lana? I should've checked before now."

"Fine, but still unconscious. She received a substantial dose as her capturer wanted no chance of her waking during transport. There's no question she's out for six hours, probably closer to twelve. She's being well cared for, as Caleb hasn't left her side."

"I imagined he wouldn't, so I hate to ask for your help, but I'm in a bind."

"I expected a call from you shortly for my assistance."

"No surprising you. Seth, I don't know where to start. Even the short version is a mess."

"There's no need. You'll find me up to speed. The Santiago family should be arriving soon for me to watch over?"

"Yes, we thought they were, I mean he allied with Black Dragon, but then ... "

"He didn't, but they took his family hostage and, you rescued them."

"How did you know all that?"

"Why the usual. A friend shared with me and let me listen in. One who monitors his students closely, down to their words and those around them when they are on a mission. It's been dull here, but I can't say the same for your group."

"Every word, huh?" Dante glanced at Angelina.

"Yes."

"I forgot. So even the recent bit between me and Dante?" asked Angelina.

"That too." Seth chuckled. "As always you two battle hard, but you make up beautifully. Alika and I are constantly impressed."

Dante squeezed Angelina's hand. "I'm glad that's your take on it."

"It is, and you put your weapons to the best use. Those men deserved their end for their part in today's treachery, including their treatment of Angelina."

"They did. I only wish I stopped it sooner."

"You intervened in time." Seth paused, "Angelina, that's enough though. Do you mind staying clear of harm's way for the remainder of the day?"

"Yes, I'll do better. I prefer Dante's mood now with me rather than his earlier one."

Seth chuckled again. "No doubt you do."

Dante kissed her forehead before continuing with Seth. "We'll send them on their way to your watch. I don't trust anyone else now."

"I wouldn't either. Caleb or I will meet them and keep them in this room with us every second if necessary to ensure their safety. Of course, I'll examine them and provide any required medical attention. We don't know what they were subjected to while being kept prisoner."

"I wondered too. Those men were ... "

"Agreed. We'll see them soon and look for you to be close behind."

Dante got up and eased Angelina up with him. "You heard him. Time to finish this."

⸺ℓℓ⸺

Dante walked over to the troops. "You searched every inch of it. That means opening every door, every compartment, and rooting behind every box in the cargo hold."

The troops nodded and one said, "Yes, sir. If it looked like someone had even a galaxy's chance of cramming into the space, we checked it. That included a thorough inspection of the cargo hold, and we did a second go-over in case. We examined the boxes too if it seemed like anyone could hide in them. This ship is cleared, Dante."

Dante clapped the troop on the back. "That's what I needed to hear. His family endured enough."

"They have, sir."

"You and part of this group will transport the Santiagos back to the fortress in their ship. Seth or Caleb will meet you and ensure the Santiagos stay safe. Those are the only two people. You are responsible for this family reaching them. I'm counting on you."

"I promise we'll get them to Seth and Caleb safely."

Dante motioned to the other half of the troops. "This group comes with me and this young woman to regroup with Ryan and her comrade."

Dante turned to Angelina to say something and stopped. He brushed her hurt cheek, and she flinched. "I'm sorry. I should've gotten something for that earlier."

"I'm fine. It's just a touch."

"What I did was a touch. What he did to you was far from that."

"It doesn't look that bad."

"No, but it'll start hurting something terrible soon. I'm surprised it hasn't already."

"Trying to take care of me now?"

He leaned in, pretending to get a closer look at her injury and whispered, "I like taking care of you, which should be clear by now."

"It is, but I'll get it seen about later."

"Somehow I don't believe you."

"I have my medical connection."

"In case it slips your mind, I'll mention it to your comrade so you get treated."

"I give you one compliment, and now you're waving your authority around."

He hid a smile. "It has an occasional good use."

***

"That the last one?" asked Ryan as he pulled his sword from the final attacker's body.

"Appears so, and I'm ready for it to be," Alena answered as she lowered her weapon.

Turning to the prisoner, Ryan demanded, "How many did you bring for this party? Tell us! Did we get them all?"

Alena shook her head. "You're wasting your time. He's still playing dumb, or my comrade knocked something loose with that last beating on him."

Ryan said to the troops, "Nice work handling that last group and ensuring he stayed tied up. Keep alert for anymore, and don't take your eyes off him." He walked over to the table with Alena.

"Ryan, when you start putting together the number of enemy soldiers we've encountered today, this is ugly."

"And there's no way Dante's group didn't run into trouble."

"Nothing they can't handle, but it's more than that." She stopped, glancing at the prisoner.

Ryan moved them further from him to eliminate any chance of being over-heard. "What is it?"

"All red. All day. Blasters kept them down."

"He didn't use Black Dragon fighters or mutated colonists, but his loyalties are clear."

"Although these people enjoy their work, they don't volunteer their services. They've got to pay their way like everyone else." She smiled over at him. "I'm glad you chose the commanding route."

"I've earned it today, but you should claim part of it with everything you did." He shook his head and looked at her. "You're right though. There are an awful lot of blades involved in this job."

"There's only one organization that possesses that kind of a vault to take from, and they hate losing."

⁓ ℓℓ ⁓

"You set it on stun?" asked Dante as his group opened the door to rejoin Ryan and Alena.

Angelina rolled her eyes at him. "Of course, we placed it on stun, Dante. My comrade and I can work a blaster superbly as you've witnessed. Those two will wake up sooner or later, and I told them to move."

"In your usual charming manner."

"Pleasantries were not in order."

Ryan stared at her and asked, "What happened?"

"What?"

"He's referring to the story played out all over you," said Alena.

"Oh, this," she dismissed it with a wave. "We ran into trouble."

"Trouble," repeated Ryan.

"It's okay. None of it's her blood. Her own words," said Dante.

"Of course, that's what she said." Alena sighed. "So, the troublemakers must be ... "

"Dead." Angelina turned to the prisoner. "Hear that? We're eliminating your friends one by one. Take your time mulling over that."

"How's it been here?" asked Dante as they walked with Ryan and Alena to a corner of the room.

"A group of his buddies made a surprise entrance earlier, but we handled them," said Ryan.

"It looked like more bodies littering the floor," said Angelina.

"You didn't imagine it. Did you get the other captive on his way?" asked Alena.

"Yes, Seth and Caleb will supervise his care on their end once he arrives," said Dante.

"Did we lose anyone on our side?" asked Ryan.

"Not a one and mission accomplished," said Dante.

"Then time for my comrade and me to head out," said Angelina, loudly enough for the prisoner to hear her.

"That's it?" said Dante.

"Yes, remember a previous engagement. Besides, this is something for you two to clean up."

"And to put it bluntly, we don't want to be around for it. We'll leave you two great minds to work it out," said Alena.

"Figures this is when you two exit," snapped Ryan.

Angelina lowered her voice, making sure her back was to the prisoner. "Please, be careful with him. The only way I trust him is dead, and we can't do that yet. Don't turn your back on him for a second. Something doesn't feel right, but I can't figure it out yet. Don't underestimate him."

"We promise to watch our backs at all times," said Dante.

"Make certain you do," said Angelina. They didn't want to go, but the two men had little time to sort out the muddle before them.

"We'll find you again soon, but we'll see ourselves out now," said Alena as the two walked from the room.

Commander Gabe and the small group of soldiers Dante and Ryan told him to bring entered the residence of the Santiagos. He stayed on alert, checking his surroundings and made no conversation with anyone along the way. The two men gave him specific instructions when they contacted him a short time ago and asked for him to come to assist. With the limited details given, he rushed to get here as quickly as possible. Upon reaching the specified room and opening the door, he continued through it as he took in the battlefield that occurred earlier.

"I've never been so glad to see you, Gabe," said Ryan.

"Yes, we're about spent," Dante directed Gabe to a corner of the room with him and Ryan.

"You've had your hands full from what I see."

"We needed someone we could trust and," Dante paused, lowering his voice further, "you have inside knowledge no one else does that's invaluable right now."

"Really?"

Ryan nodded and kept his voice low too, "Two young women just left, both extremely skilled with regular swords. Also, they are trained with other blades, which they did not use at all while they were here for obvious reasons. As far as everyone saw they are nothing more than hired help that we detest working with."

Gabe's eyes flashed with understanding, "Yes, that's all they are. Their work speaks for itself again."

"This isn't all from them, but they arrived first to take care of the enemy soldiers." Dante paused, "There was an attack on Lana."

"Is she all right?" Gabe's voice rose in concern.

"She'll be fine, thanks to them, but the man bound is responsible for everything. We need to get him back for further questioning."

"But this whole place is compromised. He got to the administrator here, who has already been taken back to the fortress as a prisoner as far as this guy thinks," said Ryan.

"The administrator was in on it too?"

"That's the story we're sticking to with the prisoner here," said Dante staring at Gabe, meaningfully.

"There's sometimes more to the narrative."

Ryan nodded. "Our troops are aware of what happened, so ask them after we've left with him."

"You'll have to know for what we need you to do, and we'll contact you with that as well. Also, to start cleaning this up, I'll have one of them tell you what we did at the other location. Follow the same procedure here," said Dante.

"You two desperately needed a second shift to come in. Glad I can help."

Dante motioned to one of the troops to join them.

"Yes, sir."

Dante spoke quietly, "As you would expect all of you we leave behind are to take orders from Commander Gabe as you would me or Commander Ryan. Answer any questions he has about what happened today. We'll be gone with the prisoner by then, so give him a true account of the events. That information will be essential for him to do what we ask of him and clean this up. Do you understand my instructions?"

"Yes, sir."

"Also, how we cleaned up earlier after we ran into trouble, that should be done here. Do you remember all the steps?"

"Yes, and we'll repeat them here, sir."

"Thank you. Return as you were."

Dante turned back to Gabe. "We'll head out, but don't trust anybody here except our people in this room."

"You've made it clear. I've got this."

Ryan motioned to a group of troops towards the prisoner. "Get him up, and secure him for the ride back. I want full flank around him at all times, and watch your backs once we leave this room."

⁓ ℓℓ ⁓

Alika surveyed Angelina and shook his head. "They didn't exaggerate."

"Perhaps not."

"Take that bathroom, and Alena claims the other one to get cleaned up. Now, please. A change of clothes is already set out for both of you there."

Angelina peeled off her bloody gear as Alena followed suit. Alika took it in silence and dumped it straight into the machine that would begin the familiar job of cleansing the day's events from it. Despite the black uniform underneath, Angelina saw the blood had soaked through. He would be adding it to the collection. After shutting the door to the bathroom, she stripped down the rest of the way and sent the stained bundle down a chute to him. Turning on the shower, she stepped into the spray. The bright red streams cascading from her and running into the drain caused her to freeze, and her body to tremble. *It's not my blood. I had to do it. There's so much of it though. How is it possible from just that? So much red. It's all over me like last time. I can't...* She sank into the tub as the shower continued to pour over her, and she couldn't hold back the floodgates any longer.

"Feeling better?" asked Alika as Angelina joined them at the table.

"Yeah, sorry I took so long. Getting everything off proved a challenge."

"I'm certain it did." He paused, "Was there anything else?"

She looked down at her hands. "No, that's all."

"You experienced a few close calls today, and we were discussing it while we waited."

"Everyone is safe. That's all that matters. I'm fine. Besides we still have another round."

Alena said, "Right, but are you sure you're ready for it?"

"I said I'm fine. We should check his data pad before we interrogate him again."

Alika sighed, seeing it useless to push her further. "First let me examine your face where you got hit, and don't argue with me. You promised Dante you would have me attend to it." He rose and gingerly touched it before using the scanner. "A sizable bruise with swelling has formed. Give me a moment." After retrieving a few items and putting gloves on, he spread a clear cream on the area. A minute later, he inserted a tiny liquid-filled syringe there. "This should negate the swelling and bruising as well as provide substantial pain relief. You shouldn't have felt the stick with the ointment I applied. All done." He disposed of the empty syringe. "Better?"

"Yes, and Dante can be happy now."

"You gave him quite the scare today, child."

"I can't undo it any more than the rest of my mess ups, Let's see what's in this data pad."

⁓ℓℓ⁓

"Thank you, Seth," said Dante as he and Ryan walked into medical.

"Allowing you two the chance to shower and eat seemed fair."

Ryan patted Seth on the back. "It was much appreciated after earlier. How's our prisoner?"

"Still secure as you left him. Caleb insisted we set the cameras on in here as an extra layer of security in addition to the troops guarding him. We are not taking any chances."

"What about the Santiagos?" asked Dante.

"Keeping them close as promised. I provided the needed medical attention some time ago and found nothing of real concern. Mr. Santiago is working with Commander Gabe virtually to sort out the disarray on the planet. Pure genius on your part."

"That would be Angelina inspired." Dante smiled.

Seth chuckled. "Her powers remain limitless. She has you in more ways than one."

"I'm more than content with that. So, the plan is working?"

"Better than hoped. She was right. Mr. Santiago identified who belongs as part of his staff or household and who is suspect. It appears your group cleared out the impostors thus far, and we'll make certain it's safe before we allow the Santiagos to return. Until then his true trusted advisors are running affairs in his absence. Now that they understand why their administrator gave them such strange orders the last few days, they immediately moved back into their roles to resume their responsibilities."

"I bet they're relieved to know he and his family came through okay, but it must be unnerving to know somebody got that deeply entrenched," said Ryan.

"Yes for all of us. It appears under control now, and Mr. Santiago can arrange matters remotely with his staff." Seth spotted Dante checking his data pad. "Any word yet?"

"No, but we're due for round two, so they should be arriving soon."

CHAPTER SIXTEEN

Alena slid her hand over the cockpit panel to plunge them through the portal. "You still think we missed something on the data pad?"

The scold on Angelina's face returned. "I hoped it would prove helpful for this, but we had limited time to probe it. I thought at least we could uncover a location besides nowhere."

"Never fear. You're about to get another crack at him because we're breaking orbit."

⁓ℓℓ⁓

"How are you holding up, Caleb?" asked Ryan as he put a hand on Caleb's shoulder.

"Okay, I guess." He stroked Lana's clasped hand. "I shouldn't have left her by herself."

"Don't go there. Already gone through that portal, and it doesn't help," said Dante.

"But that's why I knew better. After what almost happened with your girl, we said we wouldn't let ourselves be in that position again."

"You both need to stop beating yourselves over the head. Somehow these men tuned into their target's weaknesses and got them alone. This time we make it the last time. The important thing is they're okay. Don't lose sight of that," said Ryan.

Dante's and Ryan's data pads flashed in the same instant.

Dante replied to the communication, "Yes, and Ryan is here with me. What is it?"

"Yes, sir. There's a ship asking for clearance to land, and those aboard said you or Commander Ryan would grant permission as you're expecting their arrival."

"Permission granted wherever they wish. They're friends. We'll see to them."

"Of course, sir."

Caleb stared at the viewscreen monitoring the prisoner and turned to Ryan and Dante. "Do whatever it takes, but make him talk. Don't allow him to get away with what he did today."

"He won't. Angelina doesn't intend for him to live through this second interrogation," said Dante.

—ꞁꞁ—

The instant Ryan walked into the ship he captured Alena in his arms. "Alena, I waited all day to ... " He didn't finish as he kissed her. His commander duties evaporated when her fiery response refused to let him end the kiss.

Dante headed straight for Angelina and pulled her against him. "Finally." He kissed her like he wanted to earlier, with both arms tightly wrapped around her waist, but in seconds one slipped up to play in her hair. He deepened the kiss, his yearning for her soaring and asked, "Do you know how close I came to giving in today, to letting the whole galaxy know you're mine?"

"Yes, because I almost let you, and I don't think I would've cared if I had," she said. Her whole body hummed from his kiss, one she had craved all day. Her arms wound around his neck, as she melted into his embrace.

"You should listen to that voice," he murmured as he couldn't resist diving in for a second kiss, this one as sweet as the first. When he eventually ended the kiss, he stroked her face and grinned as he heard her still catching her breath. He gazed down at her. "A little different look for me?"

"I deemed the shipping dealer attire more appropriate for the next order of business."

"Unfortunately, we still have to deal with him, but I have to say you fit into that incredibly well."

She laughed. "I remember you telling me. Is the picture or the real-life model more to your liking, Dante?"

"The real-life version for sure." He brushed her neck with a kiss before looking over at Ryan and Alena. "You two about ready?"

"We can be," said Ryan with Alena still leaning up against him.

"How about the wear they came in?"

"A surprise, but I like it too. I already told Alena. Although I held my composure better than you." Ryan grinned.

"Couldn't resist." Dante groaned as Alena and Angelina both laughed.

Alena winked. "Ryan, enough teasing him for now."

"I'm afraid so. Time to deal with our prisoner. We're back to barely tolerating each other. No more sweet words between us once we begin this next round of questioning with him, and I don't know what it'll take to get to him exactly. I'm all too familiar with his type though, so this is guaranteed to become unpleasant quickly," said Angelina.

"It already has," said Dante.

"Count on worse. You have to trust me when we're in there. I know what I'm doing. Since he's aware of Alena and me, this only ends one way for him. Don't forget that."

⸻ ℓℓ ⸻

Angelina stared through the interrogation window at the prisoner while removing her hooded cloak and handing it to Alena. "Strangely he still doesn't appear bothered in there. I mean to change that." She turned to Dante. "Showtime. All ready?"

"Let's do this."

Angelina marched through the door with Dante behind her as she railed at him, "You got nothing out of him? And you had him for more than a couple of hours? What have you and the commander been doing all this time?"

"A lot. If you recall there are two prisoners to deal with."

"You troops leave. Dante and I will handle him. Go. Now."

Dante motioned them. "It's fine. You can go now, but please keep guard outside and thank you. Her manners continue to need work."

"My manners are far from the problem here. Your excuses are, Dante."

"Says the person that didn't manage anything out of him either."

"Since the other prisoner tied you up, what precious information did you wrestle from him?" Angelina sneered at him. "That's what I thought. Nothing for all of the time spent but more excuses."

"You are unbelievable!"

"My thoughts exactly!"

"You two never stop, do you?" the prisoner burst out, shaking his head at the two.

Angelina's eyes narrowed as she pretended to become aware again of the captive. "We do, and it's time we put our energy to better use. The reason we came in here." She deliberately approached him. "Did you think I forgot about you? I had just gotten started, so I'm glad Dante's efforts fell flat. I do enjoy this process immensely."

"You failed earlier too."

"Does your body feel like I did?" She chuckled at his expression. "That's what I thought. It's still sending you a different message. How long have you been doing jobs for Black Dragon?"

"It slips my mind."

"Lucky for us, I have multiple ways to help your recall." She pulled him by the hair to look up at her. "Are you a direct supplier or a middleman?"

"As if you know anything about it."

"I'm more informed than you think. Now which are you?"

"Maybe I've been both."

"That's not how it usually works, and a hit on Lana, especially this elaborate … my guess is a direct supplier. Perhaps one of their favorites."

"Lots of assumptions there."

"And they're right, aren't they? Aren't they?" She brought his head down hard onto the table and then leaned in with a warning, "Next time I'll crack your skull on this. Answer me."

He groaned, "Fine. You've got it so far."

She let go as he painstakingly lifted his head. "What's Black Dragon up to these days?"

"I wouldn't know."

"Are you trying to give me a reason?" Her fist landed a solid blow to his mid-section, and his body lurched forward as much as possible while being shackled to the chair. "You chatted with them to do this deal, you moron. Tell me the happenings with them."

"They didn't tell me anything."

"I don't believe you."

"That's your problem."

"No, it's yours." She took her dagger out and smiled. "Remember my multiple ways to assist your memory." She bent over to trace it across the front of his shirt and then stood back up. Walking behind him, she spoke softly in his ear, "There are pressure points all over your body, and if someone hits the right ones, one of two things happen. Any guesses?"

"Maybe." He took a deep breath, dreading the next sensation.

Her hand trailed his chest from behind and moved to his shoulder, and he relaxed as she continued the motion on the back of his neck. Then her hand expertly found the spot she wanted, and he let out a groan as he fell into her spell. She whispered, "How are you feeling now?"

"Nice." His shoulders felt an instant relief from the massaging touch she placed on him, and it spread in calming waves through the rest of him.

"Just nice?" She whispered.

"More than nice."

"You liked that a lot, huh?" She paused. "Some pressure points have that effect ... "

The man suddenly howled in pain. Her hand moved, and he didn't fathom where, but his nerves screamed in agony at once. Then it ceased as he panted to catch his breath, and she stood before him with her dagger in hand again. "Other pressure points produce a profoundly different sensation. Pain or pleasure."

He stared at her. If she managed that with a mere touch, he was in deep trouble. The first interrogation had been rough, but he had a sinking feeling she meant to finish him off with this one. He glanced at the display and marked the time again of how long he had remained stuck in here. Even so he couldn't resist admiring her picture-perfect body anew as he turned back to her. The instant she stepped in the room he saw what her gear hid earlier, and with her hair down too it only added to the incredible images running through his head now.

"You were telling me about Black Dragon."

"The Black Dragon Commander and Dark Lord are dead."

"The whole galaxy knows that." Her dagger reached around to make a slash on his back, and he yelped in pain. "You've earned one slice. Tell me something I don't know."

"I don't know what you don't know."

"Where did you meet them to arrange the hit on Lana?"

"I don't know."

She dragged one cut across his pant leg, and he howled again. "Up to two now. Drop by drop I'll bleed you out. Don't give me another stupid answer." She paused. "Maybe there's a simpler solution. Black Dragon hates botched jobs. I could inform them of all the intel you've divulged and send you back to them. Let them do the bloody work. Word is they enjoy it even more than I do."

"You haven't gotten anything from me."

"They don't know that."

"You don't have any way to get me to them, because they're not on your friend list."

"After everything you've seen from me thus far, do you believe I can't find a way? Sure enough to stake your life on that conclusion?" She chuckled. "Everybody has a price tag in your business. Yes, I stay informed. It's a best practice."

"I've underestimated you, but it doesn't matter. With how this turned out, they won't be directing any further business in my direction." He glanced at the display again.

She peered at him, catching him check it again. What gives with that, she wondered? "Now I'm supposed to let you loose? That's priceless. You'll always find ways to help them."

"You're right. I know better than to try that card."

She leaned against the wall and stared at him. "However, I can be reasonable when I need to be. Even Dante has seen it." She turned to him for confirmation.

"Brief moments, but they exist."

She focused back on the prisoner. "Told you so. Look you already admitted you messed yourself up with the whole failed job. You're hopelessly out of favor with Black Dragon, so you're in no position to call the shots. I've shown you a few of the many ways I intend to make you suffer. Why not simply tell me what I'm asking?"

"I want a deal."

"A deal? Not making you hurt further should be a sufficient bargain."

"No. If you want my information, you'll need to pay."

"I can't release you. You're far too dangerous. Freedom Fighters will never allow it after what you did."

"I accepted that, but I meant *you* would have to make the payment."

"Still a no-go. I don't have the deep pockets like your last business partner."

"That's not the kind of payout I want. I'm envisioning a more personal arrangement, sweetheart." He grinned.

Dante stiffened and waited for her adamant refusal to entertain this further. Rather, he was horrified when she simply said, "Of that sort, is it?"

"Oh, it's done."

"More frequently than I'd like to admit. What would this deal look like?"

The man hesitated, certain his ears betrayed him. No, she was contemplating it. "Us in a private room."

"How long?"

"Thirty minutes."

She shook her head. "You'll kill me instead in that time."

"That's the last thing on my mind. I'll use all thirty minutes to their fullest."

"Ten minutes."

"No way. From thirty down to ten."

"Sounds generous to me seeing your current state."

"Twenty."

She regarded him as if he were a bug she wished to squish under her boot. "I'll think about fifteen, but no more."

Dante couldn't stand it for another second and stepped forward. "I won't allow this! No deal!"

Angelina said, "Ignore him. Keep going. What are the parameters for the time?"

"None. Whatever I want from you."

Dante yelled at him, "She's not doing this! You're a sick man!" He grabbed her by the shoulders and turned her around to face him. "Don't do this. No intel is worth this. You know what kind of man he is. Why are you considering this?"

She looked up at him and mouthed, *trust me*. Then she said, "You know why. Now get your hands off me. You're not a part of this deal, and I don't share your Freedom Fighter ideals." She spun from his grasp and crossed her arms over her chest.

"The Freedom Fighters won't allow this. Neither will my cousin."

"Your cousin remains unconscious, and the Freedom Fighter's stance is meaningless. I captured him, and so he's still rightfully my prisoner. Therefore, I'll make whatever arrangement I wish with him, and you have no say."

He reached towards her again, but she moved back and glared at him. "Back off."

The prisoner laughed. "Dante, you missed your chance by using every waking moment to argue with her. For the life of me I can't understand it, because I would never waste the time. You should stop chasing Black Dragon and pursue her instead. By now, you could have gotten a good time out of her ten times over. Guess I'll get the pleasure of her for you."

"Why you sorry excuse for a … " Dante advanced on the man, fists clenched.

"Dante, stop!" She stood in front of him with her hands clamped down on his shoulders and whispered, "Dante, enough." Then she mouthed again, *trust me*.

After ensuring he regained reasonable control, she walked back to the prisoner. "Why such interest in me?"

"Have you looked in a mirror lately?"

"That's all it is?"

"That's plenty. They only make a few like you."

She leaned over to stare into his face from the other side of the table. "But I've encountered many men like you, and so why would I find you mildly appealing?"

"Give me a try, and you'll discover I have what you want."

"That's supposed to get me going. One of the worst lines yet." An amused smile crossed her face. "Do you believe you're the first man that wanted me in a room alone, that proposed this to me?"

"No, I'm betting you have a running list to choose from."

She came behind him and whispered in his ear, "So why in the galaxy would I settle for you?"

"Because you've underestimated me already today. You'd be disappointed to do so again."

"No, you'll find me hard to impress, and I fail to see you doing it. You haven't so far." She laughed as she circled back around and settled in the chair across from him to prop her feet on the table.

"Do we have a deal?"

"You're asking a lot."

"Fifteen minutes."

"Enduring that with you for what I anticipate you have planned is a long time."

"It's short compared to what I asked."

"Not for me. No parameters too. That negates what you consider a brief time frame."

His eyes took in every inch of her form leaned back leisurely in the chair. "What do you say?"

"We both know that's not how this works. I'm more knowledgeable than you've given me credit. You made clear your list of demands, and what you want from this deal. However, your intel is disappointing so far. I guessed the majority of it, and I'm beginning to think you don't know anything."

Ryan grabbed Alena's arm as they watched the scene continue unfolding. "What is she doing? Dante is about to explode! I don't know how he hasn't already."

Alena put a finger to his lip. "Now is where she does her best work. Observe and listen."

"She agreed to be locked in a room with that man."

Alena turned and grinned at him. "No, she didn't."

"I heard her say it."

"No, we didn't. You should listen better, commander. Our weasel made the same mistake."

Ryan looked from Alena to Angelina and back to Alena. "She's setting him up."

"Yes, but you must get Dante calmed."

Dante leaned against the wall and then paced the area next to the interrogation glass. After earlier, he rotated between disbelief and anger at the discussion commencing. Angelina continued with the deal to give herself to this pile of garbage for intel. How could he trust her? His data pad vibrated and he ignored it, but it persisted. He yanked it out and viewed a message from Ryan, "Turn around, and listen to me." He faced the glass, and instantly Ryan's voice came through his earpiece, "Buddy, there's no deal." Dante shot a questioning look to where he guessed Ryan stood and mouthed, *I heard it.*

"No, she never agreed to anything. She's playing him. Stand back, and watch your girl work."

Dante mouthed back, *"Seriously."*

Alena said through the earpiece, "Trust her like she said. You're the only one that claims her."

Dante turned back and leaned against the wall to see it play out.

"You wouldn't have guessed any of it without me," said the prisoner.

"Really? You're Black Dragon. A direct supplier. Because why would they use a middleman for a job like this? Taking out Lana. That's got to be the hit of the century for your type, right?"

"Probably."

"I've got to hand it to you, you almost succeeded. She's tough and still out from whatever you gave her. Personally, I would've done the same thing. The whole clan of them fights like an army, so you never would have delivered her to Black Dragon conscious. That's where you were headed with her I assume."

"Of course, and we knew we had to knock her out. That's the mistake others have made, trying to take her head on."

"You must have dug deep into the Black Dragon coffers. How impressive is the price tag on her?"

"If I had pulled it off, I could've taken half the year off at least."

"I can't see how with having to compensate all your enlisted help too. I'm not the best accountant in the galaxy, but I'm still not seeing it."

"Didn't come out of my payoff. They gave me extra to cover that expense."

"Wow, for one person. They took care of you. If you played your cards right, you aimed to negotiate a sweeter payoff. The whole group arrived. Dante, Caleb, Seth, and Commander Ryan. The price tag on all of them would have you set for the next decade."

"Didn't need to risk it. Once I delivered Lana, the rest ... "

"Find themselves in Black Dragon's grasp. A touch of brilliance and they picked you to pull it off. I should give you more credit. I thought everything would be in shambles with the Black Dragon Commander and Dark Lord gone. Seems they're managing fine?"

"Enough to pay me well."

"Yes, generous is something not usually associated with them. Has leadership taken a different approach?"

"No, the head man still subscribes to the Dark Lord's philosophy."

"Although he's made himself scarcer than the Dark Lord. You're probably one of the few to meet him on the command ship."

"No, he's paranoid as anything or smarter after what happened. They had a hood on me, so I don't know where they took me."

"So, he doesn't intend to end up dead like the other two, maybe keep his promotion for a while. That's clever."

"No one is getting near enough to him with a blade. He conducted all his business with me through a viewscreen."

"Didn't trust you as much as I figured."

"From what I gathered he doesn't trust anybody."

"He'd make a fantastic shipping dealer, wouldn't he?" She grinned.

"I'd take that bet." The man laughed.

"I hope you didn't take your other data pad in there with him."

"That would've gotten me killed on the spot with how he acted."

"Left it on your ship?"

"Yeah, I have a compartment under the cockpit."

"Every ship should have at least one." She got up and patted him on the back. "You're a smart man."

"Our deal?" He grinned up at her.

"I mulled it over, but what intel can you give me?"

"What do you mean? I told you a whole bunch."

"We chatted and you volunteered information. I said I would weigh your demands with what you could offer, but I never agreed to an arrangement with you." She turned to Dante. "Dante, you've been listening. What do you recall?"

He hid his smile. "I remember a discussion about possible terms of a deal, but you didn't agree to anything with him."

The man's face turned beet red as he snarled at her, "You tricked me."

"No, I simply won this round because you misjudged me again."

"If I had kept my mouth shut … "

"Still wouldn't have worked because I never intended to take one of your deals. I'm aware they are done, but it's an area I side with the Freedom Fighters. I won't be payment for any piece of intel or anything else."

"Well played." He glanced at the display again before turning back to her. "My days of working with Black Dragon are over."

"You expect me to suddenly believe you've reformed? You are desperate."

"No, just stating facts. I staked everything on this. The supreme payoff or the end of my business."

"You came up short on your gamble."

"This isn't over. Others will take the risk. The incentive is too tempting. Lana better watch her back."

"I'll pass your message to my cousin," said Dante.

The man's eyes slithered over Angelina. "Sure you won't give me part of the time? After all, you proved your point."

"As much as you'd like that, the answer remains no."

"A shame. You are a gorgeous piece of work. It bites how this turned out. I thought I'd be on the other side of this deal, but Black Dragon is the toughest employer. Never tolerated failure."

"I've heard." She watched him, and an unease gripped her.

"New management is as unforgiving as the Dark Lord. This one didn't take any chances on this one."

Angelina's face paled as pieces fell into place. "You had check-in times which you've missed, so he knows it came apart."

"There's a saying in the shipping business. A late delivery … "

"Or an undelivered one is as good as your last." Her hand grabbed Dante's arm as terror spread through her.

"You continue to surprise me, gorgeous. You were right. That Black Dragon leader could pass for a shipping dealer, and he thought of everything." A slow, cruel smile broadened his face as he winked at her.

Her voice rose in panic, "Black Dragon insurance." Shoving Dante in front of her while racing for the door, she screamed, "Open the door now! Run, Dante, run!"

Dante couldn't tell if he was pushed or thrown through the open door because instantly the entire room collapsed from the impact of a massive explosion and the accompanying debris erupting from the room and into the adjoining corridor. He groaned as he landed back first on the hallway floor, barely conscious of something encircling his head and something else diagonal to his back. It came at the same time as a weight fell on him. His hands probed it, and immediately he knew as he murmured, "Angelina."

CHAPTER SEVENTEEN

Ryan sat up, coughing and cradling Alena in his arms. "Come on. Please, say something."

"Something," she mumbled against him.

He kissed her forehead. "Only you. Thank the Ancient One. You're okay?"

"Enough. You?"

"I'm fine."

Her eyes widened in panic at Ryan. "They were still in there!"

Ryan rushed to get up with Alena, pushing back the wave of dizziness assailing him. He yelled, "Dante! Dante!"

—ᴇᴇ—

Caleb jumped up and called, "Seth, get over here!"

"Why are the alarms sounding?"

"It blew!"

"What?"

Caleb pointed to the camera screen. "The interrogation room!"

"And they were inside. I must get to them, Caleb."

"I'm coming too." He motioned to an attendant. "Call the doctor in here now, and watch over my wife."

Seth instructed the others in the room, "Follow us to the interrogation hall. Bring at least two moving beds."

"Seth, I'm already on my way." Alika's voice broke through Seth's and Caleb's earpiece as the two ran to reach the others.

⸺ℓℓ⸺

"Ryan," moaned Dante as he rolled to his side.

"We're here. Take it easy."

His eyes refocused and turned frantic as he recognized the body slumped against him, and he whispered,. "Oh no, Angelina, please, no." His hands shook as he brushed her hair back and kissed her cheek. "Please, wake up, you can't do this to me. No ... no ... she's ... "

Ryan put his hand on Dante's shoulder. "She's not, Dante. Her pulse isn't great, but she's hanging on."

Alena whispered, "She's a fighter. Seth is on his way."

"Ryan! Dante!" yelled Caleb.

"Over here!" shouted Ryan.

Caleb and Seth were there, pushing out a barrage of orders.

Caleb commanded, "Two beds here now! I got her. Let her go, Dante." He picked up Angelina and laid her on the bed. "Seth, start working on her. Dante is next. You two troops follow Seth and help."

Dante begged, "Please, I need to go with her, Caleb!"

"You are. The next bed is yours, but you need help too. Got to pull yourself together for her." A couple of the soldiers rushed over and assisted Dante onto the bed. "Thanks, guys. Take him down to Seth too."

Caleb turned to Ryan and Alena. "You two don't look steady on your feet either."

Ryan shook his head as he kept his arm wrapped around Alena's waist. "We're okay. The two of them took the full impact of it. Barely cleared it. Scared me to death, Caleb."

Alena's voice shook. "I thought she was ... I really did this time." Tears streamed down her face.

Ryan wrapped her up and whispered, "She'll make it. She has to. Got to trust, remember?" He looked up at Caleb with worry-filled eyes though.

Caleb beckoned a couple of the soldiers closer. "Ryan and this young woman were directly outside when the room blew. They need to be assessed for injuries too. I don't believe they're as okay as they say. Make sure they get to Seth too. Understood?"

"Yes sir."

Caleb turned to the remaining troops. "Check the rest of the hall for any further injured. The four individuals I've already sent to Seth took the brunt of it, so I'm guessing anyone else should be easily treated. Assist those to medical."

"Sir, what about the interrogation room? Was there anyone still inside?"

"Only the prisoner responsible for everything here today. It's none of ours spattered all over the room. Came close though." He took a deep breath. "We'll deal with the mess later once our people pull through this. Seal it off for now, and I'm heading back to do whatever I can."

Caleb rushed back into the medical room with Alika. "Seth, your promised real help is here."

"Where are we at?" asked Alika as he came alongside Seth.

"I'm working on her. The facility doctor is checking the other three. I'm hoping her condition looks worse than it is."

"It doesn't appear these pieces hit anything major, but there's a lot of blood and debris to see through even with scanners. Do we have ... "

"They just brought the machine to start the process."

"We must be careful extracting the larger fragments from her in case we're mistaken, Seth."

"Agreed. We'll need to siphon while we do the removal."

Dante yelled, "Let me see her! I'm fine! Somebody let me over there!"

Seth said from across the curtain, "Dante, I'll have you sedated if necessary. That's not helping."

Caleb said, "I'll handle him." He proceeded to Dante's bedside. "Hey, you know he'll do it. Lie back down." Dante grudgingly laid back after Caleb's gentle nudge on his shoulders, and Caleb's tone softened, "She's in the best hands. You know that, but I get it. I almost lost it when I ran in and saw Lana lying unconscious at the Santiagos. The worst ran through my head too. That woman over there is your whole universe. We all see it, but you're not losing her. Let those two do their work."

Dante took a deep breath and nodded, as tears flowed down his face. "Can you at least peek over and find out how's it going for me?"

"I can't, depending on what they're doing. That's your girl after all. I promise I'll have you a full report once we get you checked out."

"No, not until I know she's going to be okay. That's all I'm asking. That she'll make it and not ... " Dante's voice broke.

"Seth, I believe we can give him that assurance," said Alika.

"Yes, we can. Dante, that danger has passed. Calm your spirit. Please get treated as we requested."

Dante put his head in his hands as a tremor of relief reverberated through him mixed with a sob which could not be held back. "That's all I needed, Caleb."

"I knew," said Caleb as he touched his friend's shoulder and waited for him to regain his composure. After a minute, Dante stared up at him and nodded. Caleb continued, "Let's get you seen about." He motioned for the doctor to come to the bedside and then closed the curtain. "Okay, what's first for him?"

"How's Ryan and the woman that came in with him?" asked Dante as the doctor finished the preliminary visual scan and began the next process.

"Lot of scrapes and bruises. Several ugly burns. Ryan was hurting substantially from something that hit him hard from the blast, but I administered the medication to counter it and he's comfortable now. Overall, they're fortunate with the scene left behind. They each just got out of a chamber, so the treatment healed the majority of those sorts of injuries. Both are anxious to check on you, but we need to treat you first." He paused as he used the machine over Dante's upper body for a few more minutes. His eyes assessed the machine's success on his patient, and he appeared satisfied with the results as he pushed it aside. "We got most of it from what I see. The greatest portion of the embedded shards were located in your back region, but none lodged deep enough to cause significant damage. Strangely, I found hardly any on your chest for the extractor to remove. You still need into a chamber to treat where it did rip into you. Should we bring the bed chamber one, or can you manage with a portable chamber?"

"I can do the portable one."

Dante sat up and eased himself to the side of the bed, with Caleb and the doctor assisting him on both sides. The attendant rolled the medical chamber to him. It was a rectangular structure that he could have mistaken for his walk-in bathtub and shower but with none of the luxurious space. However, he wouldn't be lounging in this one.

"Use the chair in it. I don't feel confident about your vertical," said Caleb.

"That makes two of us."

Caleb slid the door open for him. "You know how this goes. Strip the rest of the way. Send the clothes through, and signal us when you're ready. We'll start the process and pass you what you need when you're done, including the standard medical towel and patient robe. In a bit, you can exchange it for the whole ensemble, those stylish medical sweats and shirt."

"Great."

"Ordinarily I wouldn't stare at you while you're stark naked with the camera, but this is an exception. If you look like you're fading on me, I'm coming in before you do a face-plant."

"A new motivation to push through this."

"That's what I'm here for." He smiled as he helped Dante into the chamber and onto the seat, "Still stable enough for this?"

Dante nodded as Caleb shut the door. Minutes later after undressing and at his request, the spray poured over his body to eliminate the impurities left behind by the debris that had tried to impale itself into him. The human magnet, as the physicians affectionally called it, had retrieved the majority of the debris from him. However, the chamber treatment process guaranteed to extract any remaining slivers and treat the wounds most effectively.

"The flow shows clear for the doctor, Dante. We're moving to the next phase. Are you ready?"

"Yeah, keep going."

The spray poured again, and it stung initially as the medicine mix sought out the numerous places on his body threatening to turn into an infection. Soon they were silenced as the mixture took effect, and he felt the tenderness subside.

"Last one, Dante. Still hanging in there?"

"Yep."

The final spray activated, and he relaxed as it coated him. He sensed the wounds closing up, and an enormous portion of the pain diminished. The combination of healing oils did their work.

With Caleb's help, he laid back on the new bed brought for him. "When do I move up to that ensemble?"

The doctor said, "After I run this image to make certain I didn't miss something." He rolled another machine from the corner to Dante. From afar it could be mistaken for a rolling dinner tray, as it consisted of solid metal on both sides with wheels. In the middle was a flat metallic piece, but with a full display and a loaded control panel. The machine maneuvered the length of the standard patient bed. The doctor took the equipment and lined it up at the head of Dante's bed. With a push of a button on the machine's console, it slowly began at Dante's head and rolled to the foot of his bed, making soft, steady beeps as it signaled its progress. The doctor nodded. "Give me a few minutes to double-check the full body scan it provided."

As Dante waited on his results, he heard the swish of water again from behind the curtain where Angelina lay. He turned towards it, but the curtain remained up. "Caleb, what are they doing to her? You told me you would check."

"They're putting her through the medical chamber but using one of the draining beds. That's why I haven't been over there. Seth and Alika are treating her, and as her physicians they can't help but see her with nothing on. There's only one other person who should get a look at her like that one of these days, and you're not a married man yet." He grinned.

"If only I could figure out how to get her to say yes."

"Dante, you know full well she already said yes to you. It's whatever this other is that's forcing her to wait, but it's not because she doubts you. Anybody can see that. When the day finally comes for you two, it won't be in medical."

A smile crossed Dante's face. "Yeah, this place doesn't scream wedding night atmosphere." He paused as the worried expression returned. "I can't believe she hasn't woken up yet." He heard the swish of liquid stop.

"She will. Sounds like they finished. It won't be long now."

Seth and Alika stood as the final sequence poured over Angelina's bare body, and the last wounds closed. They had moved her into the medical chamber bed for the process and watched as the healing oils drained off the vinyl-padded bedding sides in the chamber to the reservoir below. A hose inside the reservoir continued to empty the substance into one of the medical room's drains. They had cleaned her hair and treated her head and face by hand.

Alika peered around the curtain. "Caleb, we need a fresh bed brought for her."

"How about clothes?"

Alika smiled. "Already gotten. She'll be dressed."

"Can I see her soon? Please?" asked Dante.

"Yes, I promise."

"Will she be awake? How is she?"

"I don't know. Another scan is in order before we have her dressed. Ah, the bed. My thanks, Caleb." He disappeared back behind the curtain.

Dante sat back in bed and ran his hands through his hair, unable to hide his frustration at the little information about Angelina's condition.

The doctor returned with Dante's scan. "The image shows your body endured a tremendous amount of trauma, but astonishingly there's nothing broken, even fractured. There's inflammation in numerous places, and I'm giving you an injection for that now." He pulled out a syringe and delivered it into Dante's shoulder. "Sorry, but you'll thank me later. I'm amazed you didn't sustain damage to your back or a concussion with the blast throwing you to the floor."

Dante whispered, "That's because they never struck the floor, at least not all the way."

"What do you mean? I thought the explosion knocked you to the ground."

"She fell on top of me to cover me and took one of her arms to cradle my head and used her other arm to create a barrier between the ground and my back. Her only concern was making sure I … " He shook his head, unable to finish.

The doctor became quiet and touched Dante's shoulder. "She sounds like an incredible young woman, and I'm sure she will awaken soon, Dante." He paused. "Although you technically do not have a concussion, internally your body received a terrible shakeup which it is not meant to endure. You will feel the effects for the next day or so as it tries to absorb what happened. That's the best way I know to explain it. You will remain under observation here and rest for that time, so we can make certain there are no lingering or undetected trauma to you from today's incident."

"You heard him. No sunspear battles allowed," teased Caleb.

"Got no problem with that. I'm thankful to everyone for my medical care, but now can I please see her? Caleb, would you use your commander pull with Seth? I've been patient long enough, but I can't stand this anymore."

Seth said, "I agree, you have." He and Alika pulled back the curtain to reveal a still unconscious dressed Angelina lying on the new bed.

Dante started to get out of his to go to her, but it proved more difficult than he anticipated. "These blasted railings. I'm climbing out."

"No, you won't. You are to rest as told," said Seth.

"No, I need to be right there when she wakes up, and I can't from here. Why hasn't she woken up? You two still haven't told me what's wrong with her." He gave up on the railing and scrambled to the end of the bed, undeterred from his mission to be at her side.

Caleb met him at the foot of it and glanced at the Elders. "He's not giving up, but I have a way for you to have a cooperative patient and make him happy. How about it?"

Alika nodded. "If you can accomplish such a feat, please do."

He turned back to Dante. "Back in bed. Don't argue with me. I got you covered, and you'll like my arrangement." He winked at Dante. "I can't do it if you're not back up there. Still waiting." He smiled as Dante warily moved back up in it. "Geez, you're impatient. Let me move the two beds up against each other. There are the railings between them but not for long." Once he had moved the beds closer, he manipulated something on the side of Dante's bed, causing the railing to release and fold under it. He repeated the same process for the railing on Angelina's bed running closest to Dante's side. Then he closed the remaining space to line the two beds up side by side. "One more step. There's a way to clamp them together, so it makes an oversized couch of sorts. It'll be like being in your quarters on the couch. Okay, not nearly as comfortable, but you get the idea, Dante. I have to make sure these parts are secure underneath though. This will jar a bit when I lock it." He climbed under both beds to slide the cylindrical pieces on each end in place and anchor the latches on either side of the cylinders, continuing to talk as he worked. "Dante, you probably don't remember this, and I'm certain it'll shock Alika, but I've not always been the responsible commander I am now."

Alika chuckled, "Is that so?"

Caleb laughed. "Yep. When Lana and I were dating and into when we first got married, I tended to be more like Dante with the whole ending up in medical. Of course, Seth put me back together each time."

"It's coming back to me now." Seth smiled.

"I'm sure it is. Several visits became extended stays, and I scared Lana to death every time. She was and is as stubborn as her cousin here. Refused to leave my side. Found out fast the chairs get downright uncomfortable if you're stuck in them long enough. So, she either crawled into the bed beside me, or the medical staff brought in another one for her. The clever one that she is discovered you could pull them together, like this." He got up from the floor. "All set, Dante."

"Thanks, Caleb, and tell cuz the same when she wakes up." Dante had already moved to lay next to Angelina and clasped her hand into his.

"I will. Behave yourself, like when you're in your quarters with her." He caught the smile Dante gave him. "Hey, we know you give her more than kisses on the cheek. Both of you got over the first date shyness in record time, thank goodness." He grinned at Dante. "And I'll be the last one to get between you two lovebirds.

I've always wholeheartedly encouraged you, and I can only imagine the kiss you lay on her once she wakes up." Caleb laughed. "I'll close the curtain for you, buddy, because I want you to keep this arrangement as well as Ryan. Yeah, this is the second time I've done this today. So, if the doctors need to tend to her or you and they say to exit for a minute, you slide back on your side and turn away. Got it?"

"Totally."

"What did I tell you? He's the perfect patient now."

Seth shook his head. "That's all it took. Caleb, our thanks. Dante, I assume you're ready to hear the results now."

"That would be great." Dante nodded as he continued to stroke her clasped hand.

"She had significant debris embedded in her. Several pieces plunged deep and narrowly missed hitting crucial organs, which necessitated we take extra care in their removal with the magnet machine. This also accounted for what seemed our slowness in the beginning as well as the frightening amount of the blood you observed covering her. Of course, she suffered from an enormous number of scrapes and bruises from the debris and explosion as well as swelling in countless areas. The machine removed most of the fragments. The medical bed chamber did the rest of the work. Also, she has a concussion."

Alika took over. "She requires a boost in her blood as it's not replenishing as needed. So, we started the transfusion now, so it doesn't reach an emergency stage." He motioned towards the blood-filled bag hooked up to her other arm. "It will take about twenty minutes. We're also giving her a powerful injection for the swelling in her back and side as well as a second potent one for the concussion. The latter one should relieve the pressure that's staying on her head, and our hope is she awakens soon after we administer it. Our suspicion is that is why she remains unconscious." Alika got out two syringes. "First the one for her back and side." He lifted the corner of her shirt and injected the syringe. "Now for the other one." Alika inserted the second one at her neck, and she whimpered at the stick, cuddling closer to Dante. Immediately, he wrapped his arms around her and whispered, "I'm right here. It's okay. You're safe, my Angelina."

"Even unconscious, she knows, Dante." Alika patted him on the arm.

Caleb said, "The doctor went back to Lana, but I really need to check on her. Do you mind?"

"Go, by all means, Caleb." Seth motioned him. "We'll see to these two."

"My cousin has to wake up soon because Caleb is going insane."

Seth sighed. "Yes he is, but he's done an amazing job keeping everything to-gether, despite his worry. In all the chaos, we haven't checked in with Gabe or seen about the Santiagos either. They must be wondering why." He shook his head.

Alika put his hand on Seth's shoulder. "Go, my friend. I will handle our patients. The situation is manageable now. If that changes, I'll call for you."

"I leave them in your capable hands, my friend."

Alika returned his attention to Dante as Seth left. "Can I get you anything?"

"I'm fine now."

Alika peeked around the corner and caught one of the attendants passing by. "Sir, could you please bring me a pitcher of water and a large cup for Dante to have by his bedside? Thank you." He refocused on Dante. "I know what you said, but you should drink something. Here's both data pads as well in case." He handed them to Dante. "They are still connected between our group." He continued as he accepted the water the attendant brought. "This will be on the table at your bedside. I'll check on the others but will return to take care of the transfusion bag once the process is finished. You'll be fine?"

"Yes, and I'll watch over her."

CHAPTER EIGHTEEN

Caleb slumped in the chair with his wife's hand clasped in his, but within minutes his restlessness at seeing her still unconscious overcame him. He climbed into the bed to lay next to her. "Lana, would you wake up already? I can't stand this." Stroking her arm, he closed his eyes to block out the mess of the day. Instead, his mind began recalling the ugliest images, and the time crawled.

"Caleb?" He barely registered the whisper, but his eyes popped open in response.

"Lana, sweetheart. You're awake for me?" He whispered back as he wrapped his arms around her.

She groaned. "A hundred blaster battles are going off in my head."

"I'm stopping that for you now. Seth, can help us over here?"

"I'm taking over for him for a bit," Alika spoke quietly as he walked up. "Your wife is back with us?"

"Yes, but she's in a lot of pain with her head."

"As expected with the drug the agent gave her." He opened a handheld cylindrical metal object and pulled out a filled syringe. "Lana, I'm sorry as this will sting at your neck." He inserted the medicine, and she inhaled sharply. "However, your head will quiet down within a couple of minutes."

Alika stood watching her, measuring the time out, as Caleb stroked her hair and back to ease her discomfort while the treatment took effect.

Gradually her body relaxed, her arms encircled Caleb, and her eyes fluttered open. "How did I get back? Alika, why are you here?"

"It's a long story that your husband can tell you. How's your head now?"

"The blaster battle inside of it ended. Many thanks, Alika."

"You're welcome. Now rest. Your husband will ensure you do. I'll check on you two again in a bit." He smiled at them before leaving her bedside.

"Lana, you had me worried sick." Caleb stroked the side of her face. "Now I know how you felt."

"Yes, you did this to me on occasion." She cuddled closer to him. "Although, it wasn't all bad."

"I'm remembering now." He pulled her over and kissed her.

"How are you two managing?" asked Alika as he walked through the curtain to Alena and Ryan.

"Well enough," said Ryan as he leaned back.

"Appears so, Ryan." He chuckled at catching them in a kiss. "Do you concur with him, my dear?"

"I do." She smiled. "Any news on everybody else? We keep asking, but no one will say a word."

"Yeah, we've been begging to check on Dante at least, but nobody will let us get near him. Haven't heard a word either on Angelina. We started imagining the worst."

"My apologies. Seth and I are to blame for that but allow me to ease your mind. We finished with the two of them a short time ago. Dante is awake, quite vocal after being treated, and resting comfortably beside Angelina. She remains unconscious, but I anticipate her awakening soon and making a full recovery. I just left Caleb and Lana. She woke up and is feeling much better after I eliminated the massive headache induced by the drug. They are celebrating, so I gave them time to themselves. I'll make my way back to Dante and Angelina. Her blood transfusion should be completed within the next few minutes."

"I thought she was okay," said Alena.

"She is, but she had substantial blood loss from debris pieces that punctured deep."

"Can we see them soon?"

"Yes, once she awakens and I examine her. Until then you two rest."

"Where did Seth go?" asked Ryan.

"To contact Gabe to see how the cleanup is progressing and check on the Santiagos. We haven't been the best hosts since the explosion."

"I totally forgot."

Alena asked, "Gabe? Why would he be there?"

"Ryan will fill you in," he paused, "and it won't sit well with Angelina. I'll keep making rounds, but I need to return to her."

❧

Dante continued lying down with his arms encircled around Angelina as he watched the bag gradually empty. He kissed her forehead. "Why does it have to be so hard for us?"

She cuddled in closer to him as he noticed her face screw into a frown, and she slightly shifted the arm hooked up to the blood transfusion. He couldn't permit her to pull it out, so he laid his hand on hers to keep her from making further movements that could interfere with the transfusion. He whispered, "You'll feel better once you let it finish, and it's almost done. I'm right here. I've got you."

Angelina hurt. Gratefully it wasn't the intense pain from before. Rather it had become a continuous ache combined with an exhaustion that refused to release its grip which she struggled to overcome with no success. Even her eyelids resisted all efforts to open. A fog had settled in her head, but she finally sensed it lifting. Dante's arms encircled around her, and she happily sunk into them. When she heard his voice, she longed to answer him, but she couldn't despite her attempts. When she shifted her arm, a jolt of pain accompanied the motion. What caused it? She started to again, but his hand tenderly encased hers with his sweet whispers of care soothing her. The questions could remain unanswered because she could always trust him. So, she relaxed and let herself be held by her Dante.

"I see it's completed," said Alika as he walked back into the curtain to Dante and Angelina.

"She moved her arm a bit and made a face. She's ready for it to be over."

"In sleep, she still shows her distaste for receiving medical treatment." He chuckled as he unhooked the bag and cord. "I'll remove the other from her. Hopefully I don't have to reinsert it." When he extracted the IV from her, he saw the slight pull of her arm in response and the expression to match. "Yes, she is glad to have this out. I wish to check her, Dante."

"Do you need me to move aside?"

Alika picked up a medical scanner. "No, I'm only concerned with checking her head for the swelling due to the concussion. If you can have her leaning this way more, that would be helpful. Although I hate to ask considering how comfortable she is in her current position."

"She is, but I'll make it happen." Dante nudged Angelina back from his chest as Alika began the scan.

"It appears the injection is doing its work but another few seconds to be certain, which I won't get." Alika shook his head as she pulled back into Dante.

"Sorry, Alika, I'm trying." He reached down to shift her again and whispered in her ear, "Come on, he needs to check you. Make sure your head is okay. Do it for me."

"For you?"

"Angelina?" He held his breath, hoping he didn't imagine the voice.

"Dante?" She lifted her head, and her eyes fluttered open. "You all right?"

"I am now." He took his time giving her a long, gentle kiss.

"I'll come back." Alika chuckled.

"What's the last thing you remember, sweetheart?" asked Caleb.

"Enemy troops came in. They outnumbered me, but I held my ground. Seth would've been proud." She smiled, but it turned quickly into a scold. "Then I got supposed help when Santiago's trusted staff member waltzed back in with reinforcements. A few minutes later something sharp sticks into my neck as he grabs me from behind, and I fall to the floor. I should've known something was up. Everyone acted strange from the moment we arrived. Mr. Santiago's child went missing while there was an attack out of nowhere, and he disappeared too right before ... " Her mouth dropped open, and her eyes blazed with new fire. "Mr. Santiago knew and helped them. I can't get a hold of him soon enough!"

"Hold back your sunspear. He's innocent in this."

"How can you say that after what I just told you?"

"Because there's more to the story, I promise. Let me get it out?"

"You better hurry."

"I will. The same man that drugged you had Santiago's family hostage. He threatened to kill them if Mr. Santiago didn't go along with it."

The flame died in her eyes and was replaced by horror. "Are they okay? Tell me we got to them in time."

"They're safe. We brought them here for now."

"I can't believe one man did all this!" The fury reignited in her eyes. "Where is he? Caleb, I get to put my sunspear through him."

"As much as I love your fire, sweetheart, you won't be doing that."

"What do you mean? We let him escape?"

"No, he's dead."

"You're sure?"

"Every inch of him. I could show you, but I'd rather not. We're still cleaning it up."

"Cleaning it up? What happened?"

"Before I tell you, everyone we care about is fine. You heard that part, right?"

"Yes, but the fact you needed to say it scares me." She sighed. "Please tell me what happened."

"We brought him here for interrogation. Dante and Angelina were in the room questioning him. Ryan and Alena stood outside the room observing." Caleb paused. "The prisoner was set to explode, and he did."

"But you said they were okay?" Tears sprung in her eyes.

"They reached the door as the room blew. Barely but they made it."

"How?"

"The prisoner said something at the last second that set off an alarm in Angelina's head, and she got her and Dante out."

"Can I see them?"

"We'll have to wait."

"Why if they're really all right?"

"Ryan and Alena are fine now from what I can tell, and they're in the curtain beside us. Dante and Angelina are in the next one over, but they took the brunt of it. I wouldn't trust Dante on his feet for too long. He got thrown hard. Angelina is ... " he stopped.

"What about her? Caleb?"

"She'll come through, but they had to work on her pretty intensely before they could say that. Gave us a real scare. The explosion knocked her unconscious, and she's still out."

Lana buried her head in Caleb's chest. "My cousin must be out of his mind."

"Close, but once he knew she'd make it his panic level dropped down from hysterical."

"It's best to wait. Tell me the whole thing."

"Are you sure you're up to it? The extended version is long, and I don't know all of it. I split my time between being here worried sick about you and trying to monitor everything else."

She pulled back up against him. "Give me what you know, and we'll get the gaps filled in later."

* * *

Alika smiled at Seth. "How is that front managing?"

"My concerns were unfounded. Between Gabe and Mr. Santiago, they sorted it out. Mr. Santiago identified his staff for Gabe, and they're now aware of what happened today. They are reestablishing order and resuming normal operations until the Santiagos can return. His family is still doing well. They continued asking about the condition of our group and felt terrible about what occurred. How about our patients?"

"All cooperative, and everyone is awake at last. They've all been seen about. I gave a couple of them time alone as they were excited when the other one awakened."

Seth laughed. "I imagine so."

Alika smiled as he turned and addressed the group. "It has been a long day for all. Although there's plenty to discuss, as one of your physicians, rest is what I require of all of you. Everyone will stay where you're at tonight. We've brought two more beds into the room for Seth and me in case you need us."

☙

"I didn't check on my mom," said Dante.

"Under the circumstances, she'll understand. Seth checked on her for you, right?" said Angelina.

"Yes, but I hate I couldn't." He paused as he looked down at her. "We talked about this earlier, but if I hadn't been there today when that guy pinned you to the ship ... "

"He only had my arms and upper body secured. My knee prepared to deliver a different sensation in him than what he imagined, but you came up at the same time."

"You didn't need me to rescue you after all." He should've been glad, but a part of him felt something else.

She smiled up at him. "Another side of me wanted you to come to rescue me. I enjoyed watching you show him he shouldn't have messed with your girl."

"I'll always protect my girl."

"I know, and I like it when you take care of me, Dante."

He kissed her. Relief poured through him that she had an escape plan earlier. At the same time, there was something wonderful about the fact she needed him, that she saw him as her protector. He realized anew how he longed for it to become his permanent role in her world.

"How's my girl feeling after everything?" He stroked the side of her face.

"Better than expected. Once I woke up, the head fog lifted quickly and the weakness started turning loose."

"Angelina, you know how you ... "

"Scared you again. I'm so sorry, Dante. I don't try." She paused. "I'm still surprised we didn't go over a little of today's information."

"I'm not. As our physicians said we needed the rest of the evening off after what almost happened. Besides, I could get used to this arrangement."

She glanced at the small area inside their curtain and hid a smile. "It's well equipped and agreeable enough for a medical facility, but you'd be more comfortable in your quarters for the night."

He whispered in her ear, "You know that's not what I'm talking about."

"Do I?" She teased.

"You do." He lifted her chin and gazed into her eyes. "Going to sleep for the night with you wrapped up in my arms and knowing when I wake up in the morning, you'll still be lying next to me. I could get used to that happily."

"Me too."

"One word from you and it happens for good. Seth and Alika would do it for us."

"If it was just us, and nothing else to consider, you know what my answer already is. Don't give up on me."

"Never, my Angelina. I'll follow you anywhere, even to the farthest ends of the galaxy," He captured her up in another fiery kiss that left her breathless.

"Goodnight, my Dante," she said as she cuddled in beside him and laid her head on his shoulders as sleep overcame her.

"Goodnight, my Angelina." He kissed the top of her head and fell asleep with his arms still around her.

"Everything all right?" asked Alika softly, coming over quietly.

"I suppose," said Dante in the matching tone. "It's the middle of the night. You should be resting after everything today."

"As should you, but you're awake too."

"She got restless, mumbling in her sleep. At first, I feared something started hurting from earlier, but I don't think so. She settled down again. Maybe if I could have understood … "

Alika sat in the chair by their bedside. "It wouldn't help, and you'll be awakened again. Do you wish me to bring in another bed?"

"No way, Alika. I don't care about my sleep." He paused. "It's always like this, isn't it? What is it that steals her sleep?"

"Her head is crowded with the visions she has seen and experienced, and they revisit her."

"Isn't enduring them once enough?"

"I'm afraid not, but not all of her visions are unhappy. Many of those with your family and especially you are the most pleasant images that pass before her. She has told us on numerous occasions." Alika smiled.

"That gives me comfort," he paused, "but I have a feeling those aren't the ones frequently revisiting her. When Trey hurt her, she admitted someone else did many times, but she wouldn't tell me who."

"There's no point lying to you. Yes, those ugly fragments of her past are constant intrusions into her slumber, and she shared that conversation with me. No, I can't give you the answer as I'm bound to respect her decision in that matter. However, remember everything she does is rooted in her desire to keep you safe for you alone have won her heart, Dante."

He kissed her forehead as she began mumbling again. "I never doubt that Alika, but I only wish I could bring a lasting calm to her heart."

"You will." Alika smiled as she ceased murmuring and pulled back into Dante. "I'll leave you to sleep now."

CHAPTER NINETEEN

"Ready to take on a new day, commander?" asked Seth as he approached the bed with Alika.

"Yes, but I'm rallying for calmer than yesterday." Ryan grinned as he kissed Alena's cheek.

"Calm is a pleasant change so far." She smiled up at him.

"This setup is one of Caleb's best ideas." He looked over at the open curtain and empty bed beside them. "Hey, where are they? Is everything okay?"

"My guess would be things are quite pleasant with those two," said Alika.

"We released Lana earlier and allowed them to retreat to their quarters. They'll rejoin us at lunchtime," explained Seth.

Ryan chuckled. "Yeah, those two are managing fine."

***

Caleb shuffled a towel through his wet hair and put a clean shirt on as he finished dressing from his shower. He smiled at Lana. "Still feeling okay, sweetheart?"

She wound her arms around his neck and returned his smile. "More than okay, Caleb."

"I enjoyed helping you recuperate." He pulled her to him, finding the sweetness of her lips again.

"I feel back to my energetic self. Although keep going with this, and we'll be back in bed and need another shower."

"You're right. Besides, I wouldn't want you to overdo it."

"I overdo it? Or maybe tire you out, Caleb?"

"Not a chance. If we had more time, I'd prove it."

"I'll make sure you do."

"Tonight, it is." He chuckled. "I love your fire, sweetheart." He brushed a strand of her hair back. "I love you, Lana. I don't know what I would have done if I had lost you."

She placed a finger on his lip. "But it didn't happen, and it won't, Caleb." She pulled him to her and kissed him.

Dante smiled at Angelina as she opened her eyes. "Did I tell you I could get used to this?"

She smiled back at him. "You mentioned it."

He took his time kissing her. "Good morning, my Angelina."

"You do know how to say good morning, my Dante." She ran her fingers through his hair.

"Only way for you. You sleep, okay?"

"I did."

"Are you sure?"

"Of course. Why wouldn't I?"

He stroked her cheek. "You mumbled in your sleep several times during the night, and I thought ... "

"Oh ... I ... did I say something ... "

He glimpsed the shadow of fear pass over her face, and he rushed to dispel it. "No, I couldn't make out anything, and as soon as I brought you in closer you settled back down."

"I'm sorry I kept you awake."

"You didn't, and would you stop with that? You realize what this means though, don't you?"

"You discovered I'm noisy in my sleep?"

"No." His voice turned seductive. "It means my idea of making this the permanent arrangement is the solution to a wonderful sleep." He kissed her again.

"You make a convincing case."

"I couldn't resist trying. Whenever I eventually persuade you, tell me." He paused. "Alika said this is normal for you."

"Honesty, it's a wonder Alena gets any rest, but she's learned to block it out. Now she only awakens if it's a vision or something over the top."

"Do you remember what woke you up last night?"

"It revolves around the same stuff every night. Scattered pieces that run together."

"Or is it you can't tell me?"

"There's that too."

He kissed her cheek. "I figured, and I'm sorry. If you change your mind though, you can tell me."

"I know, Dante."

"How's everything feeling this morning?"

"Reasonably well, considering surviving being blown up. Once I get out of bed and move, I could change my mind. How about you?"

"Fine, but you're probably right about any lingering effects showing up soon enough. Until then ... " he pulled her closer and kissed her.

⁓ele⁓

"Everyone better?" asked Seth.

"No complaints here," said Caleb as he winked at Lana who smiled back at him.

"Getting a real shower went a long way," said Ryan.

"And being back in our clothes feels good," added Dante.

Alika chuckled. "Sometimes it's the little things. We're glad you've recovered sufficiently to be up and around. You gave us a scare, some more than others."

Angelina said, "As much as I can't stand medical treatment, I'm grateful for your and Seth's expertise."

Alena gasped. "We all heard it. She confessed to being thankful for medical treatment."

Angelina's eyes twinkled as she picked up a decorative pillow on the couch she sat on with Dante and playfully tossed it at Alena. "I'm feeling fine now."

Alena caught it and stuffed it beside her opposite the side she leaned up against with Ryan on the couch. "Apparently so, and I'll keep this since you can't behave yourself as usual." She laughed as did the others.

"Generally, Lana would run these sessions, but Seth and I will navigate today for obvious reasons," said Alika.

"However, Lana, feel free to interject if we fail to cover something. We realize you have substantial missing time from what happened yesterday," said Seth.

"Caleb gave me a rundown though, so I'm caught up."

"I can't believe how much that man got around in one day," said Alena as Lana recounted her near kidnapping.

Angelina shook her head. "He only saw his payoff and didn't care about anything else." She paused as the viewscreen continued. "Are those two soldiers all right?"

Ryan interjected. "They're fine. We thought at first it was weasel's work too, but we found out otherwise."

"I assume they were on our side?" She sighed at the confirming nod from Seth. "We suspected but ran out of time to negotiate further getting past the door."

"Lana is safe because you two got there in time, and those two recovered from the blaster stun," said Caleb.

Lana turned from the viewscreen. "I've heard you two could act, but if I didn't know better, I'd be convinced you both hated Ryan and Dante to the core. That was rough to watch."

Angelina stiffened as one of the scenes started, and she couldn't hold back. "We should skip through this. Nothing useful came from it."

Dante saw the instant transformation and tightened his grip around her waist to pull her closer and looked up at Seth and Alika. "I agree. We had every reason to believe the Santiagos worked with Black Dragon when we interrogated Mr. Santiago, but once we found out that wasn't the case ... nothing beneficial comes from replaying this."

"Please, let's not," said Angelina, still staring at the viewscreen.

Alika laid a hand on her shoulders. "A summary suffices."

"Thank you. Was he okay after what I did?"

"Nothing beyond my expertise. A powerful shot and he felt back to normal. He held no grudges. You saved his family. That's the only part he remembers," said Seth.

"And so should you. Time to turn the rest loose," said Dante.

Lana continued watching and listening as Alika and Seth hit the high points, intersecting narratives and segments of video to recall the day's events. Caleb had given her an accurate recap, but seeing it like this she realized the grueling day those around her endured to save her and the Santiagos. Her blood boiled as she saw flashes of Angelina's treatment by several of the men yesterday, and she didn't miss the remaining anger that passed over her cousin's face too.

"Despite how things ended, I think we should show the interrogation of our prisoner here in its entirety," said Alika.

Angelina nodded. "Unpleasant as the whole thing was, I agree."

It played, but Lana's horrified voice suddenly interrupted it. "He didn't suggest what I think he did! Dante, why was he still breathing? How could you let her do it?"

"There's no way I would have."

"Lana, it was all my idea. I made the creep think he had me, and it worked," said Angelina.

"How far did you take it?"

"Only talk for the ploy."

"A dangerous one, Angelina," said Lana as her eyes turned to Dante.

"I know, cuz. I almost had a stroke, but she pulled it off and he never got a hand near her."

"Okay. Let's continue." She watched mesmerized and repulsed as the dialogue resumed between them. The way Angelina drew the information from the man as if they were suddenly old shipping buddies was pure genius to behold. Then the moment he realized he had been played erupted on his face. If he hadn't been shackled to the chair, there's no telling what he would have done. Yet, he settled down quickly. The reason came soon enough as Lana couldn't restrain the gasp that escaped her as the room exploded, Angelina's voice rang out through the blast, and a blur of bodies catapulted from the room. She whispered, "A second later and ... "

Seth nodded. "Angelina got everyone clear in time."

Angelina stared at the darkened viewscreen. "I should've caught on sooner."

Dante shook his head. "That they set him to blow? How could anyone know?"

"Most wouldn't." She bit her lip.

"So why you?"

"Because I know how Black Dragon works."

"What do you mean?"

"My world is different than yours. You don't want to go there." She paused, waiting for him to relent, but his gaze didn't. "I know the men we dealt with today because I've encountered them countless times across the galaxy. They no longer surprise me as they do you and your group. The Black Dragon preys on such men, and I've seen the story played out in a repeating loop, whether it be in a vision or the backroom of a bar. The accounts circulate, ones most dismiss as mere scare tactics by Black Dragon, but they're not, Dante. We've been Black Dragon when we needed to."

He put his hands on her shoulders and stared into her eyes. "I thought it only amounted to a few operations where you were undercover. How many times have you been in the heart of Black Dragon?"

"Dante, don't." She shook her head.

"Tell me, please."

"More than I can bear to admit to you. Enough to see firsthand the lengths they will go to accomplish their plans and the price of failure. Our prisoner was right. The new management did not usher in this brand of assurance." She put her head in her hands as images assailed her mind.

He stroked her hair and whispered, "I'm so sorry."

"All the signs were there, and I missed them."

"No, you got us out in time."

"This incident I did, but barely."

"And you plan on walking back in there." He gazed into her eyes. "I hated the idea before, but after this I can't let you."

"Too late."

"Wait, you've already been? Why didn't you say something? What about the mark? the black blood?"

"We didn't have a chance to tell any of you." She took her hands and discreetly loosened the tightening grip he unintentionally placed on her shoulders in his panic. "We figured out how to get around it, and our visit went fine."

He took a deep breath as he leaned her back against him.

"She's telling the truth, Ryan," Alena answered the unspoken question in Ryan's eyes and kissed him.

Angelina stared at the blackened viewscreen again. "Considering the group he managed to pull together, how can we be sure we cleared out all of them?"

"Santiago is overseeing the cleanup from here. Are you questioning your process?"

"It can only go so far. I have faith in your troops, but I'm more hands-on with this situation."

"Such as one of us ensuring everything ran as well as we're saying."

"Yes, making certain every inch is checked for anyone still left hiding to cause trouble. You know, being all take charge." She winked at Dante.

He laughed. "I'm glad I impressed you with my commando style, but I'm laying off that for a while. We did call in one of our own to coordinate the cleanup. Commander Gabe is there."

"Gabe? He's an excellent choice to take on this task." Her eyes widened. "But someone is sure to mention me and Alena. We gave the Santiagos a story, and they believed it. Gabe though? Although we were disguised, he fought by our side in that one attack. What if he puts it together?"

"He knows."

"What? How? You told him? Why would you do that?"

"I didn't."

"Then how did find out?"

"The Ancient One revealed it to him when he came here with the other commanders. Before you ask, I don't know why or how."

"Do you know what could happen?"

"Not for sure, Angelina. Only what you hinted because remember, you won't let me into this whole past life you hide away. Sorry, I didn't mean to sound ... " He took a deep breath and continued. "Nothing will happen, because Gabe won't tell. He'll keep his word."

"Another person put in danger because of me."

"Please, you can't do this to yourself." He brought her clasped hand to his lips while keeping his other arm around her waist.

Alika came beside her and rested his hand on her shoulder. "He's right, my child. The fate of every individual does not rest upon your back, though you try to make it so."

"But I ... "

"You forgot again, but we're here to remind you. You're welcome as usual." Alika winked at her.

A smile escaped her as she turned back to Dante. "I'm sorry for overreacting. Gabe is trustworthy. So, does he approve of me? I can be a bad influence."

"He approves wholeheartedly of you and Alena with Ryan too. He says you're good for me."

"Did he now?" She laughed. "I don't think he would agree, after what happened with our prisoner. Does he know about that?"

"I believe so." Dante looked up at Seth in confirmation.

"Yes, and he offered to assist here, but we need his expertise to finish the other. He sent his concern."

Dante turned to Angelina and softly kissed her. "There's a visit to Black Dragon you have yet to share with us."

"Persistent as always."

Ryan and Alena cuddled on the couch that evening in the quarters he called his own during his frequent visits to the fortress now.

"It's all safe, everything to make you two appear Black Dragon and all the reversing?" he asked.

"Yes. Alika would make certain, and our source was adamant he wouldn't help us otherwise. Angelina went ballistic when she discovered they tested it out on our source first."

"Like when she found out about Gabe knowing about you two."

"A fair comparison. Poor Dante."

"Don't feel sorry for him, because he enjoys the reining-in process with her. It ends well for him." He laughed.

"For both of them. That's probably why she does it."

"Really in and out of Black Dragon with no problems?"

"Yep, except for having grounds for a whiplash claim against them."

"Their new management won't rule in your favor, sweetheart." Ryan kissed her on the forehead. "Is it still bothering you?"

"No." Then her eyes twinkled. "Maybe a little."

"I'll take care of that." He drew her closer and planted butterfly kisses along her neck as he murmured, "Better?"

"You're on the right track," whispered Alena as she fell into his embrace.

❦

Dante and Angelina lay snuggled up on the couch in his quarters for the night.

"I'm surprised Alika cleared me from medical. He's usually difficult about that with me, Dante."

"You showed appreciation for his healing services for once in your life. That's probably it."

"A hard time from you too? Maybe I should go." She pretended to get up.

"Oh no, you don't. You're all mine for the evening, and I'm not letting you loose." He eased her back into his embrace at her teasing attempt to leave. "Anyway, he didn't completely let you off the hook. If anything starts hurting, we're back to our quarters in medical."

"I saw enough of it."

"Some of the stay suited me quite well, Angelina." He murmured, kissing her cheek.

"That's true." She smiled up at him.

"As long as you're safe with me, I don't care where we are."

"That's the challenge with me. I'm told I need to stop doing that to you or else … " she paused as she shook her head. "Never mind."

However, he caught the mischievous glint which flashed in her eyes. "No, there's something. You're not getting away with that one."

"It's not worth mentioning."

"Oh, it is, and I'm prepared to use unconventional methods to get it from you." His fingertips teased the side of her body through her shirt.

"That again?" A giggle escaped her as he began to carry out his threat of tickling her. "All right, I'll tell you. Our source was unhappy about my last visit here with you."

"Why would he be unhappy with me unless he … ?" His face darkened.

"Dante, no. He thinks you're wonderful and said Alena and I have found the two best men left in the galaxy. He got on to me about all the trouble I managed to find while here."

"That part we can agree on, but I'm still waiting."

"He suggested you resort to more creative means of keeping me from danger."

"Which is? I'm intrigued. Out with it."

"It's a terrible idea, pure insanity."

"Or brilliance which is why you're holding back." He kissed the side of her face and whispered in her ear, "Tell me."

"He said you might lock me up in your quarters. See it's craziness."

"No, I'd say it's perfect. I can see it. Let me show you all the advantages, my Angelina."

Dante engulfed her in his arms, cutting off any further discussion. She ran her hands through his hair and drowned in the wonder of his endless kiss. Being locked up here with him, yes, perfect was the only description for it after all.

He stroked her arm. "I know you're still upset with what happened with some of the interrogation. At least the Santiago mix-up. However, I'm relieved you have that arsenal hidden away, and it has me feeling better about you staying safe."

"I admit it has proved effective in the right situation."

"Normally I wouldn't be happy seeing another man howling in pain, but that wasn't any kind of man who ... " he touched his forehead to hers, "when I think of what he wanted from you, it still makes me sick."

"He wasn't getting it, Dante."

"No, I would never allow him to." He took a deep breath to calm the images resurfacing. "Where did you learn that anyway? Your skill with pressure points? Did you just decide to pair it with the interrogation?"

"You don't want that answer either."

"A part of me won't be happy with it, but I asked you to let me in and I meant it." He lifted her chin to gaze into her eyes. "Where did you learn it?"

"A great portion of it is the world I've seen. In the shipping arena, a different set of rules governs gathering intel and doing business. Although you may not practice it or at least rarely, you're aware of and witness how the other side operates. Also, we've been undercover to the most ruthless shipping dealer across the galaxy, the Black Dragon. No one thinks of them in that sense first, but it's one of the many areas their hold is felt. Failure is met with death, and they have perfected every agonizing way to reach that endpoint. Both account for a fair measure of it. However, in a controlled setting, Alika trained us on the pressure points. Mercifully, he broke it down into several painful lessons, but he decided it necessary we were able to use it. I'm surprised Seth didn't make you endure it."

"He did a little of it with us, but Caleb and I proved frustrating, to put it mildly. It ended with a trek in the woods for us as I recall. My cousin proved a better student. I assumed I could fall back on my sunspear."

"Alena and I realized early that a blade or blaster may not be our first line of defense, if we hoped to keep our cover."

"So other methods were needed. Makes sense. Not just for you two. Several of Seth's lessons for me were designed to have me depend less on my sunspear. I should do better with those." He smiled at her. "You could give me a refresher on those pressure points."

"No way. I won't have you on the ground in pain because of me. I cause you enough grief." She bit her lip.

"Don't you dare think that because it's not true. " He stroked her cheek. "I'm recalling other pressure points."

"The other ones, huh?" A smile started at the corners of her mouth.

"Yes, those."

"I've shown I know where your pleasure points are and a couple to be uniquely you." Her hand slid up his arm to caress the back of his neck. "At least most of them."

"Just most of them." He barely managed the words as the softness of her touch captured him.

"I'm certain you have a few others, but we'll have to wait for me to discover those." She whispered in his ear. "You'll be the only one though, my Dante."

"My Angelina," he whispered, "how I wish ... " He didn't bother to finish as he pulled her against him and found her lips again. If he had the means to eliminate Black Dragon on his own now, he'd do it to have the future he imagined with her and make her his wife.

She dreamily leaned on the ship's doorway and traced Dante's handsome profile as he walked away for the night. Wishing for the millionth time she could give in to his heart's desire, she finally turned to find Alika and Alena, smiling at her from the couch. "I know, tomorrow, we're off again. Time to hit the bed."

CHAPTER TWENTY

The Premier Black Dragon sat in the commander chair, mulling over the report. "She's alive. Impressive. Any idea how?"

"From what we could gather, her group reached her in time."

"Apparently my employee's ploy did not keep them busy enough like he anticipated. He had disabled her at last contact."

"Correct, sir. We heard nothing further from him, and so we had no choice but to conclude it as you requested."

"Yes, he's dead now. I took care of it myself. I'm sure the Freedom Fighters are disappointed, as I can't imagine he helped them much before he made a mess of the place."

"The word circulating from the locals report seeing two handcuffed individuals at separate times being escorted off the planet by a sizable Freedom Fighter guard."

"One of them is certainly our eliminated shipping dealer, and the other must be the administrator. What about his family? That was his incentive to corporate."

"The Freedom Fighters confiscated both ships, so they'll find his family, whether they were left dead or alive."

"There's no way to know because we lost communication with the group our inside man put together. It unraveled fast, and the Freedom Fighters weeded out friend from foe with a vengeance. I shouldn't be surprised with my chosen target, but I wish we possessed better intel on how it fell apart." He murmured. "It's becoming a pattern."

"Sir?"

"Nothing. Just thinking aloud. Keep me updated if there's anything further to explain the events."

"Of course, sir. Do you want us to contact another shipping dealer?"

"Not yet." The Premier Black Dragon turned the comm off and stared out into the stars. "Lana, how did you escape? Your cousin as well and from the Dark Lord. How do I prevent this script from playing out again?" He paused. "Perhaps a wider net is needed to catch such an impressive prize as your group. In the meantime, operations continue."

—*ell*—

Alena waved a hand in front of Angelina. "Are you paying attention?"

"We could do that. Whatever that is." She glimpsed the amused expression reflected on Alena's and Alika's faces.

"A certain young man still accompanying your thoughts today?" teased Alika.

"Guilty as charged. His goodbyes make it almost impossible to leave him." She projected a list from her data pad on the wall before them. "I'm focusing. All of these are locations we could hit, but I've no clue which portal to settle on. There's still following Drew's trail. Maybe the one our ship dealer traveled to meet with Black Dragon."

"We won't find that one. His vessel didn't travel to meet them, remember?" said Alika.

"I forgot, but his shipping routes perhaps. He's obviously been a supplier for them for a bit."

"Along with others. They didn't give a second thought about spectacularly ending him."

"It's their way." She shrugged. "It still amazes me the length of time my father lasted with all his failures. If the Dark Lord hadn't worked so hard and long to establish it as one of his favorite secret bases to run so much through, my father's days would have been numbered far sooner." She continued studying the display, and her electronic pointer rested further up on the list. "Maybe we should visit the facility again."

"The one where Abigail was held?" Alena stared at her.

Alika shook his head at Angelina's nod. "No, we agreed it would be a suicide mission. The last time you barely escaped with your life."

"We saw that crystal mechanism, but we never concluded what it did. It could be key."

"No, there are other portals to explore first."

"Our time is running out, Alika."

"It hasn't yet."

She sighed. "Which location then?"

⁓ℓℓ⁓

Dante stepped back from the bustle of the conference room in the building next door to the fortress. He rubbed the back of his neck as his eyes swept over the room.

"You think we got the right people for this?" asked Ryan.

"I hope so because we've been at this forever."

"A couple of days now, buddy."

"It's different now, like we said. Not machinery under the Black Dragon garb, but turned colonists. Flesh and blood. Can they separate it, Ryan?"

"They're doing it."

"But what it does to you, to your spirit. Someone once said to me they left us with the harder task because every day of this can take a frightening toll from you."

"No doubt who said that." Ryan paused. "Dante, you have to remember that individual has a mountain of other images running through their head to complicate things that we don't know the half of."

"True, but I'm not sure I'd hold up over the long haul, and we're pushing this awful weeding process off on a miniature army."

Ryan patted him on the back. "We agreed we had to delegate this out. The Black Dragon colonists ... in reality, we found out it's been going on for years. Those are colonists that at their core would have chosen to wear the Black Dragon uniform and serve them. Like the one person said, the Dark Lord had agents serving his cause all along in the shadows. Now it's come full circle, and we have to face it like any other battle. The colonists we serve are counting on us like always."

"So, we won't let them down, Commander Ryan."

"That's what we like to hear around here. Every once in a while I have one of those commander speeches in me." Ryan grinned at Dante. "Did your friend say where they were headed when they left?"

"No, I got the impression they are still mulling over the possibilities. How about yours?"

"That's the vibe I got too, but we usually don't talk much business with our time."

Dante grinned back. "Same here. The time is better spent elsewhere. Although with them making one successful run at it, you know they're going back. Every time I think about it ... "

"Don't. I'm trying not to either. Let's see how this task force is coming with the interrogations they did earlier. They need to have the whole process down."

⁓ℓℓ⁓

"Great place we've got here," murmured Angelina as she and Alena roamed the hallway of the Black Dragon facility.

"Big and bland. Creativity is saved for other areas best left alone," Alena murmured back. "Time to discover our next assignment." She opened the door to find another soldier, awaiting their arrival.

"Step this way. Confirm your clearance."

"Black Dragon 72064," said Angelina as she displayed her data pad.

"Black Dragon 72065," said Alena as she did the same.

He scanned the fake profiles provided. "There are recruits to assign. Half of them wouldn't last a second against a blade. It'd be an insult to put one in their hand." The soldier laughed.

"A Black Dragon sword deserves to be placed in the hand of a real fighter," said Angelina.

"And we get the pleasure of deciding who takes up that call at Black Dragon," said Alena.

"Correct. Fighters in one group. General warehouse and assemblers in another as they'll probably be directed at putting together the weapons for the soldiers. Then the tech-savvy ones as they will handle more specialized duties. Those with pilot experience, ship repair, administrator type, and down the line you go. You get the idea." He pointed to a screen in front of them. "There's the list, so I won't waste anymore of my time. Put them where they best fit. If they're capable of multiple roles, note it if you want, but assign where they're strongest and move on. I'll have you do this for a while. I see your expertise is a fighter, and we have recruits requiring training," he grinned, "or testing. I'll return to get your assistance with that after a while. We'll see if they have what it takes."

"We may need to do testing of our own before we settle someone in that category. I'm sure you understand," said Angelina.

"I like you two. Make them earn their blade, but remember this is only screening. Don't have all the fun here." He laughed as he exited the room.

"Human resources for Black Dragon. Lovely," muttered Angelina as she looked at the sea of faces.

"We have to do a decent job of it or else we're done."

"Always back to the same dilemma. Let's begin."

Alena announced, "Time to receive your assignments. Fall in now."

Angelina stared at the man through her helmet, not caring to listen to him argue his case. Who knew this would be such a mind-numbing process and simultaneously test her patience. She cut him off, "You're in the ship repair crew."

"I'm a much better pilot." The man's face reddened.

"You can do two things. Congratulations. Maybe I'll put a gold star by your name. However, I disagree with your assessment, and you're here to serve Black Dragon's needs, not your agenda. Into ship repair, you go. Now."

"I want to be up in the air."

She advanced towards him and pulled out her sword. "I don't care what you want. If you don't comply this instant, you will experience why I've earned the fighter title." Grabbing him by the neck, she had her blade come to rest on his shoulder. "On second thoughts, why don't I put you in the air? I have another way in mind."

"No, I'm good." The man struggled out at her tightening grip on him.

"Now how does ship repair look?"

"It suits me well."

"Wise of you to reconsider." She released his neck, but didn't move her blade from its frightening position on him. "Do not defy an order again. It does not end well here, recruit. Your training will be short-lived if you challenge that premise again." She put her sword aside. "You have your assignment. Dismissed."

Alena held back her laughter as she watched Angelina give the trainee his first lesson in being an obedient Black Dragon soldier. Another part of her silently thanked her friend for barring the man from the cockpit. She guessed the man to be the better pilot as Angelina did, but the last thing they wanted was to send him up in the air to shoot at their team, likely where her Ryan would be. They were still helping the enemy, a point not lost on them as they continued through the sorting.

Alena knew her luck couldn't continue. She listened to the man's experience and knew where his first choice lay. *Well, disappointment is a hallmark of Black Dragon,* she thought to herself. "Excellent, but you mentioned you had your hand in shipping?"

"For a short time."

"That business takes organization, making contacts, and keeping them satisfied."

"But that's not what I do best."

"Administrator group, now."

"I'm a fighter though!"

"You are what I say you are, and I said you are an administrator. Now locate your associates." Alena shook her head as the man remained standing there. "Fine. Since you disagree, I'll grant you the chance to prove it." She took out her Black Dragon sword. "They left us a few spares." She handed him one of them and motioned at the armor. "Suit up too. I'll make it fair, and we'll see who's right. Do it now. You're wasting time."

The man did as she instructed and attacked her with his blade. Alena effortlessly deflected the blows.

Angelina stopped her interview. "Step back everyone, and give them room. This won't take long. There's a valuable lesson to follow."

Alena grinned under her helmet as she stayed on the defensive for another minute. The man continued his advance, believing his point was being proved. He was decent with the blade, enough she didn't want him on the battlefield to test it out on one of their own. Then she made her move, no longer satisfied with lengthening the battle and went on the offensive, pushing him back. Moments later, she found the opening she wanted. Her weapon went clean through him, and he collapsed to the floor. She knelt next to him. "You knew we battled to the death, right? My assessment is confirmed as correct." She rose as the man's eyes closed for the last time.

Alena turned to the group, and her voice boomed, "Our word is final in this room today. If anyone has not learned that, you will join this man in this newly created designation."

Angelina added as she stood beside Alena, "Your only purpose now is to serve Black Dragon. That is what you chose. You will do so dead or alive. Step forward for your assignments, and do not defy us."

"What happened here?"

Angelina and Alena turned at the arrival of the soldier who gave them their charge, as he pointed to the lifeless body in the corner.

"A demonstration. He did not agree with his appointment as administrator. I provided him the opportunity to back his claim as a fighter, and he failed. Unfortunate for him that he disagreed," said Alena.

Angelina nodded. "However, we had no further issues after the exercise. It served as a most effective teaching tool. We considered using a firestone to clean up the mess."

"No, leave it. They need the reminder for longer. The fighter group awaits us."

CHAPTER TWNETY-ONE

L ana called from across the room, "Caleb!"

"What is it?" Caleb asked as he came to her side.

She pointed to the message on the data pad and spoke into her device at the same time, "You're sure? There hasn't been one for a while. Okay, we're on it."

"They don't make mistakes on these, Lana. We'll answer it like normal, but it's strange to me too that we didn't get a heads up from somewhere else."

She addressed those gathered, "Attention! We received a distress call from the planet Donoma that a Black Dragon fleet is attacking."

"Seth and Dante, you're with the ground forces. The rest to the air. Ryan, your squadron may not stay there, depending on what we find. Full gear and then let's move," said Caleb.

"You wanted a break from the other, Dante," kidded Ryan as he ran towards the hangar with his friend.

"I take it back."

The familiar adrenalin rush passed through Caleb as his ship emerged through the portal and caught sight of the Black Dragon ships prepared to engage his fleet. "They brought plenty for us. Commanders, let's not keep them waiting."

Dante checked through the scanners. "No tanks, yet."

"If the pattern holds, they'll be here soon," said Seth.

"Right now, we handle those troops coming at us. This could be ugly with those disc weapons." He raised his sunspear and motioned for the others to advance.

Lana stared at the data pad and asked, "What? Another one? Are you sure? I'll let Caleb know."

"Anything for you, sweetheart, Name it," said Caleb as he fired a shot while maneuvering the ship to dodge a blast. "No way. We've got no choice but to split our forces." He turned to his copilot "You heard her, right?"

"Yes, sir."

"Pull us back from the fighting for a minute. I've got updated orders to issue." He switched on the comm system. "Listen up, everyone. Black Dragon changed the script again. We've got another attack on the planet Nitza, so we'll move half the fleet to cover both. Commander Gabe and Austin, take your squadrons to Nitza. Commander Ryan, yours too, but manage the ground forces. Lana is working on sending us another wave of troops where needed. Commander Caleb out."

"What a day," he said to his copilot. "Let's get back in there."

⸻ ⁊ℓℓ ⸻

Dante shouted, "Seth, where did that blast come from?"

"Beyond this battlefield to the far left." Seth hollered back.

"Another army?"

"I believe so."

"We have to divide."

"I see no other option either."

Dante watched as Seth and part of the squadron disappeared past the tree line to meet the second threat. He turned back to his portion of the fighters and motioned them forward. *This feels like all kinds of wrong.*

⸻ ⁊ℓℓ ⸻

"Another army?" Lana said as she monitored the increasing battlefields. "They're splitting our forces on both fronts. Commander Ryan, what are you seeing?"

"No big artillery yet which is a plus since I've been meaning to have Dante let me practice on disarming those tanks. Much smaller force than normal. Should have it knocked out fast, which is why I'm expecting to see tanks."

"Keep me posted."

"Will do."

—ᴇᴇ—

"Dante, we spotted another string of them coming from that side," yelled one of the squadron leaders.

"We have to break through. We can't allow them to ... " He didn't need to finish the thought as he focused his attention back on the soldiers advancing on him at once. *Surround us. That's what they're doing. I've got to stop this.* His sunspear resumed its deadly spree through the Black Dragon men before him, but there were too many for him, for his squadron. The circle tightened around them to his dismay.

"Surrender now, Dante!" A Black Dragon voice commanded.

The field fell silent, and the fighting ceased as Dante faced the Black Dragon leader who issued the insane order. "Never will I or any other Freedom Fighter surrender to Black Dragon."

"You are completely outnumbered and trapped."

Taking in the scene, he realized the truth of the leader's assessment, of how dire their situation had become. However, he refused to allow the squadron leader to sense the fear creeping up inside of him. "We're been here many times, and we manage to kick your rear. Today is no exception."

"I figured you wouldn't accept my offer. What about your troops? An exchange then. You will yield, and I let them go?"

"Only to meet them in battle the next time to finish this? What kind of deal is that? Only the sort Black Dragon makes. I don't care for your bargain or you, so I'll keep letting my sunspear answer for me."

"Reconsider, Dante. We ran into someone you know." He motioned behind him. "Bring him forward."

Dante gasped in disbelief as Seth appeared bound between two Black Dragon soldiers with a blade at his throat.

"As you would guess, what's left of the squadron is cooperative now. Being responsible for something happening to your Elder would be a rough one on your conscience."

"Dante, don't worry about me! You can't do what he says!" A Black Dragon's swift punch to Seth's abdomen silenced further protest.

Dante stood there with his sunspear still raised and clueless about what to do, as he stared into Seth's face.

⁓ ❧ ⁓

Lana studied the various screens and pieced it with the communications pouring in at a dizzying rate. Her focus zeroed in on one battlefield, and a terrifying picture emerged. She said, "Ryan, I know why nothing else ever came. Divide and conquer. Get to Dante and Seth now."

"I'm on it. What's going on?"

"They got separated, and they're surrounded. I'm certain they have Seth prisoner."

"Getting there as fast as we can."

"Hurry, Ryan."

⁓ ❧ ⁓

Dante knew what Seth wanted him to do, but every part of him resisted the instructions. Seth was more than his teacher, his Elder. Seth had been a father to him, and Dante couldn't reduce him to another causality of this war. Even if it cost him everything, Dante made his choice and his next action would seal his deadly fate. He lowered his sunspear. "Let them go. Take me instead."

"An impressive exchange, one worthy of the Black Dragon's consideration. Put the sunspear on the ground now. Excellent." He motioned to the soldiers behind Dante. "Retrieve his weapon and bound him, like his Elder."

"You have me now. You said you would release Seth."

"No, I agreed to free your squadron. I indicated I would consider releasing your Elder too, but that didn't work in your favor. The both of you are quite the prize." He laughed at Dante's furious expression. "Which of you will meet your end first?"

Seth stood helpless to the events unfolding, still unable to comprehend how everything unraveled so quickly. They had discovered the enemy significantly outnumbered their forces, but a situation they found themselves in numerous times. Moreover, it appeared Black Dragon brought in additional troops after the battle started, but that hadn't sealed it. His group came upon what they initially believed to be the colony army, only to uncover it had been routed beforehand. As he realized he had led his men into a trap, the adversary captured him. Now he stared in despair as Dante's life would be sacrificed as well.

A quiet Black Dragon voice near him interrupted his thoughts, "Do you doubt now, Elder? Is it not your belief the Ancient One protects his own?"

Seth turned to his side to peer at the Black Dragon soldier who also grasped his one arm tightly and in the other hand held his staff. The soldier continued, "These are the times to test even an Elder's faith."

Lana's voice came through Seth's comm. "Yours is enough though, Seth. Be ready."

"Let Seth go. I wouldn't have agreed to this otherwise," yelled Dante.

"In that case, you will be first, so he can witness your death."

"Sir, would you allow me to soften him up for you or better yet have the pleasure of killing him?" The appeal came from a Black Dragon soldier standing near the squadron leader.

"A unique request. Tell me more."

"He got a nasty hit on me, and I don't take kindly to it, so I'm eager to return the favor. I submit he should suffer before he takes his last breath. Permit me, sir."

"Such passion for one's work is seldom seen, and I must fan the fire as one of your squadron leaders. Take your time, and then deliver the final stroke."

Dante stared into the helmet of the Black Dragon soldier who would become his executor. He couldn't recall a troop he laid a blow on and didn't finish, but it didn't matter now. What did matter was finding a way out of their seemingly hopeless situation.

"It's time to take care of you as promised, Dante," said the Black Dragon soldier.

"What?" The words caught in his throat.

"You heard me. Don't pretend you don't understand."

"I do perfectly. Do your worst. I'm not afraid of you."

"You should be. All the different ways to create pain is the area we excel."

"I've seen, but what did you expect from me? To fall apart in front of you? To entertain you at the last?"

"No, I expected this. Defiant until the end."

"Give me back my sunspear, and we'll finish this right."

"Not a chance, Dante. You forget I've witnessed your work."

"I promise to make you pay for this."

"There's no way of that considering your current situation."

"I'm not out yet, and when I get my hands on you for this one … "

"I can't wait to see how that works out for you." She smiled under her helmet, amused by the exchange from him. The Black Dragon extracted one meaning from the comments, and their delight at what appeared to be Dante being toyed with only made his impending death sweeter for them. However, it had been necessary to ensure Dante knew she stood before him. She only hoped the confidence he placed in her wouldn't fail as she reached beneath his helmet to brush the back of his neck and said, "On your knees."

To all those watching, it only solidified the soldier's further control over him. Dante gave a token show of resisting, while inside he welcomed her hand caressing the back of his neck, even with the gloved Black Dragon hand. Then he allowed himself to be brought down to his knees. The soldiers holding him wouldn't hesitate to employ excessive force to have him comply with the order, and he needed to be ready to fight again with whatever she planned.

"What a sight. The great sunspear bearer Dante suffers and dies before his whole squadron and his teacher as he kneels to the Black Dragon. Hand me his sunspear." She took it from the troop. "It will be extraordinary to eliminate you with this, Dante. An amazing weapon. I see why you prefer it."

"There's nothing like it for cleaving through Black Dragon. Hand it over, and I'll demonstrate."

She laughed. "Hold him still. My strokes will find their mark this time."

Dante stared up at the soldier, telling himself underneath the cold exterior of the Black Dragon helmet lay the woman he loved. Time slowed as his sunspear went into motion and headed straight for his neck. At the last moment, it changed course and went high. The sweep of the blade hissed above him, and in the same instant, the grip from his captors fell. Immediately, his bonds were cut.

A Black Dragon gloved hand yanked him up the rest of the way and pushed his sunspear in his hands. "Back to it, Dante."

He let out a deep breath as he went to work beside Angelina against the Black Dragon threat and hollered at her, "Why are you still using that?"

"Using what?" she yelled back.

"The Black Dragon sword!"

"To kill Black Dragon, Dante! What kind of dumb question is that?"

"Use the other!"

"No way!"

"Your comrade is! Because they figured out the obvious!"

"Which is?"

"You're all in Black Dragon. No one can tell you're on our side until it's too late! You'll get yourself killed! Now get the other! No one mistakes that weapon!"

"I hate when you're right!"

"Just do it! I won't watch you die from a friendly blade! I'll cover you!"

Angelina pulled out her sunspear, ignited it, and sheathed the Black Dragon blade. "Happy now!"

"Much!" he exclaimed while dispatching the next enemy soldier.

Lana breathed a momentary sigh of relief that Alika's earlier words through the communication system to her came true. "Do not give up hope, Lana. Help comes among the unlikely sometimes." His two accomplished the impossible again, saving Dante and Seth from execution. However, if she didn't get aid to them soon, they would be back in the same circumstances. She spoke into the comm, "Ryan, where are you?"

"Coming on it now. Did the troops get the message you sent?"

"Yes. They let the situation play out, and once Dante got free they resumed their attack on Black Dragon, minus two of those soldiers."

"I've already warned mine, but I'm still worried about their safety from one of our own."

"Tell them to watch for the sunspears to distinguish our friends."

***

"Dante! Seth!" yelled Ryan.

"Over here!" hollered Dante.

"Where's Seth? Also, I'm told we have a couple of welcomed drop-ins."

"Seth was over that way when last I saw. The other one is to my right, close by. We've been trying to get to them, but it's been impossible."

"So should we stay or go?"

"Go to them. They were covered in Black Dragon and cut off from most of the troops. Do whatever it takes to reach them."

"Got it. We'll find a way to them."

"Look for a sunspear and Seth's staff."

"Already got the word." Ryan motioned for his troops to follow.

***

Seth spun around barely dodging another Black Dragon blade bearing down on him as he finished off yet another fighter. The second Dante had been freed, Alena took advantage of the chaos to cut his bindings and return his staff to him. The other Black Dragon soldier didn't have a chance to react when the sword at his prisoner's throat suddenly became the weapon of his demise. Since that moment, a series of close calls described Seth's fighting, and he knew Alena fared no better. He dared a look at her, and to his relief, he still saw her up and swinging her sunspear.

Alena sliced through another Black Dragon soldier while stepping back to avoid another approaching blade, only to almost run straight into one behind her. She went to the ground, surprising both soldiers and reemerged behind the one to cleave through him. Without giving the other one any chance to recover, she engaged him. *I can't believe how outnumbered we are. Okay, the hangar fiasco comes to mind with Angelina.* She thought to herself. It wouldn't be as bad if they had more help from their squadron, but Seth being taken prisoner had created a gulf between him and his troops, one only a scattered number managed to breach to assist them now.

Ryan hollered, "Almost there! I don't care what it takes, but get to that staff and sunspear!" His heart sank as the sunspear vanished from sight. "I said now!" His sword found the sweet spot in another troop and charged past with new fervor. He refused to lose Alena. Relief poured through him as the sunspear reappeared.

"Seth, duck!" screamed Alena. Her sunspear caught the soldier who nearly landed a deadly blow to take off Seth's head. Acknowledging her with a nod, he continued to engage the Black Dragon at hand while she deflected a swing threatening to find her side. A few minutes later, Seth returned the favor as a blade narrowly missed cleaving through her abdomen. Another soldier fell under her blade, and she raised her sunspear to meet the next one. Suddenly, she heard the sweep of one behind her, but she moved a second too late to avoid the full impact to her shoulder. "That stung," she growled. Ignoring the pain, she sidestepped so her back was no longer to her attacker and forced her arms to keep moving with the sunspear. A sluggishness crept into her movements, and she warred against it. *Fight it, Alena. You have to, or you're not making it out of this,* she repeated to herself. She took a deep breath as another soldier met her sunspear's deadly edge. A body dropped behind her, and she spun around with her sunspear raised.

"Hey, don't do that. I killed a lot of Black Dragon to reach you," said Ryan.

"Commander Ryan, I've never been so glad to see you."

"Then it must be bad. I brought a squadron, and Seth's troops pushed through now. I got your back. You okay?"

"I'm good."

"Watch out!" warned Ryan as he struck his blade at a Black Dragon troop determined to take a swipe at Alena. "Recap's over."

"Appears so," laughed Alena as she engaged a fighter next to Ryan.

<hr>

Caleb replied to his wife's update, "The second planet served as a distraction. Gabe and Austin reported minimal fleet in the air and already cleared it out to rejoin us here, but we got this under control before they arrived. I'd say do it. The ground fight with your cousin's group needs to wrap up. I'll send Gabe with his squadron."

<hr>

"Commander Gabe, they pulled you out of the skies?" asked Dante.

Gabe answered while motioning his troops to advance. "Yes, we cleared them out on that front. Let's do the same here."

"Be careful. We've got friends in Black Dragon uniform." Dante signaled to his side.

"I've been instructed along with every member of my team. If they have a sunspear, do not touch them."

"Speaking of, I need to help my friend." With sunspear blazing, he pushed his way back to Angelina.

"We both will."

"Gabe's group is here," said Dante to Angelina.

"They're an encouraging sight. What about Seth and my comrade? Did Commander Ryan reach them?"

"Haven't heard."

"Yes, he got to them, and it's going well enough there now for Lana to direct me to assist you," said Gabe.

"That's a relief. Later we make a proper introduction, Commander Gabe." Her sunspear found its mark, and the Black Dragon soldier fell at her feet as her sunspear continued its motion for the next advancing fighter.

"I'd like that, and you've lost none of your edge since the last time." He quickly sunk his blade into an enemy soldier.

She laughed. "That would be impossible. It's one of those skill sets you never lose."

~ele~

An exhausted Ryan, Seth, Alena, Dante, Angelina, and Gabe stood apart from the squadrons as the final Black Dragon soldier lay lifeless.

"Tell us what you need. Caleb is on the call too," said Lana.

"Transport ships. The soldiers that came through this should leave the planet, but they must be briefed due to the two spear-bearers involvement with today's events," said Seth.

"We'll work on the account of you and Dante's near execution."

"Our losses today were substantial." Seth sighed. "I feel the weight of it. I did not see the trap until too late."

Dante patted his shoulder. "Neither one of us did. The result would have been the same if reversed."

Ryan said, "So transports for those we lost too. Fresh personnel to help with the effort if possible."

"I agree the men there have done enough," said Caleb.

"What about any for medical?" asked Lana.

Seth and Alena exchanged a glance. Alena said, "The Black Dragon does mostly clean kills, and today they were especially diligent even with the chaotic scene. However, our soldiers are hunting for survivors now."

"Any found would not have much time left. I advise searching further where my squadron got ambushed," said Seth.

"Transports are on the way for all of it."

"We'll leave the details to the squadron leaders while we escort the two spear-bearers back to their ship. They're anxious to disappear again," said Ryan.

"Where are you two parked?" asked Dante as the group walked along.

"I'm not sure," said Angelina.

"What do you mean?" chuckled Dante.

"I know where we were, but it probably moved once the fighting began. Our assistant will bring it around."

"I don't know that he would appreciate being demoted to your mere assistant."

"I've done worse to him. Trust me. Those Elders are made of thick skin." She laughed and heard a chuckle emerge from Seth. "Now that we're a sufficient distance from the masses, my wonderful teacher, do you mind bringing the ship to us?"

"It's the least I can do for my favorite two students," said Alika.

"We're your only two, last I checked."

"And you both continue to impress. Occasionally enough even for an Elder." Alika chuckled. "It is above you and landing now."

She laughed. "I should take compliments anyway I can get them from you."

Gabe's eyes swept over the inside of the spear-bearers' ship. "Incredible. However, I don't know that I expected less."

"Mind if we get out of these?" asked Ryan as he indicated towards his helmet.

"Go ahead. I'm over all of it, but I guarantee you the Black Dragon ones are worse," said Alena.

The others removed their head gear, except for Angelina and Alena.

Alena turned to her and asked, "You're still stuck on that?"

Dante put an arm around Angelina. "We talked about this. Gabe won't say a word."

Realization hit Gabe, and he walked over to her. "I would never do anything to bring harm to you or your comrade. I promise. There's no mistaking how much you both mean to Dante and Ryan. Please believe me."

"I do, Gabe. It's just the more people that have a description of us, the more individuals we place in danger. I'm trying to protect you."

"I will always keep your secret. Although I understand your reasoning, there's another way to see this. If I have that, there could be a time it proves invaluable in helping you two."

"I don't see that being likely." She turned to Dante.

"Come on, for me," said Dante.

"One day I must learn to say no to you," said Angelina before removing her helmet and seeing Alena do likewise. It had scarcely left her head when the scarf holding her hair released to bring her tresses cascading down. She glimpsed the mischievous grin on Dante's face as his hand slipped back down to her waist. "Dante has gotten quite talented with that, almost as fast as with his sunspear, Gabe."

"You bring out a side of him ... "

Ryan gasped, "What happened to your shoulder? There's blood everywhere."

Alena said, "I took a hit, but I'm fine."

Angelina rushed over to her. "You did what? Why didn't you say something? We could've ... "

"What? Told the Black Dragon to make a path so I could report to medical? We were surrounded. The only option was to keep swinging. You've been there, and I'm fine."

Ryan pulled her over. "During the battle, that's true. Now though, you don't get to make that call. Seth does."

Seth smiled as he approached. "Would you give in to Ryan on this request?"

Alena nodded. A minute later, she lay stretched out on the ship's moving bed with her top gear stripped. Angelina also removed her armor and gloves to better assist with checking Alena's shoulder. Seth inspected the wound. "It's a deep slice, hence all the blood and will take binding segments to pull it back together.

Another angle and it would have hit your neck. Extremely close indeed, my dear. How you kept going at the level you did with sustaining this shot is beyond me." He shook his head. "I'm continuously amazed at several individuals' pain tolerance on this ship."

"She needs to go to medical, Seth," said Ryan as he stroked the side of her face.

Angelina interjected softly as she touched Ryan's arm, "Ryan, we have our own medical, and no slight meant to Seth." She glanced at him as he nodded his understanding. "The difference is our doctor hasn't been through a whole day of fighting and doesn't have a battlefield of patients waiting for his expertise. I believe she'll be fine until we get her back. Am I right, Seth?"

"Ryan, I understand your concern, but I agree with her."

Alena teased, "Ryan, you said trust Seth. Eating your words, now?"

"You're enjoying it way too much." He took a deep breath and turned to Angelina. "Will you at least give me a courtesy call later?"

"Of course. As soon as she's all patched up. Promise. We'll give you two a minute."

He leaned over. "You should've said something, sweetheart."

"So, you'd be all worried like you are now."

"No, so you could get treated as quickly as possible. I was afraid we wouldn't get to you in time."

"But you did. Come closer, so I can thank you."

He grinned and kissed her, and Alena wound her uninjured arm around his neck. She murmured, "I feel better already."

"Leaving me again," said Dante as he pulled Angelina to him.

"That's what I do. Swoop in, save you, and disappear until you need me again."

"You're crazy if that's all you believe you are to me." He rested his forehead on hers.

"I do know, though I don't get it." She ran her hand through his hair. "But I'll come to rescue you anytime I need to."

"That was insanity what you did out there."

"I wouldn't change a thing I did. I won't lose you."

"No, you won't." He kissed her.

She opened up her eyes, all of her remaining in a happy daze from his kiss. "I should get her to medical now."

He smiled as he reluctantly pulled back. "Of course, sorry I got you distracted."

"No, you're not," She stroked the side of his face. "Once she's seen about, your group will have a chance to regroup from today. Expect to see us. We have intel to share, but she needs to get looked at."

"So, we'll see you later." He brushed his lips with hers one final time.

Dante approached Ryan. "Come on buddy. You've done your part as only you can to help her." A smile emerged on Ryan's face at his comment. "Let's go, so the doctor can do his work. They'll check in with you later. My girl promised."

CHAPTER TWENTY-TWO

Ryan sat on one of the couches, forcing himself to focus on Lana's words. The causality count proved ugly as feared, more alarming considering the absence of the disc objects by Black Dragon. He had realized the extent of the death toll when he and the others stayed to assist with the terrible task of loading the dead and locating the too few survivors. The preliminary list of soldiers already confirmed lost in this battle stared back at him, and a wave of profound sadness passed through him. How many more friends would they have to sacrifice to win this war? He tried not to think about the answer as his eyes took in the names again, and his mind drifted to the almost causalities of the day. Several minutes later his data pad flashed, and he spotted Dante's eyes drawn to his own. The two excused themselves to take the call.

"Alena is doing fine, resting now," said Angelina as the screen showed her plopped in a chair, tousling a towel through freshly showered hair.

"She's asleep?" asked Ryan, unable to hide his disappointment.

"Nope, she's right here," The view expanded, and a smiling Alena appeared, reclined in bed.

"How are you feeling, sweetheart?" asked Ryan.

She stretched her arm. "Better than ever. Bring on those Black Dragon."

"Let's not. Give it a rest, would you?" He shook his head, even as he smiled.

"My physician does great work."

"But I'm sure he hasn't cleared you."

Alika appeared. "She'll take it easy tonight, but she'll be back to her normal quickness by tomorrow. If she had to now, she could manage well. I'm relieved to see you two safe. I worried about that today, especially you, Dante."

"My angel saved me again."

"I like you in one piece. You're nicely put together." Angelina laughed as she tossed the towel aside and ran her fingers through her hair.

He watched her, entranced by the motion of the lovely strands sliding through her hand and finding himself unable to resist tracing the natural curves of her beautiful form as she lounged casually in the chair. "I'm admiring the view from here too."

"Figures." She winked.

"You mentioned the real deal."

"Yeah, I heard that too," chimed in Ryan.

"You two just saw us," teased Alena.

"No getting to count that one," said Ryan.

"Tomorrow. It'll give Alena the night to rest. Happy, you two?"

"Happier if you both were here now, but we'll take it." Dante grinned.

⁓ ⟋⟋⟍ ⁓

"Those guys are something," Angelina lay in her bed and smiled at Alena after their chat with the two men. "If you need something, holler and I'll wake up."

Alena yawned and pulled the covers up. "I will, but Alika is staying in here for the night too, in case. Everybody is overreacting. We should have a sunspear duel now to prove it."

"You'd win. I'm beat. Goodnight."

"I'd beat you anyway, and goodnight."

"She's fine, Alika."

"Seems so. Goodnight you two."

Dread passed through Angelina as a familiar figure towered beside her. She opened her eyes to discover her childlike hands.

"Not tonight!" her mind screamed in defiance, but it proved futile. She stared ahead to find her memory skipped the corridor walk and deposited her already in session with her father and the Dark Lord. This time they weren't alone, and the visit had moved to a large open room which included a rectangular meeting table, chairs, and a rolling cart with a black cloth draped over the top. Angelina noticed another man with a young boy a few years older than her standing beside them. Both she had seen previously, along with other pairs on her visits, but she and her mother had yet to confirm the identities of most she encountered. The dyad was probably equally ignorant of her and her father. Before them all sat Saber, a man who realized his answers proved steadily more displeasing to the Dark Lord.

"I gave you a job and sufficient time and resources to complete it," said the Dark Lord.

"You did, but I didn't expect the interference from ... "

"Your poor planning is not my problem. It's called a continuity plan, one you failed to have."

"I can make it work now, but I just need another day."

"Which you do not have. No, I concluded you lack the proper motivation, and I have ideas to remedy the issue." He slowly uncovered half of the rolling cart and picked up a long rod with a forked end. "Are you familiar with this item's use, Saber?"

The man nodded as his face paled and sweat beaded on his forehead.

"I could do this myself," the Dark Lord turned so his eyes settled on her, "but it would be valuable to allow someone else to do it. Take it, and show him what it means to fail the Black Dragon."

She stared at the item that would send the man to his knees, howling in pain. A part of her said to obey the order. After all, she reasoned, how many people had he hurt and even killed with whatever he carried out for the Dark Lord? If he survived, he would continue the same. If it killed him, she'd be eliminating one of the Black Dragon's agents. Deep down, she saw no possibility he would be allowed to live. No one would blame her for doing what the Dark Lord commanded. Yet she couldn't make her hand take the instrument, to become this individual's torturer. The child in her revolted against this further attempt to twist her into serving this monster. Memories of the last time she recalled the forked object used flooded her, and she forced it back. Black Beauty had been chosen to deliver that demonstration for them, and the man's agonizing death still haunted her sleep. So, she stared straight ahead and shook her head.

"His failure cannot go unpunished. Now take it, and reprimand him," ordered the Dark Lord.

"Perhaps my daughter should feel its effects, and she'll be inclined to do as told," said Draco.

"An interesting suggestion. Is your father correct?" He leaned into her face, still holding out the item. "A mere child would not bear it well for even a moment."

Yet her hand refused to grasp the object. She could not make herself one of them.

"I'll do it," said the boy to her side. She turned, knowing why he did it. However, when she stared into his eyes, horror consumed her as she assumed wrong. His eyes shone bright, eager to dole out the punishment for Saber. His next words chilled her. "I want to do it. Please let me."

The Dark Lord chuckled. "This one is coming along splendidly, and I wish to encourage his enthusiasm." He handed him the rod and directed him. "Remember placement ensures he recalls this lesson to the fullest. Proceed."

At once the man's screams filled the room, as the device delivered a powerful surge of electricity, mixed with the forked heated tips that burned into his flesh. The boy grinned as he gleefully found the exact points on the man to lengthen his agony. His attention to the Dark Lord's instructions made Angelina sick as she stood there, unable to stop the horrific scene from commencing. Finally, the Dark Lord reached over and placed his hand on the rod. "Well done. The message is sent."

He addressed Saber, "Get up. Your bindings will come off soon enough. There's the door, and outside is your ship. Head towards it. Now."

His breaths still coming in gasps, Saber managed to pull himself halfway up, stumbling from balancing his weight with his hands still bound with the metal cuffs and the recent torture. He half crawled across the room and through the door.

"Free him, girl." The Dark Lord handed her a device. "Push the button. It's the least you can do. The boy did the rest."

Angelina looked at the remote. It had to be for the bindings, but why not simply take them off here? It must be to watch the man struggle for longer. Nothing else made sense.

"Push it to release him, now. I will not repeat myself." He pointed the rod within an inch of her skin.

She pressed it, and instantly an explosion followed. The device dropped from her hands as she knelt on the ground, and the bloody remains of the man covered the ground outside.

"Freedom comes in unique forms at Black Dragon. That's one. He made a deal and didn't deliver. He knew the terms when he entered it, and he believed I overlooked it. I don't ever. Call it Black Dragon insurance." He grinned as he leaned down before her. "You did well after all today for us and will serve me yet, I promise."

Angelina screamed and bolted straight up in bed. Her eyes met Alika's, who sat at her bedside and grasped her shoulders. "Child, you're safe. Are you all right?"

She nodded, her breath still coming in gasps.

Alena sat on the other side of her. "What happened?"

"You should be resting."

"Not until I find out why you screamed like someone tried to kill you."

"A nightmare. The past."

"Which part woke you up this time?"

"Father, with one of those Dark Lord visits."

"Which one?"

"I'm fine. It's morning already ... "

Alika cut her off to repeat Alena's question, "Which one, child?"

"Where he tricked me into blowing up the agent." She whispered, "Black Dragon insurance."

"I'm sorry. Certainly, one of the uglier encounters you endured."

"But still not in the group with the worst," She glanced at the display. "There's only a couple of hours before we get up anyway. There's information I can look through." She began getting out of bed.

Alena shook her head. "Lay back down, and get more rest. Think of something else, better yet someone, like a nicely put-together guy as you phrased it earlier."

Angelina laid back and sighed. "He is and has a way of making me forget everything else."

"We could call him up."

"No way I'm waking up Dante. I've gotten up enough people for one night."

"He wouldn't mind."

"I would, and he'd be worried until we arrived. Okay, I'll try to sleep again."

"Think of him, and don't tell me he hasn't given you plenty of fantastic images to work with."

Angelina pulled the covers up, and a giggle escaped her. "Go back to your bed, Alena." She took a deep breath and closed her eyes. Her thoughts wandered to him, not the Dante who needed rescuing or the heartbroken Dante. Instead, she focused on the Dante who gazed at her with those intense brown eyes as he drew her to him for one of those countless kisses that made her melt up against him in breathless wonder, and she surrendered to a blissful sleep. Then the warmth of his lips left her, along with his solid frame and his arms that had wrapped around her. A coldness poured through her as she opened her eyes to find herself back in the memory she woke from, and yet different. She was no longer the child, as she peered down at her bound hands in front of her. Her father and the Dark Lord stood by her side, rather than towering over her. The boy and his father were replaced by two Black Dragon soldiers, dressed in full attire. *The Dark Lord's training worked,* she realized. The chair with Saber had moved, silhouetted in a darkened area of the room along with its occupant. The Dark Lord pulled the rod instrument out as before and grinned at her. "I would offer it to you, but I know there's no point." He motioned behind the chair, and a familiar cloaked woman slinked from the shadows. "Black Beauty, if you'll do the honors."

Without hesitation, she took the rod object and turned to the figure seated. With the wave of her hand, the space illuminated.

An unmistakable voice emerged, "Angelina."

Angelina rushed forward in horror, only to be firmly restrained by the two soldiers. "Dante, how did they ... "

The Dark Lord ignored her. "Black Beauty, demonstrate what happens to an enemy of Black Dragon."

Angelina screamed, "No! Let him go! Take me instead! Just don't do this!" Her frantic cries fell on deaf ears, as Black Beauty brought the rod to bear on Dante.

"Child, wake up!" Alika pleaded, and his hands gripped her shoulders as she bolted up in bed still screaming. He stared into her crazed eyes and felt her frame tremble as a sob erupted from her.

Alena sat on the other side of Angelina's bedside and wrapped an arm around her back. "You're safe. What in the galaxy? Let who go?"

Angelina shook her head. "Get up. That's what I have to do."

"No, tell us what left you like this."

"Same as before, but not. Black Beauty had it. I couldn't stop it for..." Another sob emerged, and she whispered, "Dante." She pulled herself from their grasp and stumbled out of bed. "Shower. Clear my head."

Alena murmured as Angelina shut the bathroom door behind her. "I wish I hadn't persuaded her now."

"It's not your fault. If only I possessed the wisdom to break this hold remaining on her spirit, that gives her no peace."

The display by the bed sounded, startling both from their thoughts. Alena disengaged it. "According to this, she slept for most of the time, but it never tells the true story."

"The sooner she sees Dante again, the better after this latest episode. Let's get ready too."

"Any word this morning from your two?" asked Caleb as he munched on a late breakfast with the group.

"Nope, just what we relayed last night," said Dante.

"Alena looked good though." Ryan caught the smirk on Caleb's face. "I meant her arm because she had me there from her first entrance into this hall."

Seth chuckled. "Alika is excellent at his work."

"And they give him plenty of occasions to prove it. He'd be happy for them to do less of it," said Lana.

"We all would, Lana. However, some things are beyond even an Elder."

Dante's and Ryan's data pads lit up, and they bounded up to welcome the arrivals.

Caleb laughed. "Alena and Angelina have those two in line." He caught the look from Lana and kissed her. "Which is exactly the way it should be."

⸻ ℓℓ ⸻

"How's your arm?" asked Ryan as he rushed up to Alena on the ship.

"Unbelievably fine. See." She pulled him over for a kiss while wrapping her arms around his neck.

"We should be sure," he whispered.

Dante encircled his arms around Angelina and grinned. "I told you once I got my hands on you, Angelina ... " His lips found hers in a long, fiery kiss that sent her heart racing and the rest of her swooning.

She opened her eyes when she felt only the brush of his lips on hers. "That's what I get for my Black Dragon performance."

"A good beginning. Later, when I get time with you in my quarters ... " he whispered in her ear.

"You don't know how I needed that today." She stroked the side of his face as she gazed into his eyes. "You're really okay, Dante."

"Of course, I am. You saved me, remember?"

"This time I did."

Dante stared back at her and read the story in her eyes. The specifics were unnecessary to guess the part that mattered. "You did need that. What happened since we talked last night?"

"Nothing. Alena's arm is fine, and we're here like we said."

"Your performances won't fool me."

Ryan and Alena exchanged a glance and Ryan said, "Dante, forty-five."

Dante didn't turn but motioned with his hand to acknowledge he agreed as Ryan and Alena exited the ship. "It's just the two of us now, and I won't give up."

"Though you should." she sighed and remained silent for several more seconds. "A past event revisited my sleep. A Black Dragon interrogation I witnessed with one of their agents who didn't deliver on his deal. I made the mistake of trying to return to bed. The same scenario reappeared mostly except we were bound, Black Beauty took on the role of the interrogator, and you were the one to be tortured." A tear slid down her face.

"You watched me be ... "

She whispered, "About to be. I woke just as she started to."

"My Angelina." He snuggled her against his chest and kissed her hair while stroking her back. "I'm so sorry. There's nothing to fear though. I'm here with you, not a prisoner of Black Dragon." He pulled back slightly to look at her. "I'm fine with my nicely put-together self." He grinned when a real smile surfaced on her face, then reached down, and swooped her up into his arms.

She laughed. "What are you doing?"

"Proving to you how fine I am." He gently deposited her on the couch and sat beside her, wrapping his arms back around her. "Time to get those images vanished from your mind, my Angelina." He drew her to him and began to kiss her.

He planted soft kisses on her neck as he heard her catching her breath, never growing tired of leaving her in that state. He kissed the side of her face as a contented sigh escaped her lips, and she cuddled up next to him. Smiling down at her, he asked, "How are you feeling about my nicely put-together self now?"

"Much better. Your powers of persuasion again prove breathtaking."

"They're still lacking. I want you to be able to fall into my arms the moment you need to, not have to wait hours after you've already endured something like that. If only I could convince you."

"Your persuasion lacks for nothing. You know it's not that. Dante, you topple all my defenses."

"All of them, huh?"

"Yes, all of them." The next second the warmth of his lips found hers again. Only the two of them existed and everything else, all the nightmares and ghosts from the past disappeared, as she let his care flow through her.

"There they are," said Ryan as Angelina and Dante walked into the fortress, hand in hand.

"We said forty-five minutes, and I used every second of it well," Dante grinned and kissed Angelina on the cheek.

"I'd say so." Ryan turned to a smiling Angelina and hugged her. "You doing okay?"

"Yes, Dante always knows what I need." She took Ryan's expression of concern gratefully, knowing Alena disclosed to him about her rough start this morning.

"Glad to see it was nothing to worry about, Alena." Dante hugged her.

"I told everybody, but you know ... "

He chuckled. "I heard about your sunspear challenge. Next time we'll take your word for it, and thanks again for having Seth's back for me."

"You had your troubles at the moment."

"Ready to hear what we've been up to?" asked Angelina.

Lana smiled. "We're not ever, but let's get settled anyway, and you can fill us in."

"You two have already been back to Black Dragon," said Dante as he studied the screen Angelina displayed from her data pad before them.

"We had to. Time is our enemy now almost as much as the Black Dragon. The device must be located."

"You can't be rushing in though." He squeezed her waist with the arm he had wrapped around it.

Alena said, "We're not, so no need for any of you to worry. Their security does seem to rely on the mark, and it's holding steady. The rest is unchanged as far as creating a profile and fake clearances. We have the expert in that department."

Angelina sighed, "And I wish it opened the door we hoped. We uncovered a stop-off or repair facility and supply warehouse as we told you before. We stumbled on something else this last trip, but still not it. Despite our visit being cut short to aid you, we gathered that much."

Lana said, "Your help saved the day. Although I admit I expected a warning of the attack, especially now that we know you were at Black Dragon. I'm sorry, I didn't mean ... "

Angelina waved her hand. "No offense taken. I'd wonder the same. The truth is we didn't know about it until it was already in progress. Our undercover duties at that time didn't give any reason to be made aware of the battle occurring. Once we learned of it, we mysteriously received updated orders to report for our new assignments, but we were delayed. We impressed the squadron leader we worked with, and he hesitated to let us rush off. By the time we did, things had unraveled too far. All of our efforts concentrated on having a hand on Seth and finding the means to get to Dante. We weren't nearly as confident of succeeding as what we portrayed."

Caleb nodded. "You fooled us. Although I'm curious what wonders you two performed to impress Black Dragon."

"Human resources," said Angelina.

Laughter filled the room, except for Alena and Angelina, who just smiled.

Caleb shook his head, still laughing, "All right, I'll give you that one. So, what did you two really do?"

"We followed it with training," said Alena.

Ryan grinned. "They're serious. Did you go over the code of conduct for being a proper Black Dragon soldier?"

Alena chuckled. "Thinking back on it, I'd say we did since for Black Dragon it would include the importance of following commands and the consequences if you don't."

"We delivered that message effectively to these trainees. That's how we got into the good graces of the squadron leader," said Angelina.

Alena motioned to the holographic screen above them. "Showtime."

Dante watched with the others as the two received orders from the Black Dragon leader to assign the recruits. Most accepted their designated role with no discussion. Then first Angelina showed the importance of compliance as a Black Dragon soldier, and after Alena's even more terrifying demonstration, any dissent ended. Their proclamation of the recruits' loyalty and service only to Black Dragon chilled Dante to the bone. Angelina stopped the video and glanced at Alena, knowing the effect the segment had on their friends.

"That's hard to hear, but we have to be all Black Dragon when we're there," said Alena.

"Same goes if you're the shipping dealer in a bar or the hired Freedom Fighter helping negotiate a deal with the scum of the galaxy, you have to be all in or else they see through it. The details of the script are a little different, but the process remains consistent. Staying in the role, but somehow remembering who you are underneath it when it's over." Angelina paused. "Everyone ready to continue?"

Dante squeezed her hand. "Yeah, we're with you. Keep going."

"This is their version of training, huh?" asked Caleb.

Alena smiled. "Yes. If they had our trainers, no one would survive in this group."

Seth chuckled. "I agree. This is painful to watch. Mostly."

Lana said, "Because someone with a bit of practice can still find a target if we're overwhelmed with sheer numbers. How much instruction did you provide?"

Angelina said, "None of any account, but enough to appear legit to our superior as we shared your concern. However, Black Dragon training is a punishing process and not in the sense we complain about with Seth and Alika, or Freedom Fighter troops with their commanders. Our enemy's version is a beatdown, one purely for the pleasure of the trainer. It's ordinarily a method I would never endorse. Although in this case, it proved ideal."

"Several of the recruits didn't make it through the initial drills, but we officially attributed it to their uselessness with the blade. However, our testing of them turned harsher when the squadron leader became distracted with another recruit," said Alena.

Ryan nodded. "Because not all of them were bad with a weapon from what I saw."

"That's the rub, and we couldn't send them all to other areas. We would have been found out in the first room," said Angelina.

"They all had direct combat experience in that group?" asked Caleb.

"They accounted for one segment within the fighters. Also related fields like security and the shipping dealer sorts, like Angelina," said Alena.

"They seem like they could fit better somewhere else." Ryan glanced over at Angelina.

Angelina chuckled. "Some we did, but I'm part of a rough circle. Shipping dealers settle many agreements with a blade or blaster if it doesn't go to their liking. Living long enough to negotiate the next shipment is a victory."

Dante looked at her with renewed worry. "And this is your cover. Not reassuring."

"Lucky for you this one hasn't failed in her role and doesn't ever intend to. After all, who would come to your rescue?"

"That's not ... " He didn't get the rest out before she nudged him towards her and kissed him.

"I have you, Dante, and I'm not letting go. That's the reason my shipping alibi will hold."

Lana smiled. "This is a good stopping place until after lunch."

The Black Dragon Premier sat in the command chair, his forehead creased in concentration, as he finished listening to the update from the soldier on the viewscreen. "Sunspears were spotted at this last battle? You're certain?"

"Yes, sir."

"It's the planet we sent the largest squadron?"

"Correct, sir."

"Every report I received indicated we had their ground troops, including the Elder Seth and spear-bearer Dante captured. One of those sunspears must be Dante. Perhaps his cousin and her husband joined the squadron considering the desperate situation with Dante and Elder Seth. Another possibility remains." He paused. "You're certain there's no clue on how they turned the tide and Dante and the Elder Seth escaped?"

"No, sir. Their forces must have broken loose somehow. Then we must assume reinforcements arrived later to bolster their troops, since we outnumbered them according to every report we received."

"Peculiar how they slide out of the net wrapped around them. Perhaps the link is … " he hesitated. "We'll speak again in a few minutes." He ran his hand over the mute on the console as his thoughts found a voice. "Are you the link, Dante? Because I don't believe your cousin and Caleb came to your aid. It was your friends, the spear-bearers, wasn't it? After all, they did rescue your mother. But why the interest in you and your family, with keeping you safe? Yet Seth entered the equation this time too, but he's an Elder. It makes sense they'd have a soft spot for an Elder. Yet what made them break their rule of noninterference the other time?" Running his hand over the console again, the viewscreen scrolled with data from past Black Dragon reports until he stopped on one. "There it is." He carefully read through it a couple of times. "Perhaps not. In fact, their sunspears weren't spotted anywhere near you that day, Dante, and you were in considerable trouble with twelve tanks bearing down on you. They assisted everyone but your squadron. Why they even went to the colony army and then the pathetic colonists the Dark Lord used as human shields. It should've worked too. An impossible situation with no acceptable solution, at least in the eyes of a Freedom Fighter, and outnumbered on every front. Is that what you two spear-bearers saw? And you could be the difference? Another familiar scene comes to mind." He ran his hand again over the console and unmuted the communication system. "I have another question for you."

"Yes, sir."

"Is there any update on how Lana broke free from our trap by the shipping dealer?"

"We still presume her husband's group returned in time to prevent her from being taken."

"Because all those working with our hired help were eliminated, so there's nothing to confirm that."

"Correct, sir. It fits since the colonists reported seeing the Freedom Fighters return to the residence in a frantic state and then leaving with an unconscious woman, which had to be Lana. Later they departed with bound individuals."

"Yet our last transmission indicated a successful distraction to Caleb's group, with Lana disabled and on schedule for delivery. Then no communication and it all fell apart. Were there any reports of spearbearers? Never mind." He reasoned it pointless. There were too many people there that day who did utilize a sunspear, including Dante, Lana, and Caleb, to confirm his suspicions of the two spear-bearers' extra presence. Either way, he received his answer.

"Sir, what are your orders?"

"I am adding a directive to order Hunt that is already in place. Tell those on it we still want any helping the enemy as stated in the notice, but to include individuals known only as the two spear-bearers that are aiding the group as well. If they can deliver them to us or intel that does so, the same deal goes."

"What description do I include?"

"We don't possess one, a problematic detail in locating them. They have been in full gear each time. All we know is they bear sunspears and aid the Freedom Fighters in their direst predicaments. Relay the additional information immediately."

"Consider it done, sir."

He closed the viewscreen and stared out at the expanse. "Even spear-bearers can't hide forever among the stars."

—ele—

"Time to start again," said Dante as he walked towards the couch after lunch but stopped midway and wrapped his arms around Angelina.

She smiled up at him as her arms encircled his neck. "This won't help us accomplish what your cousin has in mind."

Reaching for her was the most natural thing in the galaxy now. "Completely disagree. I'm more productive anytime I can squeeze in a kiss from you before we begin work."

"Is that so?" Any further words were forgotten as he leaned in and demonstrated.

He took his time enjoying the kiss with her, but he sensed the shift. She responded to his embraces in several ways, from being left breathless, to melting up against him in contentment, or with a passionate fire he adored. Never though had he felt this reaction, and he didn't like it. Her body stiffened, and she was pushing him away. He pulled back but still held her. Staring into her eyes, he was confused by what they reflected. Her eyes looked at him but without seeing him as she murmured, "Dante, I ... Chris ... " She trembled and began sinking to the ground, but he grabbed her up to prevent her from doing so.

"Angelina, what's happening? Talk to me. Who's Chris?"

The others drew close to the two, alarmed at whatever new crisis was starting. Alena studied Angelina's face at hearing the name Chris.

"I'm Chris, Dante." She answered as if unsure of her words. " At least when I'm with our main source, Christopher. I saw that he's in trouble." She regained her footing. "We have to go now."

"Of course, we can."

"No, you're staying here. Alena and I are going."

"No way. We can help you. There's no need for you two to do it alone."

"Dante, I don't have time for this. Christopher doesn't. This isn't your fight!"

"How can you still say that after everything we've been through?"

"Because this is part of the shipping world, and you can't be seen in it with me. None of you can." She eased out of his arms and squeezed his hand while turning to Alena. "Now, Alena, or Christopher won't make it."

Alena nodded as she quickly put on her hooded cloak. "I got it."

The two started out the door.

Dante said, "Wait! How are you going to rescue him?"

"Talk to us on the way to the ship," She threw on her hooded cloak too and hurried from the hall with Alena.

Angelina turned to Seth as the group continued to the vessel. "We can't bring him to our place, so be ready. If we get there in time, he'll need all your medical expertise and more."

"You'll have it, and we'll prepare to receive Alika."

"Alika, do you … " asked Angelina.

"I've heard everything. Inform me of what you require."

"Any clue of what he got himself into? What we're walking into?" asked Alena.

"I'm an idiot for not seeing it. Targeting. First Lana. Then Dante and Seth."

"But they don't know he's helping us, or do they? Did he break?"

"No way. He'd die before he breathes a word about us, but if we don't reach him in time … "

"We'll find a way. but why target him?"

"They didn't intentionally. From what I briefly saw they're attempting to recruit another taker for the botched job on Lana. The other piece is intel fishing, and shipping dealers are where you go. That's where he ran into trouble. The word is two spear-bearers are aiding the Freedom Fighters.."

"But they have nothing to locate us yet."

"And you're going straight to them!" exclaimed Ryan.

"This is insanity! You can't go!" echoed Dante.

"We have to!" Angelina said as they arrived at the ship.

"What are you going to do?" He grabbed her arm.

"They want the two spear-bearers? Then they're getting them, and we'll make them pay for that wish." Her eyes burned with fury as she pulled herself from Dante's grasp, but he tried to follow her into the ship.

Lana stepped in front of him and turned to her. "I'll handle my cousin. Just come back to him." Angelina nodded and ran into the ship.

Alena squeezed Ryan's arm and disappeared inside with Angelina.

Ryan started forward, but Caleb put a hand on his shoulder and shook his head.

Dante watched the door close, his fists clenched to his side, and he sensed Seth's hand on his back with the unspoken message to calm himself. He turned to Lana, his voice trembling, "How could you let her leave?"

Lana placed a hand on her cousin's arm. "I didn't let her go. No matter what any of us said, there's no stopping her. Dante, you know that better than any of us."

Alika's voice came through their data pads, "I'm putting the feed through so you can hear what's happening."

"Coming through fine, Alika. Thanks, that helps." Caleb motioned the group back to the fortress room as Dante took one last look at the departing ship.

<hr>

"We need to get changed," said Angelina.

"Into?"

"Full dress. Nothing to identify us, even gender. No loyalties either."

"Got it."

Angelina continued as she undressed and redressed in the proper attire, "Alika?"

"We are headed where you wished." A name flashed on the viewscreen.

"That's it."

"Clearances are done for a standard shipping haul."

"Perfect."

"A plan?"

"Almost done. They got him outside the bar to question him. I glimpsed an alley with a building next to it, and we use those to our advantage." She typed the name of a place into the cockpit console and studied the monitor. "Give me a visual on the area surrounding that bar. That's not the building and alley, but it must be close. They didn't waste time before they started in on him. There. Slow it down. That's the one. Those two buildings and the alley between them."

"I'm sending it to your data pads."

"They didn't care. It can't be five minutes from that pub," said Alena.

"We draw as many away from him as possible. It's bad. He won't be able to manage on his own."

"How are we getting him out then?"

Angelina disappeared into the cargo hold and pushed up a long rectangular box with slits on the sides and a wheeled metal contraption under it.

"We simply collect our cargo," said Alena.

"And hope this doesn't become his coffin."

"It won't. Once we lure them away from Christopher, we get him to safety. Although it could work better if we split up."

Angelina nodded and returned to the viewscreen. "One up there," she pointed to the rooftop of the building, "and the other one there." She indicated the alley.

"It's a solid plan to me, but do you think enough go to the rooftop?"

"They will because the payoff for two spear-bearers is too sweet to resist." Angelina continued, "Alika, what do you say? Ready to be your student's voice?"

"I know my students well enough. It will be no problem."

"Who do you think should be where?" asked Alena.

"Alika, turn the feed off to the others for a minute." Angelina messaged Alika and waited a few seconds to be sure before turning back to Alena. "You're on the rooftop, and I'm on the ground. You can get back down undetected because you have ways I don't."

Alena stared back at her as the understanding passed between them. "True, and I've already got something in mind."

Angelina signaled Alika to resume the share with the others. "I'll get Christopher to our ship, so you can get him to Seth. Then I'll retrieve his vessel."

Angelina and Alena put their helmets on and responded to Alika's request to confirm the voice changers.

"We're set?" asked Alena as Alika remotely maneuvered the ship to the planet.

"I'd say so," said Angelina as she glanced at the rolling cargo box and her hand fingered her concealed sunspear. "We must reach him in time. I won't have it happen again, Alena."

"Stop that. We've been over this."

"And he can't die because of me. Time to make them pay for today."

Dante finished listening to the exchange, but then it went quiet. "What's going on? There's nothing else?"

"They're probably getting in position, so they cut the chatter," said Caleb.

"Correct, so don't be alarmed. However, they need my assistance to pull off part of their plan, so I must focus on them," said Alika.

CHAPTER TWENTY-THREE

Christopher leaned back in the bar booth and took another sip of his fruit-flavored drink after finishing his delivery for the day. It had been sizable though and afforded him breathing room before the next one. His stomach growled, reminding him of the abbreviated dinner he ate last night and the skipped breakfast this morning to make it on schedule. He looked towards the bar area, but there were no signs of his lunch yet, so he resumed scrolling through his data pad for any new requests. A few possibilities piqued his interest, but he regarded them with the necessary dose of suspicion essential for this business. As he considered delving further, the exchange at the next table caught his attention. He cast a sideways glance and listened while pretending to be preoccupied with his data pad.

"Been an awful lot of trouble for Black Dragon. There's a nice payoff for them. Sure, you're not interested?" A big hulk of a man towered over the man in the booth.

"No way. And that group has always been a thorn in Black Dragon's side."

"Yeah, but everyone is beatable."

"I'm certain you can round up those someones to help you, but I'm not one of them."

"Or maybe you don't want us to find them."

"Shoot, everybody knows where to catch them. Black Dragon has that part, but there's a reason they're still kicking. I don't trust my luck in a fight with any of them."

"Or is it about where your loyalty lies?"

"It's right here." The man tapped his chest. "So, I'm through talking with you. I told you no deal."

The man slammed his fist on the table. "We're done when I say we are!"

Christopher looked up as a server placed his food in front of him and glanced nervously at the exchange next to him. "Here's your order. Need another drink?"

"Yes, go ahead and bring me more." Christopher used the opportunity to look closer at the men involved in the confrontation. The big hulk proved unfamiliar on either side of his dealings, so he wondered if it could be one of the new Black Dragon recruits. If so, a blaster would be worthless against him. He remembered Chris telling him of her near-deadly encounter with the one. That girl claimed more close calls than he had ever seen. With a sinking feeling, he realized he did know the man being interrogated by the ruffians. The man played his part well so far, pretending to have no loyalties. Christopher knew better having worked with the shipping dealer on several occasions. Maybe the other man would give up soon, but it didn't seem a possibility.

The man in the booth shook his head. "I'm not risking my skin to catch them, so I don't care how great the payoff is."

"You heard about the other two?"

"What other two?"

"That have been causing havoc as well? You know them?"

"There's a whole mess of them that cause trouble for Black Dragon. What two are you talking about now?"

"Intel just says they use sunspears."

"That's it? Can't say I keep that kind of company. I stick to a blaster as my weapon of choice."

"You don't know where to find them?"

"I told you no. I don't know any sunspear people." The man let out an exasperated sigh.

The hulk of a man pulled the other man up by his shirt. "I don't believe you."

I'm going to regret this, thought Christopher, but he couldn't stand it any longer. He got up and walked to the booth, fingering his blaster. "I'm trying to enjoy lunch. Just finished a delivery and haven't eaten a decent meal with making sure it got done. Why don't you ease up on the man?"

"Why should I?" He narrowed his eyes as he loosened his grip on the man and turned his attention to Christopher.

"Because he's made it clear he isn't interested in working with you."

"I don't take no."

"Then you're in the wrong business. If someone doesn't want your deal, you walk away and move on to the next one. I'd advise you to do that. Now."

The man released the other man and walked up to Christopher. "You're right, and so I've got a deal too good for you to pass up."

"I'll decline, thanks."

"You haven't heard it yet."

"I have because you only have one bargain to offer. My answer is the same as his. Move on."

"You work with Freedom Fighters?"

"I work for me, to benefit me. I'm a shipping dealer. Whoever pays, I'll ship. However, I've got a healthy sense of self-preservation too. So, I'm particular with the deals I take, which is why yours is no."

"The payoff is beyond a dealer's dream."

"Doesn't matter if you're dead."

"What about sunspear-bearers?"

"What about them?"

"You know about them?"

"The basics like the rest of the galaxy." He shrugged. "They fight with a sunspear. An Elder teaches them. Everybody knows Caleb, Lana, and Dante uses one, which is why nobody wants your deal. They're crazy good with those things in a battle. I'm sticking to shipping."

"There are two more, and the word is they're as dangerous."

"News to me. But if they're like that, more reason to say no to your deal. You're on your own for sure. Sounds like the Black Dragon does have their hands full."

"Had any dealings with them?"

"Me? I wouldn't have any reason to. What in the galaxy would spear-bearers need with a shipping dealer?" He laughed.

"Why don't you tell me?"

"I wouldn't know. Sorry I can't help you." He started to return to his seat, only to come face to face with four more men, blocking his path. He turned back to the hulk of a man. "These friends of yours?"

"They are, and I got more outside. Start walking now because we're finishing this discussion there."

The man in the booth got back up and advanced towards them. "Wait a minute. You can't come in here and ... "

The next instant, the hulk slammed his fist into the man's face, and he dropped to the floor.

Christopher winced as he imagined the pain when his fellow shipping dealer later awakened. He started to say something, but the blaster lodged in his back and the four men changed his mind. *Yeah, I'm regretting this,* he thought while following his escort outside.

⁓ oℓℓ ⁓

Briefly, Christopher thought he had a chance. Five men didn't sound too bad though the one was built like his own army. Once they cleared the bar and approached the alley, he made his move. He shot one of them squarely in the chest with his blaster before it got knocked from his hand. His dagger replaced it and to his surprise, he landed a solid run through with it to cause another man to hit the ground. *Those lessons with the two paid off,* he thought as he struck a defensive pose as the others renewed their advance. The next second though he collapsed onto his knees as pain reverberated through his leg from a blaster.

The hulk of a man sneered, "I told you I had more friends out here." At least six more men came from behind Christopher. "Bad move on your part, shipping dealer. Let's try this again. Tell me about those two spear-bearers."

"Already did. I don't know anything about them."

"I don't believe you, like with the other one." His fist landed a solid hit to Christopher's abdomen, and Christopher doubled over. "Who does know then?"

"I don't know that either."

"Shipping dealers are supposed to be connected. You're terribly uninformed for one, and I'm not buying it." His boot slammed into Christopher's back, eliciting a yell from him as he fell forward from the impact.

"Not my problem."

"Oh, it's very much so. Now tell me how to find them."

"I don't know and even if I thought I did, I'd never help you."

Taking Christopher's face between his hands, he grinned down at him. "Then we'll beat it out of you."

Christopher floated in and out of consciousness as the hulk determined to carry out his threat. The man repeated the same question to him in various ways, but Christopher vowed not to tell him though it meant his death. Honestly, he couldn't have told them anything now. The assault on him had reached a breaking point, but not in the way the man intended. His mind couldn't string together a complete thought. Someone would wander upon his dead body in this alley. The notion passed through him with little emotion now. As he floated back into awareness, he heard another voice. This one didn't sound like any of his torturers and came from far above him. He attempted to hold on, but darkness folded in on him again.

CHAPTER TWENTY-FOUR

Alena arrived on the rooftop and bent down to secure a small disk device. She stood back up and advanced a few steps on the rooftop, spying the men surrounding a motionless man on the ground. Her heart sank, but she pushed back her fear for Christopher and screamed at them, "The word is you're eager to meet the two spear-bearers. We're here."

They stared up at her, and the hulk of a man hollered back, "Finally!"

"There are much better ways to do this than how you chose."

"Where's the other one?"

Alena turned around and called behind her, "Hear that? You're just the other one now. Friendly isn't, he?" She redirected her focus to the hulk. "My comrade is here, but our policy is to watch each other's back. Considering the current situation, we won't be swayed from that. My comrade will speak with you though."

"Then let me talk to him too."

"Very well." She turned. "I gather you heard that."

"Unfortunately, I did," said a different male voice from behind Alena. "Why are you so intent on meeting us?"

"Yes, we're both wondering since you took such great lengths to get our attention."

"You two are difficult to track."

"That's our preference. From where I'm standing it's the best way to be if this is how you begin all your meetings." She motioned towards Christopher.

"Your friend here wouldn't arrange to contact you."

Alena's shadow piped up, "He's no friend but one of many shipping dealers that I imagine simply set out to make his deliveries for the day."

"Until you pummeled him senseless for no reason. I'm sure he told you, but you were too stupid to listen. You can't beat out of him what he didn't know. Now leave him be, and what do you want from us?" Alena put her arms across her chest.

"Your surrender."

"To you?" Alena laughed. "You're an oversized bully with your thugs and nothing more."

"So, stop wasting our time, and what is this really about?"

"You'll surrender to me, and I'll haul you into the Black Dragon."

"One of theirs, huh? An easy guess. We've had dealings with them, and all went badly," said Alena's shadow.

"But they have a history of not getting along with others," said Alena.

"Certainly their galactic signature. Regardless it doesn't excuse your actions today to this shipping dealer. You should've left him alone when you had the chance," said Alena's shadow.

"You're threatening me?"

"No, stating facts. You can't leave a man for dead and think it'll go unpunished," said Alena.

"Come down, or I'll kill him."

Alena's voice boomed this time, "No on both counts. The payoff must be extraordinary for us from Black Dragon. If you want it bad enough, work for it. Let him be, and come get us. See how it turns out for you."

The man clenched his fists to his side but didn't move.

"The reward isn't as sweet as we thought." Alena's shadow laughed. "Crawl back into whatever hole you came from before you settled on this lousy assignment."

The man motioned to two of the men and roared, "You two remain with me. The rest of you drag them down here by any means necessary! Do it now!"

"Can't wait to see you try!" In the same instant, Alena backed up and in one swoop retrieved and stashed the small device from the ground into her gear.

Angelina watched the exchange end from her concealed place behind the other building. She had three to take out including the spokesman, and she wouldn't chance only a blaster shot with him. If he didn't stay down with one, he'd be a handful once he bounced back up. Ten times worse than Trey. With sunspear ready, she crept behind the trio as the hulk's attention remained on the rooftop, and he continued to fume over the spear-bearers' words. Within moments of running the man through, one of his men turned and spotted her motion. Rather than a clean blow, the sunspear caught the hulk on the side. He howled in pain as he faced her, clutching the injury with his hand, "What the ... you're supposed to be inside there!"

"And I counted on you being dead," Angelina fired back.

"Get him!" yelled the hulk.

"I should at least see," she murmured. Pulling her blaster out with her other hand, she aimed for one of the men's chests. He fell straight down with the shot as she put it away again and grasped the sunspear with both hands. "Now if he stays down." Turning her attention to the assailant still advancing, she said, "You're way out of your league. Your dagger is no match for this sunspear." The man shot from his blaster, but she deftly blocked it with her sunspear. "That won't help you either." He managed one additional fire before Angelina sliced the weapon from his hand, and her sunspear ran him through, his body collapsing to the ground. She went to the man she had blasted and ran him through as well, making sure he lay dead. Then she advanced at the hulk. "These men chose their company poorly. You have much blood on your hands, so it's only right yours joins them."

"I won't be going down like them. They were a useless lot. I'll do this myself."

"I know your type. You think because you're ten men in one, you're unbeatable. Yet, you're a bigger fool than all of them put together. You'll bleed out as well as the other two. My sunspear doesn't care."

The man charged at her, livid at her words. She missed his attack as he attempted to slam her to the ground. Her sunspear located another opening, but not the death stroke. *I might have to bleed him out a piece at a time,* she thought. A glance at Christopher's motionless body reminded her of the urgency to finish this fight now. The man grinned, and she understood. She'd be trapped according to his assessment. Her back found the building wall. In a flash, she ducked underneath his arm and escaped to his side, leaving him to stare at the wall. As he turned to meet her threat, she plunged her sunspear clean through his abdomen and forced him to the ground. Looking down at him, she said, "We lied. He is our friend, and you should've left him alone." She plunged the sunspear in a second time, sliding it down the middle of the man as the last breath departed his body. Replacing her sunspear, she retrieved the cargo box and rushed to Christopher's side. Hope flickered in her as she felt a pulse.

"Hey, Christopher. It's Chris." A groan escaped him, and she continued, "Hang on for me. You'll be a part of the cargo, so I can get us back to the ship." She half lifted and dragged him into it and laid him down there as she resumed talking in the same soothing tone, "It's the only way to get you past everyone. You have to stay quiet. Christopher, promise me you'll be okay."

"Promise."

Angelina stroked his hand and released it, as she closed the box and headed for the ship with her precious shipment.

⁓ℓℓ⁓

The men rushed into the building, up the stairs, and around a corridor. One of them said, "What now? I don't see anybody here."

"They have to be. There's no other way down from the rooftop, so keep searching," said another man.

"I'm not as eager to find them anymore," said another man.

"This deal is souring on me too," said another man.

"I said we keep searching. Remember the payoff."

The sound of shuffling feet from the end of the hall drew their attention, and they ran towards it. "Now we've got you!" one of the men exclaimed triumphantly.

A hunched-over woman in a hooded cloak said, "You shouldn't startle an old woman. I don't recall any business today with you gentlemen."

"We mistook you for someone else, but maybe you can help us."

"You run up on me, scaring me half to death, and now I'm to assist you." The woman let out a tired sigh. "What is it?"

"Seen anybody else here?"

"Of course. This operation caters to shipping."

"Where is everyone?"

"In and out with the nature of this work. Mostly out now, because It's around lunchtime. You picked a bad time of day to get help. Anyone in this business could've told you." She shook her head. "I don't know what you fellows are in to not know that."

"Then what are you doing here?"

"Ideal time to do my end of it. I keep things tidy on a few fronts. Going over the shipments, making sure they check out on the records end of it. See to the day-to-day cleaning of the building too." She wagged her finger at them. "You best not have made extra work for me with all your running through today."

"We don't care if we inconvenienced your day."

"I imagine you don't. Clearly, you're only focused on yourself. What do you need, so I can resume my business?"

"You see a couple of people come through here before us?"

"What did they look like?"

"Covered head to toe."

"Like soldiers, full gear right?" She resumed at the men's nods. "Yes, they came storming through here, like your group. I thought something happened in the building, but they didn't bother saying a word. I've learned it's better not to ask, but I've never seen so much carrying on as has gone on today." She took a deep breath and leaned against the door entrance. "Is there anything else?"

"Where did they go, old woman?"

"Such terrible manners and after helping you," she said while pointing a shaky finger down the corridor further in the complex. "That way. Came in together, but when they got there, one went that way, the other went the opposite direction."

"Did they come back down?"

"Not that I saw. They were loud coming through here, so I would've heard them running back down. Must still be waiting for you. Sounds like you have a meeting with them."

"You could say that." One of the men grinned.

"They won't wait on you much longer. You should stop dallying with me, and take care of your business." She moved away from them. "Excuse me so I can do the same."

⁓ ℓℓ ⁓

Christopher stifled a groan as he felt his body transferred from the cargo box to a makeshift moving bed, and he realized he lay in Chris's and Alena's ship.

"You're a bloody mess, Christopher," said Angelina as she stroked his forehead and turned to Alena.

"But we're getting you seen about. This will sting, but it'll help." Alena inserted the tiny needle to begin the IV for him and said to Angelina. "You need to go."

"On my way out now. His pulse is fainter, Alena." Her eyes drifted to a reading on her scanner from Christopher. "Keep your promise to me, Christopher." Readjusting her helmet, she left the ship to Alena's words of caution, "Be careful."

⁓ ℓℓ ⁓

Lana's group sighed in relief as they listened and heard Alika's voice come through, "I'm already on my way."

"We're prepared here to immediately receive our patient," said Seth.

"The hardest part should be over," said Lana, stating the unspoken thought, as she glanced at Caleb.

"I'd feel better if Angelina was on the ship heading back here," said Dante.

Ryan patted his shoulder. "She'll be here soon."

⁓ ℓℓ ⁓

Angelina slowly made her way through the hangar area, which remained relatively light of bustle. Most of the shipping dealers continued keeping the local bars full, either recovering from getting rid of a shipment or making their next deal. A scattered few workaholics labored on, but she quietly maneuvered unnoticed between the ships to reach Christopher's vessel. At least she thought she had. Only the shadow the second before alerted her. She stopped at his ship's entrance, and her hand grazed her blaster as the voice behind her said, "Don't. Hands to your side now, or I'll kill you where you stand."

Dante froze as the words flowed through the audio even with the flurry of activity around him. Seth's and Alika's patient arrived moments ago in medical, and all their attention focused on him. However, Alena's concern shifted from Christopher to pull up a visual on her data pad of Angelina's current situation. "We were almost out. Where did he come from?"

"Where is it? I'll help her. I can leave now."

"No way, Dante. She'll have my head. If anybody goes back, it'll be me. None of you can be seen in that world. It's only one man, and she's resourceful. Give it a minute."

"She thinks we're abandoning her!"

"No, she knows I'm monitoring. I could say something to her, but I don't want to distract her."

"Alena is making a lot of sense. Buddy, keep it together," said Ryan.

"I won't hesitate to go if needed."

Dante took a deep breath as he listened and watched with the others.

⁓ℓℓ⁓

"What do you want?" asked Angelina.

"Do as instructed. We'll talk inside the ship. Get us in now."

"I need a device to open the door, so I have to reach inside my gear."

"I'll allow it, but if you try anything, you won't live another second."

"Understood." She reached to her side for Christopher's data pad and used it to access the ship door.

"Through it now, spear-bearer."

She walked through the entrance with her capturer. "That's who you think I am?"

"I know that's who you are." He shut it behind them. "Put everything on the table now. Data pad. Blaster. Sunspear. Yeah, don't forget the sunspear."

She reluctantly complied.

The man watched as he continued pointing the blaster at her. "The others thought the best strategy was brute force. I figured eventually one or all of you would come back this way if they failed in securing you. I've heard stories. Speaking of that, where's the other one?"

"Already gone."

"Abandoned you high and dry? That surprises me."

"We didn't have a choice. Your friends left one of the shipping dealers for dead with their intel-gathering methods, so we felt obligated to aid him."

"And your buddy chose him over you? Harsh break for you."

"I can take care of myself."

"Not from where I'm standing." He motioned towards her weapons on the table.

"Fair enough."

"No one could get a description of you two. Let's have a look."

"No."

He adjusted his aim with his blaster. "I insist. Lose the helmet before I blow it off your head."

"Fine, because I do prefer to keep my head." She removed her helmet.

His eyes widened, and he lowered his weapon slightly. "You're a she, but you sounded like a man. Voice changers. My compliments. You were totally covered and with the gear, nobody would know the difference. No wonder no one caught up to you two. We've been looking in all the wrong places." He grinned. "Are you a blond, brunette, or redhead?"

"Use your imagination."

"Take the hair thing down. I want the full effect."

"Get used to disappointment."

"Now, pretty woman." He readjusted his blaster.

"You're not shooting me now. That would completely ruin it for you." Rolling her eyes at him, she took off the scarf. "This day keeps going downhill."

"You're a brunette. A gorgeous one. I'm certain of that under all your gear." His eyes raked over her form.

"And you're severely lacking in the charm department. Why don't you start by easing up on pointing the blaster at me every second? Laying off on the death threats each minute too would be a splendid change." She deliberately walked around the area, testing her limits, but careful not to go near the table with her weapons and her end goal of having the man unknowingly relax his guard. "You haven't told me your plan, but I gathered you put more thought into it than the others in your group. They came across as dim-witted to me too."

"The payoff for the spear-bearers is impressive, so I'm going to turn you over to Black Dragon. Although now that I've seen you, it's a shame."

"You'll get over it, with what you stand to make off of me." She leaned against the end of the couch and looked at a cabinet in the corner. "It's been a long day, and I'm as thirsty as anything. Mind if I get a drink? That's not too much to ask if you're sending me off to die at Black Dragon? I'll even pour you one."

He studied her, but sensing nothing suspicious in her request, he said, "That would hit the spot."

She walked to the cabinet and opened it. "Let's see what we got."

"You don't remember what's in your stash?"

She poured a drink in one glass and took it in one hand. In the other hand, she handled a glass bottle and between her gloved fingers grasped the empty glass for him and brought it to a table in front of the couch. "This isn't my ship. It belongs to the shipping dealer the men beat up so badly."

The man raised his eyebrows. "You know your way around it."

"As you're probably aware, those types of cabinets are a common place to keep drinks, so it isn't a reach."

"I thought he wined and dined you here."

She shook her head at his suggestion. "Not the way your mind turned. Every shipping dealer knows how to do that for their customers to an extent because their whole existence hinges on making the next deal. If they're to be successful, they learn what each customer expects and they deliver or they cease to work in the business. He could do that as well as other successful ones in this trade, nothing more. On the other hand, your friends are lacking desperately in that skill set along with several others. They could take lessons from a good shipping dealer, but my guess is they'll continue down their foolhardy path."

He sat on the couch and all but laid the blaster aside. "They will or have, whatever the case may be." His eyes traveled over her form again. "Come sit with me, and we'll have that drink. Let me take advantage of your company before we make our unpleasant visit."

"My company won't be as engaging as you envision, but here's your drink." She handed it to him.

He drank it down. "I imagine you possess a softer side underneath all the gear."

She refilled his glass and handed it back to him. "I put a sunspear through people without blinking an eye, so there's no kinder me hidden away."

"I'll test that out myself."

"Afraid not. I'll give you tolerable since you stopped waving weapons at me, but charming you got no chance of reaching." She poured him another glass.

He took and downed it. "I said I want you on the couch with me now."

"So, you can enjoy yourself at my expense before you hand me over to the Black Dragon? Worst deal I've heard in a while."

"I'm not waiting any longer to claim this one." The man rose unsteadily from his seat and grasped for her. One arm started to wrap around her waist from behind to force her down on the couch. However, she had waited for the chance, and by design still held the glass bottle. She turned in his hold to smash it fully on his head and disengaged from him as he stumbled for his blaster in his disoriented state. He stared in shock as a dagger plunged into his chest.

As he collapsed to the floor, she knelt over him. "You should always check prisoners for weapons. You're not any smarter than the rest of your gang. By the way, the shipping dealer is a friend, and I decided you'd die the moment we set foot on this ship for what happened to him today. Like I said, you'll never see my softer side." She stabbed the blade a second time, ensuring his death.

Dante watched the whole scene, his knuckles white from clutching the table before him and his body trembling with a cascade of emotions. "Angelina, get off that planet now."

"Everything's red, so I shouldn't find a mark. However, let's double-check you," said Angelina.

Seeing the look from Dante, Alena said, "Angelina, someone here is insistent you return now."

"Must be Dante. No doubt a wreck after watching this." Even so, she inspected the man's neck and did a rapid search through his pockets.

"Angelina, I'll drag you back myself if you don't leave this instant," said Dante.

After retrieving the data pad, she rose and walked towards the computer console. "That would prove difficult since you don't know my location, but you're persistent, Dante. I'd be foolish to test you. No need to retrieve me though."

"You could hear me this whole time?"

"No, I expect Alena didn't want to keep relaying your messages." She winked at him as she started the liftoff and set the navigation. Pacing again, she went to the table and retrieved her blaster and sunspear. "This made such a mess."

"It doesn't matter. Get back to me before you attract more trouble."

"I'm in the air, about to clear the portal, Dante." She watched the viewscreen, staying alert for danger. "I need a place to put his ship, away from prying eyes. I debated bringing it there as the first choice. Ryan's region of space came to mind as a possibility, but that would've started more questions. Anyway, Christopher will want his vessel close to him. He'll be itching to get back to it as soon as he can."

"We'll have it worked out once you're on this side of the portal," said Lana.

"I've already got a hangar picked out," said Caleb.

"Good, and Lana, thanks for handling your cousin for me."

"I told you I would, but he's on edge. The sooner you return, the better."

"That's obvious." She paused, "Dante, I'm on your side of the portal now, and no sign of tag-alongs. Tell me where to set this."

CHAPTER TWENTY-FIVE

Despite her worry for Christopher, Angelina's eyes closed, from the combination of exhaustion and Dante's stroking of her arm as she sat on the couch with him in medical. Dante had met her, along with Lana and Caleb, the moment she landed. Ryan and Alena had stayed here as a precaution. Dante's anxieties calmed once he could see with his own eyes she was truly fine. With their help and that of a firestone, she had disposed of the dead body from Christopher's ship before they returned to medical. The disposal could've waited, but her experience with Trey's corpse wouldn't allow her to leave it there. The memory of his slain body rising from the grave to haunt her remained ever-present in her mind. She had stopped to strip off her gear for fear of bringing shards of glass into the room and taken on a hooded cloak. Upon their arrival at the medical, she and Dante switched roles, with her becoming frantic to obtain answers about her friend's condition, but it proved useless. Even Caleb's attempt netted little information. Alika and Seth were in the middle of surgery, patching up Christopher from the beating he received. He was coming through it well enough, but it would be at least an hour before Alika and Seth could speak with them. The information did nothing to ease Angelina's concerns, and only Dante's coaxing ultimately convinced her to settle on the couch next to him. She stared at the veil that refused to reveal anything further and ended up cuddling into Dante to wait out the span as his arms wrapped around her. As the time waned, her eyes drooped to soak in his assurances, and she dozed for what seemed like several minutes. She startled awake, realizing she succumbed to sleep.

"You okay?" asked Dante.

"I drifted off, but I don't know how with Christopher being so bad."

He raised her chin to gaze down at her. "I do. It's been an exhausting day for you, and you forgot how your night went going into this. I haven't." He kissed her.

She leaned her forehead into his. "I had forgotten, but that explains it. How long has it been?"

"Over an hour, so soon now." He pulled her back over, and she snuggled into him again.

"Rest will be his best medicine now," said Alika as he and Seth approached the group and smiled at Angelina as her eyes flew open. "Eventually caught up to you, did it?"

"Sorry, I guess so."

"Retrieving Christopher's ship didn't go as smoothly as planned, Alika," said Alena.

His smile disappeared to turn worried eyes back onto Angelina. "How so?"

"I got his vessel back here, so it's fine." She stood up with Dante following suit, as he loosely wrapped his arm back around her waist.

Seth shook his head. "You know full well the ship is not Alika's concern."

"Yes, you do." He advanced towards her and took her hand to begin doing a visual inspection of her. "Are you all right? What happened?"

"I'm fine. Much better than the guy that surprised me."

"And he is?"

"Dead. My dagger clean through him. Ashes now. Easy cleanup. Now the rest of Christopher's ship is another matter." She sighed.

"Much better than the other guy, who is dead. That doesn't inspire confidence." He released his grasp on her arm and looked at Dante. "However, you've been attentive to her as usual, so is she as well as she says?"

"I think she is. I worried the glass pieces hit her, but the gear caught it and she avoided the other shards." He kissed the top of her head.

"Glass? Do I want to know?"

Angelina cut him off, "No you don't. Christopher. How is he? How bad was it? What did you have to do? Is he going to recover? Can we see him?"

Alena touched her arm. "Breathe. Give them a chance to answer, okay?"

Seth smiled. "Wise counsel as always, Alena." He paused. "The injuries were extensive and the blows powerful and sustained enough to cause internal bleeding. I'm grateful for Alika as he could work on one area, while I concentrated on another. There were several ruptures to repair, so having to do one at a time, I'm not certain that would have ended in our patient's favor. He lost a significant amount of blood, so we did have to do a transfusion."

Angelina put her head in her hands. "He almost bled out, died right here."

"But he didn't. Sit back down, child." Alika touched her shoulder. "If I'm to tell you the rest."

With Dante's additional urging, she sat back down on the couch with him, as Seth and Alika settled in chairs facing the group.

Alika resumed the report. "He took an ugly blaster shot full in the leg, so we saw to that. He has a concussion. The extent of it remains to be seen." At seeing the alarm in the group's eyes, he quickly added, "We don't anticipate anything permanent, but it's difficult to determine recovery time for it until he awakens. A few broken ribs as well, which are quite painful as I've been told."

"They are. I don't know how he endured my moving him."

"Yes, you do know. Perhaps better than any of us. He withstood it because he knew the alternative to be certain death if he stayed there. Thus, he clung to the flame of life that still sparked, as you did when you fell from the rooftop." Alika squeezed her hand.

"Replayed once more." A tear slid down her face to fall on their clasped hands. "Did you ... his ribs ... were you able to ... "

"Yes, it proved more challenging with the number, and they were not all clean breaks like yours. I am grateful for Seth's expertise as well."

"How long before he's awake?"

"A miracle if three hours from now. Four is possible."

"That long?"

Seth said, "Alika is being optimistic in his effort to ease your anxiety. Five hours is the realistic estimate. Christopher will be fine though, but you will drive yourself to insanity staring at these walls for that time. Why don't you and everyone else get some rest?"

"You're right. I'll go crazy sitting here, but I need to clean up the mess in Christopher's ship anyway." She got up.

"You'll need help." Dante rose with her.

"No, I created it, and I should be the one to clean it up."

Ryan shook his head. "No way, Angelina. You didn't do that, so you can't possibly be thinking that way."

"But she can, Ryan. You have no idea." Alena turned to Angelina. "We'll all clean it up, and you're outvoted." She looked around the room to the ascending nods to stare back at her.

Angelina started to say something, but Alika cut her off while staring her down. "Excellent. Glad to see that's settled. Seth and I will remain here to watch over Christopher. If there is any noteworthy change in his condition, we'll alert you."

* * *

The group attacked the ship's floor first with the machine suction devices they retrieved on their way to the vessel. The shattered glass posed the greatest danger, so it became their priority. The shards and spilled drink mixture zipped into long suction wands. An indicator on them signaled the time to eject the contents into the reservoir bucket container placed in the corner of the room. Once the group finished the floor, they moved to the table and couch where the mess could lie hidden. Lastly, they attacked Angelina's gear to remove any embedded pieces.

Caleb emptied the contents of his wand into the reservoir again. "Think we got it all?"

"Doubtful," said Lana.

"As much as I hate to admit it, I agree. We'll go over it again before we hit it with the cleaning solution."

Dante followed Angelina's eyes to the couch. "That could take more work to return to its original state."

"No, it'll come out," said Angelina while pulling out a spray bottle in her hand. "These couches are made specifically from material to come clean in a pinch. It's one of the reasons shipping dealers have them on their ships. On a side note, they're surprisingly comfortable too."

"I'm regretting asking this, but are they ship dealers preferred choice because these messy situations happen regularly?"

She sprayed the substance on the furniture, concentrating on the blood and drink stains.

"Angelina, did you hear my question?"

"I did, and I'm figuring out how to answer so you're not further upset about this world and its dangers." She squirted more solution on the spot and let it settle. "Not all shipping dealers keep their negotiations in the bars or dining establishments. They're willing to bring it to their ship. Alena and I only do so with a select few. Christopher is one of those individuals we trust enough, and he's of the same thinking. However, if you invite them to your place and the bargaining falls apart, settling a deal can look like this. A bloody mess, but that's not all, Dante." She stopped, unsure of whether to continue.

He stepped closer to her. "Go on. I asked."

"There are all types of deals made. Certain ones aren't done by myself, Alena, and Christopher, but a segment of shipping dealers agree to them as with any other arrangement. Some ships have private quarters like mine and Christopher's, but others don't. Their open area is used for everything from arranging shipments to entertaining guests to," she paused and looked at him meaningly, "sealing agreements of the most personal nature."

"Pretty versatile piece of furniture." He stared at the couch as her words sunk in, but he already knew. He had seen pieces of her world over the past several days, and the final blinders had vanished of the type of men she encountered in it, of the sort of deals offered to her, almost forced upon her.

She whispered, "I know you know now, and I'm sorry." Focusing her attention back on the couch, she observed the blood and drink stains streaking down it. She attached a brush appendage to the end of the wand device, restarted it, and swiped it across the sofa's surface. Forcing a smile she said, "See it always comes off. Nobody would ever know what happened. There's always a way to ... " She looked down and bit her lip.

Dante pulled her over and waited for her to look up at him. "When are you going to trust me enough to tell me what happened?"

She put the wand aside and wrapped her arms around his neck. "I trust you completely, Dante. That's never been in question. Some knowledge carries a hefty price with it though, and I'm not willing to see you pay it."

"And I would not watch you delivered to Black Dragon to die. I'd go to the heart of Black Dragon if I had to in order to get you back. No one takes you from me. Ever." He gave her a long, passionate kiss that left her swooning in his arms.

⁓ꝝꝝ⁓

"Glad to see you could join us for dinner," said Alika as the group returned.

"Although, we've got to stop this pattern of dining in medical." Ryan shook his head as he sat with the others.

"It's been worse, Ryan," said Caleb.

"True, I do enjoy the company." He grinned as he stole a kiss from Alena.

"It appears all of you took the opportunity to freshen up," said Seth.

"A shower does wonders, but I had to almost drag a certain someone. Always so difficult," said Alena.

Angelina sighed. "I didn't want him waking up, and we weren't here."

"He hasn't stirred, my child." Alika patted her on the shoulder. "The rest is good for him, and you can tell Seth and me what happened while we eat."

Angelina finished recounting the retaking of Christopher's ship. "That would be how I owe him a replacement bottle of drink with fire, and I served up a meet and greet with my dagger."

"A bottle of spirits truly put to its best use. We'll gladly replace it for him. Another close call." Alika shook his head. "And the mark?"

"Clear of it. The man bled red, as should have been the case. However, with all the surprises from Black Dragon, I wanted to check. All the others poured red, so I'm assuming the same. I had to get Christopher back."

"Yes, he couldn't have stood any delay."

"They all helped Black Dragon on their own accord, no prompting necessary," said Caleb.

"Except for the lucrative payoff ahead of them," said Lana.

"There's no chance of that now because I stopped that transaction. They've been bolder though, especially that big one," said Angelina.

"There are still the ones that went into the building," said Ryan.

Alena shook her head. "They weren't so committed to the mission as you may have overheard. I'm betting half changed their mind. A couple of them already questioned it in the complex. Then if any managed to make it out, they saw Angelina's handiwork."

"Why wouldn't they have made it out?" asked Dante.

"I left a few exploding surprises near the access point to the rooftop."

"You could've been hurt," said Ryan.

"Relax. I was long gone from there, but I ensured they were led where they needed to be."

"The old woman that helped you. We heard the whole exchange as clear as day. You had to be right there."

"Yes, I was."

"How did they not see you?"

"Plenty of places for someone to hide in the shadows in a room that size. Besides they saw what they wanted. They focused only on obtaining information from anyone, even an old woman and couldn't see past that."

"So, you were there the entire time?" Ryan stared at her in amazement.

"Or I can turn into an old woman." She grinned at him.

"Really?" He grinned back at her.

"Only other possibility left. Would you still like me with wrinkles?" Her eyes danced merrily.

He laughed. "Alena, wrinkles and all, I'll take you. You're the only one for me." He kissed her forehead. "You can change into an old woman now?"

"Maybe so, Ryan."

At the look on Ryan's face, Angelina laughed and stumbled out, "Alena, you had him going. I think he believed you for a moment."

At her words, they all broke out into laughter as Ryan reached over and kissed Alena.

"This is the other part you wanted to share before you had to leave?" asked Lana as she studied the list.

"Yes. Of course, the recruits' numbers alone are useless."

"But with their photos helpful." Caleb nodded.

"Just the administrators and support personnel. Those will be the ones distributed to the colonies. Shipping dealers can help us. Give us warning, but it's a drop in the bucket."

"How many more rooms of recruits were there to sort?" asked Lana.

"No, Lana, the question is how many more facilities? Three planets and they're still processing, creating their army."

A soft moan escaped from the bed, and the group hurried to the bedside in unison. Christopher's eyes opened to see Angelina peering anxiously down at him. "Chris, where am I?"

"Safe, in medical."

His eyes took in the multitude surrounding him, his look lingering on Angelina, Alena, and Alika. "Pulled out the whole team for me."

"It was bad, Christopher. I thought you wouldn't make it."

"I couldn't die on you, especially after you forced me to make that ridiculous promise to you. Can't break my word." He began to chuckle but winced in discomfort. "Alena, make her stop looking at me like I'm breathing my last."

Alena grinned at her. "You heard him. Knock it off."

"How are you feeling?" asked Alika.

"Like someone used every inch of me as a punching bag, but they did so other than that, I'm good."

Alika took a syringe from Seth and started to put it in the IV. "Expected. This should eliminate a majority of the pain."

"Wait, I don't need any more sleep. I've been laying here forever."

"Your medical staff respectfully disagrees that further rest is unnecessary, but this is for pain only. You'll find that sleep comes on its own. May I continue?" He waited with the syringe.

"In that case, go for it."

After a few minutes, Christopher shifted in the bed and stretched out his arms. "Oh, yeah, that's better. There's the good stuff, but you know what works best now. Certain people give you plenty of practice."

"I must agree." Alika smiled over at Angelina.

"You have to be Seth. Thanks for helping put me back together again. This had to be a joint effort."

"You're correct, and we're relieved you came through. Any friend of Alika's group is ours as well."

"Same here." He turned back to concentrate on Angelina and Alena. "Neither of you is in shipping dealer ware or covered in fighter gear. You wear normal clothes occasionally. I almost didn't recognize you two."

"You are something." Angelina smiled at him, and Alena laughed.

"Oh, there was that dress. You looked nice in it." He smiled at Dante. "But you're the better judge of that than me, right? Pretty impressive first meeting with Chris?"

Dante smiled at Christopher, but turned back to Angelina, "She was ... is stunning. That's the word I managed when I first saw Ange ... I mean Chris."

"The same look from both of you. When she talks about you, everything about her changes and in the best way, Dante." Christopher paused. "So, what do I call you here? Apparently not Chris."

"I let Dante pick a name, and he chose Angelina."

"Angelina. It fits you." He focused back on Dante. "Smoothly done, Dante. You don't know me at all, only what they've told you. They confided in me the truth about what happened with your family though, your mom still being unconscious, and all that you and your family have been put through with Black Dragon. I can't imagine. I was there with them too when you went to bring your dad back and, Dante, I'm sorry for how it ended for him. Your father was a good man, a wonderful father to you, and I'm glad you got to experience it again before he passed on. I wish he hadn't been taken from you. None of that helps I know, but I wanted to tell you when I saw you. I hated it for you."

Dante touched the man's arm. "It does help, and it means a lot to me. Just hearing someone else being able to see my father for who he really was, as I saw him, is more than words can say." He paused. "Thank you, and I feel like I do know you. Angelina and Alena always speak fondly of you, and it's clearly warranted. Neither one hesitated to come after you the instant they knew the trouble you were in."

"I'm still alive because they did. They're both amazing." He turned towards Alena and Ryan. "Commander Ryan, well met, and I'm told you discovered that on your own about Alena."

"Just Ryan works, Christopher. And yes, she caught me the first day she walked in, and she hasn't let up."

"I expect not, but you've got her hooked too, Ryan. Don't allow her to fool you. She gets this dreamy look in her eyes when she talks about you like Angelina does with Dante."

He laughed. "Terrific to know."

"He could use more sleep now, Alika," joked Alena.

"Not a chance. I feel good." He winked as he turned to Lana and Caleb. "Pleasure to finally meet you two. My business doesn't keep me in the same circles as you, but I'm working on your side. Only a different angle."

Lana smiled. "We understand. Angelina's group opened our eyes to what that terrain looks like, and we're grateful to you."

"You've put yourself on the line for us. We're sick about what happened to you today, but we're glad you're okay."

"Just lucky these two reached me in time. Speaking of, how did you know?" He turned back to Alena and Angelina.

"A vision," said Angelina.

"No way." He shook his head. "Down to the alley they dragged me into on the exact colony; talk about delivering."

"I heard the planet whispered in it and glimpsed a sign for the bar. Then it flashed to you in the alley with the buildings surrounding you. I knew they didn't take you far. It took a minute of scanning the area to find the place that matched what I saw."

"You make it sound simple, but I'm beyond impressed."

"Don't be too awed. Our rescue turned out messier than I envisioned. We owe you a bottle of spirits."

"What? How in the galaxy did you manage that? You don't drink, Chris. The whole thing? For real?"

"Neither do you."

"That's true, at least not more than an occasional sip. That's not the point. You know why I keep it on the ship."

"Yes, the same reason we stash a few bottles."

"I'm still wondering how you went through an entire one."

Angelina sighed. "I got your vessel back fine, but I didn't watch my back as I should have when I went to retrieve it. A visitor insisted on boarding with me."

"He either holds his spirit like no man I've ever seen, or he passed out."

"Neither."

"So, what gives?"

"As soon as he got a look at her, he had other intentions on how to spend the time with her, before he gave her over to Black Dragon," said Dante.

"You mean ... "

"Yeah, he tried to force himself on her, Christopher." Unconsciously he pulled her closer, with the arm wound around her waist.

"Dante, you must have gone crazy." He turned to Angelina. "Are you okay?" He saw her nod. "Geez, Chris, you can't stay out of trouble for a second. Every time I see you, we have this same talk."

"Don't even. This coming from the man who had to be snatched from death's door."

"The difference is this is my first time whereas this is your millionth time."

"You haven't known me that long, Christopher,"

"You're right. I still say there's only one sure solution for keeping you out of danger." His eyes twinkled, and he grinned as he looked over at Dante.

"Back to that, are we?" She laughed. "Afraid not."

Dante encircled his other arm around her and turned her towards him. "I like his idea better and better, and I'm determined to have you warm up to it." He kissed her, ignoring the others.

True to his word, she felt her whole body heat up as she opened herself up to him until he eased back from the kiss to grin at her. She smiled up at him. "Your method of persuasion remains unmatched."

Christopher chuckled. "On the day Dante wins that deal, you'll both be happy when he does." He paused. "Does somebody want to tell me what happened, since those two are hopelessly distracted now?"

"Angelina shattered the bottle over the guy's head," said Alena.

"That'll hurt."

"Then she put a dagger through him," said Ryan.

"A whole new level of pain."

"And another time to make sure he was dead," said Lana.

"She's thorough."

"We took a firestone to him for the cleanup," said Caleb.

"You left no loose ends. At least with that one. That group was relentless, but they aren't the only ones, from what I gathered."

"You guessed it. In the last week, Lana almost ended up a prisoner of Black Dragon, and Seth and Dante barely escaped right after."

Christopher's eyes widened. "With the way this crew fights, Caleb, I can't believe that." He stopped though at the expressions mirrored on the faces of the others. "But everyone is fine. How?"

"Same way you are. Two people reached us in time to prevent the worst, and then reinforcements arrived," said Seth.

"I've missed a lot since I talked to Alena and Chris."

"The two of them are busy, and this one," Dante leaned over and kissed Angelina's cheek, "manages to land into lots of trouble in record time. How about we compare notes and get caught up?"

"Sounds like we should."

"To a point. Christopher needs rest, despite what he believes. Seth and I will decide the cut-off for the night," said Alika.

Angelina watched Christopher. He had held up well, but the day's events were catching up to him as the group continued exchanging intel. She nodded to Alena. They couldn't wait any longer. "Christopher, we can finish up tomorrow. There's something we need to work out now."

"What is it?"

"A delivery you have."

He ran his hands over his face. "How did I forget?"

❧

Angelina lay on the couch, cuddled up to Dante in his quarters. She finally had time alone with him and looked up to find him watching her intently. "You're still worried, aren't you?"

"That's putting it mildly." He stroked her hair. "Are you certain it's safe for you and Alena to handle this for him?"

"Not doing it lands us all in trouble. It's the only solution."

"Half the galaxy is hunting for you two. How do you know it's not another ambush?"

"I've worked with Christopher's shipping connection numerous times."

"We could tag along tomorrow in case."

"You can help by watching over him while we're out. We talked about this. I can't have you stepping into my shipping world."

"Christopher is a real standup guy, like you said. It would be okay."

"Dante, you don't believe your own words."

"What are you talking about? He is a good guy."

"The other part."

Dante sighed. "At least half of the universe isn't like him because they resemble more of what you put a dagger through today."

"Afraid so. Anyway, I prefer to keep you right here, in this world."

"This one, huh?" He ran his hand leisurely up and down her arm as he kept the other arm wrapped around her waist. "I'm taken with it too, with you, my Angelina." He pulled her to him and began to kiss her. His hand moved to her shoulder to play in her hair as his other hand encircled her waist more snugly, and his worries evaporated temporarily as he enjoyed the feel of her in his embrace. *She's mine, my beautiful angel.* The words sang through him, and his heart raced. Her fingertips stroked the back of his neck, causing a fresh wave of warmth to course through him.

⁓⁓⁓

Alena sat in the pilot seat of their ship. "We're set. Cargo is loaded."

"Ship is in order too." Angelina nodded, as she looked behind her while settling into the copilot spot. Anyone coming aboard would never see the quarters in the back of their vessel. It was one of the features they had incorporated, a wall that slid between the open area and the back rooms when the two saw fit. The barrier appeared solid though, designed to arouse no suspicions.

"Christopher seemed good this morning."

"I thought so too, but I'm relieved Alika and Seth stayed with him overnight."

"Impossible to ignore, isn't it?"

"No matter how hard you try. Definitely the same look on both faces, Alena."

"Ryan tried to come up with another way to do this last night. I distracted him well enough that he didn't bring it up further." A smile escaped her as her eyes focused on the figure watching their ship about to depart.

"You mentioned as much when you came back from seeing him, and I'm sure you did, Alena." Angelina winked at her before returning her gaze to the figure standing next to Ryan. "My evening went similarly with Dante. He had forgotten when we said good night, but this morning was a different story."

"Back to the beginning with them."

"I don't help our case. I can't believe that guy snuck up on me, and on the heels of the whole fiasco with Santiago and the exploding interrogation room." She slumped in her chair. "It's a wonder Dante doesn't lock me up in his quarters."

"Wow. Way to inspire confidence."

Angelina sat up and chuckled. "Message delivered with the kick in the rear I needed." She pushed a button on the console and asked, "Everyone hear us now?"

"Yes," said Alika.

"We're headed out. Should be there at least thirty minutes ahead of the scheduled drop-off. Nobody get too settled because we'll be back before you know it."

Alena grinned at her and mouthed, *Much better.*

❧

Angelina peered at the ship parked nearby and watched the shipping dealer emerge. She approached him, constantly staying in surveillance mode, as she vowed no repeats of the previous day. "Lamar, I'm here as agreed."

"Bella, good to see you, although the circumstances are troubling. Considering that, do you have something ... "

"Of course. I expected you to ask." She opened her data pad and presented the information to him. After retrieving his data pad and comparing the details, he nodded his satisfaction. "I have more questions, but this isn't the place to discuss further."

"I anticipated that as well, but you're right. Once we get the shipment loaded, I'll answer what I can."

Alena remained hidden on the ship in her quarters, her eyes glued to a monitoring screen. "No surprises thus far." She whispered into the earpiece.

"That's the last one, Lamar." Angelina wheeled the final haul to the ramp of his ship, and he unloaded the rest onto it.

"Everything checked out, but I didn't expect otherwise. You both run an honest shop. Makes sense he reached out to you for help."

"This is still a business."

"Of course, you're covering the delivery for him. You should get a cut of the profits for your troubles. Time for me to settle up, Bella."

Angelina sat in a chair on her ship and motioned him to do likewise opposite of her. He handed her a small plastic card, and she inserted it into an electronic square sleeve. The device beeped seconds later, and a message confirmed the payment transfer was completed. "Always great doing business with you, Lamar."

"Did you get your share out?"

"No, he'll take care of that." She forced a smile. She wouldn't take any out. Christopher almost died because of her, and that fact replayed in her mind. Her focus returned to Lamar.

"How's he faring? I've run with him for a while and there are close calls in this line of work, but nothing like what he sounded like he got caught in."

"He pulled through and is on the mend, but yesterday we wondered."

"It was as bad as I thought. You're sure he'll be okay?"

"Yeah, he will."

"How did it go down?"

Angelina chose her words carefully, ensuring nothing gave away her identity as the spear-bearer. "He told you some, but he had difficulty remembering. They almost beat him to death. When I found him, I thought they did."

"How did you find him?"

"I started towards the bar that I later learned is where his trouble began. I had a possible deal to check out there. On the way down one of the alleys, I spotted at least two bodies on the ground. Upon investigation, it turned out to be four, but the only one I recognized was our friend. The others were dead."

"He doesn't know who they were, or what happened at the lounge?"

"Yes and no. He remembered what happened inside the bar, but he didn't know who they were beyond leaving no question of their loyalties. Once they routed him into the alley, he endured a near-death beating. He came in and out of consciousness. That's when his memory is gone. What he told me is these guys came in recruiting for a job and wouldn't take no for an answer. There's an incredible price tag on a few of the Freedom Fighters' heads courtesy of the Black Dragon as well as for intel on two other individuals who have been giving Black Dragon fits. Our friend came to the aid of another shipping dealer being harassed by the group, and they turned their focus on him. Next thing he knows he's in the alley, completely outnumbered."

"Because he wouldn't help them."

"Yes. They were convinced he had information to locate the other two when he refused to aid in taking out the Freedom Fighter targets."

"Those are Black Dragon thugs all right."

"It's what we concluded as well."

"I've heard it too, Bella."

"Same deal?"

"Yeah, but I dismissed it as all talk. I mean, those Freedom Fighters have been yanking Black Dragon's chain for how long, and it just occurred to Black Dragon to come after them? The other two are new, but they must have really riled up the beast."

"Apparently so, but our friend paid the price for it." She reflected on his comment and dared to ask, "What do you think about their deal?"

"I've always known it's a dangerous gig, but I can't lie. This one rattled me. Our mutual friend is one of the best in the biz and is always careful. As for me, I've never served Black Dragon or lifted a finger to help them, and I'm not starting now. If they take over the galaxy, it won't be because of me. If they get a hold of me, I'll take out as many as I can before they kill me."

"I'm with you wholeheartedly, but I hope it never comes to that for either of us."

"Those men aren't playing. Bella, you need to watch your back even more. If they'll do that to him, what do you think they'll do to a woman if they capture her?"

"There's an ugly list starting in my head."

"Me too, so be careful." He got up and walked towards the exit.

"Watch your back too."

"I will, and pass my concern to our friend."

"Will do." She watched to make sure he returned safely to his ship before settling in the copilot seat and saying, "Coast is clear."

"I saw," said Alena as she plopped down into the pilot position. "Let's get back."

●●●

Alena slid up to Ryan as she strolled into medical with Angelina. "Like we said. Nothing to worry about. What do you have to say for yourself?"

Ryan chuckled. "My sincerest apologies, Alena. I'm insane to doubt the two of you."

"You'll have to do better than an apology." She slid her arms around his neck.

"Gladly." He pulled her over and kissed her.

"Held it together while I was gone?" asked Angelina as she hugged Dante.

"Barely. It's Bella, today, huh?"

"Different shipping dealer, different alias. I explained it to you, but you were distracted."

"You have that effect on me. Honestly, I don't know how you keep it straight."

"Necessity."

"How did Bella come to be?"

"The name of a drink special that day."

Dante chuckled. "Inspired by that, when you don't even drink."

"The description read something like a refreshing intoxicating drink, sweetened with a splash of fruit blend to create a fiery mix that will send you reeling. It spoke to me."

"I see the resemblance now." He leaned in closer, and one hand moved up to her shoulder.

"Should you call me Bella instead?"

He stroked her cheek. "No, I got it right. Angelina. Definitely see my angel." He kissed her long and gently. "You won't change my mind."

The doubts briefly left her as she snuggled against him, soaking in his words and the safety of his arms. She ignored all the ways she didn't fit the angel image he held, and she chose to live the lie he wished. It proved easier.

Christopher watched and smiled. "You two are good for them."

Angelina walked up to Christopher's bedside with Dante's hand in hers. "How are you feeling? Alika and Seth can give you more medicine if it would help."

"Would you stop fussing over me? I'm receiving first-class care. If anything, I'm ready to get out of this bed." He grinned. "Then there's this profit share I need to fork over."

"No, Christopher. Just talk to make it sound more legit. You know the game. I'm in your debt. You saved my life yesterday."

"What in the galaxy are you talking about? I survived only because you and Alena rescued me."

Her shoulders slumped. "But the reason you were ... " she bit her lip and stared at the floor.

"Chris, you're seriously not."

She looked back up at him and forced a smile. "Forget it. You're right. You're okay. That's what's important. We should examine the data together and see if you catch something Alena and I missed."

Christopher studied Angelina at her abrupt shift, but he shrugged and agreed.

Angelina gazed up at one of the screens displayed with information captured from a confiscated data pad. However, her eyes drifted back to her data pad. A single entry kept drawing her attention, and her lie to Christopher haunted her.

"Found anything yet?" asked Alena.

Angelina startled slightly and refocused on the displayed screen. "No, it's here somewhere though, but nothing comes out at me."

"I thought you had something because you got that intense look." She made a motion at Angelina's data pad.

"Always searching for a connection. You know me."

"Chris dug up a lead, Alena?" asked Christopher quietly as she walked over to his bedside.

"She says no," said Alena while staring up at the monitor.

"Yet you don't believe her."

"Not in the least. I caught her looking particularly closely at something, but it's merely a hunch." She pointed to the screen, and to all appearances they were in an animated conversation over the data before them.

Angelina glanced at Christopher again, and the accusations echoed in her head. With her decision made, she rose from her seat.

Dante turned to her with a smile. "What did you find?"

"Nothing, but one of the data pads we retrieved is back on the ship. I'll get it."

"I'll come with you. I could use a stretch." He got up.

"No! I mean, I got it. It'll only take a minute, and there's a ton to go over. They need you here. Anyway, it's my mistake because I missed downloading it." She whispered, "Here's something to hold you till I return." She pulled him over and slowly kissed him.

"You better hurry back." He murmured against her lips. "Sure I can't come with you?"

"Be back in a flash." Angelina winked at him as she disappeared from the room with Dante still staring after her.

"Weird."

"Where is she going?" asked Alena as she came to stand beside him.

"To the ship. I volunteered to go with her, but she said to stay here. "

"For what? Why did she go to the ship?"

"She forgot one of the data pads we collected from Black Dragon, so she went to get it."

"No, she lied to you."

"What? Why would she do that? Alena, what's going on?"

"Everything is accounted for, so that's not it. Earlier I saw her looking at an item on her data pad. I can't be certain, but my guess is she means to follow up on the lead alone. Dante, you have to stop her before she leaves with the ship."

The panic in Alena's voice sent him running out the door.

CHAPTER TWENTY-SIX

Angelina sat in the cockpit chair and stared at the viewscreen, while still catching her breath after her mad dash to the ship. It was a suicide mission and possibly wouldn't give them what they needed. They hadn't pinpointed the location, only managing to narrow it down to three possibilities from the trail he left. Basing an entire operation on a guess amounted to pure foolishness or the gamble that had the potential to tip the balance for them. The nagging voice reared its head again, causing her to second-guess herself and question her motives. The man had to be long dead, killed for his failure to the Black Dragon that day. She wouldn't find him. So, what did she hope to uncover? The machine, she argued back. The voice screeched back, "Liar." Deep down she couldn't deny she longed to be the one that finally took them out, and she should be the one shouldering the risk. She wouldn't allow anyone else to be hurt, and it had been too close lately. The image of her mother's bleeding, lifeless body appeared before her, and a tear streamed down her cheek. Impatiently brushing it aside with the back of her hand, her eyes made a final sweep of the three destinations as she chose one.

Suddenly the ship's door opened, and out of breath Dante asked, "Having a hard time finding that data pad?"

She jumped up and turned as he walked towards her. "I thought I said ... why did you follow me here?"

"Sounds like you're trying to get rid of me."

"That's insane." She put her arms around his neck and whispered in his ear, "You just wanted an excuse to come back for more."

He wished he could believe her as she delivered another slow, amazing kiss that indeed left him hungry for more, but he glimpsed the screen pulled up seconds before. It revealed projections to nearby portals, not a search for any download. However, it didn't stop him from enjoying every moment of the kiss from her and whispering, "You can't blame me."

"I suppose." She ran her hands through his hair and attempted to gain the advantage again, a difficult feat now.

"Why did you come over here?"

"For the data pad."

"All accounted for. Try again."

"I thought I missed one, but it turns out I downloaded them all. Guess you rushed over here for nothing."

"I wouldn't say that." He kissed her forehead. "But I'm still waiting on the answer to my question."

He won't budge. I have to give this up now. She said to herself. Then the recent days in all their ugliness returned to her. Lana's unconscious body. Seth and Dante at blade point. Lastly, Christopher's motionless, bloody form. No, she had already decided, and for the sake of those she cared about, she must see this through. "You're right. I needed a break from that whole scene for a few minutes, but everyone shouldn't stop because of me. Although I realize now how much I wanted time with you, so I'm glad you didn't listen to me." Sliding her hands down his arms, she took his hands and maneuvered him away from the cockpit. "Sit on the couch with me."

Dante knew she hadn't told him the truth but questioning her proved useless. Reluctant to push further since he succeeded in keeping her from leaving, he gave in to her request. She eased him down to sit on the couch, smiling as she settled into his lap and curled her arms around his neck. "Much better with you here." Her lips found his again. "How about I get us that drink you like so?"

"You'd have to leave my lap. The drink isn't worth the trade," he teased.

She giggled. "I'm offering you refreshments and me. Promise I'll only take a minute, and then we'll pick up where we left off."

"Fine, but if you take too long, I'm dragging you back over."

"Deal." She kissed his cheek and got up. After retrieving two cups, she frowned when she opened the cooling box with the drink. "That can't be all of it."

"Don't worry about it. Come on back."

"No, I promised your favorite, and there's more in another place for sure. You're not the only one who likes it."

Dante chuckled at her persistence. He watched her head towards a cabinet further back, rummage through the contents, and emerge with a jar of liquid in victory. She poured a portion of it into a small pitcher. In another motion, she grabbed two glasses with the sweet drinks and handed one to him. After taking a long sip, he placed it on the table beside the couch and said, "Perfect combination."

She did the same before laying her drink aside and returning to his lap. Her hands slinked around his neck as his arms encircled her waist, and she began to kiss him again.

"Put it down now, Angelina," Alena commanded from behind the two.

Angelina broke off her kiss with Dante to see Alena and Ryan towering over them.

"What's she talking about?" His voice struggled for composure at being interrupted mid-kiss with Angelina.

"You heard me, Angelina," repeated Alena, holding her hand out.

Angelina had already sprung from Dante's embrace and looked from Alena and Ryan to her hand.

Dante glimpsed the syringe about one-fourth of a way filled with a clear liquid substance in her grasp. He understood and sat there, his mouth gaping open.

Angelina stood there as her world shattered for what felt like the millionth time. It seemed so logical in medical, but now she couldn't fathom how. The look from Alena and Ryan made her want to crawl into the darkest corner of the galaxy, but the expression from Dante undid her. Her whole body trembled, and the syringe dropped from her hands. "I'm so sorry. I didn't mean ... Dante, it wouldn't hurt you ... just made you sleep for a little, enough for me to leave."

Stumbling back a couple of steps, her eyes fell on the syringe again. "What have I done? How could I ... " She collapsed to her knees, and her palms rested on the ship's floor as a sob erupted from her.

Recovered from his initial shock, Dante rose from the couch and knelt beside her. When he attempted to put his arm around her, she shook her head. "After what I did, how can you ... " Another sob escaped her.

"Because my care for you never wavers, and nothing you do will ever change that. I believe I've also pieced together why you did it." He tried again to slip his arm about her waist. This time she didn't resist the motion, and he took the opening to ease her over to him completely. Her arms wrapped around his neck as she buried her head in his shoulder and a wave of relief flowed through him. "Come on. Let's take this back to the couch." He helped her from the floor and guided her to sit on the couch beside him.

Angelina dared a look at Alena and Ryan, expecting angry faces. Instead, their expressions reflected the opposite. "You two should be furious with me."

"No, I'd wager the why you did it makes perfect sense in your insane thinking," said Alena.

"But we couldn't let you go through with it. I'm not crazy about your method either."

"Ryan and I will be in my quarters to give you two privacy to sort this out." She touched Angelina's shoulder and smiled.

"Surely you can find a couple of ways to make up to Dante for trying to knock him out. I've got faith you two can work out something." Ryan grinned and winked at her as he strolled off with Alena.

"How did you settle on the idea of chasing after Drew's trail alone, my Angelina?" Dante stroked the side of her face.

"I wanted a way to keep everyone safe."

"Who is keeping you safe?"

"I didn't care about that."

"I care about that the most, so no more solo missions, got it?" He lifted her chin. "Got it?"

"Okay."

"Don't make me lock you up in my quarters."

"You wouldn't."

"I would, and I'm seeing it as the reasonable option, with stunts like this from you."

She sighed. "Trying to drug you went pretty far."

"Convincing seduction too. How much of that was real?" A grin lit his face.

"All of it. There's no pretending with you when it comes to that."

He leaned in closer. "I can find it in me to look past what you did."

"You're too good to me," she said as she drew him over and kissed him at first tentatively with her latest episode still painfully fresh in her mind. The next second though it retreated as she sunk into the kiss with him, and the familiar warmth tingled through her body he always awakened. She opened her eyes and stared at him as the kiss ended. "You forgive me?"

"Already did, but if it's not apparent after that, then I'll keep at it until I've assured you." In one motion, he pulled her into his lap and found her lips in a fiery kiss anew, sending Angelina's head spinning most wonderfully.

∼ℰℓℓ∼

"It'll be okay," said Dante as the two walked hand in hand back into medical, followed by Ryan and Alena.

"Everyone may not be so forgiving."

"You underestimate them." He squeezed her hand.

Alika smiled at the group. "You caught up to our runaway in time."

Angelina began, "I'm sorry. You must be so angry."

"Not angry. Surprised, yes. Although I shouldn't be, but I admit a degree in this case. Your resourcefulness reached a new level." He shook his head. "You're fine, Dante?"

"Yes, Ryan and Alena have excellent timing."

Silence filled the room as all eyes fell on Angelina. "I have explaining to do, but I don't know where to start." she looked down at the floor.

"Tell us what went through your head. Nobody is mad at you," said Christopher.

She stared up at him. "If anybody should be, it's you."

"Why would you say that?"

"The reason you needed rescuing, that you almost died is because of me. Knowing me. Anyone who gets near enough to me eventually ends up ... " her voice broke.

"Chris, you can't do that." He reached over for her other hand but winced at the effort as she stood just beyond him.

Recognizing the flash of pain on his face, she quickly moved closer to his bedside. "I didn't mean to cause you to hurt. I'm sorry. I didn't think. What can I do?"

Christopher spoke to the group with his eyes still staring at Angelina. "You mind giving me and Chris the room for a bit?"

"Take all the time necessary. May she take your words to heart," said Alika.

The group filed out with Dante hesitantly moving from Angelina's side. Christopher said, "Except for you, Dante. Stay, but move those couple of chairs closer to this side of the bed."

Dante did so.

Christopher gently commanded, "Come on, Chris, you two sit, and let's figure this out."

Angelina sat in the chair, and Dante followed suit in the seat next to her, as he encircled his arm around her shoulders.

"Isn't the rest enough, Chris?"

"What are you talking about?"

"What you're doing again. Don't play that game with me. You've got to stop this, deciding every bad thing that happens is somehow laid at your feet."

"The pattern runs true though."

"No, it doesn't. I don't know who warped your view so much, but I'd like to string them up and use them for target practice. I know I'd get help." He glanced at Dante before focusing back on Angelina. "You didn't get me beat to a pulp. In fact, without the training session from you and Alena, I would've been a goner and then the two of you saved my skin. This is not just your war, no matter how determined you are to make it that way, but you refuse to see. Why?"

"There's more to it, Christopher, but I can't." She bit her lip. "You got into this mess because you wouldn't tell them about me."

"There's nothing to tell because I don't know what you have locked up tighter than a ship hatch that scares the crud out of you. I just see it in your eyes. You didn't do this though, but I'll tell you who did."

"This isn't necessary."

"Me. I did this, Chris."

Her eyes widened, and she shook her head. "You're not making sense."

"I chose this."

"You didn't choose those men to almost kill you, Christopher. That's insanity."

"Some call this business that. But yes, Chris, I did choose it and everything that comes with this business when I entered it years ago. It's hard, and the Black Dragon danger gets worse as their reach increases with each passing day. Yet I stayed in despite that. Why? Because I decided from the first where my loyalties are and where I would never place my allegiance. I made my decision before I ever met you, and I understood the cost. I'm not helping them take down anyone, and I didn't know where to find you. You know even if I did, I wouldn't tell them."

"It shouldn't have happened to you."

"As long as Black Dragon lives, it will always be a possibility. You know that. Yet when I look at you and the rest of this group, I see the best hope for the galaxy being rid of Black Dragon one day. You can't give up, but it's going to get ugly. Chris, it's not on you though, and you have to accept that."

"I don't want to lose anyone else I care about, Christopher."

He clasped her hand. "None of us does, but there are no guarantees. We look out for each other and trust it's enough. Chris, I don't blame you for whatever happens. No one does. Let it go."

"I can't." Her voice broke.

"Yes, you can."

Angelina released Christopher's hand and cried. Christopher nodded, and Dante pulled her over, murmuring, "He's right, my Angelina, and I've got you as always."

She looked up at him through her tears and whispered, "You do."

He whispered back, "I do." Then he kissed her.

The others rejoined them in the medical room, and Alika wasted no time. "Angelina, you are aware of what I think of your insistence on following Drew's whereabouts, but," he put his hand up as Dante started to protest, "if you have valid reasons to believe it will prove fruitful in our search, we're willing to lay aside our reservations and hear you out."

Dante pleaded, "Alika, please don't."

"Dante, I've agreed to nothing, and she must make a compelling case."

She stared back at Alika, and her shoulders slumped. "I can't, but you knew. His trail could lead us to the machine, as could numerous other avenues. I don't know which one to trace any more than I did a week ago."

"But walking straight into the arms of Black Dragon isn't the answer," said Dante.

"A part of me believes it is. Drew represented something from them I could put a sunspear through and eliminate. For everything they've done, they deserve to be erased from the galaxy. I'd take the path to the center of Black Dragon if I could be the one to plunge my sunspear through it. Today, it wasn't about finding the machine."

"It got personal for you. We've all been there, Angelina," said Caleb as he wrapped his arm around Lana and kissed her forehead.

"But lucky for you, my cousin won't back down on this one."

"She's right. Are you going to let me win?" teased Dante.

"You earned it after today." She laughed and kissed him.

Christopher focused back on the viewscreens. "You haven't gone through much of the confiscated data pads and downloads. Sounds like every time you try, something happens. You know, like exploding rooms and rescuing people."

Angelina said, "We've had our share of endless delays, but to still be this clueless is crazy frustrating."

"What about tracking it through the shipping? Chris, we threw that around before."

"They're not still building it though."

"You're right. It's sitting somewhere until they use it again. The last known facility they had it stored is blown off the star chart." Christopher rubbed his chin. "There must be a reference to where they moved it to that we missed."

"Likely. I mean we mistook the storage or launching pad for the device, and I'm still baffled how we managed that blunder." Angelina pulled up the download of the device they retrieved from their trip to Black Dragon. "Something still doesn't look right to me."

"We settled on it being an earlier sketch of the machine," said Alena.

"That makes sense, but nothing on that contraption you dragged back?" asked Christopher.

Alena shook her head. "You're welcome to take a look."

He slowly climbed out of bed. "A short outing sounds great, and don't you try to stop me, Chris. I've got it covered." He motioned towards Alika and Seth.

"I know where my energies are wasted, Christopher." She rolled her eyes.

CHAPTER TWENTY-SEVEN

The group walked into the huge containment room in the other building. Christopher let out a low whistle as he took in the mammoth metal cylinder filling the center of the room. "Now that's a launching pad. Three planets are the beginning of what trouble that device is capable of." He traced the outside of it and craned his head to the top to turn. "Chris, the drop on that is truly terrifying, and you tried to do a nosedive from it. You are one lucky woman that Dante has a secure grip on you."

"I find creative ways to challenge him."

Dante kissed her on the cheek. "It'll hold, so don't worry."

"You searched every inch of it? The inside checked out the same too?

Caleb nodded. "Yeah, we watched them from there." He pointed to a movable platform above the cylinder. "It ended up being crazy slow work. I don't know how they stood it."

"I do. Just the two of them in the cylinder. They managed fine down there." Christopher chuckled.

Dante laughed. "You got us there, Christopher. I admit my focus being on Angelina more than the cylinder while we were there, but not only for the usual reason."

"To prevent another plunge. I'd been the same way, Dante." He knocked on the metal and listened. "Nothing out of the ordinary, and you scanned it too." Even so, he used his scanner to test it. "Material rings true. Where's the place you cut the hole?"

Ryan answered and motioned to Christopher. "Around the other side."

"I see it." He knelt and traced the opening with his hand and scanned it. "Nothing unusual about it either, and none of those downloads showed it?"

"We never came across it that we saw, but our host kicked us out before we got all of it," said Alena.

"They're always an unfriendly bunch." He ran his hand over the cylinder in thought. "So, it's yet to be found, or no one cared enough about only this piece to merit a visual of it." Alika and Seth assisted their patient as he rose. "You said you cut the lid off too?"

Ryan nodded. "Yeah, another puzzler. A top that doesn't open? How did they launch the thing?"

"Three planets prove they discovered a way." He looked up at the cylinder again and groaned. "I'm not eager to check that out. Do you have a view or something of the top?"

"Give me a minute to pull it up." Ryan manipulated his data pad and projected a series of images before the group of the cylinder's top, with and without the lid and those with only the lid. "Take a look."

Christopher studied the holograms and traced the edges of the imagined cylinder with his fingers in midair. "You did have to slice it off. No sliding opening. No latch anywhere. No seam in the middle to indicate two halves spread to open it." He shook his head. "We've overlooked something."

"It's a recurring theme."

Christopher smiled as he patted Ryan's back. "One we're all sick of by now, but we're going to change that somehow. Where's the top you guys chopped off? Mind if we take another look?"

Lana pushed a few buttons on a console in the room. "We stored it behind here." The door opened into a large adjoining room to reveal a huge metal circular object that fit on the top of the cylinder.

Christopher walked over to it with the others. "You two came up empty on this too?"

"Dante and I never examined it. Dante's group checked it when they removed it. They didn't see anything."

"There's probably nothing, but we're here and it doesn't add up to me either." As he knelt to inspect the perimeter closer, he carefully ran his fingertips over it. "Seems to be pure metal. I don't see wires or something to indicate a sliding mechanism. Checks out clean too." He got back up and looked up at the cylinder again and back at the top on the floor, and his eyes trailed between the two several more times.

"I've glimpsed that look before on my husband's face, Christopher. Care to tell us what you're thinking?" asked Lana.

Christopher winked at her. "About ready to, but this may sound nuts."

"We've seen plenty of that around here, so hit us with it," said Caleb.

"What if we're looking at this wrong?"

"Add it to our count," said Dante.

"No, we're literally looking at this wrong." He motioned one hand to the cylinder and the other to the disk.

"We're not following, Christopher," said Alika.

"What if this piece never slid or opened, because the device didn't launch from this end."

Ryan said, "But when we went in we saw the case up like this with the top on it. That leaves them exploding it through the ... "

"No, there's another way."

Dante said, "What about Angelina and Alena? They saw the launching pad and the device at the facility."

"Exactly, but they never caught a glimpse of the top of the cylinder. What if the top is the bottom? How did Black Dragon launch it? Think about how you brought this here."

"The whole facility was a floating hangar. We opened the room up and transported the cylinder here. Pretty simple actually." Caleb's eyes lit up.

"So, do you think they didn't have the means to turn the entire thing whatever way they wanted and move it once they packed it full of poison?"

"There's no doubt the Dark Lord did," said Seth.

"If your theory is right, the other end gets removed when they approach their big day and then reattached for the next go around, or maybe there's no other end as we have in our mind," said Ryan.

"Exactly." Christopher pointed back to the cylinder at its floor level. "That on the bottom which is really your top appears solid, but I'll venture it's a 'false bottom' of some kind. This cylinder doesn't do anything when you consider the damage we've seen the device is capable of. However, I can't believe a piece this size doesn't connect somehow to the machine itself." He paused. "Do you have a metal image detector?"

"We can have one in your hands in a minute," said Caleb as he retrieved the item from a cabinet across the room.

"Yeah, a scanner may not be sensitive enough to pick it up," said Christopher, as he took the device Caleb offered. It had a five-by-eight-sized screen with several controls situated on the bottom. The machine hummed to life with a flick of a button, and Christopher knelt to trail it over the disk surface. After a couple of minutes, the handheld device only revealed the expected metal composition. However, he still had a large surface to examine, so he persisted with it.

"Christopher, that can't be doing you well. Let one of us take over," said Dante.

"No, I'm feeling better than you think. My doctors are amazing at what they do. Anyway, the time wouldn't pass like it did the last session for you." He grinned up at Dante.

"You're right, but I'm willing to take a turn for you." He wrapped his arm around Angelina's shoulder, and she leaned into him.

"Christopher, don't overdo it. Our talents only extend so far," said Alika.

"You and Seth underestimate yourselves, as you routinely perform miracles because of certain people. I had no reason to be worried. Wait, this doesn't look like the rest." He paused the device on one spot. "There's something here." Using the handheld detector, he enlarged and sharpened the image. "Maybe the tag or chip for it."

Angelina stooped alongside him. "Is there a signal from it?"

"I'm not reading anything yet."

"But the looks of it beg to differ," said Alena as she moved to get a closer view.

Angelina worked with her data pad and the embedded object. "Nothing, unless we're working with the wrong key. Perhaps it needs the real deal."

Christopher turned to her. "Considering what it's connected to, I'm taking that wager."

Dante knelt beside Angelina. "For all of us not in the biz, could you clue us in?"

"We need a Black Dragon data pad."

"Lucky for us, we have a few on hand. Any could work, but one whose owner showed himself to be above average in his devotion to Black Dragon is a safer bet," said Alena.

"Trey's data pad."

"Sorry, ahead of time." Alena touched her shoulder. "I'll get it."

Ryan nodded. "I'll come with you, Alena. We'll be right back, guys. Promise."

Angelina shook her head. "I can't believe it. We scanned the entire cylinder, but it didn't occur to me to check this. Maybe we had the answer all along."

"If so, that's on us, since we gave you the all-clear on it," said Caleb.

Lana sighed, "And put you and Alena in great danger for no reason. I'm so sorry."

"It's not your fault, and we don't know yet what we have or if it will be of any use." Angelina smiled at Christopher. "The true hero today is Christopher. I'm glad we let you out of medical now."

"Ended up being much easier than the other jobs you bring me."

"We got it," said Ryan as he handed the data pad to Angelina.

"We always come back to Trey." Angelina turned back to the embedded image with Trey's data pad. "Let's see if this is worth everything he put us through." Using her own data pad, within seconds she hacked back into the data pad and scanned it over the implanted impression. "I don't see anything. Maybe when we severed it from the cylinder, we cut something else. Hold up. Is that it?"

Christopher nodded. "It's faint though."

"What are we seeing?" asked Dante.

"A signal of sorts which is what we hoped to find. Yet the fact that it's barely registering with a Black Dragon data pad isn't what we anticipated," said Alena.

Angelina stared at the spot, her hands clenching at the hidden piece of intel. She heard Trey's laughter and voice in her head again, "*I know a great many things. I offered to tell you, Kate, but you didn't want to hear, remember?*"

She stood up and answered aloud before she could restrain herself, "I won't let you win, Trey."

Dante jumped up and put his arm around her waist. "Is he here again?"

"No, he's not. I'm sorry. I didn't mean to scare you." She took a deep breath, unclenched her hands and wrapped Dante in a hug. "We have his data pad, and it led us so far, but we've hit another roadblock. I'm just frustrated."

"I get it. You could do much worse than yelling at dead people." He slid back from her and looked at her. "This is us making progress, though. Together, remember?" He kissed her.

"But I do like your reminders." She leaned her head on his shoulder, her spirit settled again by his embrace. Her mind continued working as she stared at the disk. The data pad gave them a signal, but not enough. Maybe they needed something to boost it? No, it wasn't that. Suddenly she knew. Pieces of how Black Dragon operated that only she understood resurfaced, an unfortunate reality of her childhood. A memory stirred now of the visits to the Dark Lord with her father, but it didn't involve what happened to her during the visit. So, she allowed it to the forefront. The same part replayed in her mind. She heard her father grumble about the inconvenience of the routine, and the Dark Lord dismissed his complaint with a wave of his hand or a glare. "That's it," said Angelina.

"What is it?" asked Dante as he stroked her hair.

She stared up at him. "It's not only the data pad. We need a Black Dragon port. A direct interface."

"Are you sure? I mean ... "

"Yes. We've got half the puzzle. The corresponding one will be on the device itself. There's certain information with Black Dragon you must hook up to one of their ports to retrieve, but we have the means to unlock it now. "

"Which is another undercover mission into Black Dragon for you and Alena." Dante sighed, as he pulled her over again.

"I'm afraid so, Dante."

Ryan embraced Alena too. "Not again, Alena."

"Yes, again, but we'll be fine, Ryan." She smiled up at him.

CHAPTER TWENTY-EIGHT

A short time later the group stood inside Alena's and Angelina's ship, all reflecting identical worried expressions on their face, except for Alika who seemed unfazed by the turn of events.

Dante shook his head. "This is too fast. You didn't prepare at all."

"He's right. Start this tomorrow morning to make sure everything is in line before you go marching back, " said Ryan.

"Dante, we were just there, so we know the lay of the land. We need the port for the device's location," said Angelina.

Alena added as she leaned into Ryan, "This is the easy part. Trust us to do this like we've always done."

Dante and Ryan exchanged a look, and almost in unison, a sigh of surrender escaped them.

"There's no stopping you." Ryan kissed Alena.

"So be careful." Dante kissed Angelina as well.

The group returned to medical, and Alika settled in one of the chairs again. Once he had projected several images before him from his data pad and arranged everything to his satisfaction, he set to monitoring his students.

"How do you do this every time, Alika?" asked Dante.

He smiled as he continued watching the screen while his fingers moved across the bottom half of the data pad. "I must for them. These operations potentially hold enough trouble on their own. Among other roles, I'm to be the calm for them. to remind them their fear cannot cloud their minds. Don't allow it to rule you, young Dante. Come, you and Ryan, sit with the others and, let's do what we can for Angelina and Alena so they hurry back."

"We're approaching the facility again. Think we'll run into the same Black Dragon guy?" asked Alena.

"Likely we will. Either way, we know our way around the place, so locating a port isn't a problem."

"Duty calls," murmured Alena as they walked from the ship and approached the guards.

Angelina stifled a groan as a soldier shoved her forward after conducting the standard whiplash check for her mark, and she passed inspection.

"Never getting used to that," said Angelina as they continued down the corridor.

"Something's wrong if you do."

"This is where our instructions say to go, right?"

Alena nodded as they stopped in front of the door. "Yes, it's the same room as last time thanks to our commanding officer. Lucky us." She opened it, and another soldier greeted them.

"What's your business here?"

"Recently we helped with sorting recruits but got called away to another assignment. We completed it and received orders to return to resume our previous duties," said Alena.

"We also worked with one of the squadron leaders in training those placed in the fighter group."

"Step inside. I'm certain of who you assisted, and I'll inform him you've returned."

Once the soldier exited the room, the two sprang into action. Alena eyed the door as Angelina pulled out the Black Dragon data pad, along with the embedded impression they had carefully extracted from the disk. In seconds, she accessed the port, stuck a transfer drive into it, and the search began.

Come on, pleaded Angelina as she willed the screen to pull up what she needed. An image of the launch pad appeared. *I'm on the right track. Give me the other half now.* Moments later a new picture emerged under the screen. It was cylindrical shaped too but included controls on the outside, and the schematics indicated it possessed a reservoir to contain a substance inside. *This is it. I just need the where.* She scrolled down to spot a location and held back a scream. *That's not it. That's its previous site. Where did they move it?*

"Time's almost up," said Alena.

"I know. Still working on it." She continued to scroll frantically and finally glimpsed a name. Sikata. *Could it be? There's nothing there.*

Suddenly Alena gripped her arm and whispered, "Zero" as the door opened.

Angelina's hand eased out the transfer drive and slid it into her gear as her other hand did the same to the piece of disk and data pad. Her hand tried to slide over the console to switch to another image, but too late.

"Come to assist with the recruits again? You were most helpful before." He pointed to the monitor. "However, that hardly appears to be the case."

Angelina waved dismissively at it while attempting to calm the alarms sounding in her head. "I started switching to the other, but I thought it would be wise to see how the recruits were already distributed out." She turned it to a blank screen. "Perhaps get an idea of where we needed to send more, but I'm sure you have insight to offer."

"I do." He walked closer to the two. "We all must be clear to our place at Black Dragon. It can become troublesome when we overstep our bounds, and maybe you two require a reminder. Is that what should happen here?" He drew two swords and slid them between where the helmet and front armor break laid on each of them.

"No, sir," said Alena and Angelina in unison.

"Do I need to make sure?" His blade on Angelina's neck pressed enough to produce a tiny stream of blood.

"No, sir. You delivered your message, and your orders will be followed." Angelina stood motionless, watching the leader under her Black Dragon helmet and knowing as Alena did he could end them both with a swipe of the blade. The steady trickle of blood continued its leisurely path down her throat and chest.

"Excellent as it would be a pity to lose capable soldiers like you." He looked between them before lowering the blades to his sides. "I like your initiative but tread cautiously. Other squadron leaders are not as understanding as me."

"Our sole desire is to serve Black Dragon, and we are grateful for your leadership today," said Alena.

"No doubt you two will fulfill that wish and be used to your fullest potential with the upcoming attack, one that promises many recruits for us."

Fear struck Angelina, and she knew Alena's thoughts plunged to the same place as their near-death experience seconds before vanished from their minds. Somehow in an even Black Dragon voice, Angelina said, "Yes, the upcoming attack. Our chance to prove our worth."

"It won't be long now. The Premier Black Dragon is focused on preparing the troops for this approaching offensive and making certain the weapon is ready for it. Rather surprising it's only one planet this time."

"It does seem peculiar after the last hit," Alena echoed as she processed the bombshell the troop had delivered.

"From what I surmised, he only wants a reminder of what we're capable of. It's been quiet here. All the activity is where you pulled up a moment ago."

"At Sikata," said Angelina.

"Yes, that facility and the surrounding area is an organized chaos now. With wanting to launch the offensive in three days, it's pushing it. Nobody dares disappoint him though, so it will happen on schedule." He paused. "You two would be more useful assisting there than remaining here."

"That sounds like a wise decision. After all, you have this well under control, sir," said Angelina.

As she hoped, the squadron leader snatched up the compliment, and she could almost see the smile beneath his helmet. "I do, and it will remain so while I am in charge here." He looked down at his data pad. "There are several items they could use help with, and you two have the skills to match. The list is growing, so you won't be disappointed. In particular, the device needs examining and final checks run before it's launched. Once done, considering your fighting abilities, fall into line with the ground troops. Report to Sikata now."

"As you command, sir," said Alena.

"And we will heed your words from earlier, sir," said Angelina.

"See that you do. Dismissed."

—ele—

"Do you see what happened? They almost got their throat slit," railed Dante.

Ryan continued, "Too close, and he spared them because he's one of the nice ones? That passes for nice? Alika, tell them to come back, please."

Alika put his hand up as he prepared to answer Angelina and Alena.

"A perfectly timed list," said Angelina as they sat in the cockpit of their ship again and maneuvered it clear of the Black Dragon facility.

"I determined it the appropriate item to make its way to his data pad from what you learned and the direction the conversation turned," said Alika.

Angelina stared at the information she captured earlier and displayed it on the viewscreen for the two of them. "Let's hope this facility doesn't have added security because we don't have time to prepare before going in. With what it's holding, I'd expect it to be better protected."

"We went through this last time, and it was all the norm. The sketch of the site isn't too detailed, but nothing screams extra clearances. Besides, I didn't think Sikata had anything worth mentioning," said Alena.

"Everyone shares our opinion on it, which is what makes it the perfect hiding place."

Alena nodded. "Alika, do we have everything together to pull this off?"

"Your authorizations are done for the ship, so you shouldn't arouse suspicion on that front. As far as a plan, you have your orders regarding the device. Stick to them to avoid any questions. To complete the necessary testing and ensure it's working properly, you'd have to access solid intel on how it operates."

Alena said, "So no one should question our probing into the database. And a detailed blueprint of the facility needs to find its way on our data pad."

"Because I envision a return visit," said Angelina.

"This definitely qualifies as that rushing into things you promised you wouldn't do," said Dante.

Ryan piped in, "Yeah, I wish you could use tonight to prepare, and wait until tomorrow morning before you go."

"We all know we don't have that time to spare, and I'm positive the squadron leader checks that we made it over to Sikata," said Alena.

"Remember, he's one of the nice ones too. If I didn't have a sword at my throat at the time, I might have laughed when he said that."

"Nobody laughed here," whispered Dante.

"I expect not, Dante," she whispered back. "It's looking to be a long night for all of us when we return, but we'll make time to catch up."

"All we want is you two back safe."

"Once we get what we need, we'll deliver on that request." She paused. "My sensible half here says we're approaching the portal to place us in Black Dragon company again."

Caleb came up behind Ryan and Dante. "None of us likes this, but you know they're right. Telling you to relax is a waste of time, but they've got this. A lot has to come together with the timeframe too."

Lana sighed. "We have to start formulating that plan because no matter what they say, they'll be spent once they return."

"Getting back isn't a done deal, Lana." Ryan stared at the screen.

Lana touched Ryan and Dante on the shoulder. "They have two amazing reasons to make sure they do."

CHAPTER TWENTY-NINE

"Both times." Alena shook her head as they meandered down the corridor of the Sikata facility and passed Black Dragon soldiers.

"I'm lucky like that today," muttered Angelina as she rolled her aching neck.

"You'll forget about it later."

Angelina stifled a chuckle at Alena's teasing. "You're right." She turned her thoughts from Dante to refocus on the current task. The complex was impressive, tucked away from what the galaxy considered a desolate corner of the planet, consisting of mostly a desert landscape. Beyond that, the planet fared better with a mountainous terrain and a multitude of caverns which combined to unearth a lucrative mining industry. However, the stretch between the two proved considerable, enough that this place stayed away from curious eyes. Still, it amounted to an astonishing feat with the size of the facility, and she glimpsed another structure next to this one. They passed several doors as they continued, but the simplified schematic they discovered with their limited time indicated the prize lay ahead. She murmured, "Crowded everywhere."

"Like everyone is on top of each other which could prove challenging to check our list off if the hallways alone are like this."

Angelina stopped in front of a huge metal sliding door at the end of the corridor. "We'll find a way. We have our orders."

"Your orders?" asked the soldier.

"As requested, sir." Angelina supplied them as asked.

"Proceed and file your report upon completion. Notify the squadron leader of any potential issues you uncover."

The two nodded and approached the device.

Angelina said, "It's massive. It needs another whole hangar to contain it."

"Like before."

"Impressive isn't it?" asked a soldier who came to stand beside them.

"It does take your breath away," said Alena.

He laughed. "The colonists will say that again soon."

"All thanks to us, and we're here to ensure that's the case, that it's working properly. If you'll excuse us?" said Angelina.

Instead, he continued walking with them. "I'm in charge of this area and headed to do similar work, so we'll be seeing more of each other today."

The three made their way to the cylindrical weapon as they weaved their way between the other soldiers strolling throughout the room on task. Angelina spotted a portal attached to the device and steered the group towards it. "I'll get preliminary readings, and then I can perform a full diagnostic on it. This could take time."

Alena nodded as she stationed herself directly in front of Angelina to provide cover for what information Angelina accessed. However, the squadron leader for this area proved more hands-on than previous ones and seemed intent on getting a closer look. "Does it appear ready to launch so far to you?"

"I just started the checks on it, so I can't give you that answer yet."

Alena moved to conceal Angelina's work again and reengaged the soldier. "We know it works. Three planets are proof. Did something come up to have us believe there's a problem?"

"No, to my knowledge the Premier is simply being thorough. Refilling it with what's needed each time is quite the task too. Every planet is a little different, with population and size, and the like."

"And we're striking ... "

"Only the Premier knows, and our job is to simply fill the device to his specifications. When we land, that's when we'll know too."

"It worked last time, so there's no reason to change. If everything shows perfectly with this, I wonder if he would move up the attack?"

"No, he made it clear his timeline is set either way."

"You're right, and he's patient when he needs to be. Always a valuable asset for someone in his position."

"He's like the Dark Lord and the Black Dragon Commander in that way. I still can't believe they're gone and dispatched by that Freedom Fighter, Dante. I've heard about him in battle, like everyone else, but still if they ever get a hold of him, they'll hack him to pieces with his sunspear."

"Then he better hope we never capture him."

"What do you think, over there? Think he had it in him?"

Angelina continued working at the port, detesting the turn the conversation took. Yet she had no choice but to give a response that fell into line with her current role. "He's the Black Dragon Commander's son, and he showed he had more of his father in him than anyone credited him. It's still hard to fathom how he managed it, but he'll pay for it one day."

"I want to be there to see it."

"Us too." She paused. "After we get baseline readings and examine them, we'll run a few simulations."

"But we've got several more measurements to obtain before we're prepared for the simulations," said Alena.

"I'll be on the other end, doing visual checks. Let me know when we're ready."

Alena nodded. "Yes, sir." Once the Black Dragon soldier walked away, she knelt beside Angelina and asked, "How are we coming?"

"Judge for yourself." She indicated toward Alena's data pad.

Alena turned her attention to it while Angelina took over the lookout role. The first screen showed a long list of values within the normal range of the device, and they continued to come in like clockwork. That would be Alika's doing upon Angelina supplying him with the sample data from the device. The next screens displayed the detailed schematics of the weapon they hoped for and the blueprint for the facility. "It's in order so far."

"Is it?"

"Scrolling through the last of it now." The information switched to intel about the nearby building. "There's that."

"Yes, that."

"Do we need to check it out?"

"I don't think it a wise move this time."

"Agreed." Alena stared down at the data pad as she realized the truth. The temptation to scope it out today beckoned but giving in would arouse suspicion, a risk they couldn't afford. They already escaped one close call earlier. As she continued the inner battle, she reasoned Angelina downloaded the detailed schematic, and it would have to suffice. That day there would be added security measures. The slightest hesitancy or misstep could reveal it being their first time there. She looked up and met Angelina's gaze underneath the Black Dragon helmet, knowing the same thoughts abounded. They would be forced to go in blind, a scenario they both hated. Yet they reached the identical conclusion. "We leave it alone."

"We must. Any other readings we should get?"

"No. If we're to stay on schedule, we start the simulations."

Angelina nodded as she stood up with Alena, and they searched for the Black Dragon leader.

⁓ℰℓℯ⁓

Caleb watched one of the overhead screens Alika projected as the information scrolled across. "Dante, the intel your girl wrestles out of a machine never ceases to wow me."

Dante glanced over at the screen, but his eyes returned to the one tracking Angelina's and Alena's movements as he forced an uneasy smile. "Yeah, she's amazing with that."

Lana put an arm around Dante's shoulder. "She won't return any sooner because you and Ryan stare at the monitor. Alika has done this countless times."

"But this is my first time seeing her in the heart of Black Dragon, and I'm scared that she won't come back, cuz," said Dante.

"Dante and Ryan can continue assisting Alika, and the rest of us can begin planning the next phase," said Seth.

"Thanks for coming so quickly," said Caleb as he walked alongside Commander Gabe toward the medical room that had transformed into a strategy room.

"Of course. Are the other commanders here?"

"The aim is tomorrow with them. However, your inside knowledge about two individuals allowed us to bring you ahead of schedule."

"Makes sense now. We're in the medical wing though. This isn't reassuring."

"He's okay, but it was scary at first. You haven't met him yet, but there's no time like the present. We're just getting to know him ourselves."

"I'm guessing how that happened, so I'm sure I'll like him." He paused. "Where are the other two?"

Caleb opened the door to the room and promptly shut it behind him. "Still undercover. Expected back tonight. We're all worried, but you can imagine Dante and Ryan right now. They've been glued to the screen, monitoring their two."

"As I would expect. Has everything gone smoothly?"

"Mostly. Had one time that made us panic. Nearly got their throat slit, and Ryan and Dante almost had a heart attack watching."

Gabe shook his head. "Poor guys."

"Yeah, but so far their two are staying far enough away from the blade point." He pointed to a screen being projected ahead of them.

"In full Black Dragon again? Where are they at?"

"Deep in one of the enemy's facilities. We'll fill you in."

Gabe came behind Ryan and Dante. "How are you two holding up?"

"I've been better," said Ryan.

Dante nodded. "Ask me again when she's back."

Without turning from the screen, Alika said, "My two students will return to us soon, and these two men's hearts will be at ease again, Gabe."

Caleb smiled. "And this is their Elder."

"A pleasure to meet you ... " Gabe grasped Alika's hand in greeting.

"Within this circle, it is Alika. Apart from here, I'm either unknown entirely, or I adopt a variety of other names. You understand, Gabe?"

"I've been briefed on how your group works and the importance of it remaining so for everyone's safety. You've done great work. Your two are exceptional."

"I agree." Alika chuckled as he continued to watch the screen. "They make the best use of their training."

Gabe turned to Christopher. "I'm told you're lucky to still be with us, my friend. For any friend of theirs is mine as well. If you don't mind me asking, what happened?"

"It went something like this." He proceeded to hit the high points of the deadly encounter with the Black Dragon loyalists. "There's the shortened version of how I ended up in medical."

"I have a renewed appreciation for the dangers of the shipping business, and I'm thankful the two of them reached you in time. It's good to know you, Christopher or whoever you happen to be today."

Christopher laughed. "You catch on fast."

"It's necessary around here. All of you will be relieved to know the Santiagos' transition back continues going well. Our troops remain there as a precaution as requested. From all reports we've received, we cleared out the Black Dragon elements there."

"Encouraging news." Seth looked over at Christopher. "However, they almost succeeded with this last attempt. It is one of the reasons Alika's group insisted on keeping their identity quiet. We're seeing what they've always kept at the forefront."

CHAPTER THIRTY

Angelina stared down as the reading registered from the fourth simulation, and she calmed herself with a reminder she didn't truly witness a whole planet of people erased from existence. *If you don't stop it in time, it will be for real.* A dreaded voice whispered inside her head. For an instant, her mind revisited the planet after the devastation and heard the woman's agonizing cry emerge from the ashes. Forcing it back, she said, "Another successful run. Shall we do another?"

The Black Dragon leader asked, "That was the fourth one?"

Alena nodded. "Yes, sir."

"Which is what we agreed to."

"We did, sir. Of course, we'll do as you command if you think more are in order."

"We should be through." He scrolled through the information from the simulations. "Nothing from the readings points to any potential problems. I'll file the report, along with my recommendation to proceed as planned. Soon another planet will be reminded of who rules the stars."

"They will feel that power crushing them," said Angelina.

"And we get to be a part of it," said Alena.

"An amazing time to be Black Dragon. Both of you are dismissed to join the ground troops and begin preparing with them."

"Yes, sir," said Alena and Angelina in unison.

Angelina stared down at the other building as the ship lifted off. "You think we should have tried?"

"No, we made the right call."

"In a couple of days, will we still say that?"

"It's done now. Leave it alone."

❧

Dante and Ryan breathed a sigh of relief in unison as the two went through the portal.

Dante asked, "Can we talk to them?"

"Yes, you two have been patient," said Alika.

"Feeling good about this last run?" asked Ryan.

Alena chuckled. "We are. The question is how did you two do?"

"We managed. Sounds like it went reasonably smoothly on your side. You want us to come meet you?" asked Dante.

"After we make a needed wardrobe change. Black Dragon armor doesn't get you a warm welcome around here, and showers are in order after this last trip," said Angelina.

"You're back safe. That's what matters."

"We know, but you thought Freedom Fighter armor didn't breathe. Black Dragon gear is tons worse. We'll call when we're ready."

Seth motioned Dante and Ryan to bring their seats into the circle. "In the meantime, it's time to get input from you and Alika."

After listening to the recap from the group, Ryan said, "That's a lot to pull together by tomorrow, but we don't have a choice."

"Are all the commanders on board?" asked Dante.

"We'll convince them when the rest get here early tomorrow morning," said Caleb.

❧

With her fingertips, Alena traced a path on the blueprint. "This one takes us all the way. Rear exit too."

Ryan cut off the rest of her words as he arrived to engulf her in his arms. "Alena, I don't know how Alika stays calm watching you. I thought I'd go out of my mind." He didn't give her a chance to answer before he kissed her.

Dante wrapped one arm around Angelina's waist, and his other hand stroked her cheek. "Back safe where you belong." His eyes zeroed in on something at her neck, and his hand slid down to brush it. "What's that?"

"Nothing. Just the reminder from the Black Dragon squadron leader to know my place."

"I thought the blade didn't get you."

"Not in any way to be concerned. Now stop." She pulled him closer. "Show me how happy you are I made it back."

"That I can do." He took his time enjoying a long, gentle kiss with her.

She stared up at him, her eyes reflecting the dreamy state his embraces transported her and murmured, "I could stay like this with you all evening happily."

"You'll get no objections from me."

"I know." She ran her fingers through his hair and sighed. "But there's a lot of work ahead of us before that happens. So, we need to get started."

"You're right, but once more." He kissed her again.

<hr>

"I'm relieved it's as complete as it appeared." Angelina scanned the projected data with the others while leaning up against Dante on the couch in medical.

"Under the scrutiny of Black Dragon eyes always poses a challenge," agreed Alena as she sat on another sofa next to Ryan. "How about our timetable?"

Lana nodded. "We beat it. Tomorrow morning we'll have the commanders caught up and be issuing their orders, and they'll return for the remainder of the day to gather their troops. The following day we head out. It's tight, but we'll be there the day before they launch the attack."

Caleb said, "The schematics look a little different, and there's a couple of twists to work out."

"But essentially we've done it once before. This go-around we know this is the device. So, we don't have to redraw the battlefield blueprint. In fact, we're in better shape. We have a few more blades we didn't have and some of the best I've seen," said Gabe, as he smiled at Dante, Angelina, and Alena.

"I won't be on a solo mission this time, so you can count on me." Dante looked over at Christopher. "Christopher may even feel well enough to join us."

"I'll help, but I'm leaving the blade work to you. I wouldn't mind taking out Black Dragon from the air though."

Caleb grinned. "I'll make that happen for you."

"Our strength is undoubtedly our blades, but our ability to get behind enemy lines is the greater need first," said Angelina.

Dante shook his head. "You and Alena got what we needed and almost had your throat sliced open for it."

"The other building must be breached, so your group can retrieve the device."

He took her face in his hands. "This isn't your group and my group. We do this together, Angelina. I won't have it any other way."

She stared at the fire radiating from those dark brown eyes of his. "Neither will I, Dante. We've always done it together. Every battlefield we've ever been through, I've been by your side."

"And you would not leave me now."

"I would not, my Dante," she said. "Sometimes there are tasks meant for each of us, but they're all part of the same vision. You know that. The Elders Hall." She paused. "Alena and I must be the ones to clear the path for you and the others to accomplish the other. Once we've done that, our blades will be beside you."

He dropped one hand to her shoulder. "Although I know you're right, I'm not happy about it."

"I'm not either, but you have to stop worrying about me, Dante."

"I'm trying." He brushed her lips with his. "I know you can handle yourself, and you've made your case for this one too, so I'm stuck." He encircled his arm back around her waist and with his other hand entwined his hand with hers.

"I too harbor misgivings about their returning with everything that will transpire. Are we certain this is the wisest path?" asked Seth.

"Yes, why not send a small ground troop to penetrate or attack it from the air and then direct troops in?" asked Ryan.

"Because it will throw up every alarm," said Alena.

"Which is what we must avoid at all costs at the initial stage. It's understood, once the attack commences our element of surprise vanishes. However, we need specific items taken care of from the other building before they realize our true intent. A Black Dragon soldier will not arouse any suspicion. As much as I abhor the idea of them disguised as the enemy again, it is the best strategy," said Alika.

"We'll present the plan to the rest of the commanders tomorrow. If you see any issues, we must address them now. Anyone?" Lana's words were met with silence.

"Great, because the day after we're the Black Dragon's wakeup call. We attack them and retrieve the device. This time we do it right," said Caleb.

Alena and Ryan sat cuddled on the couch inside the quarters Ryan claimed as his when at the fortress. "We didn't get much time left for each other, Ryan."

"That was expected with how today turned out, but I'll take whatever time I get with you."

"Me too." she grinned. "Did you really stay glued to the monitor all the time?"

"Couldn't tear me away from it."

"I never dreamed Black Dragon armor could be that mesmerizing."

He pulled her closer. "Teasing me again, Alena. You know full well, that it's you, the beautiful woman underneath that armor which claims all of me." Without hesitation, he captured her in his arms and began to kiss her.

Dante lay nestled on the couch with Angelina, one arm encircling her waist and the other rubbing the back of her neck. "Feeling better?"

"Absolutely, I'm here with you."

"I'd like to strangle the Black Dragon soldier that dared hurt you."

"You're making it all better."

"I'm just getting started." His warm breath tickled her ear as he kissed a leisurely trail up and down her neck.

"How you take care of me, Dante ... " she breathed out.

"Is what, my Angelina?" he murmured.

"There are no words."

Christopher and Alika grinned as Dante and Ryan left the ship after giving their company for the evening a goodnight kiss that still had the two smiling dreamily.

"Is it always like this, Alika?" chuckled Christopher.

"Without fail."

Angelina and Alena turned at the teasing and sat with the two as they all laughed.

"Enough from both of you. Christopher, will you be comfortable in the extra quarters tonight?" asked Alena.

"Should be and thanks for putting me up for the night. I hoped to move up to my ship, but I'm inching closer, right?"

"Yes, and your physician's confidence to release you to our care is a plus."

"Or they're having an off day." Angelina's eyes twinkled. "I don't do well supervising myself most of the time, let alone someone else."

"That's true, Chris." He chuckled as he turned to Alika. "Is this a test you and Seth engineered?"

Alika laughed. "It's not. Fortunately for you, I'll be close by inside my vessel if you require attention, and I can call for Seth if necessary. However, with the commanders' arrival tomorrow, you should be here with us. We all must get some sleep now."

"Yes, but I wonder if ... " Angelina bit her lip as she trailed off.

"What's bothering you?" asked Alika.

"It's different this time. We know it, but they don't."

"Have you seen anything, a vision prompting us in a separate direction?" asked Christopher.

"No, nothing from the Ancient One to intervene on another front. Our place is by their side for this battle."

"Then that's where we'll be," said Alika.

"If we don't stop it this time, it will be the fulfillment of every nightmare we've envisioned. The others only think they've witnessed it, but we know the truth. Nothing holds it back this time." Tears streamed down her face as she put her head in her hands.

Alena put her arm around Angelina's shoulder and rested her head there. "We'll stop them in time."

CHAPTER THIRTY-ONE

The next morning Lana stood in the meeting room of the fortress, making final preparations with Caleb, Seth, and Gabe. She turned as Ryan and Dante reentered it. "Are we all set for today?"

Ryan said, "Probably twenty minutes or so until the rest of the commanders arrive, but we checked in on our friends."

Dante grinned. "It made for a pleasant start to our morning."

Caleb laughed. "I knew you two wouldn't mind taking that task on. I believe in starting my day the same way." He encircled his arm around Lana and kissed her.

⁓ ✐ ⁓

Angelina analyzed the blueprint of the facility while she sat with the others on the ship, waiting for Lana to begin the meeting.

"All work again, huh?" asked Christopher.

A small smile appeared. "I switch gears quickly."

"It's still nice to see the side of you Dante brings out."

She turned to him. "I like that side of me too. I like me better. Perhaps one of these days I can ... " She sighed as she focused on the screen. "Lana's starting."

⁓ ✐ ⁓

Lana and Caleb prepared for questions, as they concluded their report along with what needed to happen next.

"One of our squadrons has to gain control here before we can make substantial progress, right?" Commander Cephas pointed to the building situated near the facility.

"Someone does, but it won't be one of our squadrons," said Lana.

"Then who will?"

"The two spear-bearers."

"They've agreed to?"

"Yes. You can ask them yourself since they are here for this meeting."

The newly arrived commanders looked around the room in confusion.

"Audio only gentleman, and it's relaying through a scrambler, so it will sound computer generated." She paused. "Spear-bearers, welcome and I trust you heard the question."

Angelina's scrambled voice rang through the fortress's comm system. "Greetings to all. I wish it were under different circumstances, but we are committed to helping you stop the Black Dragon from launching this attack. So yes, we will be the ones to breach the building to enable you to retrieve the device."

"You forgot something basic to first meetings," joked Dante.

Angelina laughed. "You're right, Dante, but I'm told I've been known to skip through introductions. I'm one of the spear-bearers."

Another voice emerged, "And I'm the other spear-bearer, and I echo my comrade's greeting. I'm also the better of the two of us with the blade."

The group laughed and Angelina returned, "You wish. We have our Elder with us too that we owe our fighting skills as well as our ego. There is also another individual who will be assisting us in some capacity with this operation. Is that to your satisfaction, Dante?"

"Yes, you did well."

"Thank you. We'll gladly answer any questions to accomplish the task before us, but we'll pass the lead back to Lana now."

The meeting continued with Angelina's group adding their expertise to the discussion and pulling out the high points in the data they had recovered.

"There's nothing to reveal which planet they're striking?" asked Commander Austin.

Lana sighed. "No, there's not. The troop the spear-bearers spoke to appears to be correct on that point."

"How can we warn the colonies, if we have no idea where Black Dragon will strike?"

"We have to stop them before the attack happens. That's the only solution," said Caleb.

Angelina spoke up. "They're right. Do as they ask in this area. Spreading the word of an assault when the location isn't known will only make things worse and possibly bring to pass what we mean to prevent. It will only cause panic among the people, and there's nowhere to tell them to go because there is no safe zone. In that sense, we are where we have always been since we discovered Black Dragon had the device. Even if we did uncover the target, it wouldn't be our best strategy to announce it. If the Black Dragon detected a mass exodus from a planet, they would be alerted we knew where they planned to attack. Rather than call it off, they would simply choose a different mark, and it is one of the few scenarios that would prompt them to move up their attack. In the end, a whole planet of colonists would still be killed. So, it's imperative, that you remain silent about the impending attack. You must stick to the script Lana gives you, if we're to retrieve the device in time and prevent the unthinkable from becoming reality."

⁓

Lana leaned into Caleb on the couch in the fortress. "Glad that's over. I hope the commanders have enough time to pull it together."

"They'll get it done." He kissed her forehead and turned to Ryan. "I know you need to leave to gather your fleet for tomorrow too. As soon as you're finished though, I want you to head back for a final go-over tonight. If you don't mind, of course."

He grinned. "I'll fit it in, as I counted on making a trip back this evening." He focused on Alena and wound his arms around her waist. "It'll be late, but I want to see you for a little bit."

"I'll always make time for you, Ryan. I knew what I got myself into when I started dating a commander. Take care of everything for tomorrow, and I'll see you this evening, no matter the hour."

"Waiting up for me. You're the best, Alena." He enjoyed a long kiss with her. "See you, then."

"Absolutely," she said as he took his time releasing her and walked out of the fortress.

Dante came over to Angelina and sat beside her. "I don't want to distract you, but I thought I should check on you. You've been at it for a while nonstop." He put an arm on her shoulder. "How's it coming?"

She rubbed her forehead as her eyes remained focused on the screen, and her fingers found their place on the keypad again. "Slowly and carefully. Everything is riding on me getting this perfect."

"You will. I have complete faith in you."

"For unknown reasons."

"No, because you always come through for me." He kissed her on the cheek as he got back up. "I'll leave you to it, my Angelina."

❦

Simon settled in the cockpit seat of his ship and prepared to answer the communication awaiting him. He cleared his throat and said, "I'm here. My apologies for the delay."

A familiar male voice came through, "You always have an excellent reason."

"Of course. I've been doing field work but trying to maintain my presence at home too."

"A delicate balance indeed. How does it progress?"

"I'm sorry to report everyone is staying exceptionally quiet. There's a fear of saying too much and what that gets you."

"Yet there's a hefty payoff for not keeping silent. That's not persuasion enough?"

"It will always prevail with one group of individuals. Others are concerned about saving their skin more than the payoff, and they're steering clear of any entanglements with that risk factor."

"Your suggestions?"

"There are plenty that care about the payoff, and soon one of them will be successful with taking out the desired targets. Greed is a powerful master."

"What about Commander Austin? What is he busy with currently?"

"My father has stayed in the commander role. He goes back and forth to the fortress regularly now and is spending more time with training exercises. Seeing those three planets destroyed put him and everyone else on edge."

"Nothing new then?"

"I'm afraid not, and anytime my brother or I try to pull anything from him he winds up tighter."

"Where is he now?"

"I just got back from field work, but my mother mentioned his conducting another training exercise today with the troops. He's adamant we're as ready as possible for a Black Dragon attack."

The man laughed. "How do you believe that works out for them?"

"I'd say a waste of time, but nobody pays attention to me."

"You ensure it stays that way. Eventually, someone lets something slip, and you'll alert us accordingly."

"As always I will, sir."

"Keep in touch, and goodbye for now."

Simon turned off the communication and erased any record of the conversation. He took a deep breath and muttered, "Yeah, pure joy. Back to the house to check in for a bit. I can already hear Sanders."

CHAPTER THIRTY-TWO

Angelina and Alena sat on their ship's couch, staring out the cockpit as the morning light streaked across the sky the next day.

Alika emerged with a medical bag in hand alongside Christopher and said, "This must be done before the armor goes on."

The ship door opened as Dante and Ryan strolled in. Dante said, "Thought we would ... "

"It'll be a minute. We're making sure they pass inspection," said Christopher.

"Forgot about that part for them," Ryan said as he and Dante approached the two women and sadness reflected on their faces.

"I wish they didn't have to do this every time," said Dante.

Christopher brushed the clear substance on the back of their necks. "Us too, but this insures you get them back."

Alika gathered the last used syringe for disposal elsewhere. "We're done."

"Are we certain it took?" asked Dante.

"Have a peek. At least the mark. Unless you want to draw blood, you'll need to take our word on the other," said Christopher.

Ryan stepped closer to the back of the women's necks, "We'll trust your word." He leaned down to examine Alena's neck. She wore a tight black shirt that clung to her as did Angelina, but its back swooped down sufficiently to give an easy view of the Black Dragon image that now appeared on her.

"It's a replica of the design we saw." Dante stared at the same mark on Angelina.

"It's unnerving to see it on them the first time," said Alika.

"But the alternative is unthinkable," said Dante.

"Agreed," said Ryan as they came around to sit next to Alena and Angelina.

"We got this, okay?" Angelina answered the unspoken question in Dante's eyes as she stroked the side of his face. "How about the two of you help us get our gear on?"

He grinned. "My specialty is helping you take it off, but I'll make an exception."

"We're not down in the cylinder still, Dante." She laughed as the group got up.

"Only the helmets left," said Ryan.

"We should do those because we can't chance messing up our hair," joked Alena.

"That's what you're worried about today?" said Dante.

Angelina smiled. "In this case, we can't have a strand come out of place."

"Then no playing in it before you leave?"

"Afraid not. You should've thought of that earlier."

"You're right, but before you put the helmet on and leave ... " He pulled her over and kissed her, but it wasn't enough and he kissed her again. He murmured, "Tonight, you're mine, my Angelina."

"Yes, my Dante," she whispered as he released her. She smiled as she caught Alena and Ryan saying their goodbyes. Moments later the helmets completed the wardrobe.

Alika did a final inspection of their appearance, down to tugging on the back collar of the armor to be certain no hair would fall and double-checking that their marks were clearly seen. Thankfully, he didn't mimic the roughness of the Black Dragon inspection. "Let's hear you now."

"That part is creepy too," said Christopher to Dante and Ryan, as two Black Dragon troop voices emerged.

Angelina and Alena watched from the cockpit as the group hurried back to the fortress.

"Do you think the commanders followed the script as they were instructed?" asked Angelina.

"Lana told them, and you were adamant on that point too."

"Same question."

"We hope they did." Alena paused. "Maybe it helps when they realize about the first time."

"That they'll somehow understand what I kept from them."

"Not you, what we held from them. It will always be the right decision for all the reasons you gave yesterday and ones we didn't even know. Besides, it was never our choice."

"Will they see it so clearly?"

"We have to let it go." She settled in the pilot seat and motioned for Angelina to take her position. "Today is a new battle, and I need you with me."

"I am with you, Alena." Angelina touched her on the shoulder and sat in the copilot seat. Her hands swiped over the console. "Can you hear us now? Perfect. We're headed for the portal."

Lana watched with Alika and Seth at her side. Her voice came through the comm system to all the fleets. "This is Lana. Do not shoot at the ship appearing to be Black Dragon. They are part of the operation for today, so I repeat do not shoot at that ship." She turned to the two. "Now it begins."

—ele—

"Stand still before I break your neck in two," barked the Black Dragon soldier with the stranglehold on Angelina. The armor in the front dug into her neck with the whiplash he intended on leaving the instant she and Alena stepped from their ship. "This one checks out."

"Yeah, he passes too. All day of this. I'm already sick of it." Another troop shoved Alena forward. "Get to work now."

"I thought he'd go through with his threat. That was brutal," said Angelina as they walked towards the building.

"I'm sure mine left a bruise too. Seems we're checking everyone today."

"If this is morning, by afternoon, nobody survives inspection." Angelina started to finger her neck but stopped the motion.

"Then you get them in their bad mood." Alena shook her head. "It's busier than before. Do you think they could have moved it?"

Angelina's steps slowed to match Alena's. "We tossed it around and decided no."

"We did. The last time is coming to mind though."

"The Premier is running things now, and he's more paranoid than the Dark Lord." She sighed. "We can't talk ourselves into a side trip." However, her eyes drifted to the larger building where the device had been stored on their last visit.

Alika's voice came through, "Do not second guess yourself. Put the former time behind you where it belongs. Carry out the task at hand. Once you get into this building's system, you can check for any significant change, including a relocation."

Angelina chuckled as the two resumed their pace. "The words of reason. " She turned to Alena. "That's supposed to be you."

Alena waved her hand as if dismissing Angelina. "The occasional slip up. It won't happen again."

Angelina lowered her voice, "An awful lot of personnel stacked at that door."

"I could do with less too."

"You have business here?" asked one of the soldiers stationed at the door.

"Yes, sir," answered the two in unison.

He motioned to two troops who came behind Angelina and Alena, and seconds later the troops gruffly reported, "Clear." Turning back to Alena and Angelina, he said, "Orders, now."

Ignoring the fire engulfing her throat for the second time today, Angelina said, "Final checkup for tomorrow." They showed him the Black Dragon instructions from their data pad.

He examined them. "I thought they completed all these."

"Irregular fluctuations were spotted in the last readings that came through. Slightly out of range, but they want it checked. It's coming from one of the system checks on this end rather than on the device."

"I'm not going through all this tightened security for any longer than we have to. The faster that blasted thing," he motioned toward the other building, "puts on its show again, the better." He signaled the two closer and sneered, "If there's a problem, you best find it and fix it. Because if this oversized explosive is still grounded past tomorrow, I'll hunt you both down and skewer you with my blade. Understood?"

"Yes, sir," they said in unison.

Alika said through the comm system. "The morale today at Black Dragon is unlike anything I've ever witnessed."

"Truly something to behold," muttered Angelina, as they walked through the corridor with the confidence sprung from memorizing the blueprint in record time.

Dante stood on the ship with Ryan, as his fleet along with the others waited on the other side of the portal. Only the commanders received regular updates on the progress of the spear-bearers. However, Ryan and Dante insisted on being afforded the additional linked-in monitoring of the two and now watched nervously as they entered the room to set in motion the first piece of the operation.

"You're here for what?" asked the squadron leader as he examined the order now on his data pad.

Angelina started again, "As I said, we're here to ... "

"I heard you, troop!" he yelled. "You told me there's a problem, and I'm just being informed. How did this report not get relayed to me? That device is scheduled to demolish a planet tomorrow, and it'll be our heads if it doesn't happen. I'll be sure the premier starts with you two, if I don't beat him to it!" His hand went to his blade.

Alena said calmly, "None of us want that, sir. We all have the same goal, to see it do its work as the premier wishes."

The squadron leader shouted behind him, "The rest of you, get back to it before I use a blade point to motivate you too!" He turned back to the two. "Continue. I'm still considering it as a solution for you."

"The fluctuations are barely registering. I'm sure there's no real problem, certainly not one that delays tomorrow's event. I already have a few possibilities of the cause, and they're all easy corrections," said Angelina.

"Sir, I've worked with him for a while," Alena glanced at Angelina, "and he's one of the best at sorting this situation out, which is why they dispatched us. This device will do its work as scheduled, if you allow us to do our job."

The squadron leader turned to Angelina. "You can deliver like he says."

"Yes, sir."

"You better, or we're back to our first solution, troop."

"Understood, sir."

"I'm supposed to alert the Premier of any problems."

Alena said, "What problem, sir? The Premier can't be bothered unnecessarily considering all the arrangements he's busy with. He left you in charge for a reason. You're an outstanding squadron leader, completely capable of handling this situation as you've already shown."

"And as you said, it'll be fixed, so there's nothing to report to him."

"Exactly, sir."

"You two have an hour to resolve it completely. If not, it gets sent to the premier, and you both," he tapped his sword hilt, "pay for your failure."

⸺ℓℓℓ ⸺

Dante took a deep breath. "How many times is that now?"

"Too many," said Ryan as he shook his head. "And he's going to be right up under them."

"How does she get it past him now?"

Alika said, "Already doubting them? I'm surprised by you two. Perhaps this is too much, and I need to update you with the other commanders."

Ryan and Dante jumped in at the same time. "No, Alika ... don't ... we mean ... "

Alika chuckled, "Seth, should I grant them another chance to formulate a proper response?"

"I believe so. Would you like to attempt again, gentlemen?"

"We'll calm down, but I don't know how you keep it together, monitoring all of this," said Ryan.

"It's the identical way you remain composed when directing your fleet in battle, commander. You trust yourself as you've been given the tools and abilities to lead them, and so you have confidence those you command are equipped to accomplish the task placed upon them. Correct, commander?" asked Seth.

"Yes, it is," said Ryan.

"Point made," said Dante.

"Excellent. Alika assures me you'll retain your current access." Seth paused. "Although, we do understand being on this side of it, not being in a position to directly intervene when it seems it could be helpful. However, this role has its season, so remain focused while in it. You'll both be in the thick of battle as you're accustomed soon enough."

⁓

"Well?" asked the squadron leader eyeing the two.

Angelina fumed. This guy had way overstayed their company as he had continued to stand over them. "Another minute for the readings to come in. We have to confirm we're seeing the same issue in this system before we start."

"Sir, we'll update you every few minutes if that's your wish until it's corrected. You must have a long list to see to with tomorrow, and this is keeping you needlessly tied up," said Alena.

Immediately the measurements came through. *Perfect timing, Alika*, thought Angelina as she projected them on the Black Dragon screen. "Same variations in the one area. I'll proceed now."

"Sir, it will be resolved. You have our word," repeated Alena, sensing the leader relenting.

"No more than ten minutes pass before I'm updated until it's settled."

"More than reasonable, sir," said Alena as he walked off.

⁓

"Excellent job with the camera too. I received it, and it verifies what the troop indicated when you first arrived today," said Alika. "Commanders, the two spear-bearers have confirmed the device is still at the presumed location."

"Perfect. Continue to hold your position and wait for the signal," said Lana.

❧

"I found it. Now to fix our issue." Angelina stealthily pulled out the transfer drive from her armor and slid it into the port. Her hand hung over it as if it naturally settled there while she worked.

"We're good." Alena blocked the rest of the port and pretended to be focused on the Black Dragon screen before them.

"I hope this works," said Angelina as the transfer drive silently deposited its prepared solution into the system. They had run the simulations at the fortress when she completed it, and everything appeared to go as it should. Those weren't real though. If she did it perfectly, the proof would be within the hour. *Dante, be right this time*, she pleaded inside as the download continued.

"It'll work. We have to keep our word, remember?" Alena pointed to the screen, making every appearance the two were figuring out a remedy.

"Did you update him?"

"Yes, it's covered. We stay in one piece for another ten minutes at least."

As the display approached the fifteen-minute mark, Angelina whispered, "It's done."

"Check it. Don't doubt yourself now."

"A lot is riding on this."

"There always is, but it's the business we're in. Make sure it took."

Angelina took a deep breath, and her hand moved over the console. She and Alena spotted it buried deep in the path, ready to make its full impact on the Black Dragon system. She slipped the transfer drive from the port to close it in her hand.

Alena turned to Angelina. "I stand by my earlier words. You are the best, so I don't know why you second-guess yourself."

Angelina already glided the screen to something else, as she slid the transfer drive back into her gear. "We both know that answer."

"No going there today." Alena paused. "We finished in time. I updated him, and he's en route to us. He'll be here any second now."

The squadron leader's voice boomed behind them. "I'm told you two may keep your head attached to your body."

Alena and Angelina turned and in unison replied, "Yes, sir."

"Let's hear it."

"We had a few working theories running for the source of the problem and discovered it to be a simple issue in the interface between this system and the device. It created what appeared to be irregularities, when in fact they were in range. The interface is connecting flawlessly now, the readings are showing true, and register well within the desired parameters," said Alena.

"I want to see it, now."

Angelina nodded. "Of course, sir. We already ran these." The screen showed readings well within the limits. "Although considering the importance of this, no doubt you wish to see it submitted yourself, so we'll do so again now. We fully expected those would be your orders." Angelina's hands slid over the console, and new readings scrolled across the screen a minute later.

The squadron leader studied the screen. "None are even bordering on the limits. I see nothing of interest to report to the premier, and I need to return to my long list. You two are lucky you're as competent as you boasted because you almost didn't survive the hour. Dismissed." He laughed as he left them.

Angelina walked briskly down the corridor with Alena. "That's what gets a laugh out of him for the day. Unbelievable."

"Black Dragon humor at its best or worst. I haven't decided."

CHAPTER THIRTY-THREE

Alena and Angelina stepped in front of the console on the pretense of reporting for their shift. Angelina murmured, "Here's where all the action starts."

Alena faked a yawn. "We have it easy today. If we blast anything with this weapon system, it'll be tomorrow's watch."

"Shouldn't then either. The device will be out of here for the day. Nothing worth protecting." Angelina's fingers slid over the panel, pulling up what she needed as they continued the chatter among the hum of the consoles and the other troops moving between them.

"Sounds like a boring couple of days."

Caleb announced, "Commanders, take your fleets through the portal. It's time."

"There's what?" Angelina and Alena heard the yell of the squadron leader from across the room. A mixture of rage and disbelief colored his voice. "How many? Are you sure? Don't just stand there! Get our fighters out there and in the air! Kill every last one of them!"

"We're trying, sir. It's completely unexpected though, so we're responding as quickly as possible," said one of the troops.

"You better get it together this instant." the squadron leader stopped, as a communication came through. "Of course, I see them. Agreed. All of us are goners if anything happens to it." He paused. "Get the troops in the skies and on the ground on your end. We should be able to give you the time you need. Have you gotten word to him?" He ended the transmission at the answer and muttered under his breath, "At least I'm not making that call." He turned back to those in the room. "Fire the weapons, now. Provide them a demonstration."

"Doing great, everyone. We surprised them, and they're scrambling. Ground troops, make your descent. The rest of you stay in the air, and do your worst," said Caleb.

Commander Austin saw them first and announced through the comm system. "You heard Caleb. We hold the skies. Right on schedule, there they are. Let's destroy them before they take us out. After all, we have their number."

The sky blazed with blaster fire. Ships sped to the ground in a fiery heap, all being Black Dragon. In contrast, the Freedom Fighter ship controlled the skies, and their ground troops were landing at an alarming rate. The turn of events didn't go unnoticed by the Black Dragon squadron leaders on Sikata.

"Our weapon system should be blasting them to shreds! What in the blazes is going on?" hollered the weapons squadron leader.

"Sir, they … I don't know how to explain it. See for yourself."

Like a wild animal, he hurled the troop across the room and stared at the screen. "How?"

The troop beside the console stumbled out a reply, "The weapon system acted like it was a step behind. One by one they've blown up most of the array. As soon as they spotted it, they went straight for it."

"They should've flown away from it as fast as they could and be nothing more than a pile of dust now!"

"I don't understand it either."

"Then you're of no use to me either!" He flung the soldier across the room alongside the other one.

Angelina continued on the console to supply the group with what they needed to finish off the weapons array. So far she had managed to, even with the constant modulating frequencies built into the system. Only one more remained, but the squadron leader became more volatile with every passing moment. Alena continued to monitor the scene unfolding without appearing to do so. A glance from her told Angelina their time reached its maximum.

"It was hidden and didn't emerge until they were right here, so how did they do it unless they somehow … " The squadron leader turned from the screen and began to go from one troop to the other. "Everyone hands off your consoles now. That's an order."

Angelina heard it, but she had almost finished and ignored it. Alena tried to obscure her efforts but to no avail.

His eyes lighted on Angelina still laboring over the console and marched towards the two. As he reached her, she dropped her hands from it. Pushing Alena aside, he stood before Angelina. "I commanded you to remove your hands from that console. The expectation is that my orders are to be followed instantly."

"I'm sorry, sir. I thought I located the problem and … "

He cut her off as he slammed her against the side of the console, "Or maybe you're the source of this breakdown. What were you doing?"

"Being the good Black Dragon soldier that I am, sir." She shot back. Immediately she knew she'd regret it. *We couldn't talk our way out of this one anyway. At least I got the last one to Lana before he caught me.* She thought to herself.

"I'll make you a good Black Dragon soldier." He put his hand around her throat and started to lift her off the ground. "A dead one."

His grip on her tightened. With one hand, she tried to loosen its vice as her other hand struggled to reach her blade. The effort proved useless as she began to become lightheaded.

"My friend says no deal," said Alena as her blade plummeted through the leader from behind, and she yelled to Angelina, "Get up and fight!"

Angelina sprang up with a blade in hand and shook off the dizziness. "I ticked him off."

"That just occurred to you. His throwing two people across the room like rag dolls didn't clue you in?" Alena brought her blade up against the group advancing towards them. "Staying?"

"Agreed. Not an option." Angelina pushed forward with Alena to the door out of the room. "I don't always think before I say stuff."

"No kidding. I didn't notice."

"Thanks," said Angelina as Alena eliminated a soldier who almost got a nasty shot at her. "You're the one that said it would be a boring day."

"And you had to prove me wrong. Hope you're happy with yourself." Alena pulled Angelina through the door into the corridor.

"The quiet exit?" said Angelina.

"Lost in a black hole, so let's work with what we have." Alena yelled and waved her blade in the air, "Out of the way! Freedom Fighters breached the building! Prepare to face them!"

Angelina followed her lead and added, "Spread out, and take them down!"

They rushed past the scrambling Black Dragon soldiers in the hallway, who now looked baffled as to where to go.

A Black Dragon troop voice boomed through the corridor, "Why are you standing here? Where are they?"

"We don't know. They got through, but we haven't spotted any yet," said a troop as he scanned the corridor.

"Are you blind? They had to come running through here!"

"We've seen no Freedom Fighters, maybe they're further inside."

"They're in Black Dragon armor, you idiot!"

⸺ele⸺

Dante took out another Black Dragon soldier with his sunspear. "Going as expected so far."

Ryan ducked to miss a sword and used his blade to take the legs out from under the soldier. "I like our chances. The others are slicing and dicing too."

Ryan's observation proved true as Caleb's and Gabe's squadron plowed through the enemy troops with the two commanders leading the way.

"Black Dragon will send reinforcements though. Let's hope it doesn't tip our advantage. Speaking of reinforcements, we should have a couple of our own by now," Dante said as his sunspear continued in motion.

"Yeah, an update would be great," Ryan pushed his sword through another soldier.

Alika said through their earpiece, "They've run into a situation and are stuck in the other building."

"I don't like the sound of that."

"They've kept their heads thus far, and we're working on it staying so."

Dante said, "I'm with Ryan. Do we need to help them?"

"If you do, you'll know, but I must assist them now."

Angelina sped through the corridor with Alena as they blended into the chaos that already erupted in the building and had further escalated with their performance. "Quick thinking, but we can't keep running through the hallways"

"And going through the front door is out of the question, and this has run its course." Alena shook her head at the angry Black Dragon voice echoing down the hall.

"A route that's not ... " Angelina looked up.

"No rooftops. That's not always the exit plan."

"Not that. What else runs above us?"

Alena groaned. "Tight fit with the armor. Can we do it?"

"I don't know. Can we?"

Alika's voice came through the earpieces. "Yes, there's enough room, and I've found an entry point."

The Premier put his hand up to silence the troop mid-sentence in his briefing. "Stand by." He switched over to another viewscreen. "There's a problem?"

"Premier, the Freedom Fighters are attacking our Sikata facility."

"Onscreen now." He stood up, taking in the scene, his calm demeanor never faltering. "Indeed, they are. Why am I only now been told of this?"

"Sir, we didn't realize what was happening at first. Then we saw the size of the force they brought, and it's larger than what we perceived initially."

"Now we must address the threat at hand. Discussing the importance of timely updates will wait until this situation is resolved." Another viewscreen appeared alongside the one and the Premier spoke into it. "Your duties have shifted for the day. Our operations in Sikata are under attack. Move your fleet there now. The Freedom Fighters mean to test it before tomorrow's event. Make them regret it."

"Yes, sir," said the Black Dragon commander.

He returned to the first troop. "Save your briefing for later. You'll find you have new orders." Dismissing the troop, he went back to the viewscreen with the Sikata scene. "Twice now. Right as we're set to strike, you try to stop it. How does that keep happening? Either I have a leak, or I've significantly underestimated your intel-gathering abilities. You dismantled the whole array as if it were child's play. Impressive."

CHAPTER THIRTY-FOUR

Alena crawled behind Angelina through the maze of ducts making up the air conditioning system and a miniature storage area for the Black Dragon. She whispered, "I can't believe you talked me into this."

"We've been in tighter places."

"I'm just hard-pressed to recall them at this moment. However, now I know what their attic is like. Just when I thought my expectations for this day couldn't sink further."

Angelina held back a chuckle. *Leave it to Alena to manage humor in this mess I got us into. Thank the Ancient One for Alika, for locating an entry point on the schematics in time.* The Black Dragon group had been at their heels and were completely perplexed by their disappearing act. Eventually, they would figure it out, and the thought propelled her to quicken the pace. Her mind began entertaining the numerous unpleasant ways Black Dragon could flush them out if they discovered their whereabouts.

⸺ele⸺

"Reinforcements still missing," said Dante as they went deeper into the facility.

"What's the word?" asked Ryan.

"It became necessary to take the long escape route," said Alika.

"Because?" asked Dante.

"Their cover is compromised."

Ryan groaned. "How badly?"

"Enough to reveal two people are assisting the Freedom Fighters in Black Dragon armor. They had to make a scene."

Dante asked, "Are you sure we don't need to go now?"

"Not yet, Dante."

—ₑₗₑ—

Lana tracked the movements of her troops in the air and inside the facility, redirecting troops where needed as hotspots surfaced. Thus far her group held the advantage with her husband leading the charge to edge them closer to the prize for the day. She paused in her efforts to turn to Alika and Seth who stared at the screen displaying Angelina and Alena. "How much further before they reach it?"

"Quite a bit of crawling left," said Alika.

Seth traced the path with his finger. "Their targeted end is here near a lesser-used exit."

Lana's face fell as she measured the distance in her head. "Are you certain you don't want to send Dante and Ryan to pull them out? I don't like what I see."

"Me either, but sending anyone right now could only make matters worse, draw attention to them," said Alika.

—ₑₗₑ—

The Black Dragon soldier stood in the corridor and attempted to explain his actions to the superior officer. "Sir, they could be anywhere in the building. We were under attack from Freedom Fighters, and they're only two individuals."

The Black Dragon leader calmly put his hand in the air to signal he had heard enough. "Silence. Reinforcements are on their way to even the odds. This frenzied state hasn't helped from what I've observed, which is why my instructions are to take charge of the situation. The Premier is convinced those two are key to the events that unraveled today, so he wants them found."

"And we'd have them, if these idiots had not allowed them to run right past them," raged one of the officers from the weapons room.

The Black Dragon leader turned to him as he motioned for quiet again, "Yes, Premier, you have our attention."

"Excellent. I have words of wisdom or warning, whichever one applies to you. If your squadron leader maintained a cooler head, none of this would have happened from what I understand. Do not make the same mistake. It will not go unpunished. The two you consider insignificant are far from it, for they used your chaos to their advantage to escape what should have been their cage. They will be captured or die today. Now assist in the effort, or you will no longer be in Black Dragon's service. Do I make myself clear?"

"Yes sir," said a sea of voices in union.

"Continue as you were, now that everyone is inspired to cooperate. I want the two brought back as prisoners or dead."

"Of course, Premier." The Black Dragon leader turned back to others. "Prisoners or dead. You heard him."

The Black Dragon leader stopped in the middle of the corridor, ignoring the soldiers rushing past him who had not been a part of the two spear-bearers' escape. "Between here? You're certain?"

"Not completely, but fairly sure, sir," said the soldier.

"That's more helpful than anyone else so far, but that places them further into the building which doesn't make sense. They should be trying to get out. Unless they have other business here, but that would be almost impossible after the scene they made. Even with the chaos, they couldn't be walking out the front entrance," he stared down the corridor again, "No, I don't see it. So, if they remain on this stretch, then ... " He motioned to a group of ten behind him. "Spread out and keep guard on this hallway. The rest of you come with me. We'll tear apart each room in this hall if needed. Only one explanation remains. It's time to close in on our prey."

"Sir, this room is clear," said the soldier.

"Appears so," said the Black Dragon leader as he strolled the room and eyed those working it. He turned to them and asked the same question he had a few times now, "Did two Black Dragon soldiers come rushing in here?" They responded in the negative to his inquiry. "Anyone in here that wasn't before?" Again, he received an identical response. "As you were," he said as he walked out the door and motioned his group to follow. *Still no luck.* In a couple of rooms, a few soldiers rotated in, but his group verified them as Black Dragon. Presumably, the two would try to blend in if they reentered a room. Maybe the soldier recalled wrong, and they got past this area. If so, they could be anywhere in the building or escaped from it altogether, but he wouldn't give up yet. There were several more rooms on this corridor, and the other soldiers remembered the two being trapped in this hallway once both groups realized the impostors tricked them. He opened the next door, and only the hum of machinery greeted him. "It's deserted." Nevertheless, he continued through the door with the others following.

"Sir, this is used as a utility or supply room, so it's common for it to be empty or for only a couple of people to drop in and leave."

"Making it an excellent place to hide. So, it's worth checking."

A couple of minutes later another soldier said, "Sir, I've found something or better yet someone." He knelt over something on the ground inside a closet.

The Black Dragon leader stared down at the discovery. "One of ours, and it's the work of a blade. They tried to conceal it. Smart on their end to not leave him out in the open." He turned around and walked vigilantly through the room with his raised sword. "The question is, are you two still hiding here? Anything is possible, but this room is small. I can't imagine we wouldn't see you by now. It's a sensible choice as far as traffic. One troop happened to be in the wrong place at the wrong time. Other than that, what does this room have going for it?" He lowered his weapon after making a satisfactory sweep of the room. "They're not here, but they were. Maybe they go right back out, but that returns them to the same trouble. They can't vanish though." Resuming his walk through the room, he studied each corner for an answer until his eyes lighted on a chair with a couple of boxes stacked on top at the side of the room. "Seems out of place." He walked to it and looked all around and then up. "Perhaps a makeshift ladder. Where does this vent go?"

"All through the building, like most of them. You could become lost in it."

"Unless you have the roadmap, which these two do somehow. One of those trails leads out of here, near an exit?"

"Yes, sir, it does."

He already pulled it up on his data pad. "It makes sense they would be heading for a less frequented one. Any of those would be a distance and uncomfortable, but I'd do it too if death is the alternative. However, they won't make it out now."

"Sir, how do you mean to get them?"

"Simple. I'll show you."

Alika watched multiple screens from the building where his students remained. Yet his focus stayed on two of them, one of his students crawling through the duct system and the other of a Black Dragon group making their way from room to room in the hall where his students were last seen. He observed the group exit the room where they spent considerable time after finding the fallen soldier, and he waited for them to search the next room. To his dismay, they didn't. He had hoped they would settle on the idea his two escaped to another part of the building altogether, and he tried unsuccessfully to cling to that comforting theory. Instead, as he continued to track the group's movements, another thought gained strength along with the sinking feeling in his gut. "What is he doing?" He watched the leader point to something onscreen.

Seth studied the monitor with him "I have a few possibilities, but none we want to entertain."

"My concerns too, my friend."

"Has this space gotten smaller all of a sudden?" asked Alena.

"No, it's probably just how long we've been stuck in here, but it does feel like somebody increased the heat to sweltering," said Angelina.

Alena wiped the back of her neck. "You're right. That's what it is. How much farther?"

"Still a long way." One of her arms suddenly buckled under her for an instant, and she stopped and took a deep breath.

"I don't feel so good," said Alena.

"Me either."

Suddenly Alika's voice came through their earpieces. "Get out now. They know you're in the ducts and mean to overcome you by the fumes or by burning you up inside it, whichever comes first."

Angelina said, "We're nowhere near the end."

Alika shot back, "You won't make it! I'm monitoring your vitals. You'll stand a better chance against Black Dragon troops than dead in those vents. Whatever it takes to get out, do it while you still have the strength to lift your sunspear. Now!"

Alena pulled out her sunspear, "Forging a new path with our sunspear."

Angelina followed suit as her vision swam before her eyes. "Where does this drop us?"

Alena took a shaky breath. "We'll find out."

In unison, the two plunged their ignited sunspears down to carve a hole through the ceiling. In less than a minute, the space collapsed, and they came tumbling down. In their weakened state, they found themselves on the floor and groaned at the impact. Angelina coughed, struggling to stop the raging fire coursing through her lungs. *It's like when I tested out those fake chemicals,* she thought. Behind her, she heard Alena encountering the same battle. To make matters worse, the fall succeeded in prolonging the dizziness that began in the ducts, and it overcame her desperate need to get up. Eventually, the ground settled, and Angelina started to rise.

However, an icy voice stopped her, "Don't move another inch."

Angelina recognized Black Dragon boots directly in front of her, but her sunspear lay only slightly out of her reach. She stretched out for it, but the motion was interrupted as the boot slid the sunspear beyond her grasp and he said, "I warned you." He motioned behind her, and Angelina recognized a yell of pain erupt from a familiar source.

"What are you doing? Stop!" hollered Angelina.

"A simple demonstration. Your comrade will suffer further if you fail to follow instructions again. That's what I thought." The Black Dragon leader signaled again. "Keep the blade trained on them at all times. We may have to use it if this one becomes stupid again." His eyes focused back on Angelina. "You can get up now, but I remind you to make better decisions, for you and your comrade's sake."

Angelina painstakingly got up, using a stationary table nearby to assist her as she fought against the lingering dizziness. Taking in her surroundings only painted a drearier scene of their predicament. At first, she thought it could be the medical room, as the room contained a few more long tables, like the one she used to steady herself. However, they could undeniably be used for other purposes, like assembling specialized items or mixing up unpleasant chemicals. Cabinets dotted the wall, hiding their contents. A shiver went through her body as she considered the possibilities. She also now realized how outnumbered they were. A group of at least fifteen stood in the room, which seemed impossible for the size of it. She and Alena had fought through a whole facility before, but not like this. Their bodies were still recouping from the effects of the poison, so this handful was worse than an entire Black Dragon army. Worst of all, they held Alena with a blade at her neck. Angelina couldn't know for sure if she had been hurt. Angelina asked her, "You all right?"

"I'll manage," said Alena.

The Black Dragon leader nodded. "Your comrade put up a commendable fight, considering the state our concoction left the two of you. However, it proved too much to overcome, even for ones of your mastery. Oh, I've been warned not to underestimate you two, and I didn't." He paused. "The question is, who are you two?"

Angelina froze at the inquiry, as the man focused on her helmet, his intent obvious. Knowing what had to be done, she pleaded Alika would understand what needed to happen. She stared back at him through the Black Dragon helmet and shot back, "Isn't it clear? Few use a sunspear that fight you so openly. You don't recognize the head of the Freedom Fighters?" She motioned to Alena. "And my husband is as quick with the sunspear. Perhaps you're not as knowledgeable as you presume."

"Lana and Caleb. However, I know what those two sound like, and you are not them."

"Technology. Are you that arrogant to believe Black Dragon owns all of it? I hate to disillusion you, but the Freedom Fighters have a fair share of it too. You require convincing though. So, I'll speak to you in a voice you're familiar with." She paused and pretended to modify something inside her helmet. "As I said I'm Lana, and it's your problem you didn't recognize me." Her voice came through as Lana, and she turned to Alena. "Caleb, why don't you adjust yours for the Black Dragon gentleman? Our charade is up."

Alena slowly moved one hand to her helmet and mimicked Angelina's performance. "It was a good run while it lasted, sweetheart." Relief passed through her as she sounded like Caleb.

⁓ele⁓

Alika's voice blasted through to Dante and Ryan, "Now they're in deep trouble. Take a group of your best, most trusted to them before it's too late."

"What happened?" yelled Dante.

Alika cut him off, "Now, you two."

Ryan turned to Gabe and Caleb. "Dante and I have to go. Now. Our reinforcements are in dire straits, but we need to take some help."

Gabe yelled while sending an alert with his data pad, "Special ops A here now! You're with Dante and Ryan from here on out!" He waved to the two. "Go! Do what you have to!"

"Fill us in!" commanded Dante as the group fought their way from the one building into the next one.

"Black Dragon forced them from their escape route, that being the vent system. The method used to draw them out left them in a state too weak to fight. They're prisoners in a room and have convinced their captors they are Lana and Caleb thanks to the voice changers. You'll be able to hear what's transpiring now."

Ryan said, "This is bad. Who is who?"

"Angelina is Lana and Alena is Caleb."

Fear gripped Dante's heart as the audio continued, and he yelled to the group, "Move it! We have to get to the other building now! Whatever it takes!"

"You heard him! That's an order!" added Ryan.

"A prize indeed." The Black Dragon leader removed his helmet and laid it aside to reveal a pair of brown eyes and dark brown hair. A triumphant grin crossed his face. "Couldn't resist assisting in this operation, Lana. A critical mistake on your part."

"I don't believe so."

"How do you figure, Lana? You and your husband are prisoners of Black Dragon. He has a blade at his throat, and so you will do whatever you are told. Your group fights, but what happens when they discover we captured their leadership?"

"Let me tell you what I see. A Black Dragon army is scrambling to wipe themselves off the floor because they still can't understand how they got ambushed in their facility. Then what truly gets under your skin is a mere two people started it all. Now you've got a whole army breathing down your neck that's poised to take you down. You ask what my people will do when they find out I'm here? They'll do what they know to do, which is to keep fighting you because they don't need us to tell them. We've already accomplished what we set out to do today anyway. You're the one with the blade at your throat."

"The passion of the Freedom Fighters all embodied in one woman. I had forgotten. I wish I could dismiss everything you said as rubbish, but you two have caused substantial disruption. It's time to restore the balance. As head of the

Freedom Fighters, you can be useful to us since you possess information it's time you shared."

"We're not helping you! We won't betray our people! You do have screws loose!" yelled Alena.

"Spoken like the true commander you are, Caleb. The united front. Typical. No, willing neither one of you would, but there are numerous ways to break people. The answer doesn't always lie in beating them to a pulp." He grinned as he stepped closer to Angelina. "Caleb, what do you like most about your lovely wife?"

Alena stayed silent.

"Give me something. I'm growing impatient." His eyes traveled over Angelina.

"The way she can sunspear a whole army of you in record time. It's an adrenaline rush like you wouldn't believe," said Alena, as her response resulted in the Black Dragon soldier slamming her against the wall.

"You've been married long enough that I know you have something better to say about Lana." His hands grabbed both of Angelina's shoulders and leaned in closer to her, "Or perhaps I should explore for myself."

"Get your hands off her, now!" yelled Alena.

"I have another idea, Caleb. You're going to tie her up for me. On this table."

"No way! I won't so you can.. Let her go now!" Alena tried to struggle, but the blade point reminded her of the hopelessness of their current situation.

"I figured that would be an impossible sell." He motioned to the soldiers near Alena. "Get him seated in the chair." He turned back to Alena. "Cooperate, Caleb. If that blade slips, things get messy fast, and none of us wants your sweet wife to see that." Satisfied Alena was contained, he instructed the troops. "Secure him to it."

"What are you going to do to him?" screamed Angelina. "If you hurt him, I promise you, I will ... "

"No worries, Lana. As long as he stays quiet, he should be fine for now." He asked the troops. "Is he secure?"

"Yes, sir."

"Perfect." He shifted his focus back to Angelina, with his blade inches from her throat. "On the table now."

"No, I won't do it."

The blade found her throat as two soldiers tightened their grip on her arms. "This is not a request rather a command. Remember, you hold your husband's life in your hands too. Consider carefully your next move."

Angelina realized with a sickening feeling she had no other option but to cooperate. She sat on the table and waited, knowing what would follow.

He leaned into her. "Waiting. Lie down, Lana."

Every part of her screamed not to comply, but an image of Alena in a pool of blood overpowered her resistance. She warily laid down and desperately tried to see an escape route in vain. Even if she could overpower him, they would finish Alena in a second. Maybe if she could turn the tables on him, she could make a trade. Unfortunately, that's not how the Black Dragon mind worked. They could care less for each other. As long as they held Alena, she didn't see any viable options. The last bit of hope forsook her when the Black Dragon leader said, "Tie her up. Yes, like that." A muffled groan escaped her as they secured her arms and ankles on either side of her.

"They're bound to my liking. You five remain. The rest of you, outside to stand guard." He turned back to her once the others left and the door shut. "I'll thoroughly enjoy this interrogation, Lana." He removed his gear as he spoke.

"Why are you doing this?" asked Angelina.

"A silly question. You're a Freedom Fighter and all, but you're still a beautiful woman. So why not? As I said, there are numerous ways to break someone. Could I choose from one of the many traditional methods of torture the Black Dragon gravitates toward? Yes, but I think we should strive to break both of your spirits. What better way than this? It will be my pleasure to administer it."

She stared up at him through her helmet. He was either a turned colonist or one who had always been loyal to Black Dragon. Maybe one of those she crossed paths with in one of the Dark Lord's visits as a child, one he succeeded in corrupting. She could have ended up on the identical path he now walked. They were closer than one wished to believe. "You still didn't answer me. Why are you doing this? Why choose the Black Dragon?"

"A new ploy. Bring me into your flock. Have me renounce the Black Dragon. I never took you for a desperate woman."

"I'm not. Why do you wish to be bound?"

"Now your eyesight is going. You are the one strapped to the table."

"No, these are easily undone. The bonds encircling you the strongest blade cannot cut through. You believe you master them, but you do their bidding."

"I am controlled by no one, but do as I want as you're about to see."

Lana listened in horror along with Alika and Seth as the scene with Angelina and the Black Dragon leader crept towards the unthinkable becoming reality. "We never should have let them do this. If he does this to her, Dante will never be the same." She took a deep breath. "Where are they? They should be there by now." She paused and forced herself not to yell into the comm link, "Dante, Ryan, where are you? Angelina needs you two now."

"I know! Remember, I'm hearing all of it!" yelled Dante.

"We'll get there, Dante!" said Ryan.

"We better, because if he touches ... I'll chop him into pieces with my sun-spear." He yelled back, "I said bring these Black Dragon down faster!"

"It looks so intimidating and bulky, but it always surprised me how easy it comes off. Lots of pieces to unclasp though," said the Black Dragon leader as he removed Angelina's armor. "Caleb, any pointers for me to get the most out of this? Likes? Dislikes?"

Alena struggled to get loose from the chair, ignoring the blade digging into her skin. "Stop! Don't you dare lay a hand on her, or I will ... "

"Lana, you need to control your husband, before he says something he'll regret."

"I won't sit here and watch you have your way with her. It doesn't matter anymore what happens to me."

Angelina turned to Alena. "But I care about what happens to you with everything in me. Please, Caleb, I'll be okay. This isn't over yet, but we can't win this battle. Not like this."

"I vowed to protect you."

"You always do, but we can't protect each other dead. We'll endure this battlefield together as well. I love you."

"I love you too.." Alena's voice broke.

"How touching. I'll enjoy this more now."

Angelina turned back to the Black Dragon leader and realized only one piece of armor remained. She had to make sure it stayed to sustain the ploy. "I'm still the leader of the Freedom Fighter and will see the face of the man with my own eyes, not through this helmet, that would do such a despicable act. I command you to give me this one thing. It's the only way I have any hope of getting through what you're about to do. You owe me that."

"I owe you nothing, and you're in no position to demand anything."

"You will do as I've commanded."

"Wrong, Lana!" His hand went around her neck in a vise, and he leaned close to her. "I could choke the life out of you this instant. You never should have told me that because now I'll make sure it's the one thing you keep on. I don't need it off for what I intend to do to you." He released his grip on her neck as her breathing began coming in gasps. "You can drown in your tears inside of the helmet. I'll still be able to hear your screams fine."

"You're a monster," whispered Angelina.

"Finally, you see."

"You don't realize it, even as it consumes you. None of you do until the end."

"You should be concerned about yourself, Lana."

"I can't stop you from what you're about to do. But do you think by taking from me like this, you suddenly have a hold on me? That you've claimed me? I know who I am, and after you're done with me, that remains unchanged. I know who I belong to, who I've given my heart to and all of me with it. You are not that man."

The Black Dragon leader flared with anger for the first time, and his fist found Angelina's abdomen. She screamed in agony but could do nothing in defense. Taking a moment to catch her breath, she said to him, "You will not break me."

He sneered, "Don't be so sure, because you've inspired me, Lana, to make this worse for you."

Angelina knew her time was up. She felt him slide up on the table and tower above her as he straddled her body, preparing to finish undressing her. The blow to her abdomen only added to the discomfort of his weight. A part of her automatically started to retreat in her mind, to think of anything except what he purposed to do to her. She had done it on countless occasions. It became one of the few ways she maintained her sanity during her terrifying childhood and endured the visions over the years, but this was new. She feared this would happen with the operations they ran, but she had escaped this particular nightmare until now. Forcing herself to treat it like the numerous other horrors from her world, she started to withdraw in her mind again. The good times with Alena or Alika came to mind. Better yet, those wonderful moments in Dante's embrace. Then she realized that would be the worst thing she could do. She couldn't taint those memories created with Dante while this monster assaulted her, as she'd hate herself forever if she did. As remote as it might be, there could be a chance of finding an advantage, a way to get free with his distracted state. Nothing in her believed that, but she clung to the sliver of hope. That meant she must be aware, completely present with everything this man would do to her. The thought repulsed her, and she forced back the bile threatening to escape. He slowly untucked her shirt from her pants, and her body shuddered involuntarily at the action, as his hands continued their deliberate, leisurely pace. One hand reached inside her shirt at her right waistline and started to trail up her body. He leaned down and said, "Lana, I can't wait to ... "

Suddenly, the door burst open with a squadron of Freedom Fighters. The Black Dragon fighters in the room had no chance to recover from their surprise.

The Black Dragon soldier holding Alena looked up as a Freedom Fighter came charging towards him with blade and blaster in hand. "Don't do it. I'll kill him, stay back."

Ryan continued rushing him. "Over my dead body, you will!" He shot the soldier and knocked the blade from the soldier's grasp and away from Alena's throat. Wasting no time, he ran the soldier through several times.

"He's dead, Ryan," said Alena.

"He is now." He touched her armored shoulder. "Let me make sure we cleared them out. Then we'll get you loose. Promise."

The Black Dragon leader looked up to see a Freedom Fighter with a sunspear towering over him and heard him growl, "You sorry piece of Black Dragon filth!" In the same second, the Freedom Fighter threw him from Angelina onto the ground. "I should hack you to pieces, but I'll settle for this." Dante's sunspear plunged into the man's chest to cut him open.

Dante turned to find the room cleared, and a glance told him Alena was safe. Still trembling with anger, he pulled his helmet off while rushing back to Angelina's side. "I'm here, now. Everyone else is okay too." He saw her nod in understanding as he took her hand. He motioned to the Freedom Fighter troops in the room. "The rest of you join the others stationed outside that door, and no one gets past you into this room. Ryan and I will alert you when we're ready to leave with these two." He waited until the group filed out the door, and it closed. Focusing his attention back on Angelina, he carefully slid her helmet off and laid it aside to stroke her tear-stained cheek, "I'm so sorry. Did he ... "

She shook her head and said, "He just started to, but ... " her voice broke.

"Shh, you don't have to say anymore." He leaned his forehead on hers and kissed her cheek. "I'm getting you loose, and Ryan is working on Alena. Hold on another minute for me. These are on tight, but I've almost got them. I don't want to accidently cut you with my blade taking them off. You've been through enough today." He stroked Angelina's hand as he finished removing one of the restraints.

Ryan didn't hesitate to pull Alena over when she threw her arms around his neck and buried her face there. "I'm so glad to see you, Ryan."

"I've got you. You're safe now." He pulled back slightly and kissed her. When she melted into it, he deepened the kiss.

Dante put his arms around Angelina and eased her into a sitting position to maneuver her body so she faced him. One arm encircled her waist again, and the other stroked her cheek.

Her arms encircled his shoulders, and her forehead leaned against his. "You came for me." A tear slid down her face.

"I'll always come for you."

"Because I belong with you, to you, Dante."

"Of course, you do. You're my heart. You're trembling all over still, my angel." He stared into her eyes, and they pleaded with him to bring calm to her in a way he could only do. He pulled her to him and kissed her, anticipating any moment she'd ease back with the remembrance of the Black Dragon still close. Instead, she drew him in for a second kiss. Her desire for reassurance from him canceled out everything else for once as her shaking eased. He kissed her another time, focusing only on her to remind her that he held her secure.

"You always know what I need."

"I'm supposed to, and we both needed that."

"We've been here for a while, though, Dante. It's an invitation for trouble."

"You had to get calmed down though, and you couldn't go out as you were. Come on. Let's get you off the table and down here with me." She did so, but Dante felt her stumble slightly as she stepped onto the floor. However, his arms had snuggly encircled her waist, so the misstep guided her into his embrace. "A little unsteady there. We can stay for longer If necessary." She shook her head at his suggestion. "You're sure?"

"Yes, being strapped down to the table and everything, it ... " She looked down, but he lifted her chin to stare into her eyes. The strength and reassurance she read in them comforted her. "Circulation and the rest are coming back. I need to get moving again, and I'll be fine."

"If you're certain, but you can't go out like this. Ready to get help putting the armor back on?"

"I am, Dante." She ran her hands through his hair.

"If you say so because I can't have anything happening to my girl." He kissed her forehead and assisted her with the gear. As he did, he glanced over at Ryan, "Is she okay?"

"I'm good. Ryan gave me a thorough examination."

Ryan grinned. "I did for her, and she passed well enough."

"One more piece left for us. Ready?" said Dante.

"Yes," Angelina smiled at him.

"All right." He kissed her softly one last time before replacing his helmet and helping her with hers.

Angelina turned around. "It was over there."

Alena walked over to her with a sunspear in hand. "Missing this?"

"Yes. Thanks." She took her sunspear from Alena.

Alena nodded. "I reclaimed mine too."

Without warning, Angelina engulfed Alena in a hug.

"You scared me to death too." Alena hugged her back. As she stepped back from Angelina, she motioned at the sunspear. "Together again." But then she looked up at Angelina and Dante. "Always good to see."

"It feels good too." Angelina reached over and took Dante's hand. "We're set except for one thing. Getting back into role." She paused and suddenly her voice changed. "Everyone is back to taking orders from me, including you, Dante."

"You're bossier than the original Lana, and no more special treatment, huh?" He leaned into her.

"Certainly not, and I'm in full armor again anyway." She squeezed his hand before releasing it and moving away from him.

A soft chuckle emerged from Alena in Caleb's voice. "There's the end of that."

Angelina stopped in front of the Black Dragon leader's body. His words rang in her head, his vow to break her spirit and his pleasure at being her torturer, at having her drown in her tears, and reveling in hearing her screams. Then the horrible feel of his hand beginning its assault on her body returned. Instantly, her boot slammed down on his shoulder with enough force to break it, and she leaned down to his lifeless form. "You didn't break my spirit. Far from it. Every Black Dragon soldier will suffer for what you did to me today." She rose, her voice taking on a darker tone. "Monster, indeed. Now they will see it." Without hesitation, she severed the man's head from his body with her sunspear and marched for the entrance to face the army outside.

A stunned silence enveloped the room, but the group quickly recovered from their shock and rushed to meet the soldiers awaiting them. Dante made it to her side first, but the scene had left him rattled. Despite all the roleplaying he watched her do, the person didn't seem like his Angelina. This had been different, in a frightening way. He ran up to her now. "Wait. Are you okay?" However, she ignored him and continued blazing a trail through Black Dragon soldiers like a fire consuming every living thing.

"What's the plan?" yelled Ryan as he and Alena caught up to Dante.

"This, but not." His eyes went frantically from the two to Angelina who had almost disappeared from sight of the group.

"Dante, stay with Lana, no matter what. When she's like this, she gets carried away. We're right behind you," said Alena.

"I'll catch up to her." With new fervor, he pushed through with his sunspear.

CHAPTER THIRTY-FIVE

Angelina heard him calling her name, or rather Lana's, the first couple of times but ceased to register it anymore. He was as proficient if not better than her with the sunspear she reasoned, so she no longer concerned herself. She saw nothing but the Black Dragon soldiers in her path, and her sunspear became living and breathing in her hand as every stroke reverberated through her. One slain body being nothing more than the stepping stone to reach the next soldier to fall to her sunspear. Her boots continued squishing through the bloodbath she left in her wake. She entered a corridor and opened the first door to a room full of enemy soldiers.

One of them in the room looked up. Seeing the Black Dragon garb but paired with the sunspear, he stammered, "What are you..."

She cut him off as she advanced, completely unfazed by the army coming towards her. "Freedom Fighters are taking over this place. Starting with here."

Dante kept slicing with his sunspear at Black Dragon soldiers while struggling to hold Angelina in his vision. Concern resurfaced for Ryan and Alena too, but he trusted they managed with the help of the other troops. He also wondered how the others progressed in the next building, which is where they were supposed to head back to once they rescued Angelina and Alena. It all fell apart though. As he sensed a letup in the soldiers in the large open area he fought through, he soon realized why. The incredible carnage littering the floor before him showcased her handiwork where she had cleared a path for him, but he had lost track of her amid battle. He entered a corridor, but didn't see her, only scattered slaughtered troops. "Where did she go? She was right here," he murmured. Rushing down the hallway, he halted when he heard the sounds of clashing swords and blaster fire behind one of the doors he passed. "You've got to be kidding me!" He ran back to the door and opened it to reveal Angelina in a sunspear battle with the entire room of Black Dragon troops. "Why in the galaxy would … " he yelled in frustration, even as he didn't hesitate to add his sunspear to hers.

Angelina swung her sunspear, cleaved the soldier in half, and already turned as the body crumpled in two pieces to the ground. She scanned the room to find it cleared of Black Dragon and marched back towards the door. A figure stopped her progress though.

Dante caught his breath, stood facing Angelina, and started to touch her shoulder between the armor and her neck.

"Take your hands off me!" She backed away from him.

He released her shoulder but remained in front of her. Pushing aside his worry, he reached out and took her hand. "Hey, it's me, Dante." When she didn't pull away, he stepped closer. "I'm not the enemy, remember?"

"Of course, you're not." She looked down at their clasped hands and back up at him. "Dante, I'm sorry, I don't know what came over me."

"It's okay. Why did you come in here?"

"Because we have to destroy all the Black Dragon."

"No, that's not why we're here. We came for the device. Somewhere that got lost for you today." His voice held no condemnation, only gentleness, as he stroked her gloved hand.

She surveyed the room again but as one through different eyes. "We need to get back to the others. How did I abandon them?"

"You didn't abandon anyone, and we both know how this happened. I should have found a way to reach you sooner back there, before he … "

"This isn't your fault. You got there in time."

"Right now, it doesn't feel that way." He wound his free arm around her waist, as she moved into him for her free arm to encircle his neck.

Even with all the armor separating them, the calm settled on her spirit he always touched in her.

"We'll put this day behind us soon. Once we get back, just you and I," whispered Dante.

"Like you promised?"

"Yes, like I promised."

✧✧✧

"A little concerned. We couldn't find you two for a minute," said Ryan with Alena at his side as they rushed into the corridor.

"My fault. I detoured, but he set me straight," said Angelina.

"Great work, Dante," Then Alena turned to Angelina, "And don't you go running off again."

"My cousin slips up on occasion, but we're back on course again," said Dante.

✧✧✧

The Premier finished listening to the update while watching the images from Sikata. "One of the squadron leaders indicated the two fighters mostly responsible for today's events were cornered. Have you heard anything further from him and his group?"

"No sir." The troop stared down at his data pad. "That group all went dark, no signal from any of them."

"Yes, that's what I see as well. For the whole lot of them to be in that state, my assumption is they were eliminated. Once again those two fighters have somehow escaped our snare." He wouldn't give up on capturing the two, but he always had to look at the big picture as head of Black Dragon. "Our reinforcements have evened the odds, but not overpowered them."

"We're seeing the same, sir."

"I could send more and outnumber them. That's the simplest solution. However, they have caught us unaware from the start, and that's our larger issue. Are the troops and fleet ready for tomorrow's operation?"

"Yes, sir. They only await your orders and the location."

"Today is why one must always anticipate these situations. I abhor changing my plans, but it's time we surprised the Freedom Fighters. Force their hand. Make them choose."

"Sir, are you giving the order to commence now?"

"I am. I'll send another troop of reinforcements, but their only duty is to direct the device. Then I'll relay the location to them as well as the rest of the army standing by. Prepare to strike. They thought to stop me, but they only sped up their destruction."

⁓ℓℓ⁓

Caleb and Gabe continued fighting their way through the facility alongside their troops. However, they suddenly stopped in their tracks and Caleb yelled, "Did you hear that?"

"Yes, whatever it is sounds close by."

Caleb said into his earpiece, "Dante, Ryan, are you back over here yet?"

"Just made our entrance a minute or so ago," said Ryan.

"We heard something crazy loud from inside the building."

"Yeah, like something shifting. Don't know what it could be." Ryan suddenly stopped in mid-sentence and yelled, "They're doing what? Got our answer from a couple of Black Dragon troops we know."

Dante came to Angelina's side and asked, "You're sure?"

"Yes, hear for yourself."

A distorted Black Dragon voice came through the communication system, "This is your Black Dragon Premier, and our operation will go forward sooner than scheduled. All those involved in tomorrow's operation, we will strike now. The device is being retrieved, and once it's launched you will be supplied with the location. Await my orders. The Freedom Fighters will pay for today's attack."

"So, what we're hearing is the door opening on the top of the room where the device is," said Caleb.

Lana listened, staring at the screen. "They know we'll follow the device to try to stop them from hitting another planet. We'll divide our forces."

Seth nodded. "That's what he's counting on."

"It's the only situation that would prompt him to move his attack up, and we put it into motion," said Alika.

Angelina grabbed Alena's arm. "This is what I feared."

"You must not doubt now," whispered Alena.

—ele—

The Premier asked, "The door is fully open?"

"Yes sir," said a Black Dragon troop.

"The weapon is ready?"

"Yes, sir."

"Launch it, now."

"Yes, sir."

—ele—

Caleb and Gabe continued to press with their men through the facility, smashing through Black Dragon troops, desperate to reach the room with the device. The entrance to the room was only feet ahead of them now as the rumbling of the room's top door opening grew louder until it stopped altogether. Realizing what that meant, their efforts became frenzied.

Lana stood there with her hand clasped in Seth's and her eyes focused on the monitor. "Seth, it won't happen again. It can't."

Seth squeezed her hand but said nothing.

"There is a play yet, Lana. Trust," said Alika.

CHAPTER THIRTY-SIX

The Premier watched the screen and asked calmly, "Why has the weapon not moved from the room?"

"Sir, it's not responding."

"What do you mean it's not responding? Explain."

"Sir, it showed armed and ready, but once we attempted to retrieve or launch it from the room, it didn't respond anymore. Connected systems began slowing down too."

"That doesn't make sense. What does your screen display?"

"It appears strange, sir. I'm going to different places, but it's as if it's going in a loop or something."

"Let me see, now." The Premier watched the soldier at the monitor and zoomed into his workstation. "Attempt to tap into the device again." The screen flashed though working but quickly switched to another screen. Running across it appeared to be a random sequence of data. However, they could have been lists of readings or reports streamed together in a chaotic mess. There was no deciphering it. Then it flashed to a blank screen, next displaying a screen from a completely different department, followed by nothingness, and random characters again. The pattern resumed its dizzying loop, despite the soldier's efforts to have the system respond. "Are any of those your strokes?"

"No, sir."

He continued to watch the meaningless pattern and the strange behavior. Suddenly, he understood. "No, this isn't your work. We launched something, but not the device. Our system's linking to the device is corrupt. This intruder in our system activated as soon as the launch countdown began."

"Oh no, sir, if that's the case ... "

"It is. The only way that device is leaving is if it's manually towed with ships, and I have doubts it releases its contents for us even if we could move it. There's no way to know how far this intruder has rooted itself into the interface with the device."

"We can start work to get it, sir."

"It will take substantial time if it can be done at all. There's only one person who can extract the unwanted visitor from our system."

"Who is that, sir?"

"The one who I'm certain placed it there, and that individual has foiled all our traps to date."

"Sir, what are your orders?"

"To await my next ones. This development complicated the situation." He closed the screen and went back to the squadron leader he spoke to at first. "Another change of plans. There's a delay in the attack."

"Of course, sir. How long?"

"That's uncertain. The two Freedom Fighters have been busier than I realized and have found a way to ground the device."

"Sir, we can send more troops to the building."

"That won't help us with how they have managed to disable it. They have control of the system to launch it. Possibly other systems."

He nodded, finally understanding the extent of the issue. "We'll wait on your next commands, Premier."

"You'll hear them soon. I'll let the troops know to stand down."

<hr>

Alena stared at Angelina. "What did I tell you? You did it."

Dante turned. "What is it?" Suddenly he heard it coming through his earpiece, and he saw Ryan pause too.

The distorted dark voice came through again with a new message, "This is the Black Dragon Premier. I decided it best not to rush our operation, and so we will delay it. Those involved in the operation, please stand down. I will alert you when we resume it. The Freedom Fighters will not be allowed to dictate my plans."

"Yet one Freedom Fighter did," said Dante as he turned to Angelina.

"I can't believe it worked, Dante."

"I told you it would." He put his arm around her shoulders, "You always come through for me."

Lana closed her eyes and took a deep breath. "The attack is delayed."

"Because they can't do it now," said Seth before turning to Alika. "Do you think they can somehow?"

"No. It's called off. The Premier won't dare admit the truth over an audience, and there's no getting the poison purged from their system which Angelina unleashed."

"Any luck?" asked Dante as he ran into the device room with Angelina, Alena, and Ryan at his heels.

"Haven't found the end all yet." Caleb trailed his hand on the metallic cylindrical structure, his eyes scanning it for the answer still eluding them.

"But it's been stopped today from its intended purpose," said Gabe.

"Everyone okay? Took you longer to get here than I thought," asked Caleb.

Dante motioned towards Angelina and Alena. "They're both fine. A lot more complicated than anticipated. The closer we got to this room, the less Black Dragon we saw."

"Guess your group took care of most of them for us," said Ryan.

"Or they're following orders," said Alena.

Caleb stared at her. "You sound like me. What's going on?"

Ryan waved his hand. "We'll explain later, Caleb." He turned back to Alena. "What now?"

"All the ground troops are supposed to be cleared out of this building."

"Who ordered it?" asked Dante.

"The Premier issued it about a minute ago," said Angelina.

Caleb said, "And you sound like Lana." he shook his head. "Later. I get it."

Dante nodded and addressed Angelina, "They're retreating?" Only silence greeted his question so he pressed. "Hey, did you hear me?"

"Sorry, I did. It's odd. Giving up is not his strategy. He gave the order but not the reason."

"Maybe they're bolstering the ground troops outside or taking to the air," said Alena.

Caleb answered back, "Better guess than anything I've got." He paused. "Lana, did you get all this? What's your take on it?"

"I did, and it's the logical assumption. It also means our troops will find themselves outnumbered if it hasn't already started."

"They need to head outside the building to face the Black Dragon soldiers rather than staying with us," said Ryan.

"Agreed. Send them all out," said Caleb.

"I'm giving the order," said Lana.

Gabe motioned to the side of the device. "We've locked into the port where the device is now and tried to decipher it, but as Caleb said we're not seeing how to permanently disable it."

"Maybe someone with a knack for that could take a shot at it." Caleb glanced in Angelina's direction.

"I'll give it my best try now, but I think we're taking this back like last time." She ran to the port with Dante at her heels.

"When do I get the story behind Lana and I doubled?" teased Caleb.

Angelina sighed. "We'll have to save the full version for later. You and Lana ended up being the only way for us to escape the trouble we ran into until Dante and Ryan could find us."

"Both of you took care of business as always. Although you two ticked off Black Dragon majorly this time. They don't like to be told they're getting their tails whipped," said Alena.

Caleb laughed. "Never stopped us before, and we aim to keep it going."

"So, who do I take commands from today now?" Gabe chuckled.

Caleb slapped him on the back. "Still me. Let's get this job finished once and for all, so we can all go home."

"Seeing anything?" asked Dante as he knelt beside her and touched her shoulder between her neck and the armor.

"Not enough to know I'm disabling it completely. I've grounded it as far as the Black Dragon is concerned. The poison is still inside though, and I haven't found a clue how to neutralize it. Honestly, I'm doubtful I will."

"Why wouldn't they know how to undo it?"

She asked softly, "Dante, why would they care because when would they ever be neutralizing it?"

The answer hit him like a space cruiser and he said, "Never."

"There's a way to counter it. There must be, but I don't believe we will find it with the Black Dragon or if we do I'm not sure how." She squeezed his hand. His mother remained asleep from the poison, and Angelina had vowed to discover the means to awaken her. She would somehow keep her promise. "You can't give up. I won't let you."

He squeezed her hand back. "Not with you at my side."

An uneasiness seeped through her at the Premier's command as she continued working with the screen. He didn't walk away from a battle. The feeling of being suffocated in the air ducts returned to her with a vengeance even as she glanced around the huge room. "What's the progress with our troops clearing out of here?"

"All out by now," said Caleb.

"One victory." She shook her head at the port near the device. "I wish I could say I had the answer for this, and I'll keep plugging at this, but I'm not seeing it."

"We came in knowing how it would probably go, so we'll prepare to take it back." Caleb stopped as a thunderous rumbling overhead drowned him out along with the air battle outside. He looked up with the rest of the group as the door above them reclosed.

Ryan turned to Angelina. "Did you hit something by mistake?"

She slowly stood up with Dante. "No, I didn't."

"We'll be fine. We have the clearances for this place," said Alena.

However, the unrest that had crept up in her became a full-blown alarm in her head, and she didn't believe her next statement. "True. We don't have anything to worry about…"

Her words were cut off by a familiar distorted Black Dragon voice booming through the building. "Greetings, Freedom Fighters. We haven't been introduced. I am the Premier Black Dragon, the head of Black Dragon now. I had a change of plans today due to a couple of you. Those of you responsible know exactly what I'm referring to and who you are, but I'm a reasonable leader. Therefore, I'm making you an offer. Give me those who arranged today's chaos, and I'll spare the rest of you. Although I understand this can't be easy for you, this generous proposal is only for a short time as you can see by the display. It's also worth noting, you're sealed in and if you reject my bargain, I've found a way to make the last of your stay most unpleasant. Something you won't walk away from. Not a second time today. I eagerly await your answer."

Angelina wasted no time as she ran to the door and tried to open it with no success. She attempted every clearance, but they all failed. "He means to make this our coffin."

Lana stood in front of the viewscreen, her eyes flashing fury. "We have to get them out! He has all of them!"

"Are you certain none of the clearances work?" asked Seth.

"We're sure. Cycled through all of them," said Dante.

Alika nodded. "They're right. The Premier hasn't changed them but blocked all of them for now. Even if it's a genuine Black Dragon soldier still left in there, they're not escaping."

Lana's fist hit the desk. "I don't care if it means blasting a hole as big as the Black Dragon command ship through that building, do it. I will not see them die. Alert the commanders in the air. Rescuing them comes first. We'll worry about the device once they're safe."

Angelina ran back to the port. "I'll see if I can bypass something, override the hold he's put on it."

"Anything we can do?" asked Dante.

"No, I just need to concentrate." She watched him walk off to rejoin the others before she dared return her focus to the port. Under her breath, she whispered, "Forgive me, Dante." She knew only her recipient would see the message that she now typed out directly into the port, and none of those in the room with her would let her do this.

"This message is for the Premier, the head of Black Dragon only. My comrades don't know I've sent it because they would never agree to it. You have my attention. Answer me back so I know you received this. You gave us little time." She waited, her heart racing as the seconds dwindled.

The response came across the port. "This is the Premier, and I'm listening."

She took a deep breath and began typing again.

CHAPTER THIRTY-SEVEN

The others looked up as Angelina walked towards them.

"Anything?" asked Dante.

"I'm afraid not," said Angelina as her voice came out in the Black Dragon one she started with this morning. "I thought it best to change back."

"Lana is working on our escape. She'll have the whole fleet blast us out of here if need be," said Caleb.

"From what the Premier said, it's got to be the poisoning angle again. The masks will work for a short time, but he means to put enough in this space to overcome us," said Alena.

"If we figure out where the release point is maybe we can stop it," said Gabe.

"Unless it's in this room, I don't see a way we get to it." Angelina scanned the room. "He has to be releasing it through the air system."

The Premier's voice resounded through the room. "Greetings again Freedom Fighters. I'm delighted you made a decision. Your group is wiser than I thought."

"Our time isn't up yet! Your memory failing you today too, Premier? I'll volunteer to knock it back in place with my sunspear!" shouted Caleb.

"Commander Caleb, I'm aware of the time. You've lost none of your Freedom Fighter spirit despite your current situation. A testament to you." He paused. "Spear-bearer, I agree with you. They will not be happy with our deal."

Angelina stepped forward. "No, they won't."

Dante grabbed her arm. "You made a deal with him? What were you thinking?

She pulled her arm away. "Dante, don't." She advanced further from them and spoke to the room. "The details of our agreement again. Let's hear them. I want no misunderstanding, Premier."

"An understandable request. The others go free in exchange for the spear-bearers."

"A crucial detail wrong, but you know full well. Try again, Premier."

"Oh, yes. At your petition and because I'm particularly generous today, we modified it further. Are you sure you are the spear-bearer responsible for creating such havoc in my system? You're not lying to me to save your friends?"

"I told you the truth. Now what we agreed, Premier."

"Very well. Only you as we decided. If I have you, I possess the means to retrieve what I need. There's a chance you die in the effort, but perhaps it doesn't come to that. I think you'll be more cooperative than you let on. After all, you came to this contract with me easily enough. Now have I stated our agreement accurately?"

"Yes, just me, that's our deal."

Dante ran forward and grabbed hold of her, shouting to the room. "No deal, Premier. The spear-bearer doesn't decide this one. You asked us all, and we reject your arrangement."

"We won't sacrifice one of our own to save our skins," said Ryan.

"We don't follow your rules of war," said Gabe.

Dante continued, "We know why they made the deal with you, but it changes nothing. We won't allow it. The spear-bearers stay with us."

Caleb finished, "Now you have our answer. We'll die together in this room before we hand either one of them over to you."

The Premier said, "Most disheartening, but you have time to reconsider, and I'll still honor the deal with the spear-bearer. I am granting you twenty minutes once we end this call for the spear-bearer to be surrendered to me. Otherwise, all of you die in that room as promised. I offer you one possible death in exchange for the rest of you to live. Is one life worth all yours forfeit?"

"No, it's not!" yelled Angelina.

Dante hollered, "You're not doing it, and that's final! So Premier, you're wasting our time!"

"As you wish. Spear-bearer, you have your instructions if there's a change. You know how to contact me. I look forward to meeting you."

"No, Premier! Wait! Answer me!" pleaded Angelina, but there was only silence. Turning in Dante's grasp, she continued her tirade, "What did you do, Dante? How could you?" She beat on his armored chest.

He didn't feel any of the onslaught through the armor but wound his arms around her, pulling her close to him. "I'm not ever giving you up. Certainly not to be tortured by Black Dragon. Who do you think I am?"

"I'm trying to save us. It was the only way." She stopped the beating and slumped against him.

"Save us by losing you? No way I'm making that trade." He pulled her tighter. "I can't. We'll find another way."

"He's right. No one lets you go through with that," said Ryan.

"And you even think about another insane stunt like that, and you're getting restrained," said Alena.

Angelina looked up, realizing the damage exacted. Her actions had made it worse and squandered time finding a real solution. If they all died in this room, it would be her fault. "I deserve that after what I did. I'm so sorry, but I'm done. Let's figure out how to get all of us out of here."

"Although we can't stop him from releasing the poison on us, there should be a way to keep it from this room," said Caleb.

Gabe nodded. "Buy us time until Lana can bail us out."

Dante wrapped his arm around Angelina's shoulder. "What do you say?"

"I'll reroute what I can, but it won't be enough. He'll see through it. We need another play. I know you hate what I did, but ... "

"I told you no." He grasped her shoulders and stared at her.

"Dante, please."

CHAPTER THIRTY-EIGHT

Angelina looked down at the bodies laid out before her, unsure of what she had done. The others were adamant in their refusal to turn her over. Would she be able to convince the Premier of her handiwork, that she overpowered them? Of course, she could. They trusted she would not pursue it further. That had been their mistake. She would save her friends as she intended.

The Premier glanced at the message and murmured, "Cutting it close aren't we, spear-bearer?"

She anxiously waited until the Premier's voice boomed through the room, "I hope this is not another false alarm, spear-bearer. I grow impatient to conclude this."

"There will be no more interference. I'm surrendering to you," said Angelina.

"I can't fathom your friends changed their position."

"They didn't. When they awaken they'll be furious to discover what I've done. My comrade will take my betrayal the worst considering how long we've worked together, but they left me no choice."

"You expect me to believe they simply moved past this? I heard their defense of you, and they would die rather than hand you over."

"They're Freedom Fighters, and we have helped them enormously. In several cases, we've been the difference for them in their battles with you. They acknowledge that and owe us, Premier. A couple of individuals more than others. One of them is Dante when we rescued his mother from Black Dragon. Even if she never awakens, we still snatched her from your grasp, and that's what matters to him. The Freedom Fighter thinking is completely lost on us, but it's what places them into these doomed situations. They would prefer to all die than sacrifice one and will cling to their noble ideals to the end."

"You sound like a Black Dragon soldier rather than a Freedom Fighter, spear-bearer."

"Perhaps to you, but don't make that mistake, Premier. Although I do not share the Freedom Fighter's archaic principles, I'm not Black Dragon."

"Then why do you help them?"

"Simple. Despite my distaste for the Freedom Fighters' ways, I see a galaxy ruled by the iron fist of the Black Dragon far less to my liking. Enough of this. I'm surrendering myself as agreed."

"How are they all down?"

"Blaster shots on stun, but they'll be unconscious for more than sufficient time to allow for your escort. Caleb thought our troops outside would be outnumbered once you evacuated the building of your soldiers, so he ordered ours to follow suit. Due to that, only a few of us remained behind with the device."

"Yes, but those left are among the best of the Freedom Fighters, so you understand why I'm questioning you."

"Normally, they would be, but they did not expect the shot to come from friendly fire. It has happened twice today for them now. You would be surprised how easily I overcame them. Can we get on with this?"

"That is a hard dagger to take, but I'm not ready to move on. Show me proof of your deed."

"Fine. You're thorough. More so than the Dark Lord by some accounts." Retrieving her data pad, she aimed it at the bodies on the floor. Then she went to the port and sent the images to the Premier. "Satisfied?"

"I see five bodies. Four of those are in Freedom Fighter gear, but the other appears as Black Dragon."

"The Freedom Fighters are Dante, Commander Caleb, Commander Ryan, and Commander Gabe. The Black Dragon one is my comrade."

"Where did you shoot them?"

"Places where there was a break in the armor mostly. I couldn't be particular with overpowering five of the best fighters in record time."

He inspected the images further, glimpsing blaster shots along with a fair amount of blood scattered on the armor. "Quite bloody, aren't they?"

"Pardon me, but you sent several squadrons for us to handle today. I'm not sure what else you expected."

"Let me see the faces under the helmets, now."

"No, this has gone on long enough. I've done everything you asked and held up my part of the deal."

"Or we call it off, spear-bearer."

"Fine." She growled. "The Freedom Fighters yes, but not my comrade. I've kept my comrade safe thus far, and I'm not letting you have a face to hunt down. I won't budge on that. We both know why you're asking to see their faces. You don't know what my comrade looks like, so it won't help you confirm my words."

"You continue to impress me. I thought to slip you up, but it appears not. Just the Freedom Fighters then."

Less than a minute later, Angelina went to the port again and sent the additional pictures. "Are you satisfied now?"

He trailed his fingers over the new images. "Be at the agreed place for your escort."

"As we determined. I'll be waiting." She ran to the top of the device using the platform beside it and heard the rumble of the door above her opening.

The Premier grinned. He would have one of the spear-bearers shortly and obtain what he needed from this one, no matter what it took to break him. As for the others, he couldn't have done it better himself. The best of the Freedom Fighters lay immobilized for him, and a costly lesson remained for the spear-bearer about Black Dragon deals.

Angelina faced forward with her hands secured between two Black Dragon soldiers and more behind her on the ship as she readied herself to face the Premier again.

"Sir, we have the spear-bearer as you ordered," one of the soldiers that held Angelina reported.

"Excellent. This is a long time coming." After a moment, a bound Angelina on a Black Dragon ship appeared. "Spear-bearer, we'll finally meet face to face. I'm excited."

"I can't say the same, Premier."

"I suppose not. You've shown yourself to be formidable today, but you made one miscalculation."

"At least one. I wouldn't be in the current situation if not."

"Well said. You're far too trusting, spear-bearer. An unfortunate and in this case deadly character flaw for your friends."

"What are you talking about? You can't mean!" Instantly she struggled in her captors' grasp.

"I can't pass up such an opportunity. Never trust a Black Dragon. You will always be disappointed."

She yelled as she tried with all her might to get free. "Let go of me! We made a deal! I surrendered to you to save them! You sorry piece of Black Dragon trash!"

"See you soon, spear-bearer." He turned off the viewscreen and laughed. "That one does have spirit. Now to finish this." He focused on another viewscreen and announced, "We're ready to proceed. I have my prize. Shut the overhead door and release the poison."

⁓⁓

"Lana, they're shutting the door," said Commander Austin.

"Don't allow it."

"Squad is already on it."

Harpoon hooks launched from multiple Freedom Fighter ships and latched onto the door. The ships pulled it in the opposite direction, refusing to let it close.

"It's right where we want it, Lana," yelled Commander Austin.

"Launch the projectiles and take the shots," ordered Lana.

"Yes, ma'am." Seconds later numerous explosions tore off the overhead door. "Woo-hoo! Now that felt awesome!"

Lana laughed. "Looked great from here too, Commander. That door won't be shutting again. One way or the other, we're claiming the device."

*　　*　　*

"You have an update?" asked the Premier.

"Yes. I mean, yes, sir, you should see this," said the Black Dragon troop.

"The poison completed its work so soon." The Premier flashed on the viewscreen in response.

"It didn't have a chance. There was an explosion."

He peered closer and interrupted the troop, "With the door. Is that what I'm seeing?"

"Yes, sir."

"A desperate attempt by the Freedom Fighters to save their best. I'd expect nothing less, but I don't intend to pass up this opportunity. We'll take them all prisoner or finish them off here. I'll send a group to fetch them."

A beep came from another viewscreen, and the Premier sighed as he brought it into focus, "What is it?"

"Premier, the overhead door was blown apart."

"I'm already aware."

"Sir, we believe the spear-bearer fell from the device in the impact. It's the only conclusion that fits."

"What are you talking about? We have the spear-bearer."

"No, sir. We came to retrieve him as you ordered, and he's not here."

The Premier stood up and forced calm into his voice. "How is that possible? I saw him on a Black Dragon ship between Black Dragon troops being brought to me."

"Sir, I don't know who you saw, but it wasn't us. What are your orders?"

The Premier stared at the screen for a full minute before issuing the next instructions in an icy voice, "Kill them. As many Freedom Fighters as you can." Closing the viewscreen, he sat back down and slammed his fist on the chair.

CHAPTER THIRTY-NINE

"You think he bought it?" asked Angelina.

Ryan groaned. "Convinced me. Could you quit already? Geez, I thought I'd have to wrestle you to the ground."

"Sorry, it didn't hit me I stayed in role." She stopped jostling between the two.

"Was the kicking necessary too?" asked Dante from her other side.

"It had to look authentic, so yes. You didn't feel it with the armor anyway. You're just giving me a hard time."

He wrapped her up in his arms. "I'm relieved you're safe, so I can give you a hard time."

She hugged him back. "Me too."

Caleb opened the cargo hold and called, "All clear."

Christopher clambered out. "I got a whole new appreciation for that space on this ship."

Caleb patted him on the shoulder. "Thanks again for everything."

"Not a problem. Is everyone okay?" His eyes trailed over the group.

"Everyone's fine." He motioned at Angelina. "I thought Lana was difficult to rein in, but Angelina may rival my Lana." He leaned down and whispered to Christopher. "I'm glad she's Dante's watch." They both laughed.

"He's good with it. I'll steer this while you figure out the next move with them." He nodded towards Angelina and the others.

Caleb walked over. "Christopher is keeping the ship under control. What about here?"

"We need to get changed back. Dressed in Black Dragon won't get us far," said Gabe.

"You're right, and I'm about to burn up in this." Ryan pulled the helmet off and put it aside.

"No joke. I don't how you two stand these," said Caleb as he did the same.

Alena answered back, "It's called necessity, but we'll note your complaint to their management the next time we see them." She laughed along with Angelina.

"We told you their armor doesn't breathe. Now you believe us," said Angelina.

Dante ran a hand through his sweat-soaked hair as he joined the others in removing the helmet. "We believed you before." He began to remove the Black Dragon gear he took from the dead Black Dragon soldier, but he paused when he noticed Angelina still standing there with only her helmet removed. "What are you waiting on?"

"I'm wondering if something happens and if I'll still need to be in this gear."

"There won't be. We already covered that." He moved over to her and grinned. "Or do you want me to help you take that off?"

She grinned back at him. "You have your own to manage, so no, Dante." She set to work removing it from her.

"Just offering. Anyway, I'll have mine off before you're finished over there."

"We'll see." She winked at him.

He stripped the last piece of Black Dragon gear from him. Underneath he wore the standard lightweight shirt and pants typical of a soldier. A glance at Angelina found her taking off the final segment as well to reveal the black shirt and pants he saw when she suited up.

"I caught up to you, Dante. I've done countless lightning-fast changes with operations."

"I stand corrected." They needed to quickly suit back up in Freedom Fighter gear, but another side of him won. He drew her to him, winding his arms around her waist and kissed her. No armor separated them this time, only her soft, beautiful form melting into his. He never grew tired of the feel of it. As he gradually ended the kiss, he murmured against her lips, "What I'd give for this day to be over and have you cuddled up to me in my quarters."

"Me too." She smiled up at him and stroked the side of his face.

He kissed her forehead before releasing her. "We better finish suiting up."

Caleb shook his head and grinned at the two. "Distracted again." Then he turned solemn. "But from the little I heard about what happened, I'd hold my girl close too, Dante. Glad they made it in time to you two, Angelina. You think he figured it out by now?"

"No doubt he has, and he's furious."

"You kept a step ahead of him as far as knowing what he'd want."

"And Alika is an expert at creating fake documents and transmissions as well as making alterations to images or switching them when needed. Today he came through beautifully."

Alena patted her on the back. "He perfected a lot of that with your help." She cut off Angelina's protests. "It's true. He's amazing with it, but you've always had a natural talent for all of it."

"Hopefully, it was worth it," said Angelina.

"It will be." Dante slid one arm around her waist. Despite the armor on the two of them again, it felt wonderful having her beside him rather than the alternative. "Are we ready to get started again?"

"We are." Caleb paused. "Lana, how are we looking?"

Angelina and Alena moved to the viewscreen of their ship, and the others followed them as Lana said, "Everything took longer than anticipated, and our element of surprise vanished. The scene we hoped for near the device is gone."

"Definitely a lot more fighting where we need to be than we aimed for. A simple grab-and-go won't cut it anymore," said Christopher.

"This is our best chance though. We can't leave here empty-handed," said Ryan.

"Agreed, but enough shots to the device and the poison comes busting out," said Gabe.

"And the Premier will sink his feet into holding this place to the last man. We've set him off now," said Caleb, glancing at Angelina. "For a good cause, but still."

"True," said Angelina. "So, his falling for another ploy ... "

Christopher shook his head. "Impossible, seeing how that ship leaves the hangar."

"Lana, we're left with the original plan, and our forces will have to defend it while we get it out," said Caleb.

Lana said, "If only we could draw their fleet away from that building."

Angelina stared at the screen and said, "Yes, if only we could."

"What's whirling around in that head of yours?" asked Dante.

After pulling another image from the database, she placed it side by side with the current one. "The means for the ship to leave the hangar."

CHAPTER FORTY

"What's the verdict, Alika?" asked Alena.

"A small amount of the poison made its way into the room, according to the readings from the probe. Angelina's efforts worked better than she anticipated. What did come through is further diluted because the top is open. However, keep your mask on underneath your gear, and I wouldn't advise a long stay in that room."

"All words to live by. Thanks," said Ryan.

"Of course."

***

"Yes, sir?" answered the Black Dragon squadron leader.

The voice of the Premier rang through his comm system. "Why have the Freedom Fighters not been stopped? I have a visual showing they managed to retrieve the device and by all appearances are about to make their way through the portal with it."

"We're certain that's their aim, but we haven't seen anything to indicate they've done so."

"Let me enlighten you."

The squadron leader's hand trembled as his monitor showed a mass of Freedom Fighter ships hauling an object, which had to be the device, and it clearly was nowhere near the building where it had been stored. In fact, he didn't even see the building as the Freedom Fighters made frighteningly impressive progress with inching it closer to the portal. "I see it, Premier."

"Now, you and every ship we have at this facility remedy it immediately. This day is full of enough failures. I will not lose that device as well. All of you already have plenty to answer for, so you do not wish to have this added."

"Understood, Premier. They will not leave with it." He ended the communication and opened a channel to the fleet. "The Freedom Fighters have retrieved the device and are attempting to leave with it. Here are their last coordinates. All Black Dragon ships head for them and block their retreat through the portal. Take the device back by whatever means necessary, per the Premier's orders."

❦

Angelina and Dante landed one speeder in the Black Dragon room with the device, and Caleb and Gabe landed another one.

"We avoided Black Dragon's radar as hoped," said Angelina as she jumped from the bike with the others and stared up at the open door. "Here it comes. Give them room."

Several large Freedom Fighter ships lowered metal clamps that extended down to the bottom of the cylindrical device. The clamp bent in to form a flat scoop. It began to dig under the device and the base of the floor.

Caleb said into his earpiece, "Easy with the underneath. We can't puncture this thing."

The scoop continued its work but at a noticeably slower pace.

Angelina's eyes were drawn back up to the open door.

Dante took one of her hands. "Hey, you'll tangle them together like that permanently if you don't stop."

"What? Oh, that." She had been wringing them obsessively as her mind conjured up all the ways this could go wrong. "I didn't realize I was doing it."

"I know, but we're on track again. No panic is needed yet. Save your energy."

She nodded as she squeezed his hand.

"How's it look?" yelled Caleb.

The four of them got an equal distance around the device and now inspected the clamps' hold on it from each angle.

"This side is secure, Caleb," called Gabe.

Dante and Angelina answered in the affirmative as well.

"With the substance inside, it's heavier than the other, Caleb. Are we sure this holds?" asked Angelina.

"Yep. You got the dimensions on it from your last visit, and even if it's filled to the brim with either mixture we accounted for that and more." He paused. "My side is anchored too."

"You heard Caleb. Begin the lift. Slow and careful. The rest of you, formation around it. Protect it at all costs. This must make it through the portal undamaged," commanded Lana.

Angelina watched with the others as it lifted from the room, surrounded by a swarm of ship escorts. "We wait now."

Gabe nodded. "Enough time not to arouse suspicion. We don't want to be caught here again bargaining with the Premier."

"There's no chance he's in the dealing mood anymore," said Angelina.

⁓ℓℓ⁓

"We've got their ships cornered with the device. Drive them back, whatever it takes. Do not allow them to escape with it. The Premier wants it returned to its proper location." barked the squadron leader.

"Lana, they have us cornered with it in tow, and they are bearing down on us," said Commander Cephas.

"You know what to do. We will leave here today with our prize. Play this through, commander," said Lana.

"Troops, you have your orders. Make them work for it," said Commander Cephas.

The sky lit up as two fleets fought for ownership of the cylindrical object. The Black Dragon had either called reinforcements or the warnings of the Premier assailed their ears. The result was that the Freedom Fighters found themselves driven further from the portal and back towards where the battlefield began for the day. The Freedom Fighters tried to keep a fleet of protection blanketing every side of the cylinder, but it began to break down as more ships were too damaged to remain in the fight.

~ele~

Angelina looked around the room as an explosion rang out from outside. "That sounded close."

Dante nodded. "I felt that one too."

Caleb pointed up as a craft appeared at the edge of the opening. "Look who is here though."

"You two go ahead, and Dante and I will pull up the rear," said Angelina.

"Are you.."

"Yes, go now."

Caleb and Gabe jumped on a speeder bike and made their way to the ship. The entrance opened, and they flew in. Caleb turned and motioned them to come. However, in the same instant, the ship suddenly swooped out of view, and Gabe grabbed Caleb to prevent him from falling out at the abrupt movement.

Dante stared up and gasped, "What in the galaxy?"

Angelina screamed, "Out of the way," as they ran from the opening and tackled each other to the ground, trying to brace the other's unavoidable impact with it.

Dante groaned and turned in panic to see her still body wound into his. "Angelina, my angel, please ... "

"Okay, I'm okay, Dante," whispered Angelina.

"Thank the Ancient One." Taking in a deep breath, he pulled her tighter against him.

"That was close. Another second and we'd be smashed under that thing. Are you sure you're okay? I came down on you hard."

"I'm good. Armor, remember? Although this keeps happening with us, and I can imagine a million better ways I'd rather have you rushing into my arms."

Despite their situation, she laughed and stared down at him from his armored chest. "I can too, and I'll surprise you with one of those next time I tackle you to the ground."

"I like where that takes us, so I'll hold you to it." He chuckled as he eased her up into a sitting position with him. "What happened?"

"The cylinder. It had a rough landing." She stood up with him.

He held her hand as he scanned the room. "It almost did us in. We have to get out now." He looked up. "I thought the top got blocked, but our escape hatch will still work."

Angelina pointed to the bottom of the cylinder. "Not so fast. Our means of reaching it is nothing more than flattened parts."

"The speeder. Great."

"And take a look at the platform near it where we climbed before."

"As helpful as the other."

She looked around the room for other possibilities, but her eyes returned to the top of the cylinder and the open space where the overhead door had been.

"Agreed. It's the only way. We'll make it out of here, I promise," said Dante, squeezing her hand.

⁓⁓⁓

Caleb ran over to the cockpit and yelled, "What happened? They're still down there."

Ryan hollered back, "We get it, Caleb. Alena, anything from them?"

"No, not yet. They must have seen it in time."

"But did they clear it in time? We barely did."

"Cleared what? Would one of you make sense?" Caleb threw his hands up in frustration.

"This." Ryan displayed an image of a huge cylindrical object plummeting down into the room.

Gabe whispered, "Oh no. It would crush them instantly."

"We have to get back to them, Ryan," said Caleb.

"No one is debating that, but we don't know what condition they're in." Ryan switched the viewscreen to real-time to reveal a crowded arena near the opening, and the majority of the ships were Black Dragon. "And this is the scene now where we need to be."

Caleb leaned closer and rested his hands on the cockpit. "Any effort to get them out will be a bust the second we try."

"Unless that's not what it appears we're trying to do," said Alena.

"What do you mean?" asked Ryan.

"Wait. I think I got them. Angelina, Dante is that you? Can you hear me?"

"What did they say, Alena?"

She held up her hand. "I don't think they can hear me yet, but it's them." Her hands moved over the console, attempting to clear up the signal as she continued listening. A smile broadened her face, and she laughed. At the bewildered expression of the others, she shook her head. "I'll tell you later, but they're both perfectly fine." She listened another minute. "Unfortunately, their means of getting out got caught in the impact. No speeder or platform."

"At least they cleared it in time," said Gabe.

"Dante, Angelina, can you hear me? Awesome." Alena turned to the others and gave them the thumbs up. "Must be from the impact, the debris. Sounds better. We're figuring it out. Hold on and be ready."

"I never thought I'd want a bullseye on my back," said Caleb as the ship flew closer to the open door.

"Depends on which side of it you're on though. Perspective, Caleb." She carefully maneuvered the ship.

"No trouble so far," said Gabe.

"Because we belong with the rest of the group. Just another Black Dragon vessel in a sea of others. As long as we fire enough shots to look like we're in the fight, we should be able to pull it off."

⸺ℓℓℓ⸺

Seth watched the viewscreen. "Everyone received the target from Lana, and her instructions are clear?"

"Yes sir," The commanders in the air battle answered in unison. Cephas added, "And with every member of our squadron."

"I hope so because some of the finest of our Freedom Fighters' lives hang in the balance. Time to finish this gentlemen."

The Premier turned to the monitor. "I assume an update."

"Yes, Premier. We're pleased to report we recovered the device from the Freedom Fighters, and it's back in our possession."

"You recovered it?"

"Yes sir. It's back in the room, but it took a tremendous drop. We've been unable to inspect it for damage it may have incurred with the impact."

"How did they take it? We had a whole Black Dragon army here and practically on top of it today."

"We haven't determined that either."

"Why am I just being informed of this?"

"Premier, we only confirmed a few minutes ago we regained the device."

"No, I'm asking why no one told me the device had been taken in the first place. Didn't you merit that an essential development to alert me to immediately?"

A long silence ensued from the squadron leader.

The Premier stood. "When I ask a question, I expect an answer."

"My apologies, Premier, but I'm confused since you're the one who relayed the information to me the device had been confiscated and commanded me to engage our forces to retrieve it. How can I update you with intel you already knew?"

"From me, you say? How did I impart this to you?"

"Through the communication system, sir."

"What else convinced you the message originated from me?"

"As I said it came directly through the Black Dragon communication system. The instructions were direct, precise, much in the tone, I mean the manner you would give. You supplied me with coordinates and a visual of the Freedom Fighters with the device in tow. I didn't think to question it."

"Of course, you wouldn't. By the Dark Lord, those cursed Freedom Fighters." He shook his head in disgust. "Where's the recording I sent? I want to see how they managed to retrieve it. Onscreen for me now."

"Of course, Premier."

The Premier studied the video, watching it play through once. "Where's the rest?"

"There's no more."

"Where is the footage showing their retrieval of it from the room? This only shows after it's been taken, and they headed to a portal with it."

"All I received from you showed after they confiscated it."

"I see." He replayed it, slower this time. "They are maintaining a tight circle of protection around it. For such a massive object, you can barely make it out for all their ships. It appears they almost escaped with it." He zoomed in on the picture of the prize amid the surrounding swarm and stepped closer to the viewscreen and muted his comm. "To be so close and not make it is inconceivable. Yet when they faked the call, they failed their mission. They had to anticipate we would pursue them and retake it. Their strategy makes no sense, but it has all day. I'm missing a critical piece." He brushed his fingertips over the monitor where the object stood in midair covered by a fleet of Freedom Fighter ships and unmuted the comm. "Where is the footage of our recapture of it?"

"I can send it to you, Premier."

"Do so from the beginning."

"From the start, sir? The fight went on at length before we emerged victorious."

"I'll skip through as I see fit. Send it in its entirety as I requested."

"Of course, Premier."

He watched, scanning through the initial frames. The Freedom Fighters maintained supremacy, and the device remained in their grasp. However, as the battle raged more of their ships became damaged enough to necessitate leaving the battle. Other Freedom Fighter ships directly filled in the gaps, but eventually, a shift occurred in which the Black Dragon army gained the advantage and steered the group back to the original location where the device had been kept. "Wait.

Something looks different there." He froze the frame. "For a moment ... there's still too many Freedom Fighter ships around it." He resumed the video but allowed it to proceed agonizingly slow. The Black Dragon finally broke through their enemies' defenses as the Freedom Fighters lost hold of their prize, and it plummeted down into the facility. "It appears as ... " he stopped the footage and replayed the scene of the falling item and stopped it in midair. "It cannot be, and yet it is. How did they manage it?"

"Premier, what is your command?"

What did he order? For the first time in a long time, he didn't know for certain. Yet that was not the Black Dragon way. Strength, poise, and mastery of every situation were the tenets of Black Dragon. He dared not emulate less to these troops. "Continue with your attack until they retreat, or I give you further orders."

"Yes sir, Premier."

CHAPTER FORTY-ONE

"I don't like the sound of that, Dante," said Angelina.

"Me either. This room took more of a beating than it can handle." The larger chunks of debris began to crumble down on them, and he wound an arm around her waist and pulled her to him. "Stay close. We're almost out."

"Yes, you are," said Alena through their earpiece as the shadow of a ship lowered itself to cover most of the opening.

"Careful. This room is coming apart for real. The vessel could finish it off," said Dante.

"Got it. Don't cause the building to fall in before we get you two out," said Ryan.

The entrance to the ship opened, and Caleb dove down on the speeder to them. Dante nudged her towards the speeder. "You first."

"What if it falls on you?"

"Now, Angelina. I won't have you caught down here." His nudge became solid, and she hesitantly slid on the speeder with Caleb while staring back at him in worry.

Caleb lifted them and headed for the ship entrance. Debris rained down rapidly, no longer a trickle. She watched, horrified at the mounting flood. "Caleb, you won't make it back in time. You have to get him now."

"I have to get you safe."

"No!" She loosened her grip on Caleb. "Slow down!" Jumping from the speeder onto the top of the cylinder, she reasoned that she was high enough the falling large debris chunks would miss her. Hopefully, if the room itself collapsed she had time to escape before the cylinder toppled with her on it. "Get Dante, Caleb!"

"What about you?"

"Now, Caleb! It's coming down!"

He dove again and yelled in frustration, "Hurry, Dante!"

Dante jumped on. "Why did you let her do that?"

"I didn't let her do anything! You know better than anyone she can't be ordered around!"

Angelina yelled into her earpiece, "Alena, how about dropping me the harpoon attachment and hauling me up?"

"Already on its way."

The hook dropped within reach. Angelina pulled it in front of her and grabbed the cord with both hands while placing her feet on either side of the solid curved hook, as Dante and Caleb whizzed past her. Making one final check her feet were firmly planted on the anchor, she yelled "Haul me up!" At that moment, a thunderous rumble erupted, as a wall caved in and came crashing down in the room. It triggered a domino effect, and she stared down as her heart raced with the realization, *Dante would have been dead. I almost lost him.* A sob threatened to find release at the thought as she lifted from the room. Another wall slammed into the cylinder, but somehow, she cleared it in time.

Christopher turned to Alena. "Will it hold her?"

She nodded. "This is the kind of thing we have it for. Okay, not this exactly, but it's equipped to handle harder tasks, certainly one person will be no problem."

As soon as the speeder hit the ship entrance, Dante yelled, "I'm going back for her!"

"No, she's almost up now," said Ryan.

He bounded from the speeder. "What are you talking about?"

"Look!" exclaimed Gabe at the entrance.

He saw her, hanging below, in slow motion inching closer to them.

An explosion reverberated through the ship, and Angelina screamed, as she lost hold of the cord and her boots slipped from their foothold on the hook. Her frantic efforts to grasp it again proved useless as her body prepared for freefall.

"Angelina!" Dante's heartbreaking cry rang out as he fell stomach-first onto the entrance of the ship while desperately stretching out his hands to her.

Her descent stopped, and she heard Dante call, "I got you! Don't you dare let go of me!"

Yet in the same horrifying moment, Dante's own body slid towards the edge of the ship as the momentum threatened to plunge him forward to follow her original course. Caleb rushed over in that instant, "Stop Dante! He's hitting the edge! He can't … "

Gabe yelled back, "No, I caught him!"

Dante's deadly dive came to an abrupt halt, and he took a deep breath as he tightened his grip on Angelina's hands.

Caleb, Ryan, and Christopher were there, adding their strength. "Hold on you two," shouted Ryan.

"I'll never forgive you if you let go, Angelina!" hollered Dante as her grip felt frighteningly less secure.

"You know I'd never let go of you, Dante, but my hands are slipping." A sob erupted from her.

"Please, Angelina, we're almost up. Hold on for me," his voice broke," your Dante."

Ryan whispered, "It's okay."

Caleb finished, "We got her."

Ryan and Caleb had firmly grabbed Angelina's upper arm on each side now. Gabe and Christopher heaved Dante the rest of the way onto the ship, and their full attention turned to assisting with hauling up Angelina the remainder of the way.

Breathing heavily, Ryan said, "Alena, shut this door before anyone else gets another awful exit idea."

"Done, Ryan."

Dante wasted no time, as he sensed her trembling form through the armor. Yanking off his helmet, he eased hers off too and pulled her to him, whispering in her ear, "I got you. I told you I always have you, my Angelina."

Another low sob escaped her as her grip around his neck tightened, and she burrowed her face there.

"No tears, my angel." He kissed the side of her face several times, coaxing her to look at him and she did. His lips found hers, and he dove in as he needed the kiss more than anything else now. She responded with an equal yearning for him as she left today's near-deadly fall behind and allowed herself to be held in the safety of his embrace.

Caleb waved his hand in their direction. "Let them be. What's our getaway plan? I thought we had one."

"It's still the same one," said Alena.

"I thought we got hit earlier."

Ryan shook his head. "No, we got caught in the crossfire. Black Dragon doesn't have the best aim. Almost shooting one of their own isn't a reach."

"So as Lana instructed, our team kept this ship on their radar," said Gabe.

"Yes, as the only Black Dragon craft not to fire on during battle." Alena smiled as she flew the ship further from the building. "They haven't noticed our gradual retreat, and there's no indication they will."

⁓⁓⁓

"Lana, we have it," reported Commander Austin.

"On what side of the portal, commander?"

His voice trembled in excitement. "On ours, Lana."

She turned to Seth and grinned. "On ours, commander?"

"Yes, ma'am, and it's secured in the containment room. I made certain myself."

"It feels amazing to be a Freedom Fighter today. Stand on alert though, in case Black Dragon are bold enough to attack here."

"We're ready, Lana."

"We did it! We finally did it!" She engulfed Seth and Alika in a hug.

—⁓—

The Premier sat, staring past the viewscreen. The image of the massive cylindrical object plummeting from the sky continued to replay in his mind. How did they switch the two? He still couldn't fathom it. Now the Freedom Fighters had their prize, stolen from his grasp. What did they leave him with? The worthless shell he laughed at them previously for sacrificing so much to obtain. Now their fortunes seemingly turned. A transmission flashed on the screen, and he asked, "Yes, what is it?"

"The Freedom Fighters have retreated. We pushed them back."

"Of course, we did." He resisted the urge to laugh at the assessment.

"Do you wish us to check for damage on the device? We're able to now."

"I've already assessed the object in the room myself and determined it's unsalvageable. This facility is compromised, and it's of no further use to us. Have the troops pack anything of worth like supplies, and transport them to another location."

"We're abandoning this one, Premier?"

"Yes, we're unable to do further substantial operations here after today's events. It will make sense once I've briefed the troops. Follow orders as expected of a Black Dragon soldier."

"Of course, Premier."

The Premier stood up and made one final transmission for the day.

—⁓—

"Should be clear now," said Ryan.

Alena swiped the console, and the ship went from Black Dragon to a Freedom Fighter ship. She moved it from the tree cover she had located to join the rest of the Freedom Fighter fleet starting to pass through the portal. "I always like this look better."

"Don't we all?" Dante smiled at Angelina who remained wrapped up in his arms.

Suddenly a familiar voice boomed through the Black Dragon comm system, and the group turned to the ship's viewscreen where Alena now relayed it.

"Spear-bearer, I know you'll hear this as I made it readily assessable for your listening pleasure. Yes, you know who you are, and you know who this is. This has been amazingly well played on your part, far beyond the stories told to me about you two. I'm still not sure how you engineered it all, and I'm intrigued. You're formidable enemies, one's worthy of the Black Dragon's respect. Today proved that to me. You may believe the day has gone one way but remember a planet can be reduced to ashes in a blink of an eye. That is the power of the Black Dragon. Do not be fooled. The dragon does not sleep. Rather it cloaks itself in darkness, and when the moment is nigh, it will pour forth its fury and you will not survive its flames. Your end nears and all those with you."

Angelina and Alena stared at each other, the Premier's words leaving them chilled. Ryan had already gotten up and put his arm around Alena.

Dante said, "Angelina, let it alone. You can't answer him back."

"I won't. That's what he wants. To get inside my head." *Worse than he has already*, she added silently.

Caleb came over to the ship's console. "Alena, I'm taking over this last shift for you." He paused as he swiped his hand over the console. "It doesn't matter what the Premier said. Today we beat him, and nothing changes that. Tomorrow, we fight the next battle whatever form it comes in. Time to go home, everyone." He smiled as the ship went through the portal.

The Premier waited, expecting a fiery response from the spear-bearers, but none materialized. Maybe they didn't survive the attack. No, he didn't believe that was possible. They simply weren't biting because they had tired of the chess match for one day or were finally confident in their victory. That didn't sound right either. More likely they were wary of a battle to retake the device and didn't feel the need to waste energy engaging him. Or could it be as they said, and they did what they wished for the Freedom Fighters and now took their leave? Did their loyalty only extend to a point as they indicated? It seemed a farfetched, strange partnership, but perhaps they had other motives or another agenda apart from both the Freedom Fighters and the Black Dragon. All he knew was what they accomplished today and on other occasions now boasted a more impressive record than he previously imagined, a dangerous one for Black Dragon's plans. His mind needed time to process the day, and so he retired to his quarters for a short time after sending out a message not to be disturbed unless necessary.

CHAPTER FORTY-TWO

Alika stood up. "The fortress is about to become too crowded for my comfort, so it's time I made myself scarce."

Lana strolled over to him with Seth. "You can't leave. They'll want to see you."

"My dear, not the planet, but I'll return to the ship until it quiets down here." He patted her shoulder. "You did an exceptional job as always coordinating the operation and ensuring everyone got back safely. Rest assured we won't be rushing off." He laughed. "There are two lovestruck men who will not see that happen."

"Quite true." Seth grinned and glanced at a nearby viewscreen. "They're landing now. Lana, your husband is with them too if you recall."

Her eyes lit up, and she practically flew to the door exiting the fortress. "Pick up the pace you two."

"That's all of it." Ryan removed the last piece of gear from him and stretched inside the ship.

"Man, I couldn't wait to get it off either. More importantly, you got to experience another of my perfect landings. Hold your applause." Caleb grinned.

"We managed, Caleb," teased Ryan and turned to slide his arms around Alena's waist. "On the other hand, you have been amazing today."

She slid her arms around his neck. "I have, and I don't recall you showing me how much."

"Just haven't gotten the chance until now." He pulled her over and kissed her as he commanded the last few hours from his mind, what had almost happened, and enjoyed the kiss with her. He murmured into her lips, "That's a start."

"I'd say so."

"Caleb!" Lana called out.

"Lana!" Caleb swooped her up in his arms in a fiery embrace.

Seth and Alika laughed as they walked into the ship. Seth said, "We won't get anything from those two for a bit, and we may not have success with other members of the crew." He smiled over at Ryan and Alena and Dante and Angelina who had their arms still wound around each other. "Gabe and Christopher, you could be the only ones who can supply us an accurate update."

"We'll give it our best shot," said Christopher.

"Considering the day, especially theirs," Gabe glanced towards the couples, "I don't blame them."

"You're staying behind?" asked Ryan.

"For a little bit. You need to go back to the fortress and make your appearances with Lana. The troops want to see their heroes." Alena kissed him.

Dante looked from Alena back to Angelina. "Both of you are a huge part of today's victory. You should be with us."

"We will be, but we require a quieter celebration. When you're done, we'll be ready." Angelina kissed his cheek.

They started to walk away, but Lana rushed over. "Wait, we have to get back, but I need to ask something first." she turned to Angelina and Alena. "We heard what almost happened in the room when Dante and Ryan had to come for you. Are you all right?"

"Yes, we're fine," said Angelina and Alena nodded slowly at hearing Angelina's rapid response.

Lana focused on Angelina and asked quietly, "Why did you do it?"

"Do what?'

"Pretend to be me. You had to know how much worse that made it for you."

"Still better than the alternative. The identity of the spear-bearers could not be unmasked."

"But what he almost did to you because of me."

"He would have done so anyway. Once he realized we were both women in that room, he would have had his way with me and then moved to Alena. At least this way, I'm the only one. He still thought he had Caleb in there, and our identity remained safe."

She took Angelina's hand. "Do you hear yourself? Reasoning out what happened, when it doesn't follow reason. I don't believe it's that way for even you."

"My world is different than yours. I've seen his sort and navigate in their circles. They're not all dressed in a Black Dragon uniform."

"I wish it didn't have to be that way, Angelina," whispered Lana.

Angelina's eyes glistened with unshed tears. "We fight for it to be so. Some days are harder than others, but I've always known." She took a deep breath, regaining her composure and whispered, "I'll be fine, Lana. Promise."

Lana reached over and hugged her and Alena. "Thank the Ancient One for you two." She released them and turned a concerned look on Alika.

"I'll make my determination once they've showered."

"Medical is open to you."

"Of course. If I feel further examination is needed, I will alert you and accept your offer."

Ryan kissed Alena on the forehead one last time.

Dante looked at Angelina, his worry resurfacing. "I don't need to stay?"

"You don't."

"I give you my word I will contact you immediately if there's anything of concern, Dante," assured Alika.

"Okay." He turned back to Angelina. "Whatever he tells you to do, please do it for me, and call me if I should come sooner."

"I will. Now go and I'll see you when I see you." She brushed her lips with his and nudged him to join the others back to the fortress.

⸻ ℓℓℓ ⸻

Alena, Angelina, and Alika relaxed on the couch after getting showered and dressed.

"I'm relieved we were wrong about Black Dragon following us back for the device. One battle too many with them today," said Alena.

"Considering the initial circumstances, it seemed a logical conclusion," said Alika.

"However, after the Premier's parting words to us he figured out our swap, but he had no intentions of pursuing it further today, " said Angelina.

"You thought about answering him, didn't you?" asked Alena.

"Initially, yes, but I decided not to, to heed Dante's advice. It would have only brought back ... made it worse."

"Because the damage was done," said Alika.

An uncomfortable silence ensued as she pretended she didn't understand his meaning. "You already checked me, Alika."

"Yes. In that way you are fine."

She met his eyes, and the words replayed in her mind from earlier she wished to forget. Yet one word from it stung like a dagger shooting through her. Monster. First from the Black Dragon leader, and she shuddered as her voice spoke it. "They had us prisoner, Alika. I used my sunspear on them like I always do."

"A reasonable thing to do."

"If I didn't strike first, they would have killed us."

"No doubt they would have."

"One of our blades would have cut them down before the day ended. Why does it matter that I did it or how I did so?"

"I never said either way. The question is why is it so important to you, child?"

"It ... " She tried to say it wasn't, but they all knew she would be lying. Her mind looped back to it all day long. It seemed impossible she beheaded the already dead Black Dragon leader who started to assault her in the room. Then her frenzied onslaught eliminated the army in a blood bath, while not caring in the least that she left her friends to their fate. Yet nothing compared to the last image when she didn't register Dante before her. The fear in his voice as he spoke to her, from a terror of her refused to give her rest, and it sickened and shattered her anew. She choked out, "Because as hard as I try, I cannot tame this ... " her voice broke, "monster inside that I am." She buried her face in her hands and sobbed.

Alena wrapped her arm around Angelina's shoulder on one side, and Alika did so on the other. "You are not the monster. This cruel creature created from your pain digs its claws deeper into your spirit. If I could break the hold it has on you, my child, I would," said Alika.

⁓ ℓℓ ⁓

Dante smiled along with Ryan as they received another enthusiastic pat on the back from one of the commander's squadron leaders. "Ryan, they're still fired up."

"Don't forget your cousin's speech, and Caleb kept it going." Ryan chuckled.

"We're being summoned." Dante nodded over at Caleb and Lana, who motioned them.

Dante and Ryan sat in the conference room with the other commanders and Seth as Lana and Caleb directed the meeting.

"It's been a long day, so we won't keep you. We know the troops are tired, but we should maintain a formidable fleet on guard over the fortress skies tonight and for the next few days at least. We have to be safe, although the indication is Black Dragon doesn't intend to strike tonight," said Caleb.

"How did we reach that conclusion?" asked Commander Austin.

"From a recording by the Black Dragon leader. He sent it at the end of the battle, directing it to the two spear-bearers. You can hear it for yourself," said Lana.

A silence enveloped the group as the audio finished, some hearing it for the first time and others for a second replay.

"He's a piece of work. The spear-bearer's efforts made the difference several times today, and it didn't go unnoticed by him. Tonight, he seems content to fade into the shadows and regroup. An immediate attempt to retrieve the device doesn't sound like his next play," said Caleb.

"The spear-bearers agree with our conclusions, and they have been correct in this area," said Lana.

Gabe nodded. "We have the guard standing by in case, knowing it's probably for naught, but it's the prudent decision in this situation."

"Where are the two spear-bearers? Are they all right? After everything they have done, I thought we would meet them. At least get a chance to thank them," said Austin.

"They are safe, although they had a few close calls today. As you heard, it's still dangerous for them, so it's imperative to keep anything you know about them quiet. The Black Dragon remains in the dark as to how closely we're working with them as well as any description of them. That must continue, which is why they did not join us tonight to celebrate this victory," said Seth.

"Next time we speak with them, Austin, we'll relay your message to them," said Dante.

"Please do." He shook his head. "I think of my own family if it hit our planet, and I can't imagine it."

"None of us can, which brings us to the next item. We have the device, but it's filled with poison. There remains the task of unlocking how to neutralize it before the Black Dragon attempts to retrieve it. We still have planets with individuals in an endless sleep that we must find the key to awaken." Lana glanced over at Dante sadly. "Black Dragon is strong and promises to strike again. There is much left to be done, but not tonight."

"So, do as you want this evening, whether that is returning home or staying the night here in one of the quarters and catching some sleep. The only thing before you leave, we'll have to ensure the guard schedule is covered for the fortress skies. We'll need to rotate fleets. Those not stationed should rest up because they'll take their turn. The new guy in charge won't keep quiet for long. He announced that today. Any questions? Great. Let's get the rotation situated and call it a night," said Caleb.

CHAPTER FORTY-THREE

Black Beauty sat on a ship along with Destroyer located on the other side of Sikata, away from the battlefield that had transpired. However, the Premier's warning to the spear-bearers reached them due to the clearances their past with the Black Dragon still afforded them.

Black Beauty smirked. "That arrogant fool. All of his talk and he thought they were so easily beaten."

"He is not the fool around here." He glared at her and continued. "The Dark Lord chose wisely, and so the Premier did not underestimate them."

"What is your explanation for today then?"

"There is more to them than simply sunspears. Somehow they understand how to play this game as well as us, if not better. They don't behave like typical Freedom Fighters."

"They have strategy." She laughed. "That's your conclusion? Perhaps you're as much of a fool as ... "

He calmly took his blade out and quickly had it within inches of her throat, but her dagger emerged to block it at the last second. "Black Beauty, you should think before you speak lest you become a bigger fool."

"I'll retract my statement. However, I estimate there's more to it than what you suggest."

"The mystery they've been able to maintain is extraordinary. To have a target that is invisible for this length of time may be their greatest weapon. Surely you can appreciate how well they've managed that element with being an assassin." He sheathed his blade.

A long silence followed before she continued, "What do you think happened? How badly do you believe it went?"

"Poorly enough the Premier is abandoning the facility and it's difficult to tell as far as the device. I can't imagine the Freedom Fighters would count it a success to leave without it. Also from the Premier's words, I'm inclined to think they found a means to confiscate it."

"He won't move past that quickly."

Destroyer smiled. "He'll fare better than anticipated. I'm tempted to tour the abandoned facility later this evening to try to piece together what happened, but I have a feeling it won't be necessary."

"Because?"

"I suspect the Premier will reach out to us again soon now that he experienced the havoc those two spear-bearers can create for Black Dragon. Yet he has a play left as he said, so he is far from beaten. Yes, the dragon only sleeps, but he is not slain." Destroyer laughed.

⸺ℓℓℓ⸺

"Is the evacuation complete?" asked the Premier.

"We are making final sweeps, but we believe we transported everything of use. Sir, that includes the room where the device is stored. We're still verifying the report, but it appears ... "

"It's not the device. Only the shell they recently confiscated from us. I already know."

"That's right. How did you know?"

"When I looked through the footage, I realized it."

"How did they do it, Premier?"

"That remains a mystery, but somehow they switched the two. However, their ploy only postponed the inevitable. The incident prompts me to make an onsite visit this evening."

"Where to, sir?"

"It should be apparent."

"We can relay you another update, sir."

"No, after today's events, I prefer to see for myself."

"Understandable, sir."

"I will leave within the hour."

"As you desire, Premier."

CHAPTER FORTY-FOUR

Ryan guided Alena through the door to the quarters he called his while at the fortress and eased her on the couch.

Alena ruffled his still-wet hair and giggled, "You didn't waste any time."

He wound his arms around her waist and looked at her. "The thought crossed mine and Dante's minds to come get you two as soon as they let us loose, but we managed a shower first."

"I'm sure you appreciated that as much as we did after today. I bet you won't complain about Freedom Fighter gear anymore after being stuck in the Black Dragon one." Her arms moved to rest on his shoulders and wrap around them.

"Right now, I don't have any complaints. Everything is perfect, Alena, for the first time today." He pulled her closer.

"Oh yeah. I'm amazing as I recall?"

"You certainly are." He kissed her forehead.

"I'd say the same for you." She stroked the side of his face. "You put the fear in that troop who had me earlier."

"All I saw was the blade at your throat, and I couldn't let him hurt you."

"You didn't, so let's forget about it. I'm here with you now, Ryan."

"That's where I always want you, Alena." The next second his lips found hers, and all thoughts of Black Dragon vanished.

Lana glanced over at the viewscreen in the living area of their quarters as the evening approached. She smiled as Caleb's arms slid around her from behind, and she automatically leaned back into him. "Feeling better, now?"

"Yeah, nothing compares to a hot shower after today."

"I feel refreshed too, and I didn't do anything compared to you."

"You do plenty, Lana, and I couldn't do what I do without you." He kissed her neck. "I'm glad Black Dragon didn't attack the fortress and draw you out with the ground forces again. Even though you can take care of yourself, the overprotective husband in me would rather avoid that whole scene, my beautiful one-wife army." He chuckled as he returned to placing another soft kiss on her neck.

"Lucky for them, they dodged me today. I still mean to pay them back for that elaborate ambush at the Santiagos."

"Always such fire. One of the many things I love about you." He turned her around in his arms, so she faced him and kissed her. "Calm skies holding for us?"

"So far. I kept checking and if anything changes of galactic proportions, they're to alert us."

"Otherwise, no disturbances." He scooped her up his arms and carried her to their bedroom, placing her on the bed as he followed her down. "In that case, I've got a couple of ways for us to celebrate tonight, my sweet Lana."

✦

Alika and Christopher sat in Alena's and Angelina's ship as Christopher studied the information Alika sent to his data pad. "Alika, is Chris sure about this? She's always been stubborn on this point, more than anyone I know."

"She is, but what happened to you shook her foundation, and she's insistent we have a way to reach you straightaway and you as well if there's real trouble. Alena and I agree with her."

"What about Lana's group?"

"We have means to monitor them consistently. Certainly, we only take advantage of it to a point as my students would get nothing else accomplished." The two laughed. "If Lana's group receives news of an attack or something of that sort, we see it within seconds since it involves a response from their forces. Besides we routinely check in with them a few times a day to make sure nothing of importance surfaced. Of course, there have been situations with running our operations, it hasn't been possible. However, it has worked thus far. If we need to reach them, we've shown we can effortlessly cut through their security and communicate with them. We want them to succeed against Black Dragon, and we have a personal interest in keeping them safe as you've seen." He chuckled. "Also, there's Chris' natural talent in that whole realm like few possess, and Alena and I boast a decent hand with it."

"I'm sure she could hack into mine if she wanted."

"With sufficient time there's no doubt, but that element is not in our favor in those circumstances. Besides it is the world you navigate with Chris which makes you the best option. You understand the necessity of encryption codes and having the right intel can be more deadly than a blade. Without being in this world, Lana's group doesn't fully comprehend it, though they try."

"It's probably best."

"Yes, they have enough to see to, and Dante and Ryan already worry plenty."

"They have every reason to." Christopher paused. "If I see an alert from you, I'll answer using this."

"If I receive anything from you, I'll do likewise. Their mind will be more at ease knowing this is settled."

"Was Chris okay?"

Alika sighed. "She manages as she can. Today affected her more than she'll ever admit. No doubt Dante will help her sort out what happened, and they should do so. There's no doubt he has pieces to process too, with what occurred with her."

CHAPTER FORTY-FIVE

Dante walked into his quarters, with his hand clasped in Angelina's and laid down on the couch while gliding her down beside him. He smiled as she cuddled up next to him, and he wound his arms around her to stroke her back through her shirt. "Got the clear from Alika, huh?"

"You heard him. He's thorough."

"But a lot happened today to you." He kissed her forehead.

"It did." She looked up at him. "I'm sorry about earlier in the room, how I acted."

"What in the galaxy are you talking about, Angelina? That man strapped you to a table and almost … " He shook his head as he pulled her closer. "When I saw him on you and his hands all over you, I could've torn him apart limb to limb. I'll protect you, whatever it takes. Don't you dare apologize for today."

"You're too good to me, Dante."

"No, I just realize what a treasure I've been given." He kissed her cheek where a tear had fallen.

"Afterwards, if you hadn't stopped me, I don't know what I would've done. The look in your eyes, I could see you were scared of me."

"Stop that now." He commanded softly, as he gently grasped her shoulders and stared straight into her eyes. "I could never be scared of you, and that includes today. I was frightened for you, what earlier did to you. What you did later was your way of dealing with what happened in that room. No one blames you for that, Angelina, least of all me. Why would you do so, my angel? You have been through too much already."

She exhaled a deep breath, one of relief as a sob erupted from her, and she tightened her grip around Dante.

Planting butterfly kisses on her neck and moving to the side of her face, he whispered assurances and lifted her chin to gaze into her beautiful blue eyes. He softly kissed her and sensed a familiar calm return to her. Her lips found his again, and this time it wasn't for reassurance. It was a kiss, full of passion and longing. He eagerly returned it with an equal fire pulsing through him, as he played in her hair with one hand and held her firmly around the waist against him with his other.

"The quieter celebration I promised you?" Dante caressed her arm when she cuddled up to him again.

She could hear his heartbeat through his shirt as she rested her head on him. Finally catching her breath from his kisses, she laid one arm on his chest and propped her chin on it to look up at him. "This is much better than sharing you."

He chuckled. "I agree. If only I had time to bring in the dessert you like so."

"A sweet touch, but I'll take you over any dessert." She laughed as Dante kissed her again.

"I'm wondering something, Angelina."

"And you must think I have the answer."

"Yeah. Promise you won't get upset if I ask?"

"Of course, I won't, but it may be one of those things I can't disclose."

"Fair enough." He paused. "You said you could tell me who you were and your past at some point. We have the device, and it seems a lot of the danger is over now as far as you going undercover constantly. Maybe we could finally have the future we talked about, or at least a part of it." He stroked the side of her face. "I don't want to see you go again, Angelina."

She stared up at him, aching to give him the response they both wanted. Yet when she searched, she knew the truth. "Dante, I don't want to go either, and I wondered the same thing. If retrieving the device from the Black Dragon would be the key for us. Alika and Alena hoped with me. The Ancient One made it clear to me that I'd know when I could reveal everything, so I don't even know when that will be. Like I said we've theories." She paused and whispered, "Getting the device isn't it."

"You're sure?"

She nodded. "We've always had another guess, and we're certain the one is correct now." She hesitated. "To the end. All of it must come down."

"All of what, Angelina?"

"Black Dragon. It's total destruction. The Dark Lord is dead with your sun-spear and your father's sacrifice, but the Dark Lord's legacy lives on through this new Premier. Black Beauty remains alive and whoever the other mysterious one accompanying her. The Black Dragon stands strong with or without a device. As long as they do, the spear-bearers can be manipulated to get to you and your circle."

"But the opposite is as true. We could be used to trap you. Like they could use Caleb to capture Lana because they know they're married. If they're in the same place though, they're also able to protect each other. It cancels the other out, Angelina."

"No, it doesn't, because there's more you don't know, and it makes the differ-ence. I'm sorry, Dante, and I wish I could change how it has to be."

"I know. What about a secret marriage?"

"That would never work."

"You haven't heard me out yet before you shot it down." He grinned.

"I owe you that. Let's hear it."

"Alika and Seth perform the ceremony for us, right here in my quarters or over in the fortress. You choose the place."

"That's sweet of you."

"Whatever you want. Your crew stays here. We keep separate places for ap-pearance's sake, but you really stay here with me. We adopt suitable covers for all of you, which is no big stretch as you've done it previously, as Lana's advisors. Those roles take you for the long term. With Alika's medical expertise alone, he continues sliding into that position when needed. Nobody will suspect anything who visits. Then when all of this is over with Black Dragon, we'll have a proper wedding as you wish."

"You've put thought into this. I'm impressed."

"I'm highly motivated on this one."

"Dante, you don't even know who I am."

He cupped her face between his hands. "Of course, I do. You're my Angelina, my angel, my heart, my treasure."

"You truly would, wouldn't you?" she whispered.

"You never have to wonder," he whispered.

For an instant, her heart leaped with the possibility of now having a piece of the future they envisioned. It sounded doable as he laid it out. Then reality returned. He thought he understood, but without the full picture it wasn't fair to him. He always had the option to walk away from her now, despite the thought sending a dagger through her. Once they took the vows, it all changed. The marriage vows were not to be tossed aside or promised in an unworthy manner. Either way, he deserved to go into the bond with all of her, one with no secrets between them. How could they build a marriage, even one as he suggested, on lies though they were to protect him? Moreover, when the truth spilled out, how would he feel about those sacred promises he had pledged? No, she couldn't allow it. "I know you would, Dante, but I can't let you. When the Ancient One says it's time, I'll give you all the answers you seek. If this is the path you still wish to take with me, we will."

"Nothing absolutely nothing could ever make me change my mind or heart, my Angelina. Do you hear me? I'll convince you yet." He pulled her to him and continued to kiss her, deepening it to elapse a soft moan of pleasure from her.

"You're not angry with me?" asked Angelina.

"What part of that possibly felt like anger to you?" he teased and shook his head. "Why in the stars would I be upset with you?"

"I can't stay with you, at least how you want. Plus, you're still in the dark about so much."

"I admit I thought I masterminded an awesome solution before you blasted it to pieces." He winked at her. "However, you told me in the beginning how this had to be, and I agreed. I haven't regretted that, and I still don't. Although as soon as you can tell me, you will and then no more excuses from you." He grinned at her.

"I won't even attempt."

"I'll remind you of those words if you try." He paused. "All of Black Dragon destroyed. That's a tall order."

"I don't know for sure, but it feels like that's the ... "

"The what?" He waited for her to answer but in vain. Instead, he felt her body stiffen and heard her sudden labored breathing. "Angelina? Say something." Still receiving no response, he slid further down so he faced her side by side on the couch. The look in her eyes confirmed his fear. A vision. *After everything else today, why?* Easing them both in a sitting position, he lifted her into his lap as he spoke softly to her, "I'm right here. I've got you. You're safe. I won't let anyone hurt you. It's only a vision. Please can you say something to me?" She squeezed his hand, and he squeezed it back. "At least I know you can hear me."

"I'm fine, Dante," she whispered as her eyes continued their faraway look.

"Is it over?"

"No. Still seeing."

"Okay. I've got a hold of you, and I'm not going anywhere." He watched her nod her head in acknowledgment. Her expressions changed, but he read mostly puzzlement on it. Although he felt fear as well, it wasn't the heart stopping brand as from the vision in the Elders Hall that sent her into convulsions.

She murmured, "Why show me that? That's me, and it's not new. It didn't make sense, but it never did. They're different. One is ... no, that still isn't it. What are they talking about? Always for both. What did he mean?" Her forehead creased in concentration as she searched for the answer in whatever played before her. A minute later, her eyes widened. "No, it can't be. There's no way, but it fits."

Suddenly Dante felt Angelina's body relax, and her eyes lost the faraway state. However, when she turned to him, her eyes blazed with anger. "Angelina, are you all right? What happened?"

"Where's my data pad? I need it now." She started to spring from his arms.

"You should calm down first."

"After I have the data pad, I'll consider it."

With a sigh, he handed it to her and loosened his grip on her as she left his lap to sit beside him on the couch. She pulled up several images and projected them before her and Dante.

"Angelina, tell me what we're looking for so I can help."

"It's been in front of us the whole time. How did we miss it?"

Dante studied the projections, desperately trying to follow her discourse. "It's various images of the device. What are we zoning in on?"

Angelina closed down the projections and got up. "We have to go to the containment room where the device is."

"Now? It's late. What is this urgent need that can't wait?"

"I'm going now, with or without you." She started putting her boots on.

"You know I'm coming with you, but I wish you would make sense." He followed suit and gathered his data pad and sunspear too.

"We need the others to meet us there. I hate to get Lana and Caleb up, but they'll want to know."

"Sounds reasonable, except I haven't a clue what's wrong."

"Good," she said not registering his words as she slipped on her cloak.

"I just sent a message to Ryan, Seth, and Caleb. We should end up with everyone there you want."

CHAPTER FORTY-SIX

"What's going on?" asked Ryan, as Dante and Angelina came into the room.

Dante shrugged as he walked alongside Angelina with the others trailing them, "I don't know. She had a vision, and once it finished she was determined we must come here. However, she didn't tell me what she saw."

"Troubling," said Alika.

Dante turned to Angelina. "We're here now. Would you please tell us why?"

Angelina projected the same graphics of the device she had earlier. She looked from the images to the device before laying down the data pad and making a full circle around the device. When she came back, she had initiated her sunspear and stared at the top of the device. Unable to hold back, she screamed, "When do we get to win? Tell me! We gave it our all, and it's still not enough! How much do we have to lose and continue being left empty-handed? I should've let them take me prisoner so I could end this once and for all and take them out myself." Throwing her sunspear aside, she collapsed to her knees in front of the device.

Dante ran to her side with the others in tow. He knelt beside her to put his arm around her waist. "Don't wish such a horrible thing. I would not have you in their grasp."

"They're not coming to the fortress, Dante."

"We didn't think so tonight, but we couldn't be sure."

"They're not coming for this at all, tonight or any other night. We can call the extra guard off."

"How can you be certain?"

She laughed, but it came out hollow and despondent. "Because the Premier cares nothing for this device."

"He was going to use it to destroy a planet."

"It never made sense to me how the schematics we ran across didn't match up to what we saw at the facilities. The differences bothered me, but I kept attempting to explain them away. The first time we got the shell or the launching pad instead, so I dismissed it. I chalked it up to the fact we truly didn't know what it looked like. This time it still didn't correspond. Similar design but not it. I latched on to a few comforting theories of why, but none of them set well with me. One never occurred to me."

"Angelina, what is it?"

"The only one that explains it all. The discrepancies in the drawings and what we retrieved, the amount of supplies we know they've gotten over time, and what we see before us. I'd venture to say partly why they've held back to an extent. We had all the pieces already."

Dante shifted to kneel in front of her while maintaining the arm around her waist, and he used his other hand to raise her chin to stare into her eyes. "I'm here. We're all here, but we didn't see the vision you did. We need you to connect those pieces for us. Please, Angelina."

"They truly tested this one. That's what it was always meant to be. It's the prototype, Dante."

"And that's why it never matched."

Ryan burst out as the truth hit, "They've built another one."

"We've only put off the inevitable," said Lana.

"Any day they finish what they've started," said Caleb.

"But if they had a better one, why continue to use this one?" asked Christopher.

"Because they're still building, and whatever perceived flaws this device has, the one they're creating won't. I promise you," said Angelina.

Dante stared into her eyes. The fury had vanished that consumed them when she first stormed into the room. In its place, a story of utter defeat and hopelessness filled them. No, he wouldn't allow this. "It'll have a weakness, and we'll find it. They haven't completed it. We'll stop them before they deploy it."

She shook her head. "They could be close, and we could run out of time."

"You don't know that. They continued using this one for a reason."

"The Premier will rush to finish it now. You heard him. A dragon waiting in the shadows. That's what he meant."

"He meant that in a dozen different ways. All to mess with your head. You and I know better than anyone else how well Black Dragon's leadership does that. The Dark Lord's devious tactics endure beyond his death."

"Dante, what if we can't win this?"

"I will never believe that, and deep down you don't. I will not have you give up this fight." He lifted her from the floor with him, keeping his arm around her waist and with his other hand stroked the side of her face. "I have a vision for the future too, and I'm not abandoning it, Angelina. I won't let you either. You've already promised me." He kissed her, a long passionate one that reverberated with the strength of his vow to her.

He murmured into her lips, "All of Black Dragon down, including the device. That's what we'll do."

"We will," she whispered as her whole body hummed from his kiss, and she was grateful he held her. She never understood how he managed to undo her with a kiss.

"Every battlefield we've pulled through together and won. That doesn't change."

"It won't, Dante."

"That's my girl." He engulfed her in a hug.

Alena came over. "Are you all right? The visions take a toll, and today has been long enough."

Angelina turned to her while remaining leaning up against Dante. "I'm okay. It was different than the others were in a few ways. There's no emotionally charged event entangled in it, so it didn't have its usual effect on me. The way I acted makes that difficult to believe."

Alena sighed. "After how hard we fought today and thinking we finally had the device, it didn't seem overboard. Oh, and here's your sunspear and data pad back." She handed them to Angelina.

"Second time. What would I do without you?"

"I shudder to think. Dante took care of the harder part, but he's not complaining." She laughed.

"He doesn't. I'm sorry. I've interrupted everyone's evening enough for one night."

"This is important, Angelina. We needed to know," said Lana.

"It is late, but if you are calm now, we're agreeable to giving you more time tonight," said Seth.

"But I didn't think you would."

"We're fine, Angelina, if you are," said Ryan and the others nodded.

Dante kissed her forehead. "Sure you're up to this?"

"I am."

The group sat in the smaller room of the fortress.

Angelina began, "I saw pieces from the past, but they all revolved around the device. Whether it be when Alena and I discovered it or the repeat trips to collect intel to retrieve it. I couldn't figure out why. Yet it kept reverting to the same moments, and none of them were new to me. It wanted me to revisit those times and lock into the feeling I had when I questioned it but pushed it aside. I stood there and re-experienced those reservations. However, this time it wouldn't allow me to bury it, and it rejected every theory I tried to satisfy it. That's when it switched, and it was no longer me or any of us." She stopped.

Dante stroked her back. "You don't have to finish tonight."

"I'm okay." She smiled at him and continued, "It moved to a conversation between the Dark Lord and the Black Dragon Commander. The Dark Lord received an update from the Black Dragon Commander. The vision zeroed in on the Black Dragon Commander saying if they were successful on a smaller level they would know how to proceed so that they could create their army. Then it jumped to another session with the two. They were discussing lost supplies, and the Dark Lord was furious. Not about the items themselves, but the way they were hijacked, courtesy of your group." A small smile escaped her. "The Dark Lord doesn't appreciate being made a fool of. Anyway, the vision focused on one part of the conversation, whether the loss would affect their plans going forward. The Black Dragon Commander answered in the negative because he said, 'We always knew we gathered the supplies for both things.' The last piece was new, and it occurred tonight with the Premier. I never saw him, but I recognized the same distorted Black Dragon voice from earlier. He brought a guard with him, who expressed uncertainty the Premier would see everything he wished due to the hour. However, the Premier persisted in making the on-site visit to check the progress himself in light of the events just hours before. There was total darkness as if I stood with The Premier, and my eyes couldn't see in the room, like being blindfolded. Then the schematics from the viewscreen when Alena and I first visited were superimposed onto the darkness as if someone had drawn it line by line, using it as a canvas. His message to us echoed through the room, *You may believe the day has gone one way, but remember a planet can be reduced to ashes in a blink of an eye. That is the power of Black Dragon. Do not be fooled. A dragon does not sleep. Its cloak is the darkness and when the moment is ripe, it will pour forth its fury and you will not survive its flames. Your time is coming and all those with you.'* Before me I saw the device become two distinct ones, one rested in our containment room and the other remained cloaked in darkness with the Premier. The vision did what it typically does, flashing back through the scenes. Yet that wasn't the usual. More of an effort to help me, to make certain I connected the pieces."

"Angelina, with the part of the vision from the Black Dragon, it makes sense now. However, there's no way it did before." Lana squeezed Angelina's hand.

"It's scattered connections until the vision weaved it together. You're much too hard on yourself, Angelina, as always," said Seth.

"If I had figured it out sooner, we could have chased after the correct device today."

"Step back, and think about where that would have gotten us," said Alena.

"Alena's right. The one we retrieved is done and aimed to demolish a whole planet tomorrow," said Ryan.

Caleb nodded. "We saved countless lives now by snatching it from him. He doesn't get to take that from us."

"They speak the truth, child," said Alika.

Dante smiled at her. "Angelina, we took care of the immediate threat. The other device is still being built. It could be finished in two months, two weeks, or two days. We don't know, but we never did. Today we claim the victory for this round, hold on to it, and build from it."

She engulfed him in a hug and kissed his cheek. "You're becoming a master with those rallying speeches."

"That's because you inspire me."

Alika chuckled and elbowed Seth. "I told you the boy always had it in him."

~ele~

Two days later, an all too familiar scene arrived as the group crowded outside Angelina's and Alena's ship.

"I can't believe you two are leaving again." Dante stood with his arms wound around Angelina.

"That makes two of us," said Ryan, with his arms encircling Alena.

"After everything that happened, it feels too soon, Dante. I'm sorry," said Angelina.

"Ryan, it has been a couple of days since we got the device. We stayed for a little bit," said Alena.

"Remember how most of the time got spent, Alena."

"Yes, meetings with the commanders and rallying them again after another disappointment and scouring the device for any piece of useful information from it. Not the way any of us wanted to spend our time. We had the evenings together though, and did sneak a little time in during the day."

Ryan grinned. "Yeah. Lana was nice like that for us."

Caleb cleared his throat. "Excuse me."

Dante laughed. "Caleb helped us with that too."

"You're welcome."

"When are you coming back?" asked Dante.

"I don't know that," said Angelina.

"We'll monitor what you find and once we get a break on something important, we'll rush back. Keep analyzing the device because it's the model for the other. It should help us when we get a hold of the final product. We'll continue working with the sample we got from it, but it looks to be the same substance they put in Abigail's IV bag. We maintain close enough tabs that we'll know if Seth finds anything before we do," said Alena.

"You'll stay busy. Although the Premier doesn't have a working dispersal device yet, he has countless options to keep us battling. He possesses Black Dragon armies everywhere at his disposal, and hordes of other followers not in Black Dragon uniforms. He's got plenty of weaponry, including those deadly discs, to enable him to mount an ugly attack. The Black Dragon threat remains very much alive," said Angelina.

"And you're only two against his army, and this last round added a bigger target to your back," said Ryan.

"We all did. It's the nature of it. If we need to reach you, we can and will. You know that. We should go now," said Alena.

"Promise not too long between visits."

"I'll do what I can, Ryan. Promise. What about a reminder until I see you next time?"

"No way you're leaving without it." Ryan kissed her and then found her lips again.

"What are you thinking, Dante?" asked Angelina.

"I thought you always knew," he teased.

"No, it doesn't work that way."

"I'm crazy for letting you leave again."

"We both know I won't be stopped once I want to do something."

"But do you really want to leave me?" he whispered.

Tears glistened in her eyes. "Not ever, Dante. It gets harder each time," She ran her hands through his hair, "but I have to."

"One day we won't, my Angelina."

"I believe you, my Dante."

In the same instant, he pulled her against him the rest of the way to engulf her in a fiery kiss that threatened to dissolve all her resolve about leaving him. How could she walk away from him, even one day of being loved like this? She reminded herself she wasn't. Just for now. Pushing all the doubts from her mind, she poured herself into his kiss. Nothing else in the galaxy mattered right now, but Dante and that he loved her.

Slowly releasing her, he smiled at her and kissed her forehead as she boarded the ship with Alena.

Staring down from the cockpit seat, Angelina whispered, "Goodbye, my Dante."

Looking up at her as the ship lifted off, Dante whispered back, "Goodbye, my Angelina."

The End

Find more books by Elizabeth at: https://elizabethlavender.net

You can also catch her on any of her social media:

https://twitter.com/Elavenderauthor

https://facebook.com/elizabethlavender.author

https://instagram.com/elizabethlavender.author

ABOUT THE AUTHOR

Elizabeth Lavender is the author of the Sunspear series. Originally from the Alabama coast, she currently lives in the Dallas area with her husband, Jeff, and her two children. She has a Master's degree in counseling from Dallas Baptist University and has studied psychology and English.

She enjoys science fiction and fantasy and hopes to bring some of that same enjoyment to others. She also enjoys suspense novels. However, as long as the storyline is intriguing, she will give it a try. Her reading spans from Les Miserables to Shakespeare to the Percy Jackson series to anything written by Ted Dekker or Frank Perretti.

She works full-time and has been at the same company for over twenty years happily. She is a huge football fan and has a decent throwing arm, despite what her oldest son says when he practices with her.

Although she enjoys Texas, she does love going home to Alabama to visit. Besides visiting family and friends, it is nice to be back near the water again, where the seafood is the best.

Find more books by Elizabeth at:
https://elizabethlavender.net